BLOOD HAVEN

Magic has awoken…

ANTHONY L. SMITH

Mosaic Design
Book Publishers

BLOOD HAVEN
Magic has awoken...

First Printing – June 2015

ISBN: 978-0-9961106-4-8 *(paperback)*
ISBN: 978-0-9961106-5-5 *(hardcover)*
ISBN: 978-0-9961106-6-2 *(eBook)*

Library of Congress Control Number: 2015908590

Printed in the United States of America on acid-free paper.

Published by Mosaic Design Book Publishers
www.mosaicdesignbookpublishers.com
Dearborn, Michigan USA

0   1   2   3   4   5   6   7   8   9

*To my parents
who broke the chains on my imagination.*

ACKNOWLEDGMENTS

I've always found my life to be varying degrees of hot and cold. Things are either really awesome or really awful. Finally pushing this novel out into the world for everyone to see is definitely one of those awesome moments, and it wouldn't have happened were it not for a few very special people in my life. I can't even begin to tell them how much their support has meant to me over the years. Without them, this story would be yet another unfinished, unnamed project buried somewhere in the depths of my computer.

First and foremost, I have to thank my parents. They introduced me to the great, wide world of fantasy and science fiction at a very young age. It started with *Star Wars* before I was even old enough to crawl, continued with the *Lord of the Rings* and a bit of Monty Python, and ended somewhere in the realm of *Firefly* and Harry Potter. Without them and their undying support, I never would have found my voice as a writer.

I also have to thank my brother, Donny. Growing up military brats, we moved around just enough to where we were making new friends every couple of years. My brother was the only constant and, while I've made many other friends along the way, he'll always be the Sam to my Frodo. He's always got my back and always has an idea or two to push my way when I'm working on a new project. Even though he isn't the best at saying it, he's always believed in me.

My best friend, Donavan: He isn't much of a reader, but he still served as the guinea pig to some of my earliest drafts and some of my worst ideas. Often times, I'd spend hours bouncing ideas off him during a long shift or a boring drive. He was always patient when I'd randomly pause a movie, throw an idea at him, and then proceed to write it down in my notebook. Some of the greatest scenes in this novel came from some of our greatest talks.

My writing partner and literary brother, Mark: We met as freshmen in college, and, while I eventually dropped out and joined the military, he stayed in school. The miles between us grew, but every time I saw him, it was as if I had never left. We would often stay up late, discussing our latest reads and writing efforts over a few drinks and hot wings. Our minds always seemed to sync up perfectly when it came to ideas, and his masterpiece will likely blow mine out of the water.

My "girl best friend," Ashley, was one of the first to read my story all the way through and was the motivation I needed to make sure the ladies of this story each got their own strengths and voices. I knew if they didn't, her wrath would be the greatest of them all.

Perk, Clarence, and all my other brothers from the SOG: I have to thank them for the support they showed me these last few years. Even just a pat on the back or a single word of encouragement kept me writing, kept me striving. We suffered through a lot together, but at the end of the day, I wouldn't have had it any other way. Our experiences together shaped this book into what it is. Without them, it wouldn't be more than a blank page.

Rebecca, Rachelle, Greg, and Aaron were the chosen few who suffered through the first (and definitely rough) draft. I know it couldn't have been easy, but their constructive words and observations kept the story on track and in the direction it needed to go.

Finally, I must thank you, the reader, directly. You opened this book and took a chance. For that, I am forever in your debt. I hope you enjoy.

Then

For Jerry Fox, December 21 was a day pretty much like any other. He certainly didn't believe the world was going to end just because some ancient calendar suddenly stopped. After all, how could it end when he was so close to finally getting his promotion?

The same thing had happened twelve years ago: Y2K drove half the nation insane. He didn't put any more stock in it now than he did back then.

In truth, Jerry should have been promoted a while ago. It had been in the making for some time. Three years to be exact, ever since he had been told he was a shoe-in for the last open management slot. But things had happened and he was passed up for the promotion. Not this time, though. He had the most experience on the floor. He had the highest education level (magna cum laude at Dartmouth). This promotion was *his*.

The morning started like any other. At exactly 6:05 a.m., Jerry's alarm went off. He was already awake, though. He had barely slept all night, knowing the boss would be announcing the promotion today: *his* promotion. He got out of the bed slowly despite his excitement. His back always pained him first thing in the morning, and he had to get out of bed slowly or it would hurt all day. Once he worked out his initial morning kinks, he would be good for the rest of the day.

Jerry stretched his arms one final time before going about his morning routine. He showered quickly, brushed his teeth, shaved the patches of gray stubble that were growing across his neck, and dressed. He knew it was an important day, so he wanted to look his best. He pulled out his favorite tie, a dark maroon one his ex-wife had given him. *No need to throw out a perfectly good tie, just because she's a cheating whore,* he thought every time he tied it.

Jerry Fox had a very dry sense of humor like that. It was what kept him from having many friends and why his coworkers never invited him out for drinks after work. He knew that, and, to be honest, he was perfectly okay with it. He didn't need friends. After all, it was a friend that had slept with his wife and broken up their marriage. Friends just didn't seem that important after that.

Jerry poured the smoothie he had made the night before into his thermos (he hated coffee) and walked down to his car. It wasn't a far drive to the office; he lived only a few miles away. It was why he chose this particular apartment after his wife had won the house in the divorce settlement. He liked being close to work. It meant he was always one of the first to arrive, and being one of the last to leave really didn't matter when his drive home was a quarter of the length of his coworkers'.

The drive to work was about as average as it could get. The usual stoplights turned red just as he approached them. The green lights stayed green long enough for him to slip through the intersection. The clouds overhead threatened rain, but Jerry hoped the rising sun would clear them away. He didn't bother flipping the radio to any particular station; his drive wasn't nearly long enough to worry about it.

"Born to Run" by Bruce Springsteen hummed out of Jerry's speakers. He bobbed his head to it occasionally, not really focusing on the lyrics. He was too intent on the new office that would soon be his. He imagined what he would hang on the walls: his college diploma, for sure, and maybe that picture with Jay Leno his ex-wife had snapped all those years ago. That had been a day of days. Jerry's first and only time in New York City, and he bumped into the late night talk show host. Literally. He caused Leno to spill coffee all over himself. Jerry had half expected Leno to ring his neck, but he simply laughed it off, made a joke, and even agreed to snap a photo with Jerry, coffee-drenched shirt and all. Jerry smiled slightly at the memory as he pulled into the parking lot.

Vaguely, Jerry wondered if he would get his own parking spot with the promotion as well. He never bothered to ask Rick Dantana when he had received the promotion instead of Jerry. He had been a little bitter after all, and talking to Rick Dantana about anything, much less a parking spot for the promotion that should have been his, was at the bottom of his priority list. But maybe he would swing into Dantana's office and ask. That was if Rick was even in yet. Management never seemed to show up as early as Jerry did. *Suppose that's why I'm the one getting the promotion this year,* Jerry thought as he pulled into a corner parking spot.

Thunder clapped overhead as Jerry got out of his car, and he glanced up vaguely. It didn't seem like the rain clouds were going anywhere. He held his coat together as a strong gust of wind blew past and rushed inside as the first raindrops began to fall.

Jerry worked at a small advertising branch of a larger firm based out of Philadelphia. They specialized mostly in billboard designs for up-and-coming corporations and ventures, and business logos. He was one of the lead graphic designers, spitting out images as fast as the execs could come up with them, and, while it wasn't the most exciting job out there, it was what he had majored in at Dartmouth and what he had enjoyed doing for the last decade and a half. The time had come to move on, however. The time had come to move up.

As per usual, the rows of cubicles were empty as he entered the office. The motion-sensing lights activated as he stepped across the threshold, the third from the left giving its usual flicker before powering up. Jerry walked over to his cubicle near the back wall and powered on his computer. He took a sip from his thermos and glanced around the room. Soon it would be a bustle of activity, but for now, for the next twenty or so minutes, it was quiet. Peaceful.

As he looked around the room, he noticed the light on in Mister Eckhart's office. At first he thought the cleaning crew had forgotten to turn it off last night, but then he saw a shadow moving behind the blinds.

That's strange, Jerry thought. Mister Eckhart was usually one of the last to show up. *What time did he come in?*

Shrugging it off as nothing, he sat down at his desk and typed in his user name and password to log into the company's server. He would spend the next few minutes going over emails and any memos he might have missed, though that was very rare. Still, it never hurt to be thorough. After that, he would finish his smoothie and start working on the latest project that had been pushed his way until the morning meeting at nine.

Jerry's inbox was almost empty of new messages. A message from HR, "How to Prevent and Identify Sexual Harassment," something that looked suspiciously like spam, a daily cat picture from Janet in accounting (she sent them to everyone), and an email from Mister Eckhart marked URGENT. Jerry's brow furrowed as he clicked it open.

"Jerry, please see me in my office AS SOON AS you arrive," it read. Jerry glanced toward Mister Eckhart's office, just barely able to see its shuttered windows and closed door over his cubicle wall. He wondered what was so urgent.

Locking his computer, Jerry took a quick sip from his thermos and walked to Mister Eckhart's office. Behind him, a few other early arrivers walked in, looking tired and groggy. Jerry paid them only a cursory glance.

What could Mister Eckhart want with him? Could he be giving him his promotion personally? Last time, it had been a public announcement at the morning meeting. A sick feeling settled in the pit of Jerry's stomach. Hesitantly, he rapped lightly on Mister Eckhart's door.

"Come in," came the voice from the other side. Jerry opened the door and entered. Mister Eckhart was sitting behind his desk, his telephone cradled between his shoulder and his ear as he wrote something on a legal pad in front of him. He looked tired, the bottom of his eyes rimmed in red. Listening on the phone, he nodded every few seconds, though he spared a moment to wave Jerry into the seat in front of his desk. Jerry took it, interlocking his fingers across his lap, his feet tapping the floor with nervous energy.

Everything about this meeting said it couldn't be good. Mister Eckhart always looked so well put together. His suits were always clean and pressed. He was always clean shaven, and his hair was always combed neatly to the side. This morning, however, he looked little better than a vagrant who had stolen a necktie from someone. He had obviously not shaven before coming into work, his hair was a bedraggled mess, and his necktie was loose around his collar, barely tied.

After a few more moments of fervent nodding, Mister Eckhart finally cut in. "I understand everything. Yes. Yes. I will call you back as soon as I have the numbers. Yes. Thank you. Yes. Within the hour. Good bye."

He practically slammed the phone back down on its hook. He rubbed his eyes for several seconds before finally meeting Jerry's quizzical gaze.

"Is everything okay, sir?" Jerry asked, trying to put some confidence in his voice that he didn't feel. This was definitely not good.

"Not particularly, Jerry," Mister Eckhart responded. He regarded Jerry for several long seconds. "We've never really gotten to know each other that well, have we, Jerry?"

"Uh, no, sir."

"I get the impression that's the way you like it, though. You keep mostly to yourself, do your work in a timely manner, keep everything professional. That's good. It's that kind of attitude that gets a person promoted."

Jerry perked up at that. Maybe this wasn't so bad after all.

"I know you're expecting a promotion today, Jerry. I can tell by the look in your eye. I'm sorry to say that's not going to happen. Not for you. Not for anyone." Mister Eckhart let that sink in for several seconds, letting Jerry work out exactly what was happening. "That was corporate on the phone. They're not satisfied with the numbers we're producing. We're not bringing in enough fresh revenue. So they're shutting this branch down. Some of our people will be moving to other branches, a few to corporate. Others… I'm going to have to let go."

And that was when Jerry realized what was happening. Sure, the polite people would say "laid off," but he knew what it really was.

He was being fired. "I…" He struggled to say something, anything, but no words would come.

"I'm sorry, Jerry. Trust me when I say it's not my choice. Corporate wants cuts, and I can't justify moving a long-term staffer to another branch when they're already full. And you don't have any management experience to bump you to corporate."

"So I'm…" Again, he struggled for words, but none came. A ringing began to fill his ears.

"You'll get a decent severance package, and the branch won't be closing for another month, so there's still plenty of time to find another job and get your affairs in order."

Mister Eckhart's words didn't mean anything to Jerry. He was barely able to register them over the ringing in his ears.

"So if I had gotten that promotion today…"

"It probably still wouldn't have made a difference. Hell, I had to fight just to get Dantana moved up to corporate."

Everything was drowned out after that. Dantana got to keep his job. Dantana, who had swept in from another branch and stolen Jerry's promotion three years ago, was moving up to corporate. He was getting *another* promotion.

Heat began to fill Jerry's hands, starting in his fingertips and moving up his palms to his wrists. Sweat began to bead across his forehead. Mister Eckhart was saying something else, but Jerry couldn't hear him. He felt like he was boiling all of a sudden. He stood out of his chair, loosening his necktie as he practically stumbled to the door. Mister Eckhart called after him, but all Jerry could think about doing was getting out of that suffocating office.

More than a dozen people had shown up by now. A few looked up as Jerry half-walked, half-staggered over to his cubicle. His hands felt like they were on fire.

Was he having a panic attack? He had never had one before. Not even when he discovered his wife had been cheating on him. Was this what it felt like?

Or even worse, was he having a heart attack? He swept that notion aside almost as quickly as it had developed. He was in excellent health for his age, only sporting a slight gut that had come with age, and he had full feeling in both of his arms.

Jerry practically collapsed into his chair. At first, he tried to bury his head in his hands, but they were too hot. From his peripheral vision, he saw several other people walk over to Mister Eckhart's office. Apparently, he wanted to give the termination news to each of them personally. Not to Rick Dantana, though. Rick Dantana's job was nice and secure. Hell, he would probably get a bonus when he moved up to corporate and definitely his own parking spot if he didn't have one already. That was when Rick Dantana walked in through the front doors and something in Jerry snapped. He just couldn't take Rick's smiling face anymore, his neat, pressed suit, his polished shoes.

Jerry stood and walked down the row of cubicles toward Rick, joking with the other second-tier manager, Kristina Jaw. Jerry's hands were practically simmering when Rick and Kristina caught sight of him. Evidently, he had a scary look in his eye because they both stepped back a pace. Jerry wasn't sure what he was going to do. He squared his shoulders for whatever it was, though. He had been stepped on too many times already.

As he got within a few paces of Rick, the heat burning in his hands cooled suddenly, and he slowed his pace. He veered just to the right of Rick and Kristina and pulled a paper cup from the water jug, filling it to the brim and taking a long gulp. He vaguely heard Rick and Kristina chuckling over his shoulder.

"Damn, Jerry, I didn't know someone could be so thirsty." Rick said, still laughing lightly. "I thought there for a second you were coming at me. Didn't want to have to put you in your place."

And then Jerry truly lost all sense of self-control. He whirled around and threw both fists at Rick, barely conscious of what he was doing. He wasn't even within swinging range, but it just felt right. A ball of flame suddenly sprang forth from his outstretched fists and collided with Rick's chest, sending him hurling back against the wall behind him. He hit it with crushing force, several chunks of plaster sprinkling the floor as he landed.

Kristina screamed, and Jerry's eyes snapped over in her direction. He suddenly remembered all the condescending remarks she had made to him in the morning meetings, the way she and her little flock would always whisper as he walked by, gossiping about why his wife had left him or why he didn't have any friends.

The fireball he directed at her was even bigger than the one that had hit

Rick. He didn't quite understand how it worked, but it felt good. Several more people screamed and sprinted for the door.

"Jerry, what the hell have you done?"

Jerry turned and saw Mister Eckhart standing a few dozen feet away, staring in horror at him. His eyes fell to Rick and Kristina. Both were charred where the fireballs had hit them and neither was moving. Mister Eckhart's mouth hung slightly agape.

"I… I can't take it anymore, Mister Eckhart. I'm done being a stepping stone for others!" Jerry yelled. He would show the world he wasn't someone who could be pushed around.

"Jerry, you can't do this!" Mister Eckhart yelled. More flames began to crackle in Jerry's palms. He couldn't dispel them; the heat was so intense.

"I told you, Mister Eckhart. I'm done being stepped on! Just stay away from me! I don't want to hurt you."

But Mister Eckhart wasn't staying away from him. He raised his hands in a defensive posture and took a few slow steps toward Jerry.

"Don't," Jerry yelled.

"Jerry, I know you're mad. I know you're scared."

"I'm not scared!" Jerry yelled, cutting Mister Eckhart off as he hurled a fireball at him. It collided with the cubicle wall just to his left, and he dove for cover. Jerry would have to work on his aim, he decided. He didn't know where this power had come from or how he had gotten it, but he wasn't going to let anyone step on him anymore. He hurled another fireball toward Mister Eckhart, this one hitting the side of the filing cabinet he was hiding behind, before the heat in his hands finally started to dissipate. As they returned to their normal temperature, he turned toward the door and walked out. Rick and Kristina still weren't moving as he purposely stepped over them.

Sure enough, it was raining steadily as he walked outside, and lightning flashed in the clouds overhead. Cars were skidding out of the parking lot, and several more coworkers were running down the sidewalk. A clap of thunder practically shook the ground beneath Jerry's feet. There was another flash of lightning, and then a bolt actually struck a few blocks away, sending spots soaring across Jerry's vision. He wondered for a moment where it had struck before another suddenly hit in almost the exact same location. Then another and another.

Just what was happening?

Police cars roared down the street, sirens wailing and lights flashing. Their lights gleamed blue and red across the slick road. Jerry felt the heat in his hands begin to rise again and he suddenly understood. He had to get rid of it, and it was telling him where to throw it. Balling his hands into fists again, he hurled a fireball straight into the path of the approaching police car. It hit just in front of the car, and the driver swerved to avoid it. He caught the curb with his front tire and slammed the car into the wall of the nearby building. Two other police cars skidded to a stop, but before the officers inside could even get out, Jerry had hurled two more fireballs at them. One missed, but the other hit the hood of the car, and the resulting explosion sent it rearing up like a horse.

Jerry watched in satisfaction as the surviving officers ran for cover. His hands still hadn't cooled down, however, so he knew he wasn't finished. Loosening his necktie even further, he strode toward the police, ready to hurl more fire at them. It felt so good. Who could stop him?

His answer came in the form of a lightning bolt that slammed into his chest, sending him flying backward. What was strange was that the bolt had come horizontally, not vertically. He landed hard against the concrete, rain pattering across his face as more thunder shook the ground. His throat was suddenly very dry, and his hands burned more fiercely than ever. He struggled to see through the rain cascading across his face and barely managed to see the woman walking up to stand over him. She was out of breath, panting wildly, and her blonde hair had come half out of its bun. Small lines of electricity danced across her palm, but she barely seemed to notice.

She raised her hand in the air, palm outward, and Jerry watched in awe as a bolt of lightning soared down from the sky and collided with her hand. The last thing he saw before everything went black was the woman closing her fist around that surge of electricity and directing it down toward him. Then it was over, and Jerry Fox was gone.

CHAPTER 1

Now

The signs hadn't changed a bit.

Help us stop the spread!

Notify your local DSC office if you see anything suspicious.

Starting to feel ill?

Sun burning a little too bright?

Moon making you feel strange?

Notify your local DSC office.

Killian couldn't help but snort as he stared at them. The people in line around him weren't really paying attention; they were too busy fiddling with their passports or cell phones. He was the only one who seemed to find the signs amusing. They were all brightly colored and full of smiling faces. One even featured a grinning vampire (an actor of course) being led away by men wearing white contamination suits. Had they not worn face masks, Killian was sure they would be smiling as well.

Despite what the signs said, however, they were never that friendly, never that polite. No one ever smiled.

Even with his rucksack weighing him down, Killian stood over six feet tall and was lean almost to the point of being called skinny. He had light brown hair, chopped short to stay out of his eyes, and angled grey-blue eyes.

"So where are you coming from?" a small voice came from behind him.

Killian turned to see a young woman. She was wearing a black ball cap, her sandy hair tied into a loose ponytail and threaded through the opening in the back. Her faded makeup and the lines beneath her eyes said she had traveled some miles. Her accent said she was American. Behind her, the line stretched toward the terminal as dozens and dozens of other travelers waited to pass through customs.

"Shanghai," Killian replied after a moment. He really wasn't in the mood for conversation—he was still pretty groggy from his flight—but her inquiring gaze begged him to ask the same in return. He pushed his hands into his jacket pockets. "You?"

"Seattle. I'm visiting my brother. He's a…um…" She searched for the right word.

"Mage," Killian filled in, not too keen on hearing whatever slang the Americans were throwing around these days.

"Yeah, a mage." The word obviously felt strange on her tongue. "It's my first time seeing him since he moved over."

Killian nodded. "That's good. Well, I hope you enjoy your stay." He turned back around, doing his best to signify the end of the conversation. He really wasn't interested in hearing her or her brother's story, despite how much she obviously wanted to tell it.

The line moved forward a few feet, and Killian finally saw the customs counters ahead. Again, his eyes were drawn to the signs overhead. The grinning vampire in particular drew his attention, and he felt his hands slowly ball into fists as he stared at it. The sign had gotten one thing right at least. The vampire's eyes were red.

"Is it dangerous?"

Killian glanced back over his shoulder and saw the woman's attention had been drawn up to the banners as well.

"Is what dangerous?" he asked, sighing internally. Obviously, she hadn't taken the hint.

"The city. Blood Haven."

It was only then that Killian saw how tightly she was clutching her passport and the way she constantly shifted her weight from foot to foot. He suddenly felt like a jerk. She was just nervous and was looking for some friendly reassurance.

"What classification is your brother?" he asked, putting as much kindness into his voice as he could muster. It wasn't much.

"What?"

"Water? Fire?"

"Oh," she said, forcing a half-hearted laugh, "He's a weather mage."

This time, Killian actually sighed. He hated weather mages. "People don't usually mess with them. They don't like the idea of golf-ball-sized hail coming down on their heads or lightning getting shoved up their asses. Stick with him and you'll be fine. Just don't go around announcing you're American. People don't like Americans much around here."

"But aren't you American?" she asked, referring to his own accent.

"No," he replied evenly. "I'm a Havenite."

"Oh," she said, feigning understanding. It was obvious she had no idea what the word meant. Killian decided to let her brother explain it to her.

The line moved forward a little further, and they finally passed beneath the DSC banners. Now, the signs were much more serious. They listed proscribed spells and potions, forbidden talismans from certain countries, and banned grimoires.

All things one could get in any of the city's numerous black market bazaars if they knew where to look.

The final sign was all in black with bright yellow lettering: ALL INCOMING TRAVELERS WILL SUBMIT TO A MANDATORY HEALTH SCAN.

Apparently, the woman behind him had read it at the same time, because she immediately asked, "What's it mean by health scan?""

Killian suppressed a groan, recalling that he too had been new to the city once, back before it had been called Blood Haven. Back when it had still been known as Sydney. Rubbing the bridge of his nose, he replied, "It's a scanner you have to go through, kind of like a metal detector. It tells them if you're infected."

"Infected with what?"

"Remember those signs back there?" he asked, nodding back to the DSC banners and the grinning vampire.

She glanced back at them.

"Yes."

"There you go," he answered.

She nodded, obviously feeling stupid. "Sorry, I'm just nervous. Not really sure what to expect," she said.

"Don't worry about it," Killian replied. After a moment, he added, "We were all new once."

She seemed to take a small measure of comfort from that and nodded, a slight smile creasing the corners of her mouth. Killian nodded back and moved forward with the rest of the line. With the exception of shuffling papers and the occasional muffled cough, the next few minutes passed in companionable silence. Finally, Killian reached the end of the roped line, and the customs officer called him forward to the far right counter.

"Good luck," he said to the woman before walking away.

"You too," she called after him.

The customs officer was holding out his hand when Killian approached the counter. He handed his passport over and waited as the officer reviewed it. He paid special attention to the multitude of stamps on the inside flap. He even shot Killian a narrow-eyed glance over the rim of his glasses before scanning the passport.

"Classification?" he asked in a flat tone. He stared at his computer screen, reviewing Killian's information. He was sure it was on his passport, but he answered nonetheless.

"Level 3 Elemental," he replied.

"Reason for entering the city?" asked the officer, his eyes still fixed on the computer screen, likely reviewing Killian's status as a licensed hunter.

"Coming home," Killian said despite that.

"And where are you traveling from?" he asked.

"Beijing," Killian replied after a moment. He couldn't lie this time. Again, the officer's eyes shot up to meet his. This time, however, his gaze wasn't quite as narrow.

Killian was sure the officer had seen the news report. Pretty much everyone had. The last big nest in Beijing had been cleared. The capital of

China was now a Subby-free zone. Killian simply stared straight ahead, giving no indication as to whether or not he had been involved. The customs officer shoved his spectacles up to the bridge of his nose, glanced down at Killian's passport for several more seconds, and finally added Blood Haven's stamp to the tapestry of others.

"All incoming travelers must submit to a mandatory health scan before entering into Blood Haven. Welcome home," he said a little more warmly. He handed back the passport.

Killian took it with a nod and walked to the next line. Ahead, people were funneling through a narrow metal archway one at a time. Armed security guards stood on either side. Killian vaguely recalled the horror stories Spin used to tell him about those who failed the scan. Stories of people being dragged off, the entire terminal quarantined for several hours. It was no wonder people were shifting nervously as they waited their turns.

The edges of the arch were lit with a faint cyan glow as people entered and stood with their fingers interlaced over their heads. After a few moments, the blue aura faded, and they were called through by one of the security guards.

Killian waited his turn patiently. He knew he had nothing to worry about. The Pacific had a much better handle on the Subhuman situation than Blood Haven. But then, that was why he had come back. It was time to finish what he and Spin had started.

After a few minutes and more shuffling feet, Killian was finally called forward. They took his rucksack and set it off to the side.

"Step beneath the arch and interlock your fingers on top of your head," the security guard told him. His badge gleamed with the letters DSC, and his grey uniform was clean and pressed. Killian noted the pistol strapped to his hip.

Doing as instructed, he stepped beneath the archway and waited as the blue light began to glow. A warmth filled the inside of the arch, and Killian wondered exactly how it detected if he was infected or not. After a few seconds, the light faded, and a guard on the other side waved Killian through the archway. He stepped out, suddenly conscious of the sweat beading on his forehead. It hadn't even been that hot, yet he was drenched. When the guards were satisfied that Killian wasn't infected, they waved him along and called the next person in line.

Wiping his forehead with the back of his hand, he grabbed his rucksack and moved on. Just past the scanner, escalators led down to baggage claim. Killian walked over to them, paying only a cursory glance over his shoulder. The young woman from before was a few people back in line. She was staring intently at the archway, obviously nervous. Killian thought about sending her a reassuring smile, but he instead just ducked his head and stepped onto the escalator. He rode it down to the bottom where people from his flight were already waiting at the baggage claim. Several bags had fallen from the chute onto the conveyor belt, and his was among them. He snatched the old tan duffel, the tin jar within clanking as he slung it over his shoulder.

As he walked toward the exit with a crowd of other travelers, he caught sight of the young woman again. She was riding down the escalator, looking around the baggage claim area. He wasn't sure if she was looking for him or her brother. He decided not to find out, kept his head low, and exited the airport. It wasn't that she was unattractive or even unpleasant. He just didn't have time.

Bright sunlight streaked across Killian's eyes, and he ran a hand through his short hair.

He was a few inches taller than those around him, so he didn't have any trouble spotting his ride, a matte-black Cadillac from several decades ago. It helped that he also recognized the bull of a man standing next to it.

Jo Jack.

Killian gave his first genuine smile in weeks as he walked over to the stocky man. Jo Jack was at least a head shorter and had thick eyebrows and deep-set eyes, which were overshadowed by the wide white headband he wore. Jo Jack's hair was midnight black, and he wore a spiked leather jacket he never took off, it seemed. The pair embraced, and Jo Jack swatted Killian on the back several times, nearly knocking the breath from his lungs.

"Good to see you, Kil," he said, as they pulled away from one another.

"Good to see you too, Jo," Killian replied after regaining his breath. And he meant it. It had been some time since he had seen a truly friendly face.

Jo Jack opened the back door to his Cadillac, and Killian swung his duffel and rucksack in. He dropped into the passenger seat, and Jo Jack pulled them away from the curb.

"First things first," Killian said as they looped around the terminal toward the highway. "How's my girl?"

Jo Jack chuckled. "Your jeep is fine. Started her up last week just like you asked. Could probably use an oil change, though."

Killian nodded. Jo Jack glanced over at him. "You know, for a second there, I thought you meant Daisy," he said.

Killian shot him a narrow glance. "You know the rules, Jo Jack. We're not talking about Daisy."

"I know, I know. Sorry. She misses you, though."

"Jo," Killian said warningly. Jo Jack nodded, focusing back on the road as they merged onto the highway.

Killian looked out the window as they sped down the thoroughfare. The smell of saltwater was heavy in the air, and the skyscrapers downtown practically sparkled in the afternoon sun. In the distance, Killian saw the bay and the old Sydney Opera House. He stretched out in his seat, allowing some of the miles to seep from his bones.

"Did you get what I asked?" he asked after a few minutes.

"Yep. The movers got all your stuff in yesterday. All your gear is at the shop. Fresh cloves of garlic, UV lights, the whole nine yards."

"Thanks," Killian said.

"Sure you want to jump right back into vampires? I mean, as happy as I am that you're back, you've been out of it for a while. And what you went through… I saw a couple of pretty easy ghoul nests on the Board if you want to start out a little slower," Jo Jack said.

"Just vampires," Killian replied flatly. Jo Jack glanced between him and the road, obviously not satisfied with his response. "Look, it's been eleven months, Jo Jack. I think it's about time I finish what me and Spin started."

Killian waited for more argument, but Jo Jack simply nodded and returned his eyes to the road. After a moment, Killian asked, "Did you get the names?"

"Yeah, I've got a few. Are you sure you don't want to work with Stamp on this? Or even Dietrich? It might do you some good to have someone you can trust watching your back."

"That's a joke, right? Because you know what happened last time I decided to trust Stamp. He stole my damn girlfriend."

"Okay, if you say so," Jo Jack replied.

"What's that supposed to mean?"

"It doesn't mean anything. I'm just trying to make sure you don't run off on a suicide mission and get yourself killed. You and Spin were my number one hunters. Add Stamp into it, and you guys were unstoppable."

"Obviously not," Killian muttered, pushing the memory to a distant corner of his mind.

"Look, I just want you to take it easy, okay?" Jo Jack said, his tone softening. "I'd hate to lose another good hunter."

"Thanks for the concern. I'll be fine," Killian replied. He looked back out the window, dodging Jo Jack's probing gaze. He didn't know the truth. No one did.

"Where have you been anyway?" he asked, seeming to read Killian's mind. Killian glanced over at him, but Jo Jack seemed to think better of it before he could answer. "You know what, doesn't even matter. I'm probably better off not knowing. It's just… You know the McAuliffe brothers took out that nest." It wasn't a question.

Killian had heard the news several months back. The real question he was asking—the one he wasn't saying out loud—was why Killian was going back in if he knew it had already been cleared. Killian decided not to answer. He wouldn't understand. "So who's number one on the list?" he asked instead.

"Tough choice since you refuse to work with anyone from before. I really had to scrape the bottom of the barrel, but I think I've found a few good candidates. One in particular. Loop. She's got good recommendations and has been begging me for a job for a while now. I just don't trust her inexperience to send her out alone. She's only been on a few hunts."

"How many is 'a few'?" Killian asked.

"Um, one," Jo Jack responded hesitantly. Killian had to fight not to roll his eyes. "Hey, you said you wanted new. It doesn't get any newer than that."

"Jo Jack, when I said new, I meant someone I hadn't worked with before. I didn't mean a damn baby."

"Need I remind you that you were a baby when I gave you your first job?" Jo Jack responded coyly.

"That's different. You gave Spin the job. I was just along for the ride."

"So take her along for the ride. Just give her a chance." Jo Jack sent him a meaningful look. He added, "Skye recommended her."

That brought Killian's eyes back around. "Skye recommended her?"

Jo Jack nodded. "Yeah, I was as shocked as you. I guess they met a few months back. If Skye recommends her, you know she's legit. Speaking of which, does she even know you're back?"

"Skye?"

"No, the tooth fairy."

Killian glared at him. After a moment, he answered. "No. You're the only one."

"Well, don't I feel special? Are you planning on telling her or do I get to keep you all to myself?" Jo Jack asked quirking up one corner of his mouth.

"I'll tell her. Eventually. She's definitely not going to be happy you and I are working together again. I told her I was done when I left."

"Skye'd have to be an idiot to believe that, and she doesn't strike me as an idiot. Still, better me than Frog."

Killian nodded. "You got that right." He sighed. "Alright, I'll check this Loop chick out. She better not be a child, though."

Jo Jack snorted. "Yeah, like you're some old bag of bones yourself. What are you, twenty-six now?"

Killian merely rolled his eyes in response.

A few minutes later, they crossed the Rising Freedom Bridge— formerly the Sydney Harbor Bridge—and all of Blood Haven fell into sight. It was a magnificent spectacle, especially on a clear sunny day like this. Killian pressed his forehead against the window and let out a heavy sigh.

He was finally home.

CHAPTER 2

Skye

Killian's jeep was a tan archaic thing. The brakes were covered in rust, and the paint was chipping along the bottom of the frame. The twin black leather seats were more like holsters than buckets, with shoulder harnesses flung over the backs, and the dashboard hadn't been cleaned in close to a decade. A cracked ram guard protected the front grill, and a light bar with three spotlights was mounted over the chipped and dirty windshield.

It was the most beautiful thing Killian had seen in a long time. He smiled as he climbed in and cranked the engine to life. It gave its usual stubborn grumblings before finally revving up. He pressed on the gas a few times to make sure it wouldn't die. Jo Jack was right. It definitely needed an oil change. He could tell just by how it sounded. Probably a new timing belt as well, but all that could wait. For now, it just needed to get back on the road.

He needed to get back on the road.

It was a fairly lengthy drive to Skye's academy, but he was okay with that. Nestled up in the hills on the outskirts of the city, the academy had a wide berth of open plains around it, with tall yellow grass and even taller trees swaying in the wind like a tide. The road wound up toward the front of the large building like a snake and was only wide enough for a single vehicle. Thankfully, there were no other cars as Killian guided his jeep up the path.

The academy was a three-story tall building set on the grounds of an old orphanage; the building had been renovated and repurposed into a sort of new age school. Several wind chimes hung from the entryway, jingling a tune, and there was a soccer field on the east side of the campus. A sign reading ABSOLUTELY NO MAGIC ON THE FIELD hung from one of the goals. Killian chuckled.

He parked around the side with a cluster of other vehicles, and strode into the building. An elderly woman sat behind the reception desk, and he waved to her. She had on red-rimmed reading glasses, and her grey hair was curled at the tips.

She looked up at him and, after a moment, recognition dawned upon her. "Hey! Been a while since we've seen your handsome face."

"Figured I should finally come out of hiding," Killian replied, smiling as he walked up to her desk. "How are you, Betty?"

"Oh, same as always. The smarter the kids get, the smarter their mouths."

Killian chuckled. "She teaching in her usual spot?"

"Sure is. Does she even know you're back?"

"She's about to," Killian said.

"You always did have a flair for the dramatic. So what have you been doing with yourself all this time? The teachers and I have a little pool going. I said professional rugby in Ireland. They still let our kind play there."

"Amateur division. Never could make it professionally," Killian said, smiling at her.

She chuckled lightly. "As I said, always a flair for the dramatic."

Killian winked at her and walked down the hall toward the east wing. Classrooms filled with students lined the left-hand wall, opposite a row of windows that looked out over the grounds. Killian saw several teenagers practicing spells near an old weather-beaten tree. One had a fireball wavering between his fingertips. Another put her hand against the tree trunk, and green leaves suddenly flourished across its branches, breathing life back into the decrepit tree. Killian smiled. If only he had possessed that kind of skill at their age.

He walked to the room at the end, a sort of greenhouse with wall-spanning windows on two sides and a row of skylights overhead. Plants hung in every corner, and the only piece of furniture was an old black and white chalkboard.

Children ranging in age from five to thirteen sat in a semicircle around it, listening intently as a young woman spoke from beside the chalkboard. She was very beautiful with long honey hair that reached halfway down her back, and her eyes were the most brilliant blue he had ever seen. She had creamy tan skin, and her lips always hinted at a smile. Killian cracked the door open to listen.

"The Change brought with it many mysteries," she said, her Australian accent as thick as ever. The children listened intently, their legs crossed beneath them, enthralled by her voice. "Suddenly, people could do things like never before. They could throw great balls of fire, breathe ice, or summon *spooky* creatures from the dark."

The children giggled at the voice she used to convey the last bit, throwing out her hands and stalking about the group like a wraith. Killian smiled. She caught sight of him and, after a moment of surprise, smiled back.

"But it also brought with it a sense of panic," she continued. "People didn't understand why suddenly so many people were doing these great and wonderful things. And since the day it all started was also the day the world was supposedly going to end, a fear swept across the world like never before. Whole cities were destroyed in the chaos that followed, and nations struggled to get things back under control. But in order to do so, they had to understand *why* the Change had happened. And so they began collecting everyone with these great and wonderful abilities—children like you, parents, aunts, uncles, everyone—and they put them into special camps. Other nations followed. In fact, there was only one that didn't. Can anyone tell me what country that was?"

Almost every child in the room shot their hands into the air, practically bouncing up and down on the floor. She pointed to one.

"Australia!" he practically cooed.

"That's right! Australia, the country in which we all now live. See, Australia wouldn't stand for what was happening around the world and instead provided refuge for people like us. They declared their country free, and its eastern capital, Sydney, was renamed Blood Haven. That way everyone would know this was where they could now call home. This was their safe haven."

She smiled out over the class. One child, however, looked a little confused and raised her hand. She waited patiently until Skye called on her.

"Mrs. Skye, if Blood Haven is so safe…um…why did the Terrible Night happen?" she asked.

The smile suddenly fell from Killian's face. He caught Skye's eye and nodded out the door. She nodded back, her own smile faltering for a second before she turned back to the student to answer her question.

"Because even the safest places have a few bad eggs."

Killian closed the door. He rubbed away the sweat that had suddenly gathered across his forehead, attempting to wipe away the memory as well. He leaned against the window and looked back out over the grounds. The students were no longer practicing spells next to the tree. Heavy, grey storm clouds were gathering across the horizon. Killian doubted they were the work of some weather mage.

The door opened behind him, and he felt a hand fall gently across his shoulder. "I'm sorry about that," Skye said.

"Not your fault," Killian replied. He turned and the pair embraced, holding each other tight for several moments.

"It's good to see you," she said as they pulled apart. "It's been way too long since you stopped by and gave one of your lectures."

"You seem to be handling it okay on your own," Killian said, glancing across the grounds. The academy had come a long way since he had left.

"Still, it would be nice to see you more than once a year," she said. "When did you get back?"

"Yesterday. Wanted to get a few winks before I came over," he replied.

"You could've called. I would've picked you up from the airport."

Killian braced himself for what he knew was about to come. "It's alright. Jo Jack picked me up," he said.

A crease flashed across Skye's forehead, but she didn't let him have it like he was expecting. Instead, she simply sighed and leaned against the window, looking out over the grounds. He suddenly noticed how tired she looked. Bags hung beneath her eyes, only partially covered with makeup, and lines were drawn in her cheeks, as if her usual smile had become an effort.

"So you're working together again," she said. It wasn't a question. "Between him and Frog, I swear…"

"I'm not working with Frog anymore. Jo Jack's the only one."

"That makes me feel so much better," she replied, her voice dripping with sarcasm.

"Jo Jack's a good guy, Skye. I don't know why you've always had such a problem with him," Killian replied. This was it. This was what he had been expecting.

"Because he's also a businessman, and his business involves you going out and nearly getting killed every time."

"I'm still here, though, aren't I?" Killian asked. He had set her up perfectly for it. He knew he had, but instead of bringing up Spin like he had expected, her shoulders merely slumped, and the fire went out of her as quickly as it had appeared.

"Just be careful," she said almost too quietly to hear.

"I will." He again noticed how tired she looked. "Are you okay, Skye?"

Her usual smile flashed across her face, though there was certain falseness to it. She nodded. "Yeah, just give me a few minutes to finish up with my students, and we'll catch up, okay? There's something I could actually use your help with now that I'm thinking about it."

Killian eyed her for a second before nodding. "Only you can go from lecturing me to asking for a favor in less than sixty seconds."

Skye looked at him with a slit-eyed expression. "Just wait for me in the quad. I'll be there in a few."

Killian nodded and headed back down the hall, wondering what was troubling her. The academy seemed to be flourishing. Thanks to Skye, hundreds of children and teenagers could now control their abilities instead of being swallowed up by the streets. The academy now had more students than ever and was a nationally recognized institute. So what was it?

He strode back by the reception desk and nodded to Betty. She smiled back warmly. He considered asking her about it, but he didn't want to raise any eyebrows amongst Skye's staff.

Killian walked through the double doors behind her, leading out into the courtyard in the center of the complex. There was a large circular fountain in the center with several benches around it. Shrubs and foliage grew along the sides of the horseshoe-shaped building, accompanied by the purple and yellow of lilacs and tulips—Skye's favorites. A dragon statue rested on the edge of the courtyard, the academy's guardian. Or so Skye told her students.

Killian sat on one of the benches, watching the water ripple in the fountain. He had always found it so peaceful here. He picked up a loose pebble from the ground, closed his fingers around it, and focused hard on an image in his head. When he opened his fingers up, a stone six-sided die rested in the palm of his hand. He closed his fingers again, exhaling deeply and focusing on another image. This time, it was a stone arrowhead when he opened his hand. He balanced it between his thumb and forefinger, examining his craftsmanship. The tip was pretty sharp, but the edges were rough. He would need to practice if he was going to get back to his old level of skill.

"How'd you do that?" a voice suddenly asked from over his shoulder. Killian glanced behind him and saw a young boy standing there.

"Umm, I'm an Elemental," Killian said. "You know what that means?"

The boy shook his head. He looked to be about thirteen, though he was extremely small for his age. A few dark brown hairs were growing across his upper lip, and a mop of hair hung down across his forehead. He wore a puffy grey vest and patched jeans. His hazel eyes regarded Killian curiously.

"It means I can change the properties of an object as long as what I turn it into shares the same elements. For example, I can turn this stone arrowhead into, say, a knight."

Killian focused hard on the image, and, amidst the boy's look of disbelief, the arrowhead turned into a knight chess piece. The horse's head was a little uneven, but it was still recognizable.

"The details are the hardest. Give me something big without too much detail, and I can do it in a snap. Something small like this requires a lot more focus, or give me something really complicated."

"Like what?" the boy asked. He stared at the chess piece, and Killian handed it to him, making sure to stay focused on the image so it didn't change back.

"Anything with moving parts or a lot of different properties: A gun for example, is almost impossible. I've seen only one person able to do that."

"Who?" asked the boy in amazement. He handed the knight back to Killian, who let it turn back into the pebble. He stared at the boy for a long moment.

"Someone I met when I was your age. You wouldn't know him," he finally said. The boy's face fell. He had obviously been hoping to hear more.

"I see you two have met," Skye called as she walked into the courtyard.

"He was teaching me about Elementals," the boy said.

"Oh, is that right?" she asked, shooting Killian a glance. "Sure you don't want to start teaching lessons again?"

"I'm good," Killian replied, though the look in Skye's eyes said she wasn't convinced.

"Killian, this is Lucas. Lucas, this is my old friend Killian. I've known him since we were about your age."

"So you must know the man too!" Lucas exclaimed.

"What man?" Skye asked, looking back at Killian. He dodged her gaze.

"The man who can change a gun." Confusion flashed across Skye's face. "He said he knew a man when he was my age that could change a gun using his powers."

Skye forced a smile and kneeled down in front of the boy. "That man is no longer with us," she said in a quiet voice.

Lucas's excitement fell like an anvil, and he looked back over toward Killian. "Sorry," he said.

"Don't worry about it," Killian replied.

"Why don't you run inside and finish up your lesson with Mister Pope. He's been looking for you," Skye said, nodding back toward the academy.

With a look of dismay and several seconds of hesitation, Lucas nodded and trudged back toward the building. When Lucas was inside, Killian turned to look at Skye.

"I take it back. Maybe you don't have things under control here. How does he not even know what an Elemental is?" Killian asked.

"Lucas comes from a very unique situation," Skye said, taking a seat beside him. "He grew up in America."

"What? How did he get here?"

"The Underground. They smuggled him out and brought him here," Skye answered.

"Skye, you know how dangerous that is? If agents show up looking for him, the Overseers can protect you only so much."

"I know, I know," Skye said. "I had to get him out of there, though. The things they were doing to him. He's lived almost his entire life in a metal box. He barely knows anything about the world."

"Why? America has entire camps for people like us. Why him?" Killian asked.

"Because he's different."

"Different how? What's his classification?"

"That's the thing. He doesn't have one," Skye said.

Confusion streaked across Killian's face. "What do you mean 'he doesn't have one'?" he asked.

"He can do it all. Everything. Show him how and he can do it. Fireballs, ice shards, weather manipulation. Everything. And so fast. I've never seen anyone pick it up so quickly."

"Jesus," Killian said, his elbows falling forward onto his knees and an exhale of breath escaping his lips. "How… What…"

"I've been trying to figure it out, but it seems he just doesn't have a particular specialization."

"You know how dangerous that could be? If he ever loses control of his abilities or unlocks one he doesn't know he has…"

"That's why I brought him here, to teach him rather than just experiment on him."

"Does he remember any of it?"

"Some. Mostly it comes to him when he sleeps, but otherwise he says it's just a white void, and I'm not going to try to get him to remember. Repression may be the best thing for him until he's got more control over his abilities."

"Why do I have the feeling that meeting him wasn't a coincidence?"

Killian asked, looking her in the eye.

"It's actually what I wanted to talk to you about," Skye said, dodging his gaze.

Killian immediately shot out of his seat. "No. No way. Whatever it is, count me out. This has bad news written all over it."

"Killian…"

"Don't '*Killian*' me. I've got enough of my own crap to worry about to take on some super wizard."

"He's not a super wizard. He's a thirteen-year-old kid who needs our help, and *you* can teach him. He picks up the techniques easily; it's pretty much as easy as breathing for him, but he can't always control it. You can show him how. Elementals are the best at controlling their abilities because of what you can do, and you're the best one I know."

"I'm the only one you know," Killian said.

"Be that as it may, there's still no one I would rather have teaching him. He needs structure, discipline, and the little bit I just saw proves what I already knew."

"And you think *I* can give that to him? You're joking, right?"

"Don't give me that. We both know how you were trained. Teach him the same way. He can handle it."

"Lea, he's a baby. You yourself said it. If I teach him the same way I was taught, he'll get swallowed up by the streets. Super wizard or not."

"Would you stop calling him that?" Skye barked. "And don't call me Lea. Only my mother gets to call me that."

"Well, maybe your mother should come slap some sense into you. She'd understand why bringing me on this is a mistake."

"You're my oldest friend, Killian."

"And I'm not a babysitter."

"Killian…"

"*Skye.* I'm sorry, but I can't. I just can't," he said.

Skye met his eyes, and for a long time they just stared at one another. Finally, after several long moments, she bowed her head and nodded. "I understand."

"Thanks." Killian took a step forward and tentatively placed his hand on her shoulder. She seemed to take a small measure of comfort from it, and they just stood like that for several moments. Thunder suddenly clapped overhead, and they both looked up at the dark storm clouds gathering overhead. "I better get out of here before the rain starts coming down, but before I go I wanted to ask you about someone you recommended to Jo Jack."

Skye let out a breath. "Loop. Should've known you didn't come by just to catch up."

Killian's gaze narrowed. "Says the one who just asked *me* for a favor. I just want to know if she's worth taking on, if she's really any good."

A smile cut across Skye's features. It was obviously forced. "Why don't you go find out for yourself? You can find her at Club Ice most nights. Look for the short one with black hair."

With that, Skye turned on her heel and headed back inside, leaving Killian alone in the courtyard as the first raindrops began to fall. Despite the weather, he smiled slightly. *That* was the Skye he knew.

CHAPTER 3

The Lighter

Killian stared at the boxes stacked around his small apartment. He had opened only one and already lost all motivation to go any further. It hadn't felt like this much stuff when he packed it ten months ago. Then again, he wasn't exactly in a clear state of mind back then.

His conversation with Skye replayed in his head. He felt guilty for not helping her; she had always been there for him. He just couldn't handle teaching some kid right now, definitely not when he was some kind of super wizard. Hell, Killian could barely take care of himself right now. On top of that, he was about to take on a rookie. He was already out of his mind for that. Still, the feeling of guilt lingered at the back of his mind.

Killian cut the tape on another box and pried it open. It had been labeled BEDROOM, and he was hoping to find some bed sheets in it. He instead found a mound of junk he couldn't believe he had even packed—a baseball glove with no ball, a stapler, some old DVDs. He dug through it haphazardly until his fingers brushed across something smooth near the bottom. He pulled it out curiously. It was a photograph from a few years back. In it, he was standing next to a beautiful Native American woman, his arm around her shoulder, the harbor sparkling behind them. She had long, straight black hair and full lips. A yellow flower was tucked behind one ear.

Daisy.

Another man stood on her other side, his fingers making bunny ears behind her head for the photo. He was tall and muscular, with broad shoulders and an even broader chest. His dark hair was cut even shorter than Killian's.

Stamp.

They were all laughing. Spin had made a joke as he snapped the photo and caught them all off guard with it. Killian couldn't remember what exactly they had been celebrating, but it was a great night.

Frowning, he tossed the photograph back into the box, making sure it landed facedown.

Killian checked his watch before turning back to the first box he had opened, labeled CLOSET. The packing material already lay discarded at the foot of his bed. He pulled the flaps back and again stared at the multitude of weapons stored within. There were several sheathed machetes of varying sizes, a curved hatchet, a handful of knives. They all lay across a folded navy blue jacket. Moving the weapons aside, he pulled it out, brushing away the layer of dust that had accumulated. It had been a gift from Spin after their first hunt together. The inside was lined with the same material as diving suits, making it puncture proof and protecting him from probing teeth. The collar could be zipped all the way up to protect his neck. It had done so on several occasions. Several tears in the sleeves had been stitched back together where claws had torn the fabric but not the material underneath. Daisy sewed them back together. Vaguely, Killian wondered who would do it now.

He slipped his arms through the sleeves and pulled it on, only slightly surprised it still fit after all this time. He doubted he would ever really outgrow it. Next he pulled out a small folding knife and tucked it into his back pocket. He also grabbed the pistol from his desk and holstered it behind his jacket.

Always be too prepared, a voice echoed from a distant corner of his mind.

Spin.

Killian headed down to his jeep parked in the small lot outside, pushing the thoughts aside.

He only vaguely remembered where Club Ice was located—he had never actually been there—so he took a few wrong turns before he found his way.

Even for a Wednesday night, the club was busy. It was nestled in the heart of the Cultural District, packed to the brim with young, eager college students and new age magicians whom Killian hated on principle alone. Granted, he wasn't that much older than they were, but experiences counted, and they didn't have any.

He was forced to park several blocks away; all the nearby lots and street-side meters were full. His grumbling jeep stood out amidst the cluster of electric cars and fuel-efficient scooters as he pulled into the narrow lot.

The Cultural District was home to some of the city's greatest up-and-coming poets and artists (or so they told themselves anyway) and there was a vast array of art exhibits and galleries spread throughout the district. If this was the kind of crowd Loop frequented, Killian doubted he would be able to work with her. On principle.

Making sure his pistol didn't stick out beneath his jacket, he then headed toward the club. The line to get in was fairly long. At least two dozen people stood in front of him as he walked up, waiting for the club to empty out a little bit. A large number of them wore scarves and knit caps despite the warmth, and the girls had on gaudy makeup. Several of them sported tattoos on the backs of their hands that signified what class they were, apparently some new style: red flames for fire mages, blue drops of water, a few inverted triangles for enchanters. He saw a lot of weather mages among them and just rolled his eyes.

Jamming his hands into his jacket pockets, Killian waited. After several minutes, however, the line still hadn't moved. The people in front of him didn't seem to mind. Dust was all the rage in this part of town, and he could practically smell it coming off them. They were probably all high as kites. He wasn't so fortunate.

Killian was growing impatient. He glanced toward the front of the line The bouncer guarding the door was at least four inches taller than Killian and his expression said he wasn't going to give anyone a pass. Not even the group of pretty girls at the front, no matter how much they fluttered their eyelashes at him. Killian glanced back, and, seeing no one behind him, he made up his mind. He stepped out of line.

The club shared its right side with a fashion boutique that sold a lot of the bright clothing that the people in line were wearing. An art gallery was on the other side of that. The left side, however, was an alleyway where Killian assumed deliveries were made. It was just wide enough for a loading truck. With a backward glance at the stagnant line, he headed down the alley. As to be expected, several shattered bottles and an assortment of loose detritus lined the sides of the lane. Some vagrant had set up a makeshift cardboard hut against the side of a dumpster, but he must have been chased off because it stood empty.

About forty yards in, Killian spotted a loading door with a small ramp leading up to it. There was another door beside it marked FIRE EXIT. There wasn't a handle outside. Stepping closer, he saw a padlock secured the loading door to the ground. Someone had drawn a negating enchantment into the concrete around the door to keep it from being altered. Unfortunately for the artist, it had been smeared by tread marks, and the effect was now null.

Killian smiled. This was going to be easier than he thought.

Kneeling down, he grabbed the padlock and exhaled slowly, allowing the image to form in his mind. The padlock dissolved into a small metal ball. There were several discolorations across its surface from the different kinds of metals, and a rubber seal stood like a ring around it, but it came free from the door and allowed it to slide upward.

Killian stuffed the ball into his jacket pocket and peeked beneath the door. It was gloomy inside, all shadows and dark shapes. Nothing appeared to be moving, however. As he rose to his feet, he yanked the door up as quietly as he could. It proved harder than he had expected. The tracks hadn't been oiled in some time, and the door squealed loudly. Killian stopped when it was up to his waist and settled for ducking underneath.

Just as he had expected, it was where they brought in and stored all the beverages. Several large boxes were stacked in the corner, and a row of tall shelves were lined with wooden crates. On closer look, he saw a shadow between the shelves. It wasn't moving. Killian pushed the door up a little further, cringing at the squeal, and was surprised to see a red and yellow motorcycle parked there. It was sleek and fast and definitely did not belong in a place like this. Killian smiled. It appeared he wasn't the only outsider here.

He let the door slide shut behind him, immediately engulfing him in darkness. He couldn't even see his hand in front of his face. As he muttered a curse, he took a step toward the door on the other side of the room and immediately hit his toe on the motorcycle. He cursed again. He used his hand to feel his way until he found the wall and followed it to the door. He could hear the music from the club thumping behind it, and the handle vibrated as he grabbed it. Hopefully there wasn't another bouncer waiting on the other side. Killian really didn't feel like getting tossed out on his ass after all this effort.

Thankfully, he didn't see another bouncer as he cracked the door and peeked out. It led out into a narrow hallway. The bathrooms were right across from him, and a couple was making out a few feet away. Bright strobe lights peeked through the red curtain at the end of the hallway, apparently leading out to the dance floor. The music was much louder and assaulted Killian's ears with a plethora of tones and beats.

Slipping past the couple, he headed down the hallway and stepped through the curtain. He was immediately blinded. Strobe lights peppered the dance floor and walls. The DJ was playing up on a high stage, and several painted go-go dancers twirled on circular platforms spread throughout the dance floor. One had a foxtail clipped to her bikini bottom, and another had white feathery angel wings peeking out over her shoulders. They were both unbelievably attractive and danced sensually on their little islands while everyone else seemed to bounce up and down around them, hands raised in the air. The entire room smelled of Dust and almost made Killian sick to his stomach. He had never smelled it in such concentration before. It was practically coming out of their pores. Mixed with the heavy odor of sweat and perfume, it was almost overwhelming.

Killian gave his eyes and nose a moment to adjust before pushing through the crowd toward the U-shaped bar. He glanced around as he went, searching for a short woman with black hair, but everyone's features seemed to blend together. Blondes, brunettes, redheads, they were all the same in the haze of the strobe lights. He looked up toward the second level where tables and booths overlooked the dance floor. This was going to be harder than he thought. How could he possibly find one small woman in a sea of faces?

Killian settled for snagging an open space at the bar and peering out over the crowd. The bartender glared at him so he ordered a drink. They didn't have any beers he liked so he ordered some mixed specialty from the thin man and rolled his eyes as he turned around. He had a feeling the bartender did the same. This was obviously not Killian's scene.

The bartender tapped Killian on his shoulder and handed him his drink, indicating the charge with his fingers. It took two hands. Killian dug into his pocket and dumped several chits on the counter. The bartender had obviously been hoping for paper bills, but Killian never carried any. With all the Elementals out there, one touch could turn a stack of bills into a pocketful of tree bark. So far, Killian had been unsuccessful in mastering that little trick, though. Each was engraved with the same sigil, a marking from ancient Hindu lore that kept them from being altered. On the other side was its value. Unfortunately, these were not singles.

Killian turned back around before the bartender could glare at him again and took a sip from his drink. It was awful, somehow bitter and fruity at the same time. He held onto it just so he would have a reason for staying at the bar and continued to stare out across the dance floor. There wasn't even a guarantee Loop would be here tonight. Skye had just said she was here *most* nights. He silently cursed her. She had known what kind of bar this was and knew how out of place Killian would feel here. She had done it on purpose to spite him. That was their relationship, though. She kept him in line like a big sister, and he still wasn't quite sure what he brought to the table. Friendship, he supposed. She didn't have much of that when they had first met, but that had been a long time ago and a lot had changed. She was surrounded by friends now.

Killian took another sip from his drink, fighting the urge to cringe. How did anyone drink this stuff?

The DJ was halfway through his second set when Killian finally spotted a flash of raven-hued hair. He stared hard across the dance floor and spotted a young woman weaving through the crowd. She was pretty in a sort of girl-next-door kind of way, with an angled jaw line, full lips, and almond-shaped eyes. Her hair was cut short, the tips just barely grazing her neckline. She was gone, however, almost as quickly as she had appeared.

Loop.

It had to be her.

Killian set his drink on the bar and relinquished his spot to two college students who had been eyeing it for the past twenty minutes. They swept in like a pair of hyenas as soon as he left. Killian gave them a look and slowly began working his way around the dance floor, searching again for the short woman. He spotted her again heading up the stairs to the second floor. She didn't have a drink in her hand and glanced around the room like she was searching for something rather than just enjoying the view. Killian followed her.

He caught up to her halfway around the balcony. He tried calling out to her, but she obviously couldn't hear him over the thrum of the music He himself could barely hear. She was still looking out over the dance floor like she was searching for something. Killian glanced out as well but didn't see anything out of the ordinary.

He reached out for her just as they walked past the last table overlooking the dance floor. As soon as his fingers grazed her shoulder, however, she grabbed hold of his wrist and spun him around, slamming his cheek down across the table in an arm-bar. The shock of it sucked the air from his lungs, and he felt his arm pop.

"Want to tell me how you got in here without paying?" she asked. She had to shout to be heard over the music.

Vaguely, Killian wondered how she knew he hadn't paid. As soon as he could breathe again, however, he laughed. Now it all made sense. She stared at him in surprise, her brow creased.

"What's so funny?" she asked.

"You. You're not a customer. You're a bouncer," he said, still chuckling lightly. He liked her already, even as she tightened her grip on his wrist and caused his shoulder to give another pop. He only groaned minimally.

"So what?"

"So I've been looking for you."

"Why?" she asked, her brow creasing again. Nervousness tipped the edge of her voice. She obviously didn't like people looking for her.

"You're Loop, right? Let me up and I'll tell you," Killian said, no longer laughing. His arm was starting to hurt, and they were beginning to attract attention from the nearby tables. People were glancing out from their booths, and several couples had actually detached from their lip locks to see what was going on.

"Tell me and I'll let you up," she countered. The nervousness had disappeared from her voice and was replaced with something else.

"My name's Killian," he said, barely able to see her over his shoulder. "I'm friends with Skye. I want to hire you."

Loop released his arm so quickly Killian nearly fell off the table, his balance completely distorted.

"Technically, I'm a spotter," she said, taking several steps back and crossing her arms. "I look for whoever needs to go. The bouncers take care of the rest. So what do you want to hire me for?"

Killian motioned to an empty booth, and she nodded, following him over to it. As soon as he sat down, the noise from the club died down to a steady hum. He glanced beneath the table and saw an enchantment had been inscribed into the floor. A noise barrier. He gave the club a little bit of respect for that.

Loop sat across from him. She was thin, but her arms definitely had some strength in them he hadn't been expecting. His shoulder could vouch for that. Her green eyes were highlighted with dark makeup that matched her hair. They sat staring at each other for several moments. She was obviously sizing him up just as much as he was her.

"So I've heard you want to be a hunter," he said after another moment.

He had hoped to catch her off guard with that and he definitely succeeded. She blinked at him several times before finally responding.

"Yeah, I do," she replied slowly. Part of her obviously thought this was a joke. "You're looking for a partner or just a one-time thing?"

"Partner. It's a full time gig for me, and I need someone to help watch my back. You can obviously handle yourself in a fight, but how well do you think you'd do against a pack of vampires? Or a nest of ghouls?"

"I've done pretty well so far," she said.

"Don't bother trying to bullshit me. I know you've been on only one hunt," Killian said. He again caught her off guard. That was good. He might get some real responses out of her instead of whatever she had rehearsed at home.

Loop sighed. "I don't know. I can fight. I know that much. And I'm not afraid."

"Then you really are inexperienced. You should always be afraid. Fear gets you through way more than courage."

She nodded, though she obviously didn't quite believe him. She would learn eventually just like he had.

"So what do you need from me to make this happen? Job references, tax history?" she asked, trying to recover with a joke.

"Nothing like that," Killian said, smiling slightly. "I've got just two questions."

"Okay…" she said slowly.

"First question: Is that your motorcycle in the store room downstairs?" he asked.

Loop stared at him. "Yes."

Killian nodded. Just as he had been hoping. "Second question: What's your classification?"

Again, Loop stared at him for a long moment, her eyes narrowing. She obviously didn't understand what all of this had to do with hunting. To Killian, it was everything, however.

"I'm a Lighter."

Killian smiled again. He was sold.

CHAPTER 4

Hunter

It took two weeks of constant training and conditioning to get Loop ready for her first real hunt. They spent pretty much every waking hour together since that night at the club. When they weren't together training, she was working late nights at the club. He, on the other hand, spent most nights sitting in his apartment, watching television and sipping beer. There had been a time when he couldn't be found at home. If it wasn't a hunt, it was a dinner party at Daisy's or a fundraiser for Skye's academy. How times had changed.

It had taken a few days to get to the bottom of Loop's actual hunting experience, which was about as impressive as Killian had expected. She had been hired on as a spotter to watch for a rabid vampire that was terrorizing a local park. It wasn't a nest or even a pack. She had simply sat out for two nights until she spotted the vampire, and then another hunter had swept in for the kill and the bounty. They didn't even burn the corpse for the Dust. She said there hadn't been enough to make it worth it. The hunter paid her only fifty chits.

What Killian hadn't figured out was why she wanted to hunt so badly. Was she a dealer, trying to cut out the middle man by acquiring the Dust herself? No, that wasn't it. Otherwise, she would be focused solely on vampires like he was, and she had already told him she wasn't picky. Some personal resentment against Subbies then; he doubted that as well. There wasn't any pain or fire in her eyes when she spoke about it. No, it was something else. Maybe one day she would tell him, but for now she was perfectly content keeping it a secret. As long as whatever it was didn't affect her ability to keep him alive, he didn't really care either.

Killian gave Loop today off, though. She needed some recovery time and, frankly, so did he. The training had been rigorous: constant sparring, target practice, weapons drills; Loop never complained or gave up. She wanted to hunt, and it didn't seem like anything was going to deter her from achieving her goal. In a lot of ways, she reminded Killian of himself when he had first started. Spin never gave him a day off, though.

Killian didn't give Loop the day off just to recover, though. There was something else, something he had been meaning to do since arriving back in Blood Haven, and he had put it off for far too long already.

It took him almost an hour to get to the abandoned resort in the hills outside the city. It was intended to have been the city's greatest vacation spot, servicing the wealthy and not so wealthy, but then everything Changed. It had never been finished and was now nothing more than a concrete shell of its former vision. The main two-story building stretched back toward the top of the distant hill, ending in what was probably intended to be a grand observation tower. Wings shot off from the main building in seemingly random directions, some rising up into the hills, others dipping down into the valley it overshadowed. Vegetation, like reaching green tendrils, grew across the walls and hung down across windows. The few spots that were bare of greenery were covered with graffiti. They were mostly gang signs, a few song lyrics. One tag in particular caught Killian's attention. Staring at it sent a shiver up his spine.

Known Vampire Nest it had read before someone crossed it out with red spray paint. Cleared was now written below that.

Killian wished he had been able to write that instead of the McAuliffe brothers.

Opening his jeep, Killian pulled out the tin jar he had secured in the passenger seat. It was filled with grey Dust.

No, Killian thought. *Ashes.*

He walked over to the rusted metal railing that ran alongside the building.

It overlooked the valley and the green forest below. Slowly, and with slightly shaking hands, Killian unscrewed the jar. He stared at the ashes contained within, then out toward the valley. Blood Haven was just visible across the distant horizon.

It had been a long road—months of tracking, making connections—but he had finally made it. *They* had finally made it.

"Goodbye, my friend," Killian said, barely audible over the rising wind.

He turned the jar upside down and allowed the ashes to fall. They caught on the wind and flowed outward like a stream, disappearing as they spread. Killian fought with everything he had not to cry, but still a tear slipped from his eye and down his cheek. He brushed it away as quickly as it had appeared.

Killian stared down at the tin jar for a moment before shaking his head and throwing it down into the valley as well.

It was done.

He stared at the resort for a long while after that, the memories flooding back, before heading back to his jeep. He was climbing in when his phone vibrated in his pocket. He fished it out and answered it.

"Yeah?" he said gruffly. He was still fighting to keep the tears from his eyes, and it was evident as his voice cracked.

"Kil, it's Jo Jack. You alright?"

"I'm fine," Killian said. It didn't sound very convincing, even to him. "What's up?" he said to try to cover it up.

"I've got a job. Just popped up on the Board. Might be a good one to try Loop out on. You think she's ready?" Jo Jack asked.

"Yeah, she's ready," Killian replied much more convincingly.

"Alright. What about you? Are *you* ready?" Jo Jack had obviously heard the unease in his voice and thought it related to the hunt. In a way it did, just not *this* hunt.

Killian stared at the resort in his rear-view mirror for a long moment. The ashes had dissipated and were lost from sight. He finally nodded, more to himself than the phone, and responded, "Yeah, I'm ready."

"How many you think there are?" Loop asked, as they surveyed the loading bay door from across the narrow lane. The rain was coming down in sheets around them, and Loop's hair was matted across her scalp. She trembled slightly.

"Probably five or so. They stay pretty small when they're inside the city like this," he responded, glancing down at her slightly quivering frame. "Just keep your eyes up, and you'll be fine," he added in the best reassuring tone he could muster.

Loop nodded, staring up at the sheets of pouring rain and the dark storm clouds overhead.

Killian looked up as well. *Probably a weather mage testing out his abilities,* he thought irritably. They always seemed to favor the heavy downpours like these, devoid of any lightning or thunder, and he was pretty sure he had seen one on the ride in, standing on the street corner, arms above his head chanting as storm clouds slowly formed overhead. Killian could still see sunlight peeking over the roof of the warehouse, though, so obviously the mage wasn't very powerful, otherwise, the cluster of clouds would have spread out much further. Regardless, it was raining, and Killian was soaked. Trails of water continually dripped across his grey-blue eyes.

The warehouse was a bleak figure in front of them, the windows blacked out and the concrete cracked in several locations. The loading bay door was corroded, covered in a patchwork of red and orange rust.

"You were right," Loop said quietly beside him. Killian looked down at her. "It was inexperience. I'm scared."

"We'll be fine. Just remember the plan, and everything will be okay," he replied. He looked up the alleyway toward the distant street, gritting his teeth as rain continued to patter across his face. They should have taken out the weather mage. They would need the sun if things went badly. "Let's just get in there and get this done, alright?"

After a moment, Loop nodded, and they headed across the lane. They hopped up onto the raised loading bay and took position on either side of the door. It was heavily corroded and squealed against its frame every time the wind hit it, setting Killian's teeth on edge. He hated to admit it, but he was nervous. *It's all right,* he told himself. *They don't know we're here yet.*

A chain and padlock secured the door in place. Loop nodded to Killian. He glanced at the lock and nodded back. With his shotgun in one hand, he removed one of his leather gloves with his teeth and stuffed it into his jacket pocket. Leaning forward, he used the same trick he had used at the club. He grabbed the lock, and, in the blink of an eye, it turned into a small metal ball, falling away from the chains and sliding from the door. Killian stuffed the ball into his pocket and pulled back on his glove as Loop gently set the chains on the ground. She turned around, nodded, and trained her gun on the door. He stepped forward and yanked it upward with a grunt of exertion. It squealed miserably, and Killian cringed with each passing second until it was over halfway up and he was able to knock the first latch into place. He made sure it wasn't going to come back down on them once they were inside before giving Loop a thumbs-up and motioning into the darkness.

It was almost pitch-black inside the warehouse, and Killian could barely make out the rows of shelves and crates lining the bay floor. Cobwebs wove across them like a quilt, and he was sure he saw the beady eyes of several rodents as light hit them for the first time in probably weeks. According to the Board, the pack was in the middle of a hibernation cycle and had not been out of the nest in some time. It was the perfect time to hit them.

Killian dug into his cargo pocket and shook up a couple of light sticks, rolling them across the floor into the darkness. They barely pierced the gloom, but it allowed Killian to get a better sense of his surroundings.

Know your exits, a voice echoed from a distant corner of his mind. Not long ago, that voice had kept him alive.

There were four rows of metal shelves on the bay floor, each one well over ten feet tall, and a row of crates lined the right-hand wall. There were also the decrepit remains of a forklift in the corner, but it looked older than Killian and Loop combined. Two wooden doors stood closed on the left-hand wall. One had a frosted glass window, most likely leading into the section of warehouse offices. Killian could only guess where the second one led. Overhead, he heard the steady drumbeat of rain pattering down on the sheet metal roof.

The pair walked in slowly and quietly across the concrete floor. Killian had elected to wear sneakers this time instead of his brown leather boots. He knew from experience they weren't great for running.

They took the aisles one at a time. Killian's head was on a swivel, his shotgun always pointed out before him. Loop's fingers were wrapped tightly around the grip of her submachine gun. Shadows played across the meager illumination of the light sticks. Killian could have sworn he saw several move on their own. He hoped it was just his imagination.

There was an overwhelming scent of musk and decay the farther in they moved, and, as they reached the end of the last aisle, Killian saw why. A pile of four corpses lay in the back corner of the room. They had been there for some time, judging by the pungent smell. Killian had to force himself not to gag. This was not his first time seeing this. All of them had had their throats ripped out, along with several bite marks in the form of twin puncture marks along their wrists and calves—the sweet spots.

Killian turned to his companion, his eyes continuing to roam around the warehouse. They had to be around here somewhere.

"Loop, give me an orb," he breathed. She nodded, balling her left hand into a fist and closing her eyes for just a second. When they opened back up and she spread her fingers, a small ball of light, no larger than a tennis ball, hovered above her palm. She extended her arm out toward Killian, and the glowing orb floated toward his hand. He held it in place for a second and continued to stare around the bay floor, listening hard. After a few moments, and a long drawn-out breath, he turned and threw the orb toward the far aisle of shelves and illuminated the shadow crouched atop it. He couldn't have been more than a teenager, if he had still been alive, and when the ball of light glided past him, he bared his fangs and hissed at them.

A second later, faster than either of them could track, he leapt across the row of shelves and dove toward them. Killian and Loop rolled out of the way in opposite directions, bringing their guns to bear on the teenager and blasting him as he hit the floor. One, two, three shots from Killian's shotgun and a burst from Loop's submachine gun finally left him quivering on the floor.

"Loop, stake," Killian said, as he stood up and walked over to the gargling teenager. He choked on bubbling black blood as it pooled in the back of his throat. Loop dug into her belt pouch and produced a small silver rod. An outward flick of her wrist extended it into a pointed stake, which she tossed to Killian. He caught it and, without hesitating, drove it straight into the teen's chest. He screeched as it pierced his ribs and, a moment later, finally stopped quivering.

Killian breathed a long exhale of breath and stood back up, wiping the cold sweat that had formed across his brow.

God! That felt good.

"Holy crap, he was fast," Loop said, staring down at the teenager as she stood back up as well. "Is it always like that?"

"Pretty much. And that was an easy one. Probably the runt of the litter. We'll be lucky to get a kilo off him."

"How much is the order for again?"

"Nineteen," Killian replied, continuing to stare down at the teenage vampire. He was a fresh turn, the twin puncture marks along his neck still visible.

"Nineteen?" Loop asked in disbelief. "Kilos? Has Jo Jack lost his mind? There's no way we can fill that kind of order."

"Dust is catching on," Killian replied, quieting her with a raised hand. He finally looked up from the teen. "He's got more demands. Now come on and keep your eyes up. We've still got the…" He suddenly froze, his eyes glued to the frosted glass door. It was wide open. "…rest of the pack," he finished.

He looked around sharply, his breath suddenly caught in his throat and his heart hammering within his chest. Loop saw the door and looked around sharply as well. Her grip tightened around her gun, and she swallowed a hard lump in her throat.

A low chuckle slowly echoed from all around, deep and reverberating across the concrete walls. Sweat beaded across Killian's brow. A shrill laugh joined in, then a loud chortle, until there was a chorus of laughter all around them.

"Start backing up toward the door," Killian said, a cold tingle running down his spine, his shotgun pointed up at the tops of the shelves as he slowly backpedaled.

Loop mimicked him, the laughter continuing all around them. The ball of light was still glowing from atop the far shelf, but it was fading quickly. As it disappeared entirely, Killian turned to run for the door.

A clawed hand suddenly closed around his neck, knocking his shotgun out of his grasp easily and lifting him off the floor, bringing him face to face with the head of the vampire family. He had sandy blond hair and deep scarlet eyes. His lips were peeled back in a fanged smile as he brought Killian in close so their noses were mere inches apart. Three other vampires stepped over. One held Loop by the shoulder, his massive claws digging into her leather jacket and piercing the flesh beneath. She gritted her teeth in pain. The female of the pack would have been quite attractive had her skin not been deathly pale and her fangs not poking out from between her purple chapped lips. She sauntered over slowly, taking in Killian's scent with a long drawn-out breath.

"He smells positively delicious," she said in a seductive drawl that sent another cold tingle down Killian's spine.

"He does indeed," the master said, still holding Killian in front of his face like a plate of meat, examining him.

"They killed Chris," the one holding Loop said. He was the largest of the four, at least a foot taller than Killian.

"That's a pity. He never could handle his appetite, though," the master said. Every word dripped from his tongue like acid. "Woke me every day, begging for food. It was stupid to turn him right before the cycle, but what can you do? Sort of ironic, though. It was his lack of begging that woke me today, alerting me to *your* presence."

Killian struggled against the master's grip, tight around his throat, and tried to keep fear from showing across his face. He was sure they could already smell it; he wouldn't give them the satisfaction of showing it as well.

It was obvious they had succumbed to the insanity that often went hand-in-hand with the vampiric disease. His feet kicked helplessly as, slowly, he managed to get his head around to look back at Loop. The giant holding her tightened his grip around her shoulder and brought a bitter cry of pain to her lips. Still, she managed to lock eyes with him and nodded when he glanced up toward the ceiling. She curled both hands into fists as Killian slowly swiveled his head back around to look at the master. She just needed a little time.

He would give it to her.

"Tearful goodbye?" the master asked, smiling even more wickedly and lifting Killian further into the air. As his grip tightened, Killian had to struggle to breathe. He choked out a garbled curse. The master let out a shrill laugh. "What's that? I'm afraid I didn't catch it. Oh, you were saying you taste best with a hint of pepper. Got it. Now, who should we feast on first? This has been a terribly long cycle and I'm positively starved."

"The boy. Let's feed on the boy," the female said. She was practically bouncing around them. Killian spat another unintelligible curse, dribbling saliva from the corners of his mouth. He prayed Loop was almost ready.

"What was that? I didn't catch that, either. You really must use your words," the master said. He lowered him slightly and loosened his grip, finally allowing some oxygen to seep into Killian's lungs. "Want to help us make our decision?"

"No," Killian rasped out. His eyes shot back over his shoulder at Loop. Her hands were still balled tightly into fists and were shaking at her sides. The tiniest bit of light was peeking out from between her fingers. She nodded slowly. "I was just going to ask if you knew why—ugh!—I hate weather mages so much."

The vampire master's brow creased in confusion. He brought Killian in close, so close he could practically smell the death coming off him, before the maniacal smile slowly cracked his visage once more.

"No, I have no idea."

"Because," Killian said slowly, his body tensing in anticipation. "They never want to bring out the sun!"

Just then, Loop threw out her fists and opened her hands, releasing two massive bursts of light that filled the room and blinded the four vampires. They threw their hands up to shield their eyes, and the master dropped Killian to the ground. He landed hard on his back, his feet collapsing beneath him.

Without a second's hesitation, he grabbed his shotgun and pointed it up at the master. The vampire recovered just in time to see the blast hit him square in the face. He reeled backward, and a second blast sent him sprawling flat.

Loop dove to the end of the shelves and swept up her submachine gun, spraying the other two male vampires before they could go after him. She emptied her clip.

Killian caught the female sprinting toward the door, so quickly he could barely keep his gun trained on her. As she leapt through it, he sent two blasts trailing after her and managed to catch her in the back. She too went sprawling and slid to a halt just past the door.

Killian was breathing heavily. He ripped off his gloves and grabbed the nearest piece of metal he could find—a rusted pry bar laying across the row of crates. As he closed his hands around it, one clear image formed in his head. A moment later, the pry bar dissolved into a long metal stake, the end honed to a finely sharpened point.

He went after the master first. He would be the quickest to recover. Loop was already taking care of the big one with her extendable stake. He cried out for half a second when the rod pierced his chest before sagging a moment later and dying. Judging by the blood leaking from Loop's shoulder, Killian doubted she felt any remorse.

The master lay on his back, struggling to prop himself up on his arm. Killian kicked it out from under him and he fell back flat. Killian raised the stake over his head, still breathing fiercely, fire in his eyes.

Just then, he was tackled to the side, his world spinning as he hit the concrete hard. The stake spun away from his grasp. The female vampire was atop him, her fangs extended, and he barely managed to get his hands up in time to stop her from ripping out his esophagus. He held her throat with one hand and pressed against her chin with the other. She struggled against him; it was all he could do to keep her away from his neck. She ripped at his chest with her claws, but the diving material in his jacket kept her from tearing open his flesh.

Loop suddenly sprinted over and shoved her off him with the whole weight of her body. The vampire landed with a shriek, and Killian swept up the stake. He drove it down into her chest with all his weight behind it, missed her heart by an inch, and drove it down again. This time, he hit his mark, and with a final shrill cry, the female vampire died.

Killian yanked the stake free with a sickening squelch of flesh and stood over the master. "And *we're* the monsters," he said, the same smile slowly spreading across his lips. He breathed heavily.

"Nope," Killian responded, still breathing raggedly. He fingered the stake for a moment. "You're just the job."

And with that, he drove it down as hard as he could, piercing what remained of the vampire's heart and ending his life. His eyes flared for just a moment, like a crackling fire, before he finally sagged to the floor.

Killian bent over and ripped the stake out, the point dripping with more of the tar-like blood.

"That could've gone smoother," Loop said from beside him, holding her shoulder.

"You alright?" Killian asked. He dropped the stake, and, after a moment, it transformed into the pry bar. His jacket had two fresh tears in it where the female's claws had ripped the fabric.

"I will be, once we've got them burned and have a couple jars of vamp Dust in the car," she said.

"Amen," Killian agreed. "Amen."

With slightly shaking hands, he pulled a lighter from his pocket and, after a moment trying to get a flame to catch, lit the first one—the master.

CHAPTER 5

Promises

"How'd it go?" Jo Jack asked. He was tending to something behind the counter and didn't look over as they entered.

"About as expected," Killian responded. He dropped the heavy duffel bag onto the counter, thankful to be rid of its weight. He glanced over his shoulder, still mesmerized after all this time by the variety of magical goods Jo Jack sold. Potions and ingredients took up every available flat surface while hundreds of old leather-bound books were stacked haphazardly across the rows of bookshelves, collecting dust. Talismans and charms from around the world hung from a forest of jewelry trees spread throughout the store. Killian doubted even Jo Jack knew what they all did, though he still managed to surprise him from time to time. A strange aroma burned Killian's nostrils—a mix of pumpkin spice and rotting meat. He decided not to ask where it came from, though he could hazard a guess as Jo Jack finished what he was doing, labeling some strange glowing vials. Puffs of steam rose from them, and he corked each one carefully before turning to the pair and looking them over. His eyes gazed over the yellow and green bruises forming around Killian's throat and the cuts along Loop's shoulder.

"Well, you're alive. That's a plus," he said, clucking his tongue against the roof of his mouth. He picked up the duffel, gauging its weight. "And you come bearing gifts. At least twenty kilos. Not bad. Pretty big pack, I take it?"

"Not really. About average. There was one big one, though, that made up for it. I think we took eight kilos just off him."

"We got lucky," Loop added, daggers shooting from her eyes. She was still pretty angry over the ridiculously large order.

Jo Jack snorted. "Talk to me about luck when you've got more than a single hunt under your belt, young lady." She continued glaring at him and he continued. "Look, I know it was a big order to fill. My competitors are killing me, though. With Spin gone, the McAuliffe brothers have pretty much taken over the market."

Killian's eyes suddenly fell toward the floor. Jo Jack decided to change the subject. "But with big orders come big paydays. You want it in chits or bills?"

"Chits," Killian said, thankful for the change of topic. He ignored the sidelong stare from Loop. She had caught his downcast eyes at the mention of Spin. "You know how unreliable paper can be these days."

"True enough. You're one to talk, though," Jo Jack responded. He kneeled down and opened the safe below the counter, counting out the clay chits. In this case, they were hundreds. He slid them across the counter and looked at Loop. "How 'bout you, little lady? Chits or bills?"

"Bills," she responded. She turned at Killian's questioning gaze. "I like to live on the edge."

He snorted as he scooped the chits into a pouch and tied it to his belt. Jo Jack handed the grey paper bills over to her. She promptly counted them out before rolling them up and tucking them into her own pouch.

"Pleasure doing business with you," Jo Jack said, taking the duffel off the counter and stuffing it into the safe. Killian was pretty sure it had an enlargement charm cast on it. It never seemed to run out of room.

"I expect to get that back," he said as Loop turned and headed for the door.

Jo Jack nodded, closing the safe and spinning the dial for good measure. He stood and leaned against the counter.

"It's good to see you back in the world, Killian," he said quietly. "It's what Spin would've wanted."

Killian nodded. Loop walked out behind him, and he glanced over his shoulder at her. "Say hi to Daisy for me," he said before leaving.

The sun was beating down on the street, and Killian shielded his eyes for a moment while he adjusted. Loop walked over to the car, unbothered by it. After blinking away the spots in his vision, he followed her.

"You and Jo Jack have a very odd relationship," she said as he unlocked the driver-side door.

"What do you mean?"

"You're obviously friends, and he obviously cares about you, but neither of you *really* talks. It's just odd."

Killian chuckled. "Have you met Jo Jack? Normal isn't exactly in his DNA."

Loop snorted. "Yeah, and you're just a shining example of normalcy yourself. Two weeks and I still know hardly anything about you."

"Consider that a plus," Killian said, looking at her over the top of the car.

"Are you at least going to tell me what that was all about back there? I know Spin was your old partner. You could at least tell me what happened."

Killian sighed. He wondered when this would come up, as she had likely heard the rumors around the hunting community.

"All you need to know is that Spin and I went on a hunt. I came back. He didn't."

Loop stared at him for a long moment before simply nodding and dropping into the passenger seat. "Think you can drop me off at my bike?" she asked.

Cars whirred past them, but none of them was a taxi, and there wasn't a bus stop for miles. Jo Jack's shop wasn't exactly in the best part of the city, well off the beaten path. Killian suspected that was kind of the point, though. No one to ask questions.

"Yeah, I've got to swing by there to pick up my jeep anyway." The ancient shocks groaned in protest, as he took his seat. He glanced into the back to make sure the extra jar of vampire Dust was still there before buckling his seatbelt.

"Carson should be pleased. We didn't completely destroy his crap-ass vehicle," Loop said, a small smile crimping the corners of her mouth. She obviously regretted asking about Spin and tried to break the tension.

Killian nodded before starting the car, the old carburetor engine grumbling to life. Jo Jack's words played across his mind. *It's what Spin would've wanted.* Killian hoped he was right.

Killian sat at a high table, sipping pale ale. The bar was busy, as people crowded around him to watch the latest rugby match. Ireland had made it to the semi-finals this year despite the United Nations' best efforts to ban them. They didn't like that there were two mages on the team, even though they never used their powers on the field.

It seemed the United Nations had their hands in everything these days, though. They had gained power in the early days of the Change by blaming everything on the mage community. From then on, they were considered the world's police when it came to magic-related activity, and they ruled with an iron fist. Killian hadn't realized how bad it was until he ventured outside of Australia last year. Blood Haven truly was the last *free* city.

A familiar voice suddenly cut through the crowd, disrupting his thoughts. "I see you've been making friends."

Killian turned to see Skye standing a few feet away, her hands jammed into the pockets of a tan leather jacket. Matching boots extended up to her knees. She looked tired, but she still managed a slight smile.

Killian grinned and stood from his seat, embracing her. "You know me. I make friends wherever I go," he replied.

He ushered her to the seat across from him. As she sat down, a huge roar went up from the crowd when Ireland scored a goal. Skye visibly flinched, looking over her shoulder at the commotion. When she looked back, Killian saw fear in her eye, not annoyance.

"You alright?" he asked.

"I'm fine," she said a little too quickly. She had obviously been anticipating the question. "Just startled me."

Killian nodded, but he didn't quite believe her. The lines beneath her eyes had only deepened since the last time he saw her. He decided not to push it, though.

"Thanks for coming," he said once they had settled down and Skye ordered a drink from the spry waitress.

"Of course. Tell me now, is this a friendly call or do you have someone else you want to ask me about?" she asked.

"Very funny. It's a friendly call," Killian said. He was relieved she wasn't still mad about their last meeting. It had been out of line. He knew that now. Especially after the promise he had made her last year before leaving. It seemed she had forgiven him, though. He leaned beneath the table and picked up the jar of vampire Dust he had kept for her.

"In fact, I have a present for you," he said, handing the jar to her. She looked at it for a second before realizing what it was.

"Killian, you…"

"We had a little extra from the last job, and I figured you could do some good with it. I know it has more uses than just getting people high."

"A lot more. I take it that's how you got the bruises around your neck," she said, tucking the jar back beneath the table.

"Yeah, it got a little rough" was all he could think to say. He saw the disapproving look coming from her.

She sighed heavily. "You promised me you were done, but I guess I'm not the only one you made promises to."

Killian nodded slowly, wondering if this was a trap or not. Was he supposed to agree? "No, you're not."

Skye nodded.

That's it? Killian wondered. No scolding? No motherly tone? Twice now they had spoken of his return to hunting, and twice now Killian had walked away with minimal verbal scarring. Just what was going on with her?

"How is Jo Jack anyway?" she asked.

"Same old Jo Jack. Loop says we have a very odd relationship. I think she just doesn't understand Jo Jack," Killian said, thankful the conversation was steering away from his latest hunt. He didn't want her to know how close it had really been.

"Does anyone?" she asked, one corner of her mouth tweaking up.

Killian chuckled. "Good point."

"How'd she do?"

"Not bad. She's quick and she listens. She just needs to learn to calm down a little bit. Other than that, she's fine."

"Well, I'm glad my referral did some good," Skye said, sarcasm dripping from her voice.

"Yeah, I've been meaning to ask. Why did you recommend her? You hate hunting," Killian said, ignoring her derision.

Skye stared at him for several moments, an internal debate obviously warring within her. Finally, her shoulders slumped. "She told me why exactly she wants to hunt so badly. Kind of hard to turn a person down after that."

"And why does she want to hunt so badly?" Killian asked. Maybe he would finally get to the bottom of it.

"If she hasn't told you, I'm definitely not going to. It's not my place," Skye said.

This time, Killian's shoulders slumped. He should've known he wouldn't be so lucky. Loop would tell him when she was ready.

Just then, another loud roar went through the crowd. Skye actually stood from her seat this time, and Killian saw her reach into her jacket for something. He looked closer as she sat back down and saw the black handle of a pistol peeking out from her belt. Something was definitely up. Skye never carried a gun; in fact, she was one of the city's biggest activists when it came to changing the current carrying laws. Another difference they shared.

He waited until she was settled back in her seat before asking. "So you want to tell me what the heck is going on with you or are you going to stop jumping out of your seat every time Ireland scores a goal?"

Skye was obviously caught off guard by his question because she just stared at him for several seconds. Finally, she sighed and actually chuckled lowly. "Is it that obvious?" she asked.

"What, the fact you're nervous as a Chihuahua or the hand cannon you got tucked in your jacket?" he asked.

"Both I suppose," she answered quietly.

"Well, you're carrying the gun at a three o'clock position when it should definitely be at a five, and as for your nerves, I've never seen you like this so tell me, what the heck is going on with you?"

Skye locked gazes with him and then glanced over both shoulders at the nearby crowd. Was she afraid one of them might listen in?

"People are looking for Lucas," she said quietly, leaning across the table so their faces were only a foot apart.

"Agents?" Killian asked almost out of habit. The UN often sent agents to gather up runaways who had escaped their native countries. It was always very quiet and could never be proven, but everyone knew it happened.

"I'm not sure. The point is, people are looking for him, and it's only a matter of time before they find him. I've been on pins and needles for the last few days since I first found out. I don't know how much longer I can keep him hidden at the academy. It's literally the first place anyone would think to look," she said. Again, Killian noticed the bags beneath her eyes, the lines gouged into her cheeks. No wonder she was so nervous. This was bad.

"I get the feeling I know what you're about to ask me," Killian said carefully. He'd known it as soon as she started telling him what was going on.

"Please, Killian, I'm pretty much out of options. Just hide him for a few days until I can find a more permanent solution."

Killian sighed. Of course it had come down to this. He should've known from the start. Staring into Skye's eyes, however, and seeing the fear that was eating away at her, he could hardly say no. He bowed his head, feeling certain he was going to regret this.

"Give me tonight to get some stuff in order, and I'll swing by the academy tomorrow to get him." A wide smile broke across Skye's face, and her eyes glistened for just a second. "Just a few days, though. I'm not a babysitter."

"I know. I just need time to get in contact with the Underground. They don't exactly have an email address."

Killian nodded. Skye stood up and pulled him into a tight embrace He could practically feel the tension falling from her shoulders She really had been at her wits' end.

"Just promise me you'll keep him safe," Skye said. "Promise me you won't let anything bad happen to him."

Killian nodded, knowing he was going to regret this. "I promise."

CHAPTER 6

Nightmare

The crack of thunder woke Killian from a restless slumber. He had been dreaming. He had been running through Skye's academy, a dark shroud chasing after him. Black wings flapped from within the cloud, and static electricity buzzed all around. Then he was on the edge of a great precipice, staring out, and there was nowhere to go but down. He jumped.

A cold chill ran across Killian's spine, like tiny fingers crawling up his back, and he shivered beneath his blanket. Rain still pattered steadily outside his window, and lightning flashed through the blinds.

An uneasy feeling worked its way in Killian's chest, and he looked around his room warily. Everything looked the same. His punching bag still hung stagnant in the corner; a pair of sparring gloves lay beside it. There was a pile of dirty clothes in front of his closet, an equally large pile of clean clothes beside it. His curtains were drawn, shading the streetlights outside his window, and the alarm clock beside his bed said it was just after two in the morning. Everything *looked* normal. So why couldn't he shake this feeling of uneasiness? Was it his meeting with Skye earlier? Surely, he wasn't this nervous over watching a kid for a few days. So what was it?

With a slow sigh, Killian laid his head back against the pillow, forcing his concern off as nothing. *Probably just nervous energy from the job earlier,* he muttered.

As soon as he closed his eyes, however, his phone chimed beside him. He snatched it up, pressing it to his ear. He vaguely noticed the flashing icon in the corner letting him know he had several missed calls.

"Yeah?" he croaked, keeping his eyes closed.

"Killian, turn on the news right now," Loop's voice came through the earpiece. Her tone was serious.

Killian snapped open his eyes and fumbled through the dark room until he managed to snatch the remote from the floor. He turned on the wall-screen on the opposite side of the room. A special report banner flashed across the screen, and a reporter was standing out in the rain with an umbrella over her head. The flaming ruins of a building were behind her. Firefighters and water mages were struggling to get the fire under control; debris was everywhere. Killian turned the volume up to hear what she was saying.

"The Skye Academy of Magic was bombed just a little while ago."

Killian didn't hear the rest of the report. A ringing suddenly filled his ears, and everything else became muted after that. He slowly pressed the phone back to his ear.

"When?" His voice was barely above a whisper.

"About an hour ago," Loop replied. "They haven't said if anyone was caught in the blast or if…"

"Have you heard from Skye?"

"No, I tried calling, but I couldn't get through."

"Keep trying. Call me if you get in contact with her. I'm on my way over there."

Killian clicked off before Loop could respond. He tugged on a pair of jeans a second later. He snatched a shirt off the back of his chair and yanked on his jacket, stuffing his phone and keys into his pockets. As he pulled on his boots, he opened his desk drawer and pulled out his pistol. After staring at it for a moment, he tucked it into the back of his jeans, his heart hammering a mile a minute within his chest.

Please, God, let her be alright, he thought over and over. He couldn't lose anyone else.

He took the stairs down to the first floor two at a time, jumping the last set altogether, and was in his jeep and out of the parking lot in less than five minutes. He raced down the M4 motorway at a speed that would have gotten his jeep impounded, bobbing and weaving through the light traffic that still occupied the road.

The glow of the flames was visible long before he saw the academy. When Killian finally rounded the last corner, he saw why. The academy was still alight, flames crackling high into the night sky. It was the kind of fire that could be produced only by a magical source. The water mages and firefighters were still trying desperately to subdue it; protection wards kept it from spreading any further. A large cluster of students and faculty stood on the edge of the grounds, watching as their home burned. The red and white flashers of the ambulances, fire trucks, and police cruisers sparkled off the falling rain, dramatizing the scene even further. Killian parked beside a row of news vans and jumped out, pushing past a lone elderly reporter who looked late to the party.

"Pope!" he called out, recognizing one of the teachers. The old man turned, but a police officer ran over and stopped Killian before he could get to him, holding him back from the line of yellow cordon tape.

"I'm sorry, sir, but you can't cross the barrier." He shoved Killian back forcefully. Killian's boots sopped in the mud, and his hands balled tightly into fists.

"Killian!" a voice called over the police officer's shoulder. Killian saw Skye running toward the barrier. Her hair was a mess, and black soot clung to her cheeks, but she was okay. Killian shoved past the police officer and raced over to her. They hugged each other tight from opposite sides of the barrier tape.

"Thank God you're alright," Killian breathed, continuing to hold her. Behind him, the police officer stalked off, muttering beneath his breath.

They slowly pulled apart, and Killian saw her eyes were pink and swollen, most likely from the heat of the flames and the smoke, and from crying.

"What the hell happened?" he asked. Skye glanced over his shoulder toward the camera crews, several of which were now pointed in their direction, and lowered her head so they couldn't see her mouth.

"They came for Lucas," she said simply.

"What? Who?"

"I don't know. Whoever was in the city looking for him. When they couldn't find him, they detonated some kind of bomb in the quad. We barely managed to escape."

"Where's Lucas?"

"With a friend."

"Who?"

Skye looked over toward the cameras again, as if she was expecting to see some of the unknown assailants again. She pulled him into another tight embrace, pressing her lips against his collar.

"Stamp," she breathed.

Killian practically lurched backward, his mouth hanging slightly open. "Are you kidding me?" he asked, dumbfounded. "Of all the people in the city, you chose him? *Him?*"

"Keep your voice down," Skye said. "He was the only person I could think of when I couldn't get ahold of you. And just because you two are having some kind of bro feud, doesn't mean I have to hate him too."

Killian rolled his eyes.

"Don't give me that," Skye scolded. "You used to trust him with your life. Are you honestly trying to tell me that just because of what happened with Daisy, I shouldn't trust him with Lucas's?"

"It has nothing to do with that," Killian said. It sounded hollow even to him. "He's just not as reliable as you think."

"When it comes to his choice in women, no he's not. But when it comes to helping me out, he's a hell of a lot more reliable than you are. So cut me some slack. I'm kind of under a bit of stress here, if you haven't noticed," Skye said, pointing a thumb over her shoulder at the ruins of her school.

Killian suddenly wanted to kick himself. She was right. She was always right. "Sorry," he said faintly.

"It's alright. This night hasn't been easy on anyone." She pulled him into another embrace, her forehead resting against his shoulder.

"I'm just glad you're alright," he said.

"I almost wasn't. If Pope hadn't seen that bomb, we would all be dead right now. These people are serious. They're willing to do anything to find

Lucas."

"Then we need to hide him until we can get him out of the city," Killian said.

"Oh, it's 'we' now is it?" Skye asked, her eyebrows shooting up. Killian shot her a sidelong glare. "I'm working on it," she said. They pulled apart, if only slightly, and Killian made sure to block her from the cameras. "I managed to get hold of some friends in the Underground after I left the bar, and they said they *might* know of a place out West that can take him, but it's going to be several days before they can get him out. I told Stamp and he said he could handle it, but now I can't get him either. I'm afraid after seeing what they're capable of, he might need some help."

She met Killian's eyes, and he sighed deeply. "I told you I'd help. I'm not going back on my promise now."

"Thanks," she said. Killian nodded. "No really. Thank you. I know the last year hasn't been easy, and this isn't exactly how you intended to get back in the swing of things."

"Have to start somewhere," he replied. "I'm sure the police will want to talk to you once they get everything under control here. In the meantime, I'll head over to Stamp's and look in on him and Lucas. Figure out what their plan is."

Skye nodded. "Be careful," she said. "These guys are dangerous, whoever they are."

"I will."

With one final embrace, Killian headed back to his jeep. He trudged past the police officer and climbed in, wringing out his jacket and shaking the water from his hair. He grabbed his phone from his pocket and dialed Loop from his contact list, which was inherently short these days. She picked up on the second ring.

"Where are you?" he asked.

"Home. Is everything okay? I still can't get Skye."

"Skye's alright. I need a favor, though. I'm on my way to get you," Killian said as he eased his jeep out of the mud and back onto the road.

"Trouble?"

"Shouldn't be, but I'd still like some backup."

"Copy that. I'll be waiting."

Killian nodded, more to himself than at the phone, and hung up. This had just gotten a lot more interesting.

It finally stopped raining as they pulled up in front of Stamp's apartment.

"How does he afford a place like this?" Loop asked, staring up at the green and white building as they drove past. It was five stories tall, the first level a parking garage for residents. A quick glance at Stamp's truck parked in his usual corner spot indicated that he was at home.

Killian pulled into the visitor lot across the street. "You obviously don't know Stamp that well," he said.

"From what little you've told me, it sounds like that's a good thing." As they parked, Loop drew her pistol from the holster beneath her arm and checked the magazine. Killian briefed her on the way over, and she had been smart enough to come prepared. She chambered a round.

"Stamp's a good guy. He's just…" Killian sighed, searching for the right words. It still pissed him off, just thinking about it.

"An asshole?" Loop filled in, hopping out of the jeep.

Killian chuckled. "Sure, let's go with that."

The buzzer out front was broken, so they strode through the breezeway and up the stairs, deciding against the small elevator. Loop kept her jacket open in case she needed to draw her gun, and Killian felt his pistol dig into his lower back. If everything Skye said was true, they could expect danger at any moment. It set his teeth on edge.

They rounded the landing of the fourth floor and stopped at the door at the top. The lights were off. Killian peered into the gloom as an all too familiar tingling sensation rolled down his spine. He drew his gun; Loop did the same.

"Want an orb?" she asked.

Killian shook his head. He moved into the hallway slowly, his gun held steady before him. Loop moved right behind him. Stamp's apartment was halfway down the hall. Killian swallowed a hard lump in his throat and tightened his grip on his pistol. Loop followed right behind him, watching the other doors like a hawk.

Killian reached the door to Stamp's apartment and stared at it for a moment, preparing himself for whatever was about to come. He nodded to Loop, rapped on the door several times, and stepped to the side of it.

Nothing. After a solid minute, no one answered the door, and there hadn't been any shouts or gunshots from inside.

Killian pressed his ear against the door. He couldn't hear anything. That was when he noticed the markings carved into the frame. A negating enchantment. Stamp had even taken the time to carve out the extra symbols that would keep anyone from listening through the door. Sound could come in, but not out. Killian smiled slightly. Stamp was as thorough as ever. Unfortunately, it also meant Killian had no idea what to expect on the other side of the door. Why wasn't Stamp answering?

Killian waved to Loop and motioned to the enchantment. She stared at it a moment before digging into her pocket and fishing out a multi-tool. Killian was about to give her a look when he saw the lock pick she produced from one end. He nodded to her, and she kneeled down in front of the deadbolt while he watched the hallway.

It took several minutes and several exasperated breaths from Loop before they heard an audible click; Killian turned to see the deadbolt unlocked. He gave her an appreciative nod, and she smiled back, pleased with herself.

Killian moved back beside the door and grabbed the handle, waiting until Loop was in position as well. Slowly, he turned the handle and pushed the door inward. It creaked against its hinges. All the lights were off, entrenching the entire apartment in gloom. Fingers continued to dance across Killian's spine as he stared into the dim space.

He nodded to Loop one last time and moved into the apartment, his eyes sweeping across the foyer and the living room. He signaled for Loop to stay by the door and stepped into the living room. Very little had changed since the last time he had been here. The brown leather couch, the ornate coffee table, the giant wall-screen—it was all the same, expect for one thing.

There was now a picture beside the couch of Stamp and a very beautiful Native-American woman—Daisy. They were at some park, smiling at the camera with a beautiful blue sky overhead. It brought a bitter burn to Killian's stomach, and he turned away.

He was about to move toward the bedroom when a floorboard creaked behind him. He turned just in time to have his gun knocked from his grasp. He blocked a second blow that would have knocked his jaw off, and suddenly he and the unknown assailant were both on the ground. Killian struggled to get up, but his feet were kicked out from under him. He rolled and sent an elbow into the shadow's abdomen, knocking the air from his lungs. He took a hook to the cheek in return and succeeded in blocking a knee to his groin. Scratching at the floor, he managed to get a hand on his gun and turned it toward his attacker just as a ball of light floated over and illuminated Stamp's face. They both blinked at each other as Loop stepped into the living room beside them.

"Judging by the picture, I'm going to assume this is Stamp," she said, looking down at them. Her tone matched that of a scolding mother. "Now, if you two are done with the cat fight, maybe he can tell us where the kid is."

"Killian, what the hell are you doing here?" Stamp asked, ignoring her. He rubbed his stomach.

"Skye asked for my help," Killian replied, massaging his cheek. "What the hell are *you* doing with all the lights off?"

"Trying to get the drop on you idiots. I heard you pull up across the street and thought you were the people after Lucas."

"Didn't occur to you just to look outside?" Killian asked.

"And risk getting my head blown off? No, if everything Skye said about these guys is true, I'm not taking any chances."

"Probably should put down a rug then," Killian said, directing his attention to the loose floorboard Stamp had stepped on.

Stamp rolled his eyes and climbed to his feet, ignoring Loop's offer to help him up. She extended one to Killian and he accepted it.

Stamp walked into the foyer and opened the coat closet, flipping the circuit breaker and turning on all the lights. As the overhead light in the living room clicked on, the orb dissolved.

Killian continued massaging his cheek and sat down on the couch. Loop stood beside him.

"So where is the kid?" she asked again.

"You still didn't answer my question. What are you doing here?"

Killian shot him an angry glare. "I told you. Skye..."

"Asked for your help. I heard. I also heard she couldn't get ahold of you, so what are you doing here now?"

Killian snorted at that. "You haven't been watching the news, have you?"

A momentary look of confusion flashed across Stamp's face.

Killian sat forward on the couch. "Skye's academy was bombed," he said somberly.

"What?"

"You should probably learn to answer your phone." He grabbed the remote and flipped to the news station. They were still covering the explosion, pictures and footage of the damage littering the screen.

Stamp's mouth hung open as he stared at it. "How... I..." He dug his phone out of his pocket and tried to turn it on. The screen remained black.

"Forget to pay your bill?" Loop asked, her mouth a firm line across her face.

Stamp looked at her angrily, then back at the phone, before throwing it against the wall. It shattered on impact, a hundred pieces falling to the floor.

"Is Skye okay?" he asked, staring at the ground.

"Yeah, she's alright. She thought you might need my help, though. After what happened, she's not sure what we should expect," Killian said. He sat back, folding his arms across his chest. "So are you going to tell us where the kid is now or are we going to have to keep playing hide and seek?"

Stamp looked over at him, his face wavering between embarrassment and anger, before calling out Lucas's name. A door creaked from the bedroom, and the boy walked out slowly, his eyes darting around the room nervously until he spotted Killian.

"Hey, it's you!" he exclaimed, his mouth cracking into a wide smile.

"Yeah, it's me," Killian said, sighing heavily. He still wasn't entirely convinced this was a good idea, even less so now, but he had given his word, and he intended to keep this one. To some people that still meant something. Killian glanced back up at Stamp, the burn still in his stomach. "We should find a better place to hide him."

Stamp merely nodded.

"I might know a place," Loop said. They both looked over at her in surprise, and she holstered her pistol. "If you two are done fighting, that is."

Killian and Stamp both glared. Lucas kept smiling.

CHAPTER 7

The Reaper

Stamp had dark brown hair, cut almost down to his scalp, and a hard, chiseled jaw. Unlike Killian, who was tall and lean, Stamp had wide shoulders and a broad chest. He looked more like a football player than a skilled magician. His brown eyes were hard and focused as he stared out across the streets from the back of Killian's jeep. Killian reached up and adjusted his rear-view mirror so he wouldn't have to keep seeing him every time he looked up.

They were heading to some nightclub on the upper east side of the city. Loop said she knew the owner, and they would be able to crash in the apartment upstairs. It also put them far enough away from the academy that the people searching for Lucas might not look there, though Killian could not be sure how they had found him in the first place.

Lucas sat between him and Loop, fast asleep. The sun was starting to peek over the horizon, beams of white light shining up into the dark, receding storm clouds from the night before. In the short time since arriving at Stamp's, Lucas had already developed an attachment to Killian, refusing to leave his side. Loop thought it was cute. Killian thought it was annoying.

"He likes you. It's sweet," Loop said as Killian pushed his head away from his shoulder for the tenth time.

"He acts like he's five," Killian replied, his hands tightening around the steering wheel.

"Well, yeah, he's been raised in a box. It doesn't surprise me he hasn't developed right socially."

"And mentally."

Loop looked over at him incredulously. "What happened to you, Killian? I thought you loved kids. Skye told me you used to teach at the academy all the time."

"Yeah, well, that was before a kid got my best friend killed," Killian said angrily. He instantly regretted saying it, knowing Loop would want more information now, but she instead just lowered her eyes and looked at Lucas.

"Well, it wasn't *this* kid," she said, her voice suddenly very quiet.

"I'm sorry, I thought you were supposed to be my partner, not my therapist," he replied.

"I am your partner, but I'm also a human being, Killian. You should try it sometime."

Killian kept staring straight ahead, biting his tongue, despite the look Loop gave him that begged for a retort.

Finally, she gave up and turned back to Stamp in the back of the jeep. "So what's your classification?" she asked him.

Stamp looked up, but before he could answer, Killian cut in. "Geomancer."

"No way!" Loop exclaimed, jostling Lucas from his slumber. He locked around groggily for a moment before laying his head back against Killian's shoulder. Killian did not shrug him off this time. He just stared straight ahead, gritting his teeth.

Loop smiled at him and lowered her voice. "So you can alter the earth and stuff like that, right? I've never actually met one before."

Killian snorted.

Stamp shot him a glare before looking back at Loop. "Yeah, I can cause minor quakes and can control the geography of the land in small scales."

"Like a sandbox," Killian muttered.

Thankfully, Stamp didn't hear him this time and Loop ignored him. She looked around and pointed to a building on the right.

"We're here," she said. There were lines of bars and nightclubs along the road, accompanied by tattoo parlors, a few hole-in-the-wall restaurants, and a crop of gas stations. Neon lights shone off the puddles of rainwater and cast a brilliant pink and blue glow across the asphalt. The crowds and the traffic had dispersed, and the parking lot was empty.

"You sure this place is legit?" Killian asked, as he pulled into a spot facing the exit. He glanced over at the concrete building that housed the club. A giant blue sign on the side read THE POWER PLANT.

"Chaser and I go way back," Loop said, hopping out of the jeep. With a look at Killian, she pulled Lucas from his seat and carried him toward the entrance. "He's a Lighter too."

"I guess we can just automatically trust him then," Killian said, closing his door.

"You trust me, right?" Loop asked. Killian stared at her for a second before nodding. "Good, because I'm telling you *I* trust him. He's pulled me out of the fire multiple times."

"Alright," Killian said, rolling his eyes.

Loop locked eyes with him for a long moment before turning back to Stamp. "Hey, can you take Lucas for a sec? I need to talk to Killian."

Stamp nodded and she handed Lucas over to him. Stamp cradled the sleeping teen in his arms like a toddler. Loop nodded over to the corner of the building, and Killian followed her.

"Are you alright?" Loop asked once they were out of earshot.

"Yeah, why?" Killian asked.

"Well, because you've been at my throat since we left Stamp's, and I'm just trying to figure out why."

"I'm fine."

"Obviously you're not. You look like you're about to hurl every time that kid touches you, and you're obviously still pissed over what happened between you and Stamp. I'll admit, after everything you told me about him, I wasn't very excited to meet him, and I sure didn't want to have his back in a firefight, but now that I've met him, he's not that bad."

Killian sighed, rubbing the bridge of his nose. "I know."

Loop blinked at him. Obviously, she was not expecting that. Killian continued. "It's just still a little sore, and I guess seeing that picture of him and Daisy just brought back old memories."

"And the kid?"

"He just… He might die, and I don't want to get too attached to him. He's obviously already attached to me," Killian said.

"Jesus, Killian, you can't think that way. I know after whatever happened with Spin, it's hard not to, but you got to keep your head up."

"I know. Maybe I wasn't ready to come back after all, but it's a little late for that now," he replied. He glanced back over at Stamp and Lucas. Lucas had his face buried in Stamp's collar, fast asleep. "I'm good, though. *We're* good."

"Alright," Loop said. She nodded over to the club's entrance. "Come on, let's go meet Chaser. Even you'll like him."

Killian snorted. "He's a Lighter. That automatically means I have to."

Loop smiled.

Stamp and Lucas joined them as they strode to the entrance door. Twin Tesla coils stood on either side of the door. Killian was sure at night they glowed and sparked as people waited to get inside. Loop banged on the door hard, stood back, and waited.

Killian's eyes tracked across the parking lot and the buildings along the street, searching for any signs of trouble or anyone who looked like they might be following them. He didn't see any.

The big metal door opened behind him, and he turned back to the entrance just as a man stepped out, his arms spread wide. He had dark skin and even darker hair, cut short, with a mural of tattoos along his arms and neck.

"Loop!" he exclaimed, smiling widely as she stepped into his embrace. "It's been way too long, girl."

They embraced for a moment before Loop stepped back and motioned to her companions. "Chaser, these are my friends, Killian and Stamp. The little one is Lucas."

"Hey, Lucas," Chaser said, extending his hand to Killian with a toothy grin. Killian's eyes narrowed, and Chaser immediately started laughing. "Sorry, bad joke."

"His sense of humor has been missing lately," Loop said.

"I see," Chaser said, regarding Killian with a quizzical stare. Killian shifted uncomfortably beneath his gaze. There was something he didn't like about the man's dark eyes. They were too curious.

"Anyway, I was wondering if we could crash in the apartment upstairs for a few days. We need a place to lay low," Loop said.

"You in trouble again?" Chaser asked, his gaze returning to Loop. Killian exhaled slowly, not realizing he had been holding his breath.

"Sort of. Not with the law or anything. There're just some questionable people we're trying to avoid."

"Hmm," Chaser said, thinking about it a moment. His gaze fell back on Killian and then to the sky. "Yeah, that shouldn't be a problem," he finally said. "You know the rules: You clean up any messes you make and don't interfere with the business. Otherwise, you can stay as long as you want." He directed his attention to Killian and Stamp and, again, Killian felt himself grow uncomfortable beneath the man's gaze. "Any friend of Loop's is a friend of mine."

He extended his hand to both of them. Stamp shook it right away, shifting Lucas to one shoulder, but Killian was a little hesitant. A cold, tingling sensation ran down his spine. After a moment, he finally took the man's hand and shook it. A strange sort of shockwave ran down his back, and he had to keep his whole body from shaking. Chaser smiled the whole time. After a moment, he released his hand and directed them all into the nightclub. Loop and Stamp walked in right away; Killian hesitated a moment before following. He glanced over his shoulder as Chaser closed the door behind them and suddenly felt trapped like a mouse in a cage. His throat was suddenly very dry.

Killian splashed a handful of water across his face and stared at himself in the mirror. His hands were still quivering slightly as he gripped the edges of the porcelain sink. What was wrong with him? His breath was coming in short gasps, and his heart had yet to stop hammering within his chest.

"I take it that was your first encounter with a reaping," a voice said from the doorway. Killian flinched—he was making a bad habit of letting people sneak up on him—and turned to see Loop standing there.

"A what?" he asked, grabbing the towel off the rack and drying his face and hands.

"A reaping. It's what Chaser did to you. He likes to do it when he meets new people. I probably should have warned you, but, with everything going on, I didn't even think about it. It basically allows him to peer into your soul and see what kind of person you are. Everyone is a little shaky after it happens to them the first time. His tattoos are what allow him to do it." She let it sink in for a moment before adding, "I guess you haven't seen everything."

"I guess not," Killian said, throwing the towel back up on the rack. He felt a burn slowly build in his stomach. So that's what that had been. No wonder it had left him feeling so violated. "I take it you've had it done to you before."

"Yeah. I about hurled the first time. Sorry. I really should have told you. I didn't even think about it."

"It's fine," Killian replied. He exhaled deeply, his heart finally beginning to settle. "I guess not everyone goes around doing that kind of thing; otherwise I would've encountered it a long time ago."

"Yeah, it's pretty rare. Chaser had to go to three different continents to get all the tattoos he needed. It's also why I brought us here, though. If anyone comes looking for us, he'll know the moment they walk in."

"And we can trust him not to sell us out?" Killian asked.

"As much as I'd trust anyone in this city," she said.

Killian nodded. It wasn't the most reassuring answer, but he figured it was the best he was going to get.

He was a little mad that Chaser had basically invaded his soul, but he also understood why he had done it. In a city where people throw fireballs and breathe ice, it paid to know what kind of people were coming into his club. Still, Killian would make it a point to keep his distance.

The apartment was a fairly nice loft over the club. The slanted roof pressed down on the eastern wall, but otherwise the space was pretty airy. A two-way mirror looked out over the nightclub floor, making it seem much bigger than it actually was. A raised bedroom section about three feet higher than the rest of the apartment had a queen-sized bed and a nightstand. A plush white and black rug dominated the living room floor, with a foldout couch and two armchairs positioned around it. There wasn't a wall-screen. Instead, an old flat-panel television rested in the corner. The kitchen was comprised of whitewashed cabinets and stainless steel appliances, though they looked like they had been built at the turn of the millennium. They had already decided who would sleep where. Loop and Lucas had of course won the bed while Killian and Stamp had flipped a coin for who would get the foldout and who would get an armchair. Killian had lost and was already preparing himself for an uncomfortable night of sleep, though with how he was feeling, he doubted it would be very hard to fall asleep. Exhaustion was quickly creeping up on him.

He had been asleep only a few hours when Loop called him and, judging by the look in her eyes, she was feeling it too.

Stepping out of the bathroom, Killian looked out over the nightclub floor. Stamp and Lucas were talking in one of the booths that spanned the far wall, and Chaser and a few workers were cleaning up around the club.

"He really is a good man," Loop said, stepping up beside him. She yawned heavily, covering her mouth with the back of her hand.

"Why don't you get some sleep? We've been running on fumes the last couple hours, and you could do with some shut-eye."

"What about you?"

"I'll get a few hours after you get up."

"You sure?" Loop asked, obviously uncomfortable leaving everyone alone together. She looked back out over the nightclub floor.

"I'm sure," Killian affirmed. "Don't worry. I won't kill anyone while you're sleeping."

Loop snorted and, with a nod of gratitude, walked up to the bedroom section. She was out before she even got her boots off.

Killian smiled faintly before opening the door and descending the steps to the nightclub. Lucas waved at him, and he nodded back before taking a seat at the bar. He glanced over toward Chaser and his group of workers, and the club owner smiled at him. Another tingling sensation rolled down Killian's spine.

"Help yourself," Chaser called over.

Killian dodged his gaze and, with a nod, grabbed a glass mug from the other side of the bar and filled it with whatever was on tap. It turned out to be a pale ale. It glided down his throat smoothly, and he threw the rest back with a long gulp.

"Sure that's a good idea?" Stamp asked, walking over. Lucas still sat at the booth, staring after him.

"It's just a beer, Stamp. Relax," Killian said. "One isn't going to get me drunk."

"I remember differently."

"Yeah, well, a lot has changed," Killian said, a bit of spite creeping up into his tone. Stamp knew exactly what he was implying, but he didn't rise to the invitation. He bit back a comment and instead grabbed two sodas from the cooler behind the bar.

"You know, one of these days we're going to have to talk about what happened," Stamp said. "I know things weren't handled the best, but you've got to let it go. Daisy and I are happy…"

"Please, spare me the love song," Killian cut in. "I told Loop we're good, so we're good, but don't act like we're still buddy-buddy like we used to be. And don't try to be my shrink either. I've got enough people stuffing feelings down my throat. Let's just stay focused on what's important."

"Yeah," Stamp said, looking back at Lucas. He managed to keep the anger from his tone, but the condescension was still there. "Let's."

He walked back over to the booth, handing Lucas one of the sodas. Killian scoffed. He went to refill his own glass before hesitating. He instead sat back on the stool, rolling the mug across his palm. He stared at it a long moment, a million thoughts and feelings rattling around in his head. Finally, he managed to narrow them down to one image, and the mug turned into a small glass ornament. It was a duck, Daisy's favorite animal. The details weren't perfect, the bill uneven and the wings crooked, but it still brought a sting to Killian's heart, looking at it. With a glance over at Stamp and Lucas, he let it change back into the mug and set it back down on the bar.

"So that was the pain I sensed," Chaser said, sitting down on the stool beside him. Killian stared at him with narrow eyes. "I should've figured it was a broken heart. And the anger I'm guessing is toward your friend over there."

"Among others," Killian said quietly, continuing to stare at him.

Chaser smiled, this time not meeting his gaze. "I'm sorry if the reaping I performed on you felt unjustified, but I make it a point to know who and what is coming into my club, especially when they're asking to use my loft as a safe house."

Killian bit back a colorful comment. "I'll just make it a point never to shake your hand again," he said instead.

Chaser chuckled. "It wasn't the handshake that did it; it merely helped bridge the connection. It was when you looked me in the eye that really did it."

Killian's mouth fell slightly open. He had always thought manipulative magic like that required physical contact. It never occurred to him simple eye contact could do it. He immediately averted his gaze.

"Relax," Chaser said. "I've already seen all there is to see, and since you're sitting at my bar, you have nothing further to fear. I never would have let you through the front door if you hadn't passed the test."

"That's comforting," Killian said.

Again, Chaser chuckled. He liked to laugh a lot. The lines around his mouth and eyes were evidence of that.

"I can see why Loop likes working with you," Chaser said. "For someone who doesn't have a sense of humor, you're quite funny."

"Happy I could entertain."

"That's all any of us can do. We entertain our destinies until they decide to entertain us." Killian was not sure he understood what he meant by that, but before he could ask, Chaser stood from the stool. "Relax. As long as you're under my roof, you're under my protection, and that goes a long way."

Chaser picked up a crate of empty bottles from the floor and headed toward a storeroom in the back. Killian stared after him. He would make it a point to swing by Jo Jack's and pick up a few protection charms…just in case destiny decided he wasn't entertaining enough.

CHAPTER 8

Destiny

Killian woke with a start, his throat dry and a thick layer of gum across his eyes. He blinked it away and stared around the darkened room, panic tightening across his chest. He sat up on the couch and glanced around the loft. Light was coming in through the two-way mirror looking down on the club floor, but otherwise the apartment was dark. Someone had laid a blanket across his body, and Killian pushed it aside, swiping his pistol off the floor beside him. He stood slowly and walked over to the window cautiously, glancing down to the nightclub floor. He felt his heart steady as he saw Loop showing Lucas how to summon a light orb and Stamp cleaning one of his pistols at the bar. Chaser and the workers had disappeared, probably to sleep before the shift tonight.

Killian walked over to the refrigerator, popped it open, and found a few bottles of water. He uncapped one and downed half the bottle in three long gulps. He wiped away the thin trail of water that had dripped across his chin and put the bottle back in the refrigerator. He grabbed his jacket off the back of the couch, tugged it on, and headed downstairs.

Loop looked up as he walked by and smiled, an orb floating above her hand. "How'd you sleep?"

"Good. How long was I out?" Killian asked.

"About two hours."

"Felt like longer."

Killian rubbed the back of his neck, stiff from the arm of the couch, and watched as Lucas summoned his own ball of light, allowing it to float above his hand. It was almost perfect and was nearly as bright as Loop's. Killian could see what Skye was talking about; Lucas was quick. He nodded appreciatively and headed toward the door.

"Where are you going?" Loop called after him. She let the orb in her hand dissolve and stood up.

"Jo Jack's. I'm going to swing by there, pick up a few protection charms, and see if he has any wards."

"Can I come?" Lucas asked. The ball of light disappeared from his palm as he stared up at Killian questioningly. Loop looked between them, obviously not sure what to say, and Killian's mouth clamped shut.

"Sorry, Lucas, but you need to stay here," Stamp said, turning from his disassembled gun.

Lucas's shoulders immediately slumped, feeling crestfallen. Killian stared at him, then over at Stamp. The burning in his stomach had finally subsided and had been replaced with…something else.

"You know, he's never going to know his full potential if he doesn't get out in the world and see what's all out there," Killian said. Loop's eyes shot over in his direction, and Stamp looked at him suspiciously.

Killian could not believe he was about to say this. "You can come, Lucas."

"Whoa, whoa, whoa," Stamp said, standing from his stool. Before he could argue, however, Lucas was racing up the stairs to grab his jacket. Stamp walked over to Killian, keeping his voice low. "Have you lost your mind, Killian? There are people out there looking for him, who will *kill* you if they see you with him. You cannot take him out there."

"If I recall, we agreed this morning to focus on what's important. That kid's wellbeing is important," Killian said.

"Oh, give me a break," Stamp said. "Don't act like you're doing this for Lucas. You're doing it because I said no."

"Maybe it would do Lucas some good to get out and see a little bit of Blood Haven," Loop interjected before the argument could escalate any further. "Killian will be with him the whole time."

"Am I the only one thinking logically here?" Stamp asked, barely able to believe his ears. "Fine, fine. Take the kid out, get him killed, but you're going to be the one to tell Skye what happened. Not me."

"Fine," Killian said. He turned, barely managing to hide the smug smile across his face.

Loop stepped up to him. "Don't make me regret siding with you on this," she said quietly.

Killian nodded, and Lucas came bounding down the steps, wearing a hooded sweat jacket and his puffy grey vest. He looked positively rambunctious.

"Come on, Lucas," Killian said, trying to force as much excitement into his voice as he could muster. This was going to be good for him. It was. So why did he feel like this was such a monumentally bad idea? He pushed the thought from his mind as they walked out of the club and headed to his jeep.

Lucas stared all around, mesmerized, almost the entire ride to Jo Jack's. He took in all the details with an open mouth and wide eyes. The city changed a lot in the last thirteen years since the magical outbreak had first begun. Almost a quarter of the city had burned down during the Terrible Night, and a sort of new age metropolis sprang up in its stead. Bookstores were now spell libraries, pharmacies were poultice stores, and hospitals were healing wards. Hunting stores now carried cloves of garlic next to the salt licks, and almost every car rental company had a *"No magic while driving"* clause in their contract somewhere. Lucas took it all in, barely able to blink as they traveled across the city amidst the flow of day-to-day traffic.

"A lot to take in, isn't it?" Killian finally said after about ten minutes.

Lucas practically had his head hanging out the window. "I…I can't believe there's so many," he answered.

"So many what?"

"Of us," Lucas replied. He glanced over his shoulder at Killian. "I always thought I was the only one. The little bit I can remember, I always thought I was alone."

Killian wasn't sure what to say to that. He really wasn't sure what to say at all. "Well, you're not," he finally managed.

Lucas smiled widely and nodded. He looked back out the window, and several more minutes ticked past in companionable silence. They stayed off the highways and major thoroughfares, sticking mainly to the back roads and side streets. Killian still was not sure how they had found Lucas in the first place, and he wasn't taking any chances, especially after his promise to Loop. Skye's wrath would be nothing compared to Loop's if he let something happen.

"How come you're so mad at Stamp?" he suddenly asked, looking back over at Killian.

Killian tried to hide his surprise. He had not even realized Lucas was paying that close attention. Maybe he wasn't as mentally deficient as he had first assumed.

"He…" Killian tried to find the right words, but nothing except a tide of colorful phrases came to mind. "He did something I didn't think he would do, and it hurt me pretty bad."

"What did he do?" Lucas asked, obviously not satisfied with the response.

None of your business, Killian wanted to say, but he had promised Loop he would try to be better and instead let out a deep sigh.

"He stole the woman I love," he said after a long pause.

Lucas stared at him, then went back to looking out the window. "I think they stole my mom," he said quietly after several moments. He sniffed loudly, and Killian noticed several tears fall from his eyes.

Again, Killian was lost for words. His lips parted slightly as he tried to search for something to say, but all that came out was, "Do you remember her at all?"

Lucas wiped the tears from his eyes and looked over. His eyes were pink and distended. "I think so. I remember somebody with black hair who would come and sing to me, but I can't remember the words or what her face looked like. I think it was my mom, though. Then she just stopped coming. I think they took her away."

Killian swallowed a hard lump in his throat. He fought back the memories of his own mother and was relieved when he looked up and saw they were near Jo Jack's. The small red and tan building was a welcome sight as they parked in the back lot and hopped out. He pushed the images away and led

Lucas around to the front of the building. Lucas had dried his eyes and didn't look like he wanted to talk about it anymore. Killian was thankful. He was still trying to get over his own problems. He couldn't handle taking on Lucas's as well.

They walked into the store, the bell above the door giving a soft jingle. This time, Killian was hit with the sharp, putrid scent of fish oil. He looked around for its source but couldn't find anything.

"What's that smell?" Lucas asked, covering his nose.

"That, my friend, is the newest in acne removal potions," Jo Jack said, walking out from between a nearby row of shelves. "Something you don't have to worry about quite yet."

Killian tried to breathe only through his mouth. "Fish oil, Jo Jack?"

Jo Jack grinned, his eyes mischievous beneath the shadow of his wide headband. "Only a small part of the potion."

"Sure doesn't smell like it," Killian said.

Dust hung stagnant in the air, as it always did inside the small, congested shop. Lucas was even more mesmerized here. His head practically spun as he stared around at everything. Killian had to actively keep him from touching anything.

"So what brings you in today, Killian?" Jo Jack asked, stepping behind his counter. "I can't reverse childbirth, only prevent it."

He laughed as Killian dragged Lucas back to the front of the store. He was back to acting like a small child. Killian planted him in front of the counter and glared at Jo Jack.

"He's not mine," he said. "I'm just looking after him for a few days. Anyway, I need some stuff. Protection charms, wards, anything to lock a building down."

"Expecting trouble?"

"Something like that."

"Who'd you piss off this time?" Jo Jack asked. His eyes flickered down toward Lucas.

"I wish I knew," Killian said quietly.

"Well, you've come to the right place. I got everything you could possibly need to turn a building into Fort Knox. Magically speaking, that is."

Jo Jack stepped out from behind the counter and led them down to the aisle on the end. It was stacked with books and rolled-up scrolls, maps, and charts. Jo Jack searched through one particular stack until he found a thick leather-bound book. A heavy layer of dust clung to its surface, and Jo Jack brushed it aside with one meaty hand. He handed it to Killian who almost buckled beneath its weight. It felt like it weighed a ton.

"*Wards of the Modern Warlock*," Killian read. He turned to Jo Jack, staring at him incredulously. "Jo Jack, are you kidding me?"

"Hey, that book is over two thousand years old. I had to use a revelation charm just to translate its text and an enchantment to put it back together," Jo Jack replied smugly. "Now do you want my help or not?"

Killian merely rolled his eyes in response, and Lucas let out a faint chuckle. The corners of Killian's mouth quirked upward.

"Speaking of which…" Jo Jack said, walking over to one of the jewelry trees layered with pendants and necklaces. He removed one—a wooden pendant carved to resemble a fox head—and tossed it to Killian. He barely managed to hold onto the book as he caught it. The pendant was tied with a long leather cord, and, upon closer examination, he saw there was a strange symbol carved into the fox's forehead.

"Celtic revelation charm," Jo Jack explained. "That one is keyed to reveal any magical traps and wards people might have set up."

Killian stared at it closely before sliding it over his head. A strange sort of tingling sensation enveloped him, starting at his fingers and rolling down his spine. It lasted only a moment, but Killian knew the charm had bound itself to him.

"Thanks, Jo Jack," he said.

"No problem."

"No, really. Thanks."

Jo Jack nodded. He grabbed a few other books off the shelves—tomes on detection spells, protection charms, and basic enchantments—and a jar full of some strange purple powder before leading them back up to the front. Killian unloaded the books onto the counter, thankful to be rid of the weight for a moment, and stared at the purple powder curiously.

"Lava rock powder," Jo Jack said. "You sprinkle it across an entryway, and anyone meaning you harm gets a nice little zap when they walk in."

"Nice," Killian said, regarding the powder for a moment longer.

Jo Jack's eyes suddenly snapped over toward the front door. He stared through the glass panes.

"You were followed," he said quietly.

"What?"

Killian looked over. Two men were walking toward the front door. They were both wearing long, western-style dusters; the larger of the two had on a pair of wire-framed sunglasses, hiding his eyes. His hair was cropped all the way down to his scalp, and his muscles bulged beneath his coat. His companion was a great deal thinner, his coat practically hanging off his shoulders, and was far less imposing. His blond hair was tied back in a loose ponytail.

"You don't think they're just here to shop?" Killian asked. He felt the weight of the pistol dig into his lower back.

"Men like that don't shop here," Jo Jack said. He glanced around the store, then down at Lucas. He sighed heavily. "Hide in the back behind the shelves. I'll try to get them out of here."

Killian nodded and grabbed Lucas by the shoulder, leading him to the back of the store. They crouched down behind a row of shelves and waited. Killian's heart was practically in his throat. A moment later, the bell above the door rang, and he heard the two men enter.

"*Ow!*" one of them suddenly screeched. Killian risked a glance around the corner of the shelf. The smaller one was rubbing his chest, a confused look appearing on his face as he glanced around. The taller one didn't make a sound, though a bead of sweat rolled down the back of his head.

Jo Jack turned to the two men and smiled widely. "Can I help you gentlemen with something?"

The smaller one's eyes snapped over in his direction, but it was the big one who spoke. "We're here for the boy."

"Boy?" Jo Jack asked, a confused expression flashing across his face. "No boys here, mate. If that's your thing, though, I can recommend a few very nice establishments. Real clean…"

"Don't play dumb with us," the blond one snapped. The smile on Jo Jack's face vanished.

The larger one looked over at his partner, and his mouth suddenly clamped shut. He was obviously the one in charge. He was also pretty powerful; Killian could practically feel the magical energy coming off him.

"We're here for the boy," the large one repeated. "Give him to us, and you will not be harmed."

"I've already told you, I don't deal in that kind of merchandise," Jo Jack said, the easiness in his tone vanishing. A power slowly drifted into his voice that Killian had never heard before. It made the hairs on the back of his neck stand up. "Now, if you're not here to buy something, I'm going to have to ask you both to leave."

"Maybe we didn't make ourselves clear," the blond said, his voice hoarse and contrived. "Give us the damn kid!"

"Oh, you made yourself perfectly clear," Jo Jack replied. "You made it clear that you came into *my* store and started giving *me* orders."

"I'll make this simple," the leader cut in, flashing his partner an annoyed expression. He pulled a long chrome pistol from inside his coat and leveled it on Jo Jack's head. "We know he is here. Tell us where or you will be killed. He is ours."

Lucas gasped, and Killian immediately clamped his hand over his mouth. The leader looked over his shoulder toward the back of the store.

"Watch him," he said, nodding to Jo Jack. The blond nodded back and drew his own pistol, aiming it at Jo Jack's head.

The big one turned toward the back of the store and walked slowly. Jo Jack raised his hands in the air, his eyes darting toward Killian and Lucas's hiding spot. He gave the tiniest of nods toward a row of shelves on the right side, stacked with jars of clear liquid. Killian grabbed his pistol from his belt and aimed carefully. Beside him, Lucas held his breath.

As the leader strode past the shelf of jars, his gun held aloft before him, Killian pulled the trigger. The first jar shattered and a spiral of blue flames suddenly shot out from inside it. The leader stumbled into the bookshelf beside him, nearly knocking it over, and Killian shot two more of the cars. More flames curled out. The blond turned in surprise, and Jo Jack yanked the gun from his hands while he was distracted. He suddenly vanished in a veil of black smoke, taking the gun with him.

While the two men were distracted, Killian grabbed Lucas by the shoulder and sprinted around to the opposite side of the store. He ran to the end of the last aisle and skidded around the corner. Twin gunshots suddenly ricocheted off the shelf beside him, and he practically toppled back into cover. Several more hit where he had been a moment before. The leader had obviously recovered enough to shoot back. Killian bit back a curse.

Risking a quick peek around the corner, he saw the flames had finally died down and, with it, his chance for escape. He fired a couple shots around the corner blindly and searched for another option. A fresh wave of gunshots hit the shelf beside him, and an idea suddenly sprang into his mind.

Killian turned to Lucas. The boy was shaking, and Killian was pretty sure that Lucas he had wet his pants. He ignored it.

"Lucas, when I say so, we're going to run as fast as we can for the exit, okay?" Lucas nodded. Tears welled in the corners of his eyes and his whole body quivered. Killian dropped to one knee. "It's going to be okay. We're going to make it out of here."

This time, Lucas nodded much more confidently, summing up every ounce of courage he had. Killian nodded back and fired several more shots around the corner, driving the two men back into cover. Summing up all his own courage, Killian threw his shoulder against the nearby bookshelf as hard as he could. He grunted with the effort. Another hard shove and the shelf suddenly creaked. Putting all his weight behind the third push, the shelf began to totter and, a moment later, toppled over completely. It hit the row of shelves beside it and those shelves toppled as well, creating a domino effect. Killian heard a shout of pain as the final row of shelves toppled.

"Now!" he screamed to Lucas, not waiting another second. He sprinted from cover, Lucas right on his heels. He lunged over one of the shelves and slid across the counter. The two men were pinned beneath the final row of shelves. Killian could see only the big one, but a groan of pain told him the other one had survived as well. He contemplated shooting them on the spot, but a look back at Lucas told him this was not the time. The boy had used up about all the bravery he had left.

Killian grabbed Lucas and carried him over the last shelf, and they slammed through the entrance. An angry shout trailed after them, but Killian never looked back. He practically flung Lucas into the passenger seat of his jeep and hopped in on the other side. A moment later, he started the jeep and peeled out of the parking lot, nearly running over an old man in the process. The door to Jo Jack's shop slammed open, and the big one came sprinting out. Several gunshots trailed after Killian's jeep and one even shattered the rear window, but they were around the corner a moment later. Only then did Killian finally breathe again…and feel the fierce shockwave of pain that hit his upper arm. He glanced down and saw the blood smeared across his shoulder where the bullet had hit.

"You're hurt," Lucas practically squealed.

"Ow" was all Killian managed to say in response as he clutched his arm.

CHAPTER 9

Traced

The gunshot had scooped out a trench in Killian's upper arm, which oled through his jacket sleeve and hurt miserably as he and Lucas pushed through the club's front door. Loop was on him in a heartbeat, dashing over from one of the nearby booths. Stamp came down the apartment steps a moment later, asking what happened.

"You may have been right," Killian said simply as he was led over to one of the booths and sat down.

"We'll save the 'I told you so' for later," Stamp said. "What happened?"

Killian gritted his teeth and explained as Loop helped him shrug out of his jacket and rolled up his sleeve. A spider web of blood flowed down his arm in long, dark trails, and his entire arm burned. He practically bit off his tongue as Loop pushed a towel against it.

"He needs a healer," she said, looking over her shoulder at Stamp. Beside her, Lucas looked terrified.

"Don't bother," came a voice from across the club floor. It was probably the last voice Killian wanted to hear right now—Chaser's. He was carrying a crate full of liquor bottles. After setting it down, he placed a hand gently on Lucas's shoulder and whispered a few quiet words in his ear. Lucas nodded several times. With a final glance in Killian's direction, he turned and ran upstairs to the apartment.

"They won't be able to heal him," Chaser said once Lucas had closed the door to the apartment behind him.

"What are you talking about?" Stamp asked.

"Forgive me if I don't take your word for it. I'd still prefer going to a healer," Killian cut in. He cringed as Loop pressed the towel further against his wound. The cloth was already soaked through with blood.

"Still don't trust me, huh?" Chaser asked, crossing his arms. "Is it my personality or my abilities that set you on edge? Because my abilities might just keep those men from finding you again."

Killian's eyes shot up to his and, this time, he wasn't afraid to meet them. "What do you mean?"

"Don't you think it's a little strange that such a minor wound is bleeding so much?"

"A little, I guess. Feel free to enlighten me, though," Killian said, looking up at him.

"Well, judging by the darkening of your blood and the burning sensation you're probably feeling in your arm, there's some sort of tracer working through your bloodstream right now. The only reason those men you encountered aren't already beating down my door is because it was such a minor wound, but trust me when I say that's only bought you a few minutes. If you don't want them finding you again, you're going to need my help."

Sweat beaded across Killian's forehead. The salty taste of blood began to work its way into the back of his throat.

"And why are you so anxious to help?" he asked.

"Look, I don't know exactly what you've all got yourselves mixed up in, but from the little I've overheard it has something to do with that boy up there, and, in my city, you don't mess with kids."

"What kind of tracer do you think is it?" Loop asked before Killian could think of a response.

"I don't know. Not without running a full sweep of his system, but it's probably a blood compound, probably a capsule that was in the bullet. Bounty hunters like to use them to track their marks. Shattered on impact and latched onto him. Now it's in his blood and tracking him like a hound," Chaser said. "I can brew up a potion that might be able to hold it off until I can get it out of his system, but that's only if we start right now."

"I thought you were just a club owner," Killian groaned out. The fire was starting to spread to his chest and other extremities. "How do you know about that?"

"I'm a man of many talents."

"Should introduce you to my friend Jo Jack," Killian said. "You guys would get along great."

"I'm sure. Let's save the introductions for later, though," Chaser said. "Do you want my help or not?"

Killian looked at Loop, still not sure if he could trust him. His hands were shaking and his heart was pounding in his chest. She nodded slowly. So did Stamp. Killian glanced back at Chaser, his vision starting to shake as well.

"Do it," he said, his voice barely audible.

Chaser nodded. Not wasting any time, he disappeared into the back storeroom.

"This had better be legit," Killian said to Loop.

She nodded. "It is. He knows what he's talking about. Trust him."

"That's easier said than done right now," he replied with a groan.

Chaser emerged a few minutes later, carrying several jars of ingredients, a glass bottle filled with some sort of red liquid, and a wooden bowl and pestle. Killian shot Loop a concerned look, but she nodded reassuringly as Chaser set to work, measuring the ingredients with his fingers and crushing them together with the grinder. Once he had mixed all the ingredients, he poured in almost the entire bottle of the red liquid. It immediately began frothing, and a strange sort of scent filled the air. It smelled like peppermint, and, for some reason, Killian was suddenly reminded of the night Spin died. There was something about the smell that reminded him of the way that thing had looked at him right before it tore out his throat. His hands balled into fists at the memory.

"This will block whatever tracer is in your system long enough for me to try to get it out, but it's going to hurt like hell," Chaser said, throwing in the last ingredient and causing the liquid to froth even more.

"It already hurts like hell," Killian replied through gritted teeth. The burning was almost too much to handle now. His heart felt like it was going to explode. Loop grabbed one of his hands, and he clutched her fingers tightly.

Chaser nodded and handed him the bowl. "Drink," he said.

When Killian raised the bowl to his lips, the scent nearly overwhelmed him. He tipped his head back and allowed the liquid to slide down his throat, trying not to choke on the disgusting taste. It tasted like vomit and felt like ice, practically freezing his chest. He was surprised that puffs of white smoke didn't come out when he exhaled. His vision suddenly went spotty, and he cried out as a shockwave of pain bit into his stomach, shooting out all the way to his fingertips and toes. A spasm racked his body, and he hunched forward, clutching his stomach and trying not to retch. He gritted his teeth, forcing it back down, and bit back a cry of agony.

"Let it work. Don't fight it," Chaser said. "Breathe. Just breathe."

Killian shot him a look of pure death. His lower lip quivered, and he slammed his hand against the table. The pain was almost unbearable. He grabbed Loop's hand and squeezed even tighter. It must have hurt her—his grip was practically crushing her fingers together—but she never made a sound. She just held on.

"This had better work," Stamp threatened, his own hands clenching into fists. "If it doesn't..."

"It will," Chaser said.

Flashes of white light hit Killian's vision, and then everything that had occurred over the past few days seemed to play back in front of him. The gunfight, the explosion at Skye's, the vampire nest, and then the night Spin had died. Everything moved in slow motion as his old mentor approached the little girl. Her dress was torn and dirty, and her hair hung in tangled curls. Something about her made Spin drop his guard, and, when she turned toward him, her eyes were filled with tears. Neither of them had noticed how red they were until it was too late.

A final spasm hit Killian's body before the breath was suddenly sucked from his lungs, and he sagged against the booth. His whole body felt like it had been broken; he couldn't even lift his arms. Sweat glistened off his forehead and slid down his cheeks in long, steady streams.

"That…hurt…like…hell," he said quietly, sucking in mouthfuls of air with each word.

"Told you," Chaser said. He motioned Loop away, and she rose from the seat, massaging her hand. Chaser took her place. "Now let's see about getting this tracer out of you."

Killian nodded, too weak to do anything else, and glanced up toward the apartment windows. Even though he couldn't see him, he knew Lucas was watching, probably crying again.

"Thanks for sending the kid away," he said quietly, still gasping for air.

"I didn't want him seeing you if things went badly."

"And what were the chances of it going badly?" Killian asked, finally able to catch his breath as Chaser started examining the wound.

"About fifty-fifty," he answered, the smile returning to his lips for a moment. He prodded the edge of the torn flesh with his finger, and Killian flinched away, cursing loudly.

"Comforting," he said, gritting his teeth again.

"I was never known for my bedside manner," Chaser said. "Maybe it's why I got fired so easily."

Killian glanced over at him curiously, but the focused look in Chaser's eyes said now wasn't the time to ask. He looked up at Stamp and Loop instead, both visibly concerned, and put on his best reassuring smile. None of them felt very reassured, though, least of all Killian. He knew things were only going to get worse.

"You were a doctor," Killian said several hours later as Chaser wrapped up his wound, now freshly stitched and free of the tracer compound. It was more a statement than a question.

Chaser clipped the end of the bandage into place and brushed his hands together as if he was some artist done with a fresh painting. He wiped his head dramatically and breathed out a long, drawn-out sigh.

"One of the best," he finally said. He began collecting the various ingredients he had used to get rid of the tracer and loaded them into a wooden crate at his feet. A metal bowl off to the side contained flecks of a black metallic substance—the tracer Killian's blood had been laced with. Much longer and Chaser said he wouldn't have been able to draw it out.

"What happened?" Killian asked.

Chaser stopped loading the crate. He stood for a moment, staring at the ground, before he finally looked up and met Killian's gaze.

"I killed a kid," he said simply. With that, he picked up the crate and strode off, disappearing back into the rear storeroom.

Killian stared after him. After several minutes, he still hadn't returned, and Killian figured he must have hit a nerve. He decided to leave him be. He unrolled his sleeve, careful not to hit his wound, and stood from the barstool.

Stamp stepped up beside him, staring back there as well. "Quite a friend Loop's got," he said.

"Yeah…" Killian managed in response. He had to force himself to look away. What did he mean he had killed a kid?

"Think we can trust him now?"

Killian looked over at him, the words still playing in the back of his mind. After a moment, he nodded. "I think we can count him as a friend… for now."

"What about me?" Stamp asked. "Are you counting me as a friend again yet?"

"Let's not get ahead of ourselves," Killian replied. "I'm still pretty pissed over what happened."

"You know, one of these days…"

"I'm going to have to let you explain. Yes, I know," Killian interjected, "but not today." The corners of his mouth tweaked upward slightly, and he looked up toward the apartment windows. "Alright, Lucas, you can come down now," he called.

The door to the apartment immediately flew open, and Lucas came rushing down the stairs. He almost tripped on the last few steps and barely managed to catch himself, sprinting over.

"Chaser told me not to watch, but I couldn't help it. I saw the whole thing," he practically shrieked. "Are you okay, Killian? It looked like it hurt."

Killian chuckled despite himself and nodded. Stamp grinned as well, ruffling the boy's hair. "He'll be fine," he said. "I mean, he'll always be a tool, but physically he'll be okay."

Lucas laughed and grinned widely. "Those assholes better hope they don't run into us again."

"Whoa, where'd you learn *that* word?" Stamp asked.

"From Killian. He said it a bunch when Chaser was working on him. I'm not completely stupid. I can figure out what these words mean."

"And under the bus I go. He's growing up so fast." Killian smirked.

"You just better hope Skye doesn't hear him using those words or she'll be driving that bus," Stamp said.

"Hey, I agreed to look after him...with you. That doesn't include me watching my language too," Killian replied.

"Are you two seriously at it again?" Loop asked, as she pulled open the club door and walked in carrying several bags of groceries.

"No," Stamp replied.

"He started it," Killian said.

Loop merely rolled her eyes. She set the bags down on the bar top and looked Killian over.

"How are you feeling?" she asked, still a little concerned.

"Okay. Arm's a little sore, but I'll survive."

"Where's Chaser?"

"In the back. I...may have hit a nerve when I asked him about being a doctor," Killian said, more than a little bashfully.

Loop sighed heavily. "I figured it would come up eventually. What did he say?"

Killian looked down at Lucas who was listening intently and shook his head. "Nothing much."

Loop caught his meaning and quickly changed the subject. "Well, if you two are done fighting, you might be interested to learn the gunfight at Jo Jack's caught the media's attention. I saw it on TV while I was getting groceries. The police didn't give a statement, which means they don't have any leads, so at least we don't have to worry about *them* coming around."

"Well, that's good," Stamp said.

"What about the tracer? Was he able to get it out?" she asked hopefully, her eyebrows arched high upon her forehead.

Killian nodded, happy to be able to pass on at least some good news. Loop smiled, obviously relieved.

"Good. Maybe we can breathe a little bit now. It took everything I had to leave to go get groceries."

"We need to eat," Killian said. "And you hovering while he worked on the tracer wasn't helping."

"*Sorry,*" Loop said exaggeratingly. "You had us worried."

"I had myself worried," Killian said quietly. He still felt a slight burn in his arm and rotated his shoulder slowly.

"Well, I think this is as good a time as any," Stamp said. He raised his chin high in the air, staring down his nose at the pair of them. An extremely smug look crossed his face. "I told you so."

"Oh, my God," Loop said. She swatted him on the arm, and they all chuckled. It felt good to laugh, Killian suddenly realized. He had done so little of it the past several months; he had forgotten what a release it was.

Loop and Stamp began unloading the groceries. She had bought a variety of foods and beverages, obviously not sure what they would all want, especially Lucas. Killian doubted he had been able to pick many of his own meals before. They sat down on two of the stools, and Loop passed him a head of lettuce.

"Start breaking that up, would you?" she said as she unloaded a bag of hot dogs and hamburgers.

Killian nodded and began tearing off chunks. Lucas watched, and a thought suddenly occurred to Killian. "You know, you're going to need a new name," he said.

"What do you mean?" Lucas asked, looking up at him.

"Oh, yeah, I didn't even think about that," Stamp said, glancing up from the potatoes he was peeling.

"Whenever someone moves to Blood Haven, they take a new name,"

Killian explained. "Sort of a way of starting fresh."

"Killian's not your real name?" Lucas asked, surprised.

"It's not the name I was born with. Doesn't mean it's not my real name, though," he replied.

"When you move to Blood Haven, it's like a pilgrimage," Loop said. "You're literally starting a new life. So, as a rite of passage, you shed your old name and take on a new one. That way, you never feel the oppression of your old life. And given what you've been through, I think it's more important for you than anyone."

Lucas looked between them, his mouth hanging slightly open in wonder. "What do you think my name should be?" he asked.

"That's not for any of us to say," Loop said. "You have to be the one to decide. When the time is right, you'll know what you want it to be."

Lucas's brow scrunched up in thought, and they all stared at him in amusement, watching the wheels turn within his head.

"I know!" he said, his eyes opening wide. "Call me Destroyer!"

Killian and Stamp both busted out laughing. A surprised and somewhat sad look washed over Lucas's face, and they managed to stop after a stern glance from Loop. She leaned over to meet his gaze.

"Maybe that's not it just yet," she said in a surprisingly matriarchal tone. "But keep trying. For now, we'll just stick with Lucas."

He nodded and managed a faint smile. Killian reached over and patted him on the shoulder.

"Help me with this lettuce," he said, passing over several chunks. "Destroyer."

CHAPTER 10

Adults

The music from the club floor thrummed against the apartment windows; almost the entire apartment vibrated with the heavy beat. Killian sat staring at his phone screen, a worried look etched across his face. No text messages. No missed calls. Nothing. Concern was starting to creep its way into the pit of his stomach.

"Still no word from Skye?" Loop asked. She had just finished tucking Lucas into bed, and Killian could see he was already passed out. It had been a long day. Killian felt exhaustion tugging on him as well.

"Nothing," he replied. "The police have got to be done with her by now."

"They might be holding her in protective custody until they can figure out who bombed the school."

"Damn, I didn't even think of that." Killian sighed heavily. "We need her contacts in the Underground if we're going to get Lucas out of the city."

"Skye's smart. She'll figure out a way to get us in contact with them," Loop said reassuringly, patting him on the knee.

Killian managed a small nod in response and stared out at the dance floor below. It was practically bouncing with activity. Girls dressed in colorful outfits, some little more than bathing suits, swayed and twirled to the rhythm while the men grinded against them, rocking back and forth. The bar was packed to capacity, and the bartenders were doing a dance of their own as they tried to keep up with the onslaught of orders.

A faint orange flicker in one of the corner booths caught Killian's eye, and he saw a young mage trying to impress a girl with a weak fire spell. The ball of flame wasn't very big, barely larger than a tennis ball, and the girl was wholly unimpressed. The bouncer saw it as well and strode over, enforcing the strict "No Spell" policy every guest was briefed on when they arrived. After a brief argument, the kid was dragged out, kicking. Killian smiled in amusement. Chaser ran a tight ship. He was starting to see why Loop trusted him so much.

"So you never told me what exactly happened to Chaser," he said, turning back toward Loop. Her eyes snapped up to meet his, and he saw the sudden uncomfortableness in her expression. "Oh, he…um…"

"Killed a kid," Killian finished.

"Yeah," she responded quietly. She sighed, her shoulders sagging and her head drooping. "When the outbreak first happened, a lot of doctors abandoned ship. Too much stuff they had never seen before. Chaser was one of the few who didn't. He started using what he called 'old medicine' to treat a lot of the stuff he was seeing—you know, magical injuries and curses. Stuff like that. He started using potions when other doctors were still using penicillin, and, for a while, he was really helping. But then, one day, I guess you can say he mixed the wrong ingredients, and a kid died. I don't know exactly what happened. Chaser won't really talk about it, even to me, but I know he had his medical license taken away. Not that it would really matter now with all the healers in the city, but I think it still hurts him sometimes, knowing he can't practice medicine anymore. His potions in the beginning saved a lot of lives, especially during the Terrible Night."

A pained expression suddenly flickered across Killian's face, and he stood up, thrusting his hands in his pockets.

Loop noticed and shot a questioning glance in his direction. "What is it?"

Killian shook his head. "Nothing. I just…" His voice trailed off, unsure if he was ready to share that part of his life.

"Killian, you can tell me. Come on, we're partners now. Partners trust each other," Loop said.

"It's just…" He struggled for the right words. It still hurt even after all this time. "My mom… She died during the Terrible Night."

"Oh, God, Killian, I'm so sorry," Loop said, realizing what she had said.

Killian shook his head. He walked over to the window and leaned one arm against it, staring at the neon lights suspended over the dance floor. The crowd below was bathed in a tapestry of blue, green, and red.

"It's alright," he said. He rubbed the weariness from his eyes and walked back over to the couch, his feet sinking into the plush rug. "That night was tough on everyone. I can't go crying every time it's mentioned."

"Still, you were what, thirteen? No kid should have to see that," Loop said. She reached her hand out, and, after a moment of hesitation, Killian took it gently into his. She caressed the back of his hand with her thumb. They locked eyes, and there was suddenly a strange awkwardness between them. Loop dropped his hand and scooted back on the couch, suddenly feeling very uncomfortable. She cleared her throat, trying to change the conversation for more than one reason now. "So I take it you didn't manage to get anything from Jo Jack's."

Killian's eyes flicked up toward hers, a light suddenly coming on in his head. "Actually, I did."

He had completely forgotten about the revelation charm Jo Jack had given him. It had been bobbing against his chest nearly all day. He pulled the amulet from beneath his collar and held it out for her to see.

"Whoa," she said, looking at it closely. "That's a Celtic revelation charm. You know how rare these are?"

Killian looked down at it. It looked like a simple carving to him. "No, but I take it you do."

"Yeah, they're really hard to find. You said Jo Jack *gave* this to you?" Loop asked, more than a little surprised.

"Well, I think he had the intention of selling it to me, but yeah," Killian replied.

"Maybe Jo Jack's a better friend than I thought. You're going to have a hard time finding one for less than five thousand chits."

"What?" Killian's mouth practically fell open.

"Yeah, like I said, they're really rare. If Jo Jack gave this to you, he wanted you to stay alive."

"Could've fooled me. He bailed the first chance he got."

"Well, I didn't say he's a saint," Loop said, "but he definitely must think a lot of you if he was willing to sell it to you. He had to know you wouldn't be able to afford its usual price."

Loop handed it back to him, and Killian examined it much more closely. It still looked like a simple mediocre carving to him. The fox's head was uneven, and the symbol was crudely carved, hardly legible. Loop seemed to know her stuff, though, so if she said it was valuable, he was inclined to believe her. Maybe Jo Jack was looking out for him after all.

"I still don't like him, but there's definitely more to him than I originally thought," Loop said.

"That's Jo Jack, a bundle of mysteries," Killian replied, a small smile darting across his lips. He tucked the amulet back beneath his shirt and took a strange sort of comfort from its now-familiar weight against his chest.

They sat back down on the couch together, and a silence fell over them for several minutes. Killian tried to think of something to say, not sure why it was suddenly so awkward, but nothing came to mind. Beside him, Loop appeared to be in the same boat. What had just happened?

Thankfully, Stamp came out of the bathroom a moment later, saving them both from the awkward silence. He groaned, tucking the new phone Chaser had given him back into his pocket and rubbing the back of his neck.

"Fall in?" Killian asked, smiling slightly.

"Shut up," Stamp replied, dropping onto the armchair beside him. "You know I went in there only because I can't hear anything out here."

He looked at the windows, practically vibrating in their frames, and scoffed.

"Daisy's pissed, I take it?" Killian asked. He wasn't sure what he wanted the answer to be, but he had a good guess.

"Extremely," Stamp replied. "Something about not being able to trust each other if we don't tell each other what's going on. Your name came up a couple times. I think that's what pissed her off most. Not that I'm out risking my ass without her permission, but the fact you're here with me and she's the last to know. Women, man. They never get their damn priorities straight."

"Umm, sitting right here," Loop interjected.

Stamp shot her a slit-eyed expression. "Oh, you know what I mean. Normal girls. Not you."

"Remind me how that's supposed to make me feel better," Loop replied.

Killian watched with amusement. "Did she forbid you from hanging out with me?" he asked, deciding to save Stamp from burying himself anymore.

"No, but she wants to talk to both of us when this is all over," he replied, waving his hand in the air dismissively.

"Great. I'm not even dating her anymore, and I'm still going to get a lecture," Killian said.

Loop snorted beside him. "You both deserve worse than a lecture," she said. The corners of her mouth slowly quirked upward, and they all chuckled lowly.

Stamp's eyes slowly drew up toward the bed where Lucas was sound asleep, and he sighed. "I remember when I was a kid…before the Change and all that. My parents would have guests over, and they'd always make me go to bed early. I remember wanting to stay up so bad to be with the adults. Now that *I'm* the adult, all I want to do is sleep," he said. He rubbed the exhaustion in his eyes and rolled his neck around.

"You know, you *can* get some sleep," Loop said. "Chaser said he would let us know if anyone popped up looking for us."

"I wish I could. Truth is, between Killian getting attacked at Jo Jack's and Skye's academy being bombed, I haven't been this wired in a long time. I forgot how amped up I can get."

"Daisy not letting you out to play?" Loop asked with the twitch of another smile.

"Pretty much. Ever since what happened to Spin…" His voice trailed off suddenly, his eyes shooting up toward Killian's.

"Well, on that note, I'm going to go get a drink downstairs," Killian said, seeing where this conversation was leading and desperate to get out of its way. He rose from his seat before Stamp could go any further.

"Oh, alright," Stamp said, his tone flattening. "Try to stay out of trouble."

Killian gave a nonchalant wave over his shoulder, careful not to meet Loop's eyes. She was getting way too good at reading him. She would probably want to sit down in a circle and talk about it. Truth be told, it would probably help if they did, but he didn't think he was ready for that just yet. He still had way too many pent-up feelings for Daisy and way too many regrets about Spin to just forgive and forget all that had happened.

The sharp beat of the music blasted his eardrums the moment he opened the apartment door. He swung it shut behind him quickly, paying a swift glance over his shoulder to check on Lucas. He was still fast asleep atop the bed, however, the covers drawn around him like a cocoon. Killian shook his head. It had been years since he slept like that.

A misty haze of sweat and perfume hung over the club floor like a shroud as he walked down the metal staircase. Killian nodded to the bouncer guarding the bottom of the steps, pulled the velvet rope aside, and began threading his way through the mesh of people. Most were of the average variety, but Killian spotted a few tourists as well, looking to experience the nightlife in one of the more "dangerous" parts of the city. Killian snorted. They wouldn't know the dangerous part of town if he dropped them off in it.

Weaving and twisting his way through the crowd, he finally managed to make his way to the bar and shouldered his way next to a young mage who looked too young to drink. He turned, ready to argue, but thought better of it when he saw the look in Killian's eye. He instead went back to sipping his drink quietly, and Killian signaled the bartender for one of his own. He turned and looked out across the dance floor as he waited. There was never a shortage of attractive women in a place like this, and tonight was certainly no exception. He watched them bump and grind their way across the dance floor, trying to keep his eyes from drifting too far south and failing miserably. He was sure Loop and Stamp were watching with keen interest from their bird's-eye-view in the apartment, but he didn't care. He shot a glare up at the two-way mirrors and turned to accept his drink from the bartender.

When he turned back to the dance floor, a flash of crimson hair caught his eye. Killian stared across the dance floor and waited for the woman to reappear. A moment later, he caught sight of her, dancing amidst a swath of people on the dance floor, her arms intertwined above her head and her hips swaying back and forth sensually. Her skin was paper white, and her fiery orange hair reached halfway down her back. She had long, slender legs, and her skintight green shirt revealed a toned, rigid stomach. Her eyes were closed as she rocked back and forth to the beat of the music. After a moment, they gradually opened, as if she could sense his gaze upon her. She made a full sweep of the dance floor before she finally caught sight of him. Her bright green eyes settled on his, and, after a moment, the corners of her lips tweaked upward.

Shooting one last look up at the apartment and downing the remainder of his drink, Killian began pushing his way toward her. He had no idea what he was going to say to her. Maybe he would just start dancing. He was halfway across the dance floor when someone suddenly caught his arm.

"Killian, we might have trouble," Chaser said just loud enough to be heard over the music. His tone was serious.

"What?" Killian's whole body tensed. He looked at the people dancing around them but didn't see anything out of the ordinary.

"You're being watched. I noticed it when you first came down. Then I brushed against one of them. All I can say is they're not here to party." Chaser locked eyes with him, and his meaning hit Killian like a bag of bricks. He nodded over toward the corner of the dance floor.

Killian glanced at a young man in a brown leather jacket, eyeing them. When their gazes met, he looked away casually and pretended to be typing on his phone. Killian's head was suddenly on a swivel as he searched the club for any more. He counted at least a dozen; they were dressed in casual attire and blended in pretty well, but they all stood way too rigidly to be tourists, and their eyes followed him everywhere he looked. He kicked himself for not noticing before.

"You think they're agents?" Killian asked, careful not to lock eyes with any others. He felt for his gun tucked into his belt before realizing he had left it back on the counter in the apartment.

Stupid, stupid, stupid, an all-too-familiar voice said within his head. *How could you have been so stupid?*

"That would be my guess," Chaser said. "Regardless, you need to get Lucas out of here. There's a back exit over by the bathrooms. I'll try to distract them. Go."

Killian nodded. He immediately began weaving back through the crowd toward the apartment steps. Chaser made his way over to the DJ booth, and, a second later, the music cut off. Everyone's attention turned to the booth.

"Ladies and gentlemen, I'm sorry to interrupt this amazing beat, but I've got something to announce," Chaser called out across the crowd.

Killian ducked through a group of drunken girls celebrating a bachelorette party and snaked past two men in fraternity shirts, his eyes constantly searching for any agents who might be coming up on him. Everyone seemed to be focused on Chaser as he made his announcement. None of them paid him so much as a second glance.

"I'm proud to say that next month I'll be opening up a second Power Plant location in the downtown area!"

A loud cheer suddenly erupted from the crowd, and a man threw up his arms in excitement, nearly flooring Killian. He edged his way past him, several choice words escaping his lips, and ignored the disgruntled look he got in return.

Chaser continued by saying the opening night would feature an open bar and a discounted cover charge. Another cheer went up, and Killian ducked through the last row of spectators. His heart nearly stopped as he saw where the bouncer was supposed to be standing. In his place was a tall man in a tight grey shirt.

"Mister Riley, I'm with the Federal Protection Bureau," he said, stepping forward and blocking Killian's path. "We'd like to have a word with you."

CHAPTER 11

Protectors

Ice suddenly filled Killian's veins. This was much worse than he thought. They weren't just agents. They were Protectors, the secret police force of the United States. If they were involved, he was in serious trouble. Still, he managed to put on the best confused, innocent smile he could muster and played dumb.

"Riley? I think you got the wrong guy. My name's Jack…Jack Flash," Killian said, shrugging his shoulders.

A heavy hand suddenly gripped his shoulder, cementing him in place. "I think not."

Killian craned his neck and saw another man wearing a crisp grey and white suit, holding him in place. A nervous chuckle escaped his lips, and he glanced up at the DJ booth. Chaser was still talking; if he had caught sight of the situation, he gave no indication. He was on his own.

"We know who you are, Mister Riley. Mister *Nicholas* Riley," the one blocking his path said. He had a hawk nose and thin blond hair slicked back. It practically gleamed from all the hair gel he had on it.

"And we know you've been aiding an escaped juvenile fugitive," the one holding him in place said. His voice was much gruffer than his counterpart's, and his breath smelled like cigarettes. "Allow us to take him back into custody and everything can go back to normal for you and your friends."

"Don't and we'll be forced to take *you* into custody," the blond one said. "And I assure you, your living conditions would be much worse than his."

"Look, fellas, I really don't know who you're talking about," Killian said, fighting to keep his voice steady. He had to stall until he could come up with an idea to get out of this. So far, nothing was presenting itself, though.

"And if you'll look to the back of the dance floor, you'll see my two associates who will be handling vouchers for the night," Chaser's voice suddenly echoed out. "The two gentlemen in grey will set you up for the night. First come, first serve of course."

Killian had to force the smug smile off his face. Almost the entire crowd turned at once, and the two Protectors froze. Killian decided it was now or never, ducked beneath the suit's grasp, and drove his elbow hard into his chin. The Protector's head snapped backward with an audible crack, and Killian spun around, reaching into the Protector's jacket and praying he was right-handed. His fingers grasped metal, and he practically yelped in excitement. He pulled the gun free from beneath the man's arm and yanked the trigger. The shot ripped into his upper thigh with a thundering boom, and suddenly there was chaos everywhere as dancers dove to the floor.

The suit fell backward with a cry of shock and pain, and Killian turned toward the other one, only to meet a hard fist that rocked his jaw. He too went sprawling, stars dancing across his vision as he hit the ground hard. He recovered just in time to see the blond Protector pull his own pistol and level it on his head. People were still hitting the floor or running for the exits. All Killian could do was stare up at him. Then, two more gunshots joined the symphony of screams and cries, and the blond fell as well, a silent agonizing look on his face as he locked eyes with Killian.

Over his shoulder, Loop was sprinting down the apartment steps. She fired two more shots into the ceiling, and everyone ran for the doors. Killian could have kissed her at that moment. She ran over and helped him to his feet, the crowd rippling away from them.

"We've got to get out of here. Where's Stamp and Lucas?" Killian asked, rubbing his jaw. Blood streamed from the corner of his lip.

"They're coming," Loop said, throwing a glance up at the stairs, then around the club floor. Other Protectors were closing in, but the tide of the fleeing crowd was keeping them back for now.

Suddenly, the door to the apartment burst open, and Stamp came running down the stairs, Lucas cradled in his arms. He was down the steps in a flash, and they broke toward the rear exit. The crowd thrashed them about, and Killian barely managed to push through, Loop and Stamp right on his heels. Then they were out of the crowd and in the back hallway, running past the bathrooms. The exit was right ahead of them.

A gunshot suddenly split the air, and Loop sprawled across the floor. Killian whipped around, caught sight of two Protectors at the corner of the hallway, and yelled for Stamp to keep going. He crashed through the door, and Killian fired several shots toward the Protectors. One bullet hit the corner of the wall and concrete and plaster went flying. Three more shots drove them behind cover, and Killian sprinted forward to Loop, who was struggling to stand. As he helped her to her feet, he saw the bullet had ripped through her abdomen. She wouldn't be able to walk. Throwing one arm around her back and emptying the remainder of his clip down the hallway, Killian dropped the gun and picked up her legs, cradling her in his arms like a small child. She didn't resist. Her breathing was coming too fast, and sweat was already thick across her brow.

Killian raced for the door. Several gunshots chased after him, but none struck true, and then he crashed through the exit and was out in the cool night air. For a moment, his heart hammered within his chest as he searched for Stamp, but he saw only empty vehicles in the dark parking lot. Had he left them? A deep panic suddenly set in, and he struggled to keep his breath from catching in his throat.

"Over here!"

Killian's gaze snapped upward, and he saw Stamp loading Lucas into a nearby sedan, waving over the top of the vehicle to get his attention. Killian ran over as fast as he could, trying not to jostle Loop too much. Blood was quickly pooling across her shirt, staining it a dark crimson.

Stamp popped the rear door open for him, and Killian laid her on the seat. "It's going to be okay," he said over and over.

Several gunshots suddenly pinged off the trunk of the car, and Killian and Stamp dove into the front of the vehicle.

"Stop shooting. You might hit the boy," he heard a distant voice call out, followed by the pounding of feet as the Protectors closed in.

"Get us out of here," Stamp said from the passenger seat. Killian looked down at the base of the steering column and saw it had been ripped open, several ignition wires tied together. The motor hummed quietly beneath the hood. Without hesitating further, Killian slammed his door closed, popped the car's lever shifter into DRIVE, and floored the gas pedal. The tires spun and they sped out of the parking lot, joining the rush of other vehicles escaping the area. In the rear-view mirror, he saw at least ten other Protectors standing in the parking lot, staring after them, before Killian rounded a corner and out of their sight.

Only then did the flood of emotions kick in, and Killian suddenly slammed his hand against the steering wheel. "Fuck, fuck, fuck!" he practically shouted. "How did they find us? How do they keep fucking finding us?"

"We need to get Loop to a healing ward," Stamp said. "She won't last long like this."

Killian risked a glance over his shoulder and saw that Loop was fading fast. She clutched her stomach and was only semi-conscious, her eyes glassy and wet. Beside her, Lucas was struggling to hold it together. He was breathing almost as heavily as she was and couldn't take his eyes off the blood pooling across her stomach.

"A healing ward's no good," Killian said. "If they could track us to Chaser's, they could track us to the hospitals."

"Then we're going to have to take her somewhere shady and leave her there," Stamp said.

"What?" Killian's eyes snapped over in his direction. Surely, he had misheard him.

"I know it's shitty, but it's our only choice. We've obviously got to keep moving. That's twice they've managed to track us down."

"That doesn't mean we're going to leave her somewhere!"

"Killian, I don't like it either, but...."

"No. Fuck you for even suggesting it. We're not."

"He's right," Loop suddenly uttered from the backseat. Killian looked over his shoulder at her. Each word was a struggle. "Stamp's right. You can't stay with me. You…have to keep moving. Leave me. I'll…be…fine."

Killian shook his head.

"No. No way. I'm not losing another friend because of this thing," he exclaimed, pointing his finger at Lucas. He turned a corner sharply and merged onto the highway, ignoring the hurt look in Lucas's eye. This was exactly why he hadn't wanted to get involved in the first place. Look where they were now. Loop had been shot, probably dying, and all the kid could do was cry about it. Killian slammed his hand against the steering wheel again.

"Killian…" Stamp began, but he didn't have to say anything further. Killian knew he was right.

"We'll take her to Barker's. He'll look after her," he said, his voice dropping in volume as the fight left him.

"You sure you want to take her to him?"

"He hates mundanes *and* the U.S. I can't think of a better person to take her to," Killian replied. He omitted the fact that Barker was also pretty much their *only* option. Killian severed most other ties after Spin had died.

A quick glance in the rearview mirror told him Loop didn't have much time. He pressed even harder on the gas pedal, practically redlining the RPM gauge.

"Alright. He's just an asshole," Stamp said.

"And now he gets the chance to make up for it," Killian replied. "Just like you."

Killian banged on the door again. Behind him, Stamp cradled Loop in his arms while Lucas stood just behind him. "Open the damn door, Barker," Killian called again.

They were standing in the breezeway of a rundown apartment building. The sun had yet to show over the horizon, and there was a certain foreboding feeling in the darkness that engulfed the street. Metal bars lined most of the windows, and the silhouettes revealed several vagrants peeking out from the nearby alleys, looking for a grain of Dust or a chit. Police never came to this part of the city; they knew better. Killian hoped it would be the same for Protectors.

"Ugh, I'm coming. Hold on," Barker's voice came from the other side. They heard the clatter of several glass bottles falling over and several muttered curses.

"Bark, I'm going to give you five seconds to open the door before I turn it into a battering ram and shove it up your ass."

"I said I'm coming," Barker called before finally opening the door. "Now what is so damn important?"

His eyes fell on Loop's unconscious frame, then the blood dripping from her shirt. "Oh," was all he managed to get out.

"Yeah. Oh," Killian replied, shoving past him. "We need you to heal her. Fast. She's already fading."

"Yeah, yeah," Barker said, ushering Stamp and Lucas inside.

Barker was several inches shorter than Killian with slit-shaped eyes and high protruding cheekbones. His head was bald and flat, and his skin was dark tan. He was also one of the most talented healers Killian had ever met, probably the only reason he hadn't severed this connection as well.

"You know, I normally charge extra for house calls, but considering this is *my* house I guess I'll make an exception," he said, chuckling lowly. He led them through the cluttered living room and into his tiny bedroom in the back. Several empty liquor bottles littered the floor, and the entire room smelled like trash.

Stamp laid her down on the bed as gently as he could, and Barker practically shoved him out of the way.

"Alright, let Daddy work." he said, rubbing his palms together. Stamp's hands balled tightly into fists, but he didn't do anything. He instead just stood there, one arm around Lucas's shoulder, and let Barker set to work.

With surprising gentleness, Barker eased Loop's shirt up to just below her breasts and exposed the gunshot wound. It was still pulsing blood sporadically, and Loop's skin was growing paler and paler.

"Is it through and through?" Barker asked.

"I don't know. I didn't get a chance to look," Killian replied. "We were too busy running."

"Roll her on her side," Barker said. "I need to see if the bullet came out the other side."

"Why does that matter?" Stamp asked. "You're a healer, aren't you?"

"Because, genius, if I heal her with the bullet still inside, it's going to be stuck in there. Then what is she going to do? Crap it out?"

Stamp looked ready to knock his head off, but a look from Killian kept him in place. Killian leaned over and eased Loop onto her side. She sucked in a mouthful of air, though her eyes remained closed, and Killian tugged on her shirt. There was a bullet hole out her back as well. Blood had already pooled across the sheets around where she had been laying. Killian laid her back flat.

"Yeah, there's one back there," he said.

"Alright, let's start the magic," Barker said, rubbing his hands together again. He placed them gently across Loop's abdomen and closed his eyes. Slowly, a glow began to emit from beneath his palms and between his fingers, and warmth spread throughout the room. The torn flesh around the bullet hole began to mend itself, stitching back together slowly. After a few moments, her stomach had returned to normal, the bullet hole erased from existence. There wasn't even a scar. After several minutes, her coloring had yet to return, however.

"She lost a lot of blood," Barker explained. "I can repair the flesh, but I can't give her back what she's lost. She'll have to produce that on her own and, judging by how *much* she lost, I'd say she'll be out of the fight for several days at least, if not more. She's very lucky. Much longer and she wouldn't have made it at all."

"Thanks, Bark," Killian said as sincerely as he could. For once, he really meant it.

"Do I even want to know what you guys have gotten yourselves into?" Barker asked, looking between them.

"Probably not," Killian replied, "but if anyone shows up looking for us or her, do me a favor and..."

"Handle it," Barker filled in. "I got you. Just remember I did this for you."

"I'll remember. I owe you one."

"More like you owe me half a dozen, but who's counting?" Barker asked, a grin playing across his lips.

Stamp rolled his eyes. "Now, let's talk about compensation . . ."

CHAPTER 12

Revelations

Killian's hands still hadn't stopped shaking. The adrenaline coursed through his veins like a tidal wave, radiating outward through his limbs. He splashed water across his face and stared at himself in the mirror. Years had been added to his face. Lines that hadn't been there two days ago were now etched beneath his eyes. Anger piled up inside him. Anger at the Protectors for shooting Loop. Anger at Skye for mixing him up in all this. Mostly, it was anger at himself. He had sworn he wouldn't get attached to anyone again. It was why he had insisted on working with someone new. They were supposed to be partners. That was it. Yet here he was fretting over Loop as if he had known her for years. Against his best wishes, she had become a friend.

Killian turned off the faucet and leaned against the door. He could hear voices from the other side, Stamp and Barker arguing.

"It's bullshit!" Stamp said, trying to keep his voice down and failing miserably. "You can't expect us to pay that much."

"Hey, you think this kind of treatment is cheap?" Barker spat back. "If you wanted cheap, you should have taken her to a damn healing ward. You want to stay off the radar, you take her to me, and that isn't cheap."

"You're a fuckin' asshole, you know that?"

"Nice to see your vocabulary has improved since last time, Stamp. You've never liked me. Don't act like it's because of my price."

"You're right. It's not because of your price. It's because of your damn attitude," Stamp retorted.

Killian sighed, closing his eyes. They had never gotten along, and he honestly didn't understand why. Sure, Barker wasn't the most likeable person out there, but he wasn't the most *un*-likeable either. Some people just didn't mesh, he supposed.

"*My* attitude? Why don't you try taking a look in the mirror, you self-righteous prick. I run a business and as long as you're here you're going to pay for that business."

"Well, then I guess it's a good thing we're out of here as soon as Killian's done in there," Stamp said.

Killian's eyes snapped open at that. He wrenched the door open, and both men froze, their fingers extended toward one another.

"We're not leaving until Loop is awake," he said, his eyes darting between them.

"Killian, we've been over this…" Stamp started, but Killian cut him off.

"No. We're not leaving until she's awake. End of discussion. Got it?"

Stamp stared at him, disbelief evident in his eyes. His finger was still extended out toward Barker. After several moments, he nodded.

Killian shot another angry glance in Barker's direction. "Barker, we'll pay you what you want. Just shut the hell up."

Barker nodded as well, unwilling to argue with the look in Killian's eye.

Killian nodded back, sparing a glance in Lucas's direction. The boy dodged his gaze, hiding his head in his knees. Killian didn't bother trying to get him to look up. Instead, he turned and headed into the bedroom where Loop was sleeping. He slammed the door behind him and practically fell into the small foldout chair beside the bed.

His mind was a whirlwind of a million questions. One was almost constant: *How did they find us?* It was as if they had a giant billboard following them around, telling their pursuers their every move. It was probably what made Killian want to lash out most. Spin had taught him how to hide in plain sight, how to disappear, but it was like he couldn't hide from these people. Twice in as many days they had been found.

How?

A harsh shiver suddenly racked Loop's body, and Killian gritted his teeth until it passed. He grabbed another blanket from beside the bed and laid it across her. She was barely visible beneath all the covers, a tiny bundle that hardly took up a quarter of the bed. The occasional moan of pain escaped her lips, and Killian could tell she was dreaming. Her eyes moved rapidly beneath their lids. Killian sat back in the seat, rubbing the bridge of his nose. He hoped it was a good dream and not something like this nightmare they had stumbled into. He ran his hand through his hair and down across his face. More than anything, he was just exhausted.

"What happened?" a quiet, raspy voice asked from beside him. Loop's eyes slowly fluttered open, and Killian immediately fell to her side.

"Hey, how you feeling?" he asked, relief washing over him, his frustration all but forgotten.

"Like I got shot," she replied lowly.

Killian forced a chuckle. "Fair enough," he said. Her eyes trailed around the room in confusion, and he quickly explained, "We brought you to my friend Barker. He's a healer, a damn good one. He'll look after you until you can move on your own."

"How long have I been out?" she asked.

"A while."

"How long?" Loop asked again, focusing her gaze on him.

Killian hesitated a moment. "About four hours," he finally answered.

Loop's mouth almost fell open. "Killian!" she practically shouted before a shooting pain in her abdomen forced her to lower her voice. She gritted her teeth before looking back up at him. "You guys need to get out of here," she breathed. "If they can track him to the club…"

"I know. We are, but I wasn't going to leave you here to wake up alone," Killian said, returning her stern gaze.

"I'll be fine. I'm a big girl. You have to go." Loop's jaw tightened as she slowly sat up. She was obviously still in a fair amount of pain. All sorts of signals were still circulating through her brain, telling her she was hurt. She adjusted the pillows behind her so she was propped up and slowly relaxed backward. "I'm not the important one. Lucas is."

"You're my partner, Loop. That *makes* you important," Killian said, refusing to back down.

Loop's eyes settled on his. After a moment, she reached her hand out, and Killian took it tenderly. This time, there was no awkwardness.

"Not when someone as innocent and as powerful as Lucas is looking to you to protect him. You have to help him, Killian. It could be the most important thing you'll ever do."

Killian blinked at her, unsure what she was implying.

She lowered her voice to little more than a whisper. "It took me a while to put it together too. It wasn't until the Protectors showed up that I finally did. Why do you think so many people are after a *thirteen year old* kid?"

Everything suddenly seemed to click into place, the implications of what she was saying hitting him like a battering ram. The Change. Thirteen years ago. Lucas was thirteen. It wasn't possible. He struggled to stay in his seat.

"You don't think... No, Skye wouldn't keep me in the dark like that. He... She..." Killian struggled for words, but it all seemed to fit together. How had he not realized it before?

"You have to protect him, Killian. You have to keep him safe. For all our sakes," Loop said, her eyes all but begging him.

Killian nodded slowly. If what she was saying was true, the whole weight of the world had just dropped onto his shoulders.

Loop let go of his hand, and he let it fall to his side. Just what had Skye pulled him into?

Killian stared out the side-view mirror, replaying his conversation with Loop over in his head. When he was certain they weren't being followed, he pointed to the side of the road.

"Here, this is good. Pull over," he said.

Stamp guided the sedan over to the curb and put it in PARK. They had been driving around the city for the past few hours, taking random turns and avoiding the major thoroughfares as best they could. The gas tank was almost empty, though, and Barker had taken the majority of their remaining chits. It was worth it, though. Loop was alive and would be protected if anyone came looking for them.

"What's the plan?" Stamp asked as Killian opened the passenger door and climbed out. The sidewalk was relatively deserted. Only a few people were still walking about on their lunch breaks.

"We've got to get some money together if we're going to keep moving around," Killian replied. "I've got a stash at my apartment in a safe. I'm sure they've already been there, but I might be able to sneak in and grab it."

"You sure that's a good idea?"

"No, but it's the only one I've got. Unless you feel like robbing a bank, that is." Stamp shook his head and Killian continued. "I want you to take the remaining chits we've got and check into a bunch of different hotels, at least half a dozen. A little trick Spin taught me. Go from the north side all the way down into the slums and the hourlies. Check into three under your name, the rest under a bunch of different aliases. Then go to the Skyway Hotel over by the airport and get two rooms. Check in under your favorite baseball player's name. I'll know it's you."

"I guess I won't be checking into any of the resorts. We've barely got a hundred left in chits," Stamp said.

"Stretch it as far as you can. Most of them will probably want only a down payment. Just make sure you have enough for the Skyway."

"Will do," Stamp replied.

Killian nodded and glanced into the back seat. Lucas was staring straight ahead, his palms pressed flat against his thighs. He had barely spoken a word since leaving Barker's. Killian figured he was in shock. There was still blood on the seat beside him.

Killian closed the passenger-side door, rapped on the roof, and stepped backward onto the curb. Stamp eased the car back into traffic and disappeared around the corner. Lucas never once turned around.

If what Loop was implying was true, he really was the most important person in the city right now, maybe even the world. Killian had to force his breakfast back down into his stomach.

He walked a few blocks and boarded one of the free bus liners. It would be a long ride to his apartment, but at least it wouldn't cost him anything. He hadn't been this broke since before he met Spin, back when he was still living on the streets, scrounging for food.

Killian pushed the thought aside and focused on what was ahead of him. The bus began to move, and he grabbed onto one of the overhead metal rings. He had no doubt the people after them, whoever they were, had left a few surprises at his apartment in case he was dumb enough to show back up. The problem was he was dumb enough or desperate enough. Regardless, there were bound to be a few snares he would have to slip past if he wanted to get in, grab the chits from his safe, and make it back out in one piece. Already he could feel his heart beginning to speed up. It wasn't as if he had never faced danger before. It had been a part of his life since the first few cases of the magical outbreak, but there was something different now. There was a certain weight that had fallen upon his shoulders, and he couldn't shrug it away. Not for the first time, he wished Spin were still around. He would know exactly what to do.

He'd also probably call me a coward for feeling so jittery, Killian thought. The hint of a smile played across his lips. He steadied himself mentally and physically and set his mind forward. He couldn't afford to second-guess himself.

The ride took well over an hour before the bus finally pulled into his part of town. Just to be safe, he got off a stop early and walked the rest of the way on foot. It was shaping up to be a bright blue day. For once, Killian wished it would rain. He would look less conspicuous with his head down and his collar pulled high. Instead, he had to walk around as if it was just another day.

After three blocks, his apartment building finally came into view. It was a crumby building with grey concrete walls and external air conditioning units poking out many of the windows. A dumpster on the side of the building was filled to capacity with trash, and several more bags were piled on the ground. A few had been torn open, most likely by homeless looking for anything useful.

Killian surveyed the building from across the street. He hadn't seen anyone milling around, but that didn't mean there still weren't eyes on the apartment, magical or otherwise. After a few minutes, he strolled down another block, crossed the street, and entered into an alleyway several buildings down. When it intersected with another alleyway, he peeked around the corner and, not seeing anyone, headed toward the backside of his building. A back door led into the old community laundry room. It had been out of service since before Killian moved in and, with a hard shove from his shoulder, he was able to get the door open.

It was gloomy inside, and Killian saw several old washing machines and a dryer collecting dust. He squeezed past and peeked out the opposite door into the hallway.

Empty.

He had taken two steps out the door when a voice suddenly echoed down the hallway. He practically fell back into the laundry room.

"He's not here," he heard a voice say. It was gruff and raspy and sounded frustrated. "Be retarded to come back."

"You heard what Sax said, though," another voice replied. This one was much shriller and had a weird accent Killian didn't recognize. They were getting closer. "We have to be sure."

Shrinking into the shadows behind the dryer, he watched as two men strode past the door, not paying a second glance into the laundry room. They wore long brown dusters, western-style, and Killian saw the chrome handle of a pistol poking out from the smaller one's jacket.

Great. These guys, Killian thought. They weren't the same ones from Jo Jack's store, but they were definitely part of the same crowd. Which begged the question: How many groups were after them?

Even worse, people were still here looking for him. Now he would have to contend with these jerk-offs *and* any magical surprises they might have left for him. Killian ground his teeth. *I could just ditch, head out, and forget the chits,* he thought, *but then we'd would have no money. And we're going to need money if we want to stay ahead of these guys and anyone else who decided to come after us.*

At this point, he was starting to wonder if there was a mass email going around he didn't know about. In the end, Killian ducked out from behind the dryer and peeked into the hallway. The two men had turned the far corner. The hallway was a large square, with the lesser apartments facing the inside of the building and the higher quality units (if you could call them that) facing the outside, with at least a minimal view out their tiny windows. The way Killian saw it, the two men were making a loop, which meant he had a few minutes until they rounded the corner on the opposite side. Not wasting any more time, he dashed out of the hallway and raced up the stairs just past the main entryway

Killian took the steps as fast as he dared, trying not to make too much noise, and rounded the landing of the fourth floor. He glanced out into the hallway and saw it was empty. He stepped out into the hallway. After a couple paces, he broke into a jog. He rounded the first corner and saw his apartment door. It was closed, but as he got closer, he saw the lock had been busted open. He also saw the glowing ring of symbols that had been drawn into the door and across the floor. It took Killian a moment to realize what he was looking at. It was a detection enchantment and, thanks to the revelation charm still dangling around his neck, he could see it. It would alert the person who had drawn it to his presence. Killian stared at it closely. It was as close to perfect as one could get, with no breaks in the circle or illegibility to the symbols. Simply put, he couldn't get around it.

Damn it, Killian thought. *What am I going to do now?* He looked up and down the hallway, his eyes settling on the apartment two doors down. It was vacant. The old tenant had overdosed on vamp Dust a while back, before Killian moved in, and the landlord hadn't found a new resident yet. Killian jogged over. He tried the knob, but—to no surprise—it was locked. He threw his shoulder against it and felt the bolt give a little. A second shove and the door swung open, though it made a little more noise than he would have liked. He quickly shut the door behind him and was hit with the sharp, putrid scent of bleach and ammonia. The building manager had obviously tried to scrub away the smell of death that had settled into the apartment. To no avail, it seemed. Killian could still smell it. He paid it little mind, however, as he walked over to the nearby window, the plan still formulating in his head. It was more than a little crazy, but it was all he could come up with. A hard pull upward and the window slid open with a harsh squeal. Killian ground his teeth together. It was like nails on a chalkboard. He poked his head out. The ledge on the other side was less than a foot wide. Before he could think better of it, he swung through the window one leg at a time and lowered his feet down onto the ledge carefully. It was still wet from the rain a few nights ago.

God, he thought, *has it been that long already?* The past few days had been a whirlwind.

He made sure his boots had some traction on the wet surface before setting his whole weight down. It really was quite slick.

Maybe it would *have been easier just to rob a bank,* he thought as he slowly began shimmying along the narrow ledge.

Just then, a door opened on the ground level, and one of the trench coats stepped out into the afternoon air, directly below him. Killian froze. He watched as the man with the weird accent pulled a pack of cigarettes from his jacket and lit one. He inhaled deeply. His dark blond hair was swept back into a pseudo mullet, and he had high sharp cheekbones. If he looked up, Killian was done for; he would be caught completely in the open. All he could do was stand still, his arms pressed flat against the concrete wall behind him, his toes hanging over the edge of the narrow sill.

After several drags from the cigarette, someone called from inside the building. "Hurry up, Q, Sax wants us to check the other floors again."

"Yeah, yeah, I'm coming," Q yelled back. He took one last puff on the cigarette before dropping it to the ground and heading back inside.

Killian breathed a sigh of relief. If they continued with their earlier tactic, he had maybe ten minutes before they hit the fourth floor.

He began edging along the sill again, doing everything he could to not look down. He passed the first apartment window and heard the blare of a wall-screen. Killian risked a glance over his shoulder and saw a small child, one of his neighbor's kids, watching cartoons. She looked over and gasped. Killian brought his finger to his lips and, after a moment, the girl nodded. Killian nodded back and moved along, creeping ever so slowly.

He was only a few feet from his window when his heel caught a particularly slick spot and his foot went out from under him. All at once,

Killian was swinging away from the ledge. His heart froze and he threw his arm outward in a desperate attempt to catch the windowsill. His fingers hit the glass pane, dragged downward and, somehow, managed to find purchase on the old wooden sill. He held on for dear life, his feet dangling beneath him, and the ground a long way down.

Slowly, he raised one leg up and put his toe back on the ledge. Then he lifted himself up and got the other one back on. His heart had yet to start beating again. Making sure he had his balance, he dug his finger into the bottom of the window and lifted hard. It didn't budge.

Damn it, don't tell me I locked it, he thought as he tried again, in vain, to get the window open.

In desperation, he dug his hand into his jacket pocket and found his key ring. He closed his palm around it. Focusing hard, he turned the whole thing into a small metal strip, less than a centimeter thick. He jammed it into the bottom of the window and pushed down as hard as he dared, cautious of losing his balance and slipping again. With a harsh grunt of exertion, the window finally popped open a few inches, and he managed to slide it up the rest of the way. The strip turned back into his key ring, and he stuffed them back into his pocket.

Killian practically fell through the window. His heart had finally started beating again, but now it felt like it might explode within his chest. He immediately ran over to his closet and found three loose floorboards, which he peeled back to expose the metal safe below. He spun the combination into place and pulled it open, revealing the symbol he had chalked into the door to keep it from being altered, and his stash of chits he had kept for emergencies such as these. *Spin really taught me well,* he thought as he grabbed a belt pouch and began stuffing the chits inside. He grabbed all the hundreds he could find and several fifties before tying the pouch closed and putting it inside his jacket. The smaller denominations he stuffed into his pants and jacket pockets.

Killian closed the safe, and, giving the dial a spin for good measure, he secured the boards back into place. He grabbed a rucksack from beneath his bed and threw in a couple shirts and some fresh undergarments. He also grabbed a box of shotgun shells from the shelf. He took the pump-action that was propped up in the corner, making sure it was fully loaded before shouldering the pack and heading back to the window. A quick glance told him no one was outside, so he climbed out. He made sure to avoid the wet spot this time and gave the girl a nonchalant wave as he shimmied past. She smiled and waved back.

Killian reached the window to the vacant apartment and climbed through, careful not to snag his ruck or hit the shotgun on the window. The putrid scent hit him again, and he wrinkled his nose as he walked over to the door. He cracked it open and peeked out. No one. The trench coats were apparently still on a lower floor. He would have to take the fire escape on the side of the building just in case. He didn't want to accidentally run into them on the main stairwell.

He shut the door behind him and headed down the hallway at a brisk walk. He rounded the corner and immediately stumbled backward. One of the trench coats, Q's partner, was at the other end walking toward him. Killian ducked backward, his breath caught in his throat.

"Hey, who's there?" the man called. A million curses cycled through Killian's head. Unfortunately, none of them were the magical kind.

He pressed his back against the wall and listened as the man quickened his pace down the hallway. Killian took several steps backward, flicking the safety off on his shotgun. He aimed at the corner of the wall and sunk low to one knee. That's when, out of the corner of his eye, he saw the door to the utility closet that housed the circuit breaker boxes and the water heater. Killian immediately rushed over and opened the door, sliding inside. He closed the door.

It was like a sauna. Sweat collected across his forehead as he listened hard through the door. He heard the man come around the corner and the click of his gun as he yanked the hammer back, preparing to fire. He heard a low sigh as the trench apparently decided it was nothing and holstered his gun. A moment later, his steady footfalls began retreating away from the door. Killian sighed. That had been way too close for comfort.

His phone suddenly vibrated in his pocket.

Buzz, buzz, buzz.

It was not very loud, but in the silence of the hallway, even through the door, it may as well have been an air horn announcing his presence. He snatched it out of his pocket and silenced it as quickly as he could, not bothering to see who it was, but it was too late. The damage had been done. The footfalls were coming back in his direction, and this time they were much faster. He heard the hammer click back again on the man's pistol. All Killian could do was stand there, caught like a deer in the headlights. His heart hammered within his chest, and he clutched the shotgun tightly, his finger falling to the trigger. He didn't have a choice.

Killian burst through the door and blasted the man. He never got a chance to return fire. The spray had caught him full in the chest, and he fell backward, dead before he hit the ground. Killian immediately turned and ran. He rounded the corner and saw the fire escape at the end of the hall. Several gunshots suddenly hit the wall beside him, and he ducked, firing behind him. The other trench coat, Q, crouched behind cover as the spray caught the corner of the wall, blasting bits of concrete outward. Killian heard a cry of pain. Apparently, a ricochet had caught him. Killian didn't want to see if he was done. He turned and sprinted to the fire escape door, blasting the handle apart and slamming through it. He took the metal steps two at a time, his boots clanging the entire way down. When he reached the ladder, he hopped straight on it and let his weight carry it down. When it reached its limit, it snapped to a halt and he lost his grip, falling off. Thankfully, he landed on his back, his rucksack cushioning some of the fall.

Some.

His back was still on fire as he pulled himself back to his feet. He immediately dove to the side as a fireball flew past and hit the ground beside him. Apparently, Q wasn't done after all.

Killian returned fire, emptying his shotgun and driving the trench coat back into cover atop the fire escape. He took off at a sprint down the alleyway and erupted onto the main thoroughfare. He pounded down the sidewalk until his feet felt heavy and his legs rubbery, and then he ran some more. He ran until he finally caught sight of a cab and flagged it down. The driver pulled over to the side of the road, and Killian threw his pack inside, falling in after it. The driver seemed about to protest, his eyes falling to the shotgun in Killian's hands, but after seeing several of the larger chits, he simply rolled his eyes and asked him where he wanted to go. After several ragged gasps for air, Killian managed to spit out his destination—the Skyway Hotel.

CHAPTER 13

The Truth

"That's the last time we ever listen to one of your plans," Stamp said, crossing his arms like some scolding parent.

"Hey, it worked, didn't it?" Killian replied, rolling his eyes. He washed his face in the nearby sink before pulling on a fresh shirt.

"Barely. You almost got shot."

"Yeah, almost," Killian said.

Stamp scoffed in response.

"Look, we knew it was going to be risky, but it had to be done," said Killian. "We needed money, and I managed to take out one of their guys, maybe even two. That's a win in my book."

Of course, Killian omitted the fact he had almost pissed his pants in the process. Or how close he really came to being killed.

"Whatever," said Stamp. "That's twice, though, you've managed to walk away from these guys after a dumb decision. You might not get a third."

Killian shrugged his shoulders and slumped down into an armchair.

Stamp really had managed to stretch the chits far. He had checked into eight hotels, including this one, and even managed to get them two suites. This one had a large foldout couch, two leather armchairs, and a high-definition wall-screen. There was also a kitchenette tucked away in the corner. The bedroom hosted a king-sized mattress where Lucas was currently sleeping.

"How is he?" Killian asked, thinking of what Loop had said.

"Okay. More exhausted than anything."

"We all are."

"Yeah. He won't talk, though. I think what you said really hit him hard. When you called him a 'thing'."

"Shit," Killian breathed, rubbing his face with both hands. "I forgot about that. I was mad. It's not…"

"I know," Stamp interjected. "You might want to tell him that, though."

Killian nodded. He groaned as he rose from the seat. He still felt pretty sore; he was sure he would have a bruise the size of Australia come morning. He ignored Stamp's expectant gaze, pushed open the door to the bedroom, and walked inside, closing it behind him. Surprisingly, the bed was empty. Lucas sat in the corner of the room, his knees curled up beneath his chin.

"Hey, I thought you were sleeping," Killian said, walking over. Lucas looked up but didn't respond. Not sure what to do, Killian sat down on the bed. He cleared his throat. "Um, listen, Lucas. I'm sorry for what I said earlier. You, uh…"

"You were right," Lucas said quietly, interrupting him.

"What?"

"You were right. I am a thing. I'm not normal. I'm a freak." His voice was almost devoid of emotion, but Killian caught a crack in his tone when he said the word 'freak.'

Killian sighed. "You're not a freak, Lucas. You're not a thing either. You're just a kid who's gotten mixed up with some very bad people. That's not your fault. What's happening, what's happened, isn't your fault."

"It is, though. It all is," he replied. Several tears coursed down his cheeks and he wiped them away.

"Lucas, I need to ask you something," Killian suddenly said. Lucas dried his eyes and looked up at him. He wasn't entirely certain he even wanted the answer, but he needed to know.

"When's your birthday?" he asked.

"Umm…" Lucas hesitated, as if he had to think about it, and Killian suddenly realized he probably did. He had probably never celebrated his birthday before. "I heard her say it was December 21 a few times, the lady who used to come visit me, my mom, I think."

Killian did everything he could to keep his heart from jumping out of his chest. So it was true, what Loop had said. How had Skye not told him?

A hurt look crossed Lucas's face, and Killian recognized it instantly. It was the same expression that had crossed his face every time he thought of his own mother. He slid over on the mattress and sat down on the floor next to Lucas.

"Lucas, I want you to listen to me long and hard, okay?" Lucas looked at him, and Killian suddenly thought of his mother. She might still be alive if the Change had never happened. Spin would never have taken up hunting vampires if the outbreak hadn't made them in the first place. However, Killian also would not be who he was today if it hadn't been for the outbreak either. He leveled his eyes with Lucas's. "None of this is your fault. *None* of it."

"But I am the cause of it, right?" he asked. Killian's mouth almost fell open. Lucas wiped his eyes again as more tears threatened to break free. "I told you I'm not completely stupid. I know why you asked my birthday. It's the same as when all this happened, right? The same as when the Change first started and people starting getting their powers. I'm the cause of it."

All Killian could do was nod slowly. Lucas immediately burst into tears and fell against his shoulder. Killian wasn't sure how to respond. After a moment, he put his arm around Lucas's shoulder and just let him cry.

"Why me? Why me?" he asked over and over.

"I don't know," Killian replied, fighting back tears as a flood of emotions hit him as well. "I don't know."

It was several hours later when Killian finally remembered the phone call and thought to check his cell. To his surprise, he had over twenty missed calls and at least a dozen text messages, all from Skye. Killian immediately sprang to his feet, jostling Lucas from his slumber, and ripped into the living room. Stamp was sitting on the couch, dozing, and Killian shook him awake.

"What? What's going on?" he asked, first groggily, then wide-awake.

"Skye. She's been trying to call me," Killian said, indicating his phone.

Stamp was immediately on his feet.

"Shit, why haven't you been answering?" he asked.

"I silenced it when someone tried calling me at the apartment. It nearly got me killed. I completely forgot about it. It must have been her."

Killian dialed her back and put the phone to his ear. It was only half a ring in when Skye picked up.

"Killian, thank God, I've been trying to get ahold of you for hours. Are you guys alright?" she asked, more than a little panicky.

"Stamp and I are okay. So is Lucas," Killian replied. He switched it to speaker mode so Stamp could hear.

"Thank God. When I saw the news about Jo Jack's, I feared the worst. Then there was this report about a shootout at some club."

"Yeah, that was us too. It's been a rough ride," Killian said.

"I'm just glad you guys are alright."

"Are you finally out? Did the police let you go?"

"Not exactly. They wanted to put me into protective custody, but I managed to slip away. I'm with a friend now, someone from the Underground. He says he can help Lucas. Can you guys meet us?"

"Yeah. When?" Killian asked. Finally some good news. He looked up at Stamp, who nodded in agreement.

"Tomorrow. I'll text you the address. One o'clock."

"Is that Miss Skye?" Lucas asked from the door. He was still rubbing the sleep from his eyes.

"Yeah, it's me, Lucas. How are you holding up?" Skye asked, the severity suddenly lost from her voice and falling back into its former rhythm.

"I'm okay. Killian and Stamp have kept me safe. I just wish Miss Loop hadn't gotten hurt."

"What happened to Loop?" Skye asked, anxiety returning to her voice.

"She got shot when they showed up at the club. Don't worry; she's all right. Just needs a few days to recover. It was close, though."

"God, Killian, I'm so sorry. I never meant for her to get hurt. I never meant for any of this to happen. I... I should have... ," she trailed off, and Killian turned the phone off speaker. He put it back to his ear.

"Should have told me?" Killian asked. A confused look streaked across Stamp's face. He mouthed that he would explain later.

"What… I…"

"I know, Skye. What were you thinking, not telling me? Or Stamp?" Killian asked.

"It… I couldn't risk them finding out," she finally said.

"Who?"

Skye's voice suddenly sounded very close, as if she had her hand cupped over her mouth to keep anyone else from hearing.

"The Underground. They wouldn't understand. They might try to take him for their own purposes. They're good people, but they're fighting a war. I couldn't risk it, but now it doesn't look like I have a choice. We cannot let them get him."

"Speaking of that, you know the U.S. has sent Protectors after him?" Killian asked.

"What?"

"I guess they want him back really bad. I've never heard of them leaving the states before."

"Me neither. This is worse than I thought."

"Well, I hate to ruin your day further, but they're not the only ones after him. There's some other group too. Some guys in trench coats. I can't figure out who they are, but it looks like some guy named Sax is in charge. I can't be sure, though."

"You said Sax?" Skye asked, concern suddenly rising even higher in her voice.

"Yeah. Why? You heard of him?"

"Not sure. Maybe. Might just be rumors, though."

"Well, sharing is caring, Skye."

"Just something I heard Pope talking about a while back," she replied. "He was saying something about some cult of mages who were trying to push magic superiority over the mundanes. I think he said their leader was named Saxos, but I can't be sure. I'll have to do some research."

"Do what you can. Maybe it'll help us figure out who all we're up against.

Magical superiority, though. That doesn't sound good," Killian said. His spine tingled as he remembered the big trench coat in Jo Jack's.

"I will. Just lay low for now and meet us tomorrow. One o'clock," Skye said. "And Killian, I'm sorry. For everything."

Killian nodded, unable to come up with a response, and hung up. He shoved the phone back into his pocket.

"So you want to tell me what that was all about?" Stamp asked.

"Later," Killian said, glancing over at Lucas. He sighed heavily. "Lucas, do me a favor and go back into the bedroom. And no peeking this time."

Lucas looked about to protest, but the expression Killian gave him stopped him short. His shoulders sagged, and he walked back into the bedroom, closing the door behind him. Killian turned back to Stamp, keeping his voice low.

"This may be worse than we thought," he said.

"I'm not sure it can get any worse."

"I wouldn't be so sure. Those trench coats I keep running into, turns out they may be part of some cult bent on magical superiority."

"Superiority? Over who exactly?" Stamp asked. He could tell by the look in Killian's eye he didn't want the answer.

"The entire mundane world."

Stamp had to keep his mouth from falling open. "You're kidding me. I guess that's why they're trying so hard to get their hands on Lucas."

"Yeah, I think they want to use him as some sort of weapon. Can you imagine what that could do? We're talking World War III but with fireballs against nukes."

Stamp practically fell back onto the couch, his fingers digging into his scalp. "You're right. This is way worse than we thought."

"I'm starting to see why the U.S. wants him back so bad too. Odds are they're thinking we're trying to do the exact same thing."

"So what do we do?" Stamp asked after several moments.

"Meet with Skye and her contact in the Underground tomorrow." As if on cue, his phone chimed within his pocket. Skye had texted him the address for the meet. "Try to stay alive until then."

"That's turning out to be easier said than done," Stamp said. Killian nodded. "One thing's for sure: your shotgun and my shitty little pistol aren't going to cut it if we want to make it out of this alive."

"Agreed."

"I'm thinking we take a little trip to Carson's before the meet tomorrow," Stamp said. "Put some of those chits to good use."

Killian nodded, a slight smile tugging at his lips. "Sure you don't think he's an asshole too?"

"I think everyone's an asshole, you most of all. There are just some I'm more willing to put up with." Killian snorted. He turned to call to Lucas, but Stamp halted him. "There was something else. Something about Lucas. I've never seen you get so mad at Skye. What didn't she tell us?"

Killian hesitated. In truth, he could understand why Skye had not told them. It was dangerous. The more people who knew, the more likely it was to get out. At the same time, they had the right to know. He sighed heavily.

"Lucas. The reason he can do everything, all the classes and specializations, is because he caused all this."

"Caused all what?" Stamp asked, looking around as if he was missing something hung up around the room.

"The Change," Killian replied flatly. He was still having trouble believing it himself. "Somehow, he's the cause of all it."

This time, Stamp's jaw did drop open.

CHAPTER 14

Birds of a Feather

Carson was a short, portly man in his mid-forties. He had a cleft chin and a patch of black hair atop his head that was quickly turning grey. Before the Change, he had been a used car salesman and stuck it out even after the Terrible Night. As a result, he made a tidy profit selling weapons and vehicles to the city's less reputable population.

Initially, he was willing to give them only five hundred for the sedan, due to the fact it was obviously stolen and the multiple bullet holes, but after a stern look from Stamp and a bit of negotiating from Killian, he bumped it up to seven-fifty. They took the chits and perused his assorted merchandise, both mundane and magical. He sold everything from guns and ammunition to ceremonial knives and war axes, crammed onto ceiling-high shelves in an old singlewide trailer. There was also an assortment of less-than-glamorous vehicles parked outside. Some dated all the way back to the turn of the century. For the right amount, he would let a person rent one as long as it didn't come back with *too* many bullet holes. Killian had been shopping here for years, ever since Spin had first taken him.

"And Spin was the man who could change the gun?" Lucas asked from beside him.

Killian nodded. The trailer was split down the middle by a row of industrial metal shelves, stocked with boxes of ammunition, melee weapons, and a plethora of different caliber handguns. Killian squeezed past a particularly cluttered shelf stocked with glowing glass bottles labeled Single Use Curses, making sure not to accidentally bump any of them. They were known to be highly unstable, and he valued his eyebrows as well as his eyesight.

"He taught me a lot, but I never was able to master that trick. Too many moving parts, I guess," Killian replied. He picked up a .45 from one of the shelves and stared down the sights.

"I bet you could do it now," Lucas said excitedly.

"Oh, I definitely couldn't do it now. I'm *way* out of practice," Killian replied with a snort. He set the pistol back down.

"What do you mean?" Confusion streaked across Lucas's face as he stared up at him.

"Well, magic is just like anything. If you don't practice, you lose your skill. I'm coming off a ten-month hiatus where I basically didn't use any magic."

"Because of what happened to Spin?" Lucas asked. He moved to grab a hooked knife off one of the shelves, but Killian caught his hand before he could get to it.

"Among other things," he replied, glancing over at Stamp. He was staring down the sights of a scoped hunting rifle.

"What exactly happened to Spin?" Lucas asked, his voice taking on a much more somber tone. He had obviously wanted to know for some time. Killian could practically see the curiosity burning in his eyes.

Killian stared down at him. Even after all this time, it was still hard to think about. He picked up another pistol off the rack and squeezed it between his fingers.

"There's something you need to understand about the Change, Lucas," he began, trying to remember how Spin had first explained it to him. Back then, it had been so hard to believe, until Spin took him to his first nest. Plus, he didn't want to bring on a fresh wave of guilt for Lucas. He felt bad enough. "When everyone started getting their powers, magic wasn't the only thing that came back. A small percent of the population also caught this new disease. There was a patient zero somewhere, and it just spread from there. They called it the M Strain at first because it didn't just give people abilities, it mutated them, gave them whole new strands of DNA. Small things at first: heightened senses, stronger legs, that kind of stuff. Hell, most of them thought they had hit the jackpot. But then people started to turn. First into werewolves, then ghouls, and finally vampires."

He could see the disbelief in Lucas's eyes. The same look had crossed his own face when Spin first told him.

"Anyways, being one of these 'Strainers' pretty much made you a criminal because of the danger they posed to society. A bunch of different governments tried handling it different ways. Russia burned down whole cities to try to contain it. Japan introduced some toxin into their water supply that was supposed to kill it. Blood Haven started the DSC, the Department of Subhuman Control. This special organization's sole purpose was to control the outbreak. For the safety of the general population, it was said. That's what Spin told me anyway. It turned out to be more than they could handle, though, so they made the Board, this website where they would post known hunting grounds and nests, and allow hunters to pick up the contracts. That's what Spin did when I first met him, and he trained me to do the same. We hunted them 'for the good of the population'," Killian quoted.

He looked up from the pistol. "But it wasn't very long after we started killing vampires that it was discovered that their ashes could be converted into Dust, a powerful drug for mages. You see, it makes us way more powerful than normal, enhances our abilities beyond anything you could believe, but it's also very dangerous. Too much and it starts to fry your nervous system. Any more than that and it'll kill you.

"Before long, we were hunting vampires more for their ashes than for the good of the population. Then someone got the bright idea to start selling werewolf pelts on the black market—sort of new age body armor since they're basically bulletproof—so we added them to the job description as well. Then it was ghouls for their teeth or their eyes; I can't remember. All we cared about was keeping food on the table, and, in the first few years, that was no easy feat. So that's what we did. We hunted anything that came across the Board. Got pretty good at it too."

Killian set the pistol back on the rack and leaned against a row of shelves by the wall, folding his arms across his chest. "Anyways, about a year ago,

Spin got a tip from our fixer about a big vampire nest outside the city. This abandoned resort up in the hills. It was going to be a huge haul, the biggest we had ever heard of. Spin said it would be enough to retire off. Stamp had gotten sick the week before, so he couldn't go, but we decided to do it anyway.

"Everything was going smooth. We were almost to the basement where they were all sleeping together when we found this little girl." Killian's heart sped up a little and he clenched his fists beneath his arms. "There was just something about her. She had her back to us and was crying. Spin told me to keep watch and went over to help her. He was acting really strange, and when he finally saw her face, he called her by his daughter's name. I had heard him talk about her only once. He'd gotten really drunk and told me about her battle with cancer and how she had died a few months before the Change. I don't know what made him think it was her, but he dropped his guard and, when he did, she ripped his throat out."

Lucas's hand went over his mouth as he suppressed a gasp. Killian wasn't looking at him anymore. His eyes were fixed on the dark corner of his mind where he had kept that particular memory.

"Next thing I knew, the whole nest was coming down on me. I had to leave Spin back there with those things…to die alone," Killian finished with a grimace.

Lucas was utterly lost for words. It was obvious he hadn't anticipated such a dark tale, but he wanted to know, and Killian wasn't going to spare him from the gritty details. Not if the information could save his life one day. Not if it could keep him from falling to a similar fate. He shook his head, trying to clear the memory from his mind.

"Anyways, after he died, I stopped using magic, completely turned my back on it until a couple days before I met you when I started preparing for my first hunt back. I'm nowhere near as good as I used to be, though, and I might never be. They say magic runs off the soul, and I think I left mine somewhere back in that resort."

Lucas stared up at him for several long moments. The hairs on the back of his neck were standing up. He inhaled a long breath. "Well, you need to start practicing again then," he said as sternly as he could. "Because I don't think you left your soul behind in that resort. I think you just misplaced it for a while."

Killian chuckled at Lucas's fierce, if somewhat misguided, faith in him. He didn't understand it. "I have been," he said. "I'm getting better, but I'm still nowhere near as good as I used to be. Here, look."

Killian grabbed a bullet from one of the wooden ammo boxes stacked around the store and closed his fist around it. When he opened it back up, it had transformed into a tiny knight chess piece made of lead and brass, with smooth details.

"Wow! That's way better than the other one you showed me the day we met," Lucas exclaimed.

"See, I've been practicing." Killian allowed the bullet to change back and tossed it back in the box. It was strange. In almost no time at all, he had pushed the memory to the back of his mind and was able to smile again. Before, it would have taken him hours to even be able to move again.

"Well, I still think you'll be able to change a gun one day. I bet you could change a whole building," Lucas said.

"I don't know about that," Killian responded. "I don't want my head to explode or anything. That would take a lot of energy."

"Maybe I'll be able to do it one day," Lucas said, the possibilities already circulating within his head. "I would make myself a giant castle where only my friends could come in. You think I could?"

"Maybe, if someone teaches you," Killian replied. He ruffled Lucas's mop of dark brown hair, wondering how anyone could use him as a weapon. He was so innocent. He needed to be protected, not used. The thought of what his power could do if set loose upon the world sent a cold shiver down his spine. It just wasn't equipped to handle that. It might never be.

"Hey, Kil, what do you think of this?" Stamp suddenly called from the other side of the shelves. He was holding up the hunting rifle.

"Are you planning on going deer hunting?" Killian asked with the hint of a sly smile.

Stamp shot him a slit-eyed expression. "No, but I was thinking someone could use it from a roof, watch our backs."

"And who would that be? I'm no marksman, and you're shit with anything that requires two hands."

"You know, a simple 'no' would've sufficed," Stamp said, setting it back down and turning to a rack of pistols.

"Are you and Stamp friends again?" Lucas whispered.

"We're getting there," Killian replied with a half-hearted smile. It still hurt, thinking about Daisy with anyone else, but he was starting to understand why she had turned to Stamp. It was an effort to keep the bitterness from his voice every time he spoke to him, though.

"Good. You guys should be."

Killian turned and picked up a sand-colored pistol off a nearby table. It had a black rubber grip and fit in his hand almost perfectly. He glanced down the sights but already knew this was the one for him.

He turned and called to the back of the trailer, holding up the pistol. "Hey, Carson, how much for this one?"

Carson emerged from the trailer's tiny bathroom, zipping up his pants. A repugnant smell wafted out from behind him.

"Three hundred," he said, paying the pistol a cursory glance. Sweat glistened off his forehead. Apparently, his trip to the toilet had been a workout.

"I'll take it," Killian said. He turned and grabbed the hooked knife Lucas had been eyeing as well. "This too."

The address Skye had sent them was an old, dilapidated warehouse near the docks. It was completely remote; nothing was nearby except rotten wooden pallets and a few archaic forklifts. They drove past in one of Carson's rentals, a rusted sedan from before the turn of the century, and surveyed the area. The other nearby buildings were all in similar condition and several had been boarded up. They didn't see any other cars. Making a full sweep of the area, before pulling up in front of the building, they came up with an escape plan just in case things went south.

"I'll go in first," Killian said. "If I don't call you in after a few minutes, high tail it out of here."

Stamp nodded and Killian glanced into the back seat. Lucas obviously wasn't so sure about this plan, a concerned look pasted across his face, but he nodded regardless, and Killian gave him a thumbs-up. He climbed out.

The sky was fresh and bright again. Killian checked for the pistol tucked into the back of his pants, then the one holstered beneath his arm, before walking toward the building. His back was throbbing, the full pain of the bruise beginning to set in, and he gritted his teeth. It was going to hurt if he had to run anymore. He really hoped this was legit.

There was an entrance around the side, an old loading bay. The door had already been pulled up. Killian stepped inside, his eyes tracking around the room. It was huge. A maze of wooden crates was piled high all around, and beams of light cut through the cracked windows overhead. He suspected this place had been abandoned after the Terrible Night and no one had ever moved back in. As Killian crept along beside one of the crates, a strange tingling sensation rolled down his spine. He was starting to have a bad feeling about this. He looked around, staring up at the piles of crates. They hadn't received any other messages from Skye, so the meeting was still supposed to be here. So where the hell were they? His hand twitched toward the pistol beneath his arm.

"Don't even think about it," came a voice from over his shoulder, and he heard the distinct sound of a hammer being cocked on a pistol.

Killian froze, cursing himself. He was really going to have to work on his situational awareness. People were sneaking up on him way too easily these days.

"Hands up," the voice said. Killian slowly raised them, spreading his fingers. "Who are you?"

"I could ask you the same thing," Killian said. He moved to turn around.

"Don't move." Killian halted. He could practically feel the gun trained on him and could tell by the man's tone that he wouldn't hesitate to shoot him. "Are you alone?"

"No," Stamp said as he stepped around a nearby corner, pumping the shotgun and aiming it at the man. "He's not."

Killian immediately whipped around and pulled the pistol from beneath his arm, the man caught between them. He had slanted black eyes and shaggy brown hair that reached down to his shoulders. His skin was tanned to a golden bronze, and a feather dangled from the sleeve of his long buckskin jacket. He was definitely Native American.

"So, who are you?" Killian asked.

The man smirked, one corner of his mouth tugging upward. Quick as a wink, he drew a second gun from within his coat and trained it on Stamp. They were matching revolvers, though it looked like the cylinders had been modified to hold eight bullets rather than six. He cocked the hammer back on that one as well.

"Well, ain't this a crossroads," he said, his voice low and thick with an American accent. His pistols didn't waver.

"Put your guns down!" Skye suddenly shouted, running over. Killian suddenly felt an undeniable urge to drop his pistol. He couldn't fight it. He lowered it to his side. Stamp and the Native American did as well. Skye walked between them, looking at each of them angrily. She wore the same tan leather jacket from a few days ago and white pants. Her long honey hair was tied back into a loose ponytail. "We're supposed to be on the same side."

"What the hell just happened?" Stamp asked, staring down at the shotgun. Obviously, he had felt the same thing, complete and utter loss of will, and it shook him. He couldn't bring himself to raise the gun back up.

"Skye, I told you to never use that on me," Killian said, more than a little furiously. He knew what it had been.

"I'm sorry. I didn't want to, but…"

"You wouldn't have had to if your friend here hadn't pulled his gun on me," Killian replied, pointing at the man angrily.

"Whoa, wait a second. Am I missing something? Will someone please explain to me what the hell just happened?" Stamp interjected.

"She's a Siren," the man said. He holstered the pistols back into his coat. "Skye, you never told me."

"A Siren? Wait, that's a real classification? I thought that was made up."

"It's real. I can control people with my voice," Skye explained. She looked up at Killian who was still visibly angry. "Unfortunately, it results in people not trusting me, so I don't tell that many."

"I couldn't imagine why," Stamp said. He let out a long drawn-out breath. "Damn. Just damn."

"We can examine the logistics of it later," the man said. "Where is the boy?"

"His name is Lucas," Killian said. He still hadn't holstered his own pistol. "Speaking of which, you still haven't told us who the hell you are."

"Kestrel," he said simply.

"Kestrel leads the Underground. He's my contact," Skye explained. "He'll help get Lucas out of the city and to safety."

"And where exactly is this 'safe' place?" Killian asked, not bothering to hide his distrust of the man.

"For your safety and for the boy's, it would be best if you didn't know," Kestrel said. "Less chance of the Protectors finding out that way."

"Now, where is he?" he asked again.

Killian looked over at Stamp. After a moment, he nodded, and Stamp called out to him.

A few seconds later, Lucas peeked around the corner tentatively. Killian waved him over and he walked to them slowly. Upon seeing Skye, however, a huge smile broke across his face and he ran over to her. "Miss Skye!" he exclaimed as she hugged him tightly.

"That reminds me," Killian said, turning around to look at her. He refused to meet her eye, however. "Did you find anything else out about this supposed cult we might be dealing with?"

"They're known as the Prime Magi," Kestrel said before she could answer. Killian looked over at him. "They're led by a man named Saxos, a very powerful somatic mage. We've tangled with him before. He's tough."

"What's a somatic mage?" Lucas asked. He still had his arms wrapped around Skye's waist and looked up at her questioningly.

"It means he has magical control over his body. He can alter it, make himself stronger or faster. They're very rare," she explained.

"And very dangerous," Killian said. "No wonder that bookcase didn't slow him down."

"You've met him?" Kestrel asked, his face betraying a bit of surprise.

"I think so. At Jo Jack's store. There was a really big guy there who seemed to be in charge. I dropped a huge bookcase on him, and it slowed him down only for a second. I'd bet that's him."

"You're lucky to be alive. He's killed some of my best men," Kestrel said, not nearly as impressed as Killian thought he should be. "If he really is on Lucas's trail, we're going to need help getting him out of the city. I'll get into contact with one of the teams here in Blood Haven. They'll escort Lucas out of the city and make sure he gets to safety."

"Thank you, Kestrel," Skye said.

"Miss Skye, are Killian and Stamp going to be able to come with me?" Lucas asked.

Skye looked up at Killian, obviously not sure what to say.

"No, buddy, we're not going to be able to come," Killian stepped in. "It won't be safe if we do."

"But I don't want to go without you," he said. Hurt showed across his face. "You're my friends."

This time, Killian was the one not sure how to respond. He hated to admit it, but he had really started to like Lucas. Now he felt like he was betraying him by leaving him to the wolves.

"Lucas, you won't be safe otherwise," Skye said, dropping to one knee to look him in the eye. "We wish we could go with you, all of us, but your safety is what matters most to us. And that means us staying behind. I promise, after this, you'll be safe. You won't have to run anymore."

Lucas nodded slowly, obviously still hurt by the notion of going alone, and Skye hugged him tight.

"When will you take him?" Stamp asked.

Kestrel glanced at his cell phone. "Tomorrow most likely. I'll call the team as soon as we leave here and will have Skye relay the instructions. Think you can keep him safe for one more night?"

"We've done alright so far," Killian said, ignoring the gunshot wound in his upper arm and the searing pain throbbing in his back.

"Then wait for my word. It's almost over," Kestrel said. He looked to

Skye and she nodded. "I'll see you soon, Lucas," she said and hugged him one more time.

Stamp walked over and placed his hand on Lucas's shoulder. "We'll keep him safe. You just look after yourself," he said.

Skye nodded and thanked him quietly. She looked over at Killian, but he still refused to meet her eye. She sighed and, after a moment, followed Kestrel out of the room.

Stamp turned back toward Killian. "You want to tell me what that was all about?" he asked.

Killian looked up at him. He holstered the pistol back beneath his jacket and dug his hands into his pockets. "Not really," he said before turning and walking out the opposite way.

CHAPTER 15

Something Like Forgiveness

"How did you know I needed help?" Killian asked several hours later when his curiosity finally got the better of him. He had been wondering ever since leaving the warehouse and figured now was as good a time as any to ask.

Stamp, who was gorging himself on a cheeseburger, sighed through a mouthful of food. They were seated around the coffee table in their hotel room; food wrappers and plastic cups all but littered its surface, and Lucas was munching noisily on a basket of French fries covered in globs of ketchup. It was his first time having ketchup, he had explained.

"When *don't* you need help?" Stamp asked after swallowing his bite. He quickly took another. They had not had a real meal since yesterday.

"I'm serious," Killian replied flatly. "I told you to wait in the car for my call, but then you just showed up. Not that I don't appreciate it—he did have me dead to rights—but how?"

Stamp, still chewing, wiped his hands on one of the napkins. He looked down, obviously contemplating his response.

"Honestly," he said after a few moments, "I just had a feeling."

"What?"

"Well, you had walked into the warehouse and, I don't know, I just got a funny feeling all of a sudden that you were in trouble. So I came in through the other side, told Lucas to hide, and went to find you." Killian stared at him in disbelief, a harsh ridge slowly forming across his brow. "Oh, don't look at me like that. Look, I'm not saying I had a vision or anything. It was just a feeling. Could have just been nervous energy, for all we know."

Killian hesitated in responding. It was an effort to keep the total disbelief from leaking into his voice. "Right," he managed. "I'm, uh, just going to pretend that's not weird and say thanks. I guess I owe you one."

It sounded rather forced, even to him. Who just had a 'feeling' like that? He wondered if Stamp was putting him on somehow, but his expression said he was being sincere, even if he didn't quite believe it himself.

It was several moments before Stamp finally looked back up at him and let out a long-winded sigh. "No, you don't," he said. "Not after everything I put you through—*we* put you through. Watching your back is the least I can do." He hesitated before adding, "I think it's about time you let me explain exactly what happened with Daisy."

Lucas suddenly perked up from his basket of fries, his interest clearly piqued. He glanced between them.

"Do we really have to have this conversation right now?" Killian asked, glancing over at him with squinted eyes. Lucas had been pushing for them to be friends again ever since he had first heard about their feud.

"Look, man, we've almost died *a couple* of times," Stamp said. "I think we should just clear the air."

Killian rolled his eyes. "More like clear your conscience," he muttered. Much louder, "God, I knew I shouldn't have introduced you to Loop. She's rubbing off on you, always wanting everyone to share their feelings. Fine, just fine. Clear the air." He waved his hand across the air for him to proceed.

Stamp shot him a narrow glance but leaned forward in his seat to begin anyway. It was obvious he had rehearsed this many times before, but it still sounded more than a little strained. Guilt was obviously having a fierce battle with pride. He pulled on the tips of his fingers anxiously before beginning. "Look, man, we met Daisy at the same time," he started. "Hell, the same day, when she first started working for Jo Jack. It was right after that job we did in Blackheath, remember?"

He looked up at Killian expectantly, as if waiting for him to crack a broad smile or laugh at the memory, but all Killian recalled was a long night in a car waiting for a werewolf to show. Thirteen hours sweating in a rust bucket to find out it was nothing more than a teenager dressed up in a dingo hide. They hadn't even been paid.

Stamp seemed to catch the hint there wouldn't be a joyful trip down memory lane and continued. "My point is I've known her just as long as you have, and if she hadn't taken such an instant liking to you, *I* would've asked her out. But then you guys started dating and that was it. You were my friend, and I wasn't going to move in on your girl. But I never stopped liking her, never stopped thinking about her like that. Then, when Spin died, you just kind of shut everyone out. You disappeared off the face of the earth and didn't want to talk to or see anyone. It was the saddest and loneliest I had ever seen her. All she wanted to do was help and you wouldn't let her."

Killian felt a slight stab at that. He knew he had hurt her, but hearing it from Stamp really cemented it in place. He had been such an asshole to her, to everyone who cared about him. Maybe he deserved what he had gotten; maybe he deserved what Stamp was slowly building up to.

"She called me, crying one night," he continued. Killian knew exactly where this was leading. His heart began to speed up in trepidation. "She said she had gone to see you to try to pull you out of the hole you had crawled into, and you threw her out. She said you slammed the door in her face."

"I remember," Killian said, his voice flat and devoid of a tone. It certainly wasn't one of his finest moments. "I told her I couldn't handle her shit anymore. That she just needed to leave me alone."

At the time, it had seemed like the only way to deal with his pain was to shut her and everyone else out of his life. Losing Spin had been like losing his mother all over again, and, for the longest time, revenge was all he could think about. He didn't want Daisy to see him like that.

Stamp's voice flattened as well. "Well, after she left, she called me, said she didn't want to be alone. Jesus, man, you had broken her heart. I told her to come over. What else could I do? We talked for what must have been hours. Then she fell asleep in my arms on my couch. I know I should have handled it differently, put her to bed or something, but it just felt so right. So I just let her lay there until she woke up the next morning, and when she did, I kissed her. I couldn't help it. I expected her to slap me at any moment, but she didn't. She kissed me back. I think she was probably just looking for comfort. I know she still loved you at that point, but I didn't care. Call me a shit friend if you want, but it was all I had thought about for years and there she was. Pretty soon, she stopped crying every night, stopped mentioning you in every other sentence. She was starting to finally move on, and then you crawled back out of your hole."

Stamp trailed off.

"And we know exactly what happened from there," Killian said, looking down at his knuckles. He had cracked at least two of them on Stamp's jawbone. This time, it was his turn to hunch forward in his seat and let out a long-winded sigh.

"I'm sorry, man," Stamp said. "Maybe we were selfish. Maybe we should have tried harder to be there for you, but…"

He searched for the right words.

"But eventually you get tired of trying to save somebody who doesn't want to be saved," Killian filled in. Stamp nodded slowly.

Killian stood and walked over to the kitchenette. He gripped the edge of the counter so tightly his knuckles turned white, exhaling slowly. Stamp watched him from the couch, unsure what to say or do.

"I get it," Killian finally said. He looked over and locked eyes with Stamp. "I hate it and I hate you for doing it, but I get it."

A look of utter shock passed over Stamp's face. He couldn't find any words in response.

Killian rubbed the bridge of his nose, a bitter sting finding its way into the left side of his chest. He looked over at Lucas and let out a wan smile. Lucas smiled back, obviously pleased. Killian looked back at Stamp and locked gazes with him again. A strange fire was flickering inside his eyes, a fire Stamp had only seen a couple times before.

"If you ever hurt her," Killian said. He left the threat open-ended, his eyes filling in the rest.

"I won't," Stamp replied, managing a minute nod. He stood and held out his hand. "We good?"

Killian hesitated a moment, staring over at him. Finally, the fire simmered down within his eyes, and he leaned over, shaking Stamp's hand firmly. "As good as we can be," he said.

Stamp smiled. It was about as close to forgiveness as he was going to get. Lucas was grinning ear to ear.

"Besides, we've got bigger problems to worry about," Killian said suddenly, shoving his hands in his pockets and redirecting his attention to Lucas. It was obviously a dire attempt to lead the conversation away from Daisy.

"If what that asshole said is true," Killian tried to continue, but Lucas interrupted.

"Kestrel," he said.

"What?"

"His name was Kestrel."

Killian stared down at him for several moments. His eyes were little more than slits.

"Well, if I get in trouble for using that word, you shouldn't be allowed to use it either," Lucas protested.

"Right," Killian said, trying desperately to keep his eyes from rolling and failing miserably. "We'll come back to that later. If what *Kestrel* said is true about Saxos and the Prime Magi, we're going to need to watch ourselves."

"Like we haven't been doing that already?" Stamp asked, suppressing a snort from Lucas's comment. He let out a chuckle and directed a finger between himself and Lucas. "Well, *we* have, at least. You, on the other hand, seem to go looking for them."

"Shut up. Just because I said we're good doesn't mean I won't still kick your ass for being a smartass. My point is, these guys are serious players." He looked down at Lucas. "And with the Protectors we've got on our ass, it could get pretty rough if we don't get you out of the city soon."

The smile dropped from Lucas's face and he nodded solemnly. It was obvious by the look in his eye he was still uncomfortable with leaving them behind. Killian really couldn't blame him. He was apprehensive about it too, but what choice did they have? He wouldn't be safe otherwise.

"Well, what all do we know about somatic mages?" Stamp asked. "If we're going to survive this, we should probably get to know our enemy. I mean, other than the fact they're tough sons-of-bitches, I really don't know anything about them. Hell, before today I thought Sirens were just a myth."

Killian chose to ignore that. He knew Stamp was fishing for information about what had happened back at the warehouse, but he wasn't going to bite. It was old history he wasn't about to dig up.

"I don't know much either," he said. "I've never actually met one. I know they can change their muscle density so they're stronger, though. Tougher. Can even make them faster. I don't think for very long, though. Kind of like a cheetah. Short spans and they're spent. Although this guy didn't look like he'd need much time if he got his hands on you."

"Big?"

"He was huge!" Lucas piped up, forgetting his worries for a moment.

Killian nodded in agreement. "At least half a foot on you," he said, nodding to the top of Stamp's head.

"Great, a giant," he replied. "What about the other guys he's with? You said you took one of them down already."

"Can't be sure what classification he was, but his buddy was a fire mage. Pretty good too. His fireball nearly burned me to a crisp. The other one that was at Jo Jack's I'm not sure about either. I haven't seen him since."

"So, we've got the Nazis of mages running around the city, looking for us while the Protectors breathe down our necks. That about sum it up?"

"Basically, yeah."

Stamp looked up at the ceiling, shut his eyes, and let out a long, exasperated breath. It was only for Lucas's sake he didn't let out a long chorus of curse words to vent his frustrations. Fortunately, he didn't have to say anything for Killian to know what he was thinking. He had been thinking the exact same thing for some time now.

"Yeah," he said. "I'm right there with you. I really hope that ass—," He caught himself and glanced at Lucas out the corner of his eye. Lucas was staring at him suspiciously, waiting for it. Killian rolled his eyes this time and quickly filled in the man's proper name. "—Kestrel comes through. For your sake and for ours."

Stamp only nodded in response.

The rest of the meal passed much more quietly after that. The weight of everything they had discussed rested heavily on each of their shoulders, Killian's especially, as he replayed mentally what Stamp had told him. He had never really looked at it from anyone's perspective but his own. They had all handled it poorly, but the past was the past, and he had let it burn him up long enough. Like he had said, they had bigger problems to worry about now.

It wasn't much longer before the drowsiness of a full stomach began to weigh on each of them. Coupled with the exhaustion from the past few days, Killian couldn't keep himself awake any longer and excused himself to the bedroom. He had won the coin toss for the bed this time and was barely able to unlace his boots before crashing down on it and shutting his eyes. A few minutes later, he felt Lucas crawl onto the bed beside him and sink his head into one of the plush pillows. It did not take long for either of them to fall asleep.

The dream came again, almost right away. This time, Lucas was with him. They were running through the halls of Skye's academy. The walls were deteriorating around them, the paint flecking off and chunks of the wall disappearing into the black shroud behind them. It was chasing them and, no matter how fast they ran, they could never seem to escape it. Lucas was crying, and Killian could feel a burning in his chest like never before.

They rounded the corner to Skye's classroom, and Killian threw the door open into the greenhouse. He ushered Lucas inside before looking toward the shroud. It was quickly approaching. All he could make out of its black shadowy form was a pair of scaly wings. They flapped outward from within the shroud, and static electricity seemed to come off them.

Killian threw himself through the door and slammed it closed behind him. He turned, expecting to see the many plants and skylights of Skye's classroom, but he instead only saw a great canyon before him, his feet on the edge. The door dug into his back as he took a surprised step backward. Beside him, Lucas stood quivering. Tears continued to glisten within his eyes.

Killian turned back toward the door and saw the handle shaking as the shroud attempted to get in. Killian grabbed hold of the handle and held it in place, but it continued to shake in his hand. Any minute he would lose his grip and the shroud would get in. Somehow, he knew that would be the end of them. He looked down into the precipice below, and something told him they would have to jump if they wanted to survive.

"*Lucas,*" he began, not sure if his voice would even work. "*We have to jump.*"

Had he really just said that?

Lucas stared at him in disbelief before nodding. Killian counted to three with his fingers before letting go of the handle and jumping out. He heard the door fly open behind him but never saw the shroud come through. They were falling into the canyon and into its darkness. They seemed to fall forever, and then suddenly they weren't falling at all. Killian had never felt a landing. He didn't feel the ground beneath him or anything really. It was as if they were suspended in mid-air. Then he heard a deep voice. It reverberated across what he could only assume were the canyon walls around him. He couldn't actually see anyone. The darkness was total.

"*You have come,*" it said, and Killian instantly knew it wasn't the voice of any human. He struggled against the invisible bonds that must have been holding him in place, but he couldn't move.

"*The path was inevitable,*" it continued. "*The sacrifice will be both of yours to make. Lucas and Killian… Killian and Lucas… Killian… Killian.*"

"Killian."

Killian sat bolt upright in bed, his gun clenched tightly in his hands and trained evenly on Stamp's forehead. He stood a few feet away, his hands raised into the air. Killian breathed fiercely, a coat of sweat damp across his body. Beside him, Lucas was still fast asleep, though he had a slightly pained expression on his face. Slowly, Killian lowered his gun as the effects of the dream began to wear off. It had not been that vivid last time and had ended when they jumped into the canyon. What dark recesses of his mind had that voice spawned from?

"What is it?" he asked.

Stamp slowly lowered his hands back to his sides, and Killian noticed one of them was clutching a cell phone. Stamp held it up.

"Skye called. We're meeting with the Underground tomorrow at four. She already sent the address."

Killian managed a small nod in response.

Stamp started to say something, but after a moment he must have thought better of it because he merely turned and stepped back out of the room.

Once the doors were closed again, Killian slowly laid his head back on his pillow. It was wet with sweat. He turned and looked over at Lucas, still sleeping soundly beside him. The pained expression had vanished from his face. So at four o'clock, they would say goodbye, probably forever. Three days ago, nothing would have made Killian happier, but now he wasn't so sure, especially with what that voice had said. He couldn't help but think it was more than just a dream.

"The sacrifice will be both of yours to make."

Killian tried his best to push it from his mind as he attempted to fall back asleep. The only comfort was that maybe with Lucas gone, he would stop having these dreams. Unfortunately, it was a minimal comfort at best.

The Underground

The drive to the meet was very quiet. Killian hated to admit it, but his nerves were starting to get the better of him. The dream had left him shaken, though he tried not to put too much stock in it. Still, he gripped the steering wheel tightly to keep his hands from shaking.

If Stamp noticed, he didn't say anything. He looked to have his own concerns circulating within his head. He occasionally glanced back at Lucas and tried to put on a reassuring smile, but it wasn't very convincing. The fact was, they were all very nervous about separating. Killian just wasn't sure if he trusted anyone else to keep Lucas safe. Not just for Lucas's sake either, but for the whole world's. If this cult, the Prime Magi, really were intent on using Lucas as a weapon against the mundane world, as Kestrel had implied, there could be all-out war.

Again Killian tried desperately to push the thought from his mind. He glanced into the rear-view mirror. Lucas was sitting with his head slumped, obviously sad he would soon be losing his first two real friends. Not for the first time, he felt more than a little sorry for him. He had just begun to experience this great world he was a part of and now he was being shipped away, probably to somewhere remote and absent of anything fun or exciting for a child his age.

All at once, Killian began to despise Skye for ever introducing him to Lucas. At least then, he wouldn't feel so attached to him. It was so strange. He had promised himself that after Spin, he wouldn't grow attached to anyone, least of all a child because of what had happened.

Damn Skye, he thought as they approached the address she had sent them. As they rounded the final corner, he thought of seeing her again and felt his anger begin to ebb away. She was just doing what she thought was right, and she was a far better person than he was.

The address was a seven-story apartment building constructed of sand-colored brick. Small balconies looked out over the street. Clothes hung from drying lines on many of the overlooks, and a few sported old charcoal grills. Killian supposed the apartment, 6B, was one of the Underground's safe houses. They drove past the building a few times to get a feel for the area before Stamp pointed to a small alleyway a block away. "Park in there," he said.

Killian nodded and guided the vehicle into the narrow backstreet. It was gloomy inside the alley. Tall buildings towered on either side, and the trio was entrenched in shadows as they climbed out of the vehicle, despite the sun still being well overhead. Lucas glanced around uneasily as Killian and Stamp headed around to the back of the vehicle. They popped the trunk. At least a dozen different guns were stored inside—two submachine guns, a double-barrel sawn-off shotgun, a pump-action, eight pistols of varying sizes and calibers, and the scoped hunting rifle. Killian shook his head amusedly as he picked up a pistol and holster. He made sure the pistol was fully loaded before holstering it to his ankle beneath his pant leg. He also holstered one beneath his arm. The tan pistol was tucked into the back of his jeans.

"You know, it's a good thing the cops haven't connected us to all this yet," Stamp said as he grabbed a shoulder holster and pulled it on. He tucked a silver, snub-nosed revolver into it. "Because we would definitely be branded as terrorists if they found us with all this heat."

Killian snorted.

Stamp picked up one of the submachine guns, but after a moment he shook his head and placed it back in the trunk. If all went well, they wouldn't have to fire a single shot. Once they were all loaded up, Killian closed the trunk.

Stamp waved Lucas over. "Alright, we all know the plan," he said. He looked down at Lucas. "You're going to stay by my side the whole time. Is that understood?"

Lucas nodded. Uncertainty was still splashed across his face. Killian placed a hand on his shoulder and gave it a reassuring squeeze, trying his best to look confident as they turned and headed down the alleyway. They checked their coats to make sure the guns were hidden from view before walking out. The sun was beating down on the asphalt with an unforgiving glare, and they squinted to look up the street. This was it. In just a few minutes, they would say goodbye forever. Killian let out a breath he had been holding for the better part of a minute and led the way.

They were quite the sight to anyone walking on the sidewalk in front of them. Their gazes were hard and obstinate, focused on the apartment building before them. They walked on either side of Lucas like a protection detail. Killian had to force himself not to grind his teeth.

He entered through the glass doors first and surveyed the tiny lobby before waving them through. The elevator had an Out of Order sign taped to the metallic doors, so they headed up the stairs. It was quite a climb and took a while. They stopped at every landing so Killian could peek out and make sure it was clear before proceeding. Finally, they reached the sixth floor, and Killian glanced around the corner down the hallway. He didn't see anyone and nodded for them to follow.

The wallpaper in the hallway was a bright sunny yellow, with wood paneling along the bottom half. It hadn't been polished in some time, however, and chips and scratches were evident along its surface. The grey carpet was also torn up in several spots along the baseboards. It was still a league above Killian's own accommodations, though, so he didn't judge too harshly. The hallway remained devoid of activity as they headed to the designated apartment. It was fortunate because Killian was a twitch away from drawing his gun at any given moment.

Finally, they reached the apartment. It was near the end of the hallway. Sunlight peeked in through a window on the far wall. Killian nodded to Stamp and Lucas, and they flattened themselves against the wall by the door.

Gathering his wits about him in case this went south, Killian raised his fist to knock. Before he could, however, the door suddenly swung open He didn't even have time to react. A young man with dirty blond hair stood there in the doorway, a friendly smile on his face. He stood at least a head shorter than Killian and wore a black leather biker's jacket.

"Killian, we've been waiting for you," he said. At the mention of 'we,' Killian looked past him and saw a group of people standing in the living room—three men and two women, all dressed in similar clothing. The two women looked to be in their mid- to late twenties. One of them, a brunette, had a set of brilliant green eyes he could see from the doorway.

"Come in," the man in front of him said, waving him inside. He peeked around the corner at Stamp and Lucas and smiled again.

"Where are Skye and Kestrel?" Killian asked flatly. None of them moved.

"Uh, yeah, I'm afraid they can't make it. They picked up a tail—we think Protectors—and couldn't shake 'em in time. Don't worry, though. They're safe and Kestrel already briefed us. We're still prepared to escort Lucas out of the city."

Killian stared at him. He didn't like it. Skye was supposed to be here. He again looked over the man's shoulder at the group standing in the living room. They all regarded him with the same neutral expressions. Glancing back toward Stamp and Lucas, Killian knew they really didn't have any other choice but to trust them. They had to get Lucas out of the city before the Prime Magi or the Protectors could close in on them again. After a few silent moments, he nodded, and Stamp and Lucas stepped into the apartment with him. The man closed the door behind them.

"Thanks," he said, sighing in relief. "I wasn't sure how you were going to react. Skye said you can be a little jumpy."

"After what we've been through the past few days, you'd be jumpy too," Stamp said. He rested his hand on Lucas's shoulder.

"You're probably right," he replied. He led them into the living room to the rest of the group. "I guess we'll go ahead and introduce everyone. I'm Ridley for starters, wheelman for this little shindig."

He pointed to the three men. They all stood about average in height and build, and two of them had very bland faces. The other had a jagged pink scar beside his left eye and seemed to wear a permanent sneer across his mouth.

"That's Silver, Skiff, and Zipper," he said, pointing to each of them in turn. The one with the scar was Zipper. He then pointed at the two women. The short dark-skinned one was named Lilac.

"And finally, we have Winter," he said, nodding to the one with the brilliant green eyes. "A bit of a joke since she's always so pale."

"Uh, good to meet all of you," Killian said awkwardly. He wasn't really sure how to handle this. Skye was supposed to help them through this. He turned and directed a thumb at Stamp. "This is—."

"Stamp. Yeah, we know who you all are," Zipper said. He looked at Ridley pointedly. "You going to do it or what?"

"Ah, yeah," Ridley said, his voice taking on a slightly awkward tone. "I'm sorry about this, but we're going to need you to hand over your guns while you're here. Kind of a rule we've got for anyone who's not part of the Underground. Helps keep things running smooth."

Killian looked at him in disbelief. "You're kidding, right? You've heard what we've been through. There's no way we're giving up our guns."

"You will if you want us to help you," Zipper said, stepping forward.

"Hey, was I talking to you?" Killian snapped at him.

"Look, dickhead, you can either give us your guns or we can take them. Rules are rules," Zipper said, not backing down.

"That wouldn't be wise."

"Which part?" Zipper asked, acid dripping from his voice.

"Trying to take our guns."

"Oh, yeah? Why is that?" He locked eyes with Killian fiercely.

"Because if you do, I'll turn that chip on your shoulder into a battering ram and shove it up your ass," he replied. Beside him, Stamp suppressed a snort. That was the second time in two days Killian had used that line. He needed to come up with something new. Zipper continued staring at him menacingly.

"Oh, for crying out loud," Winter suddenly interjected, drawing all their attention toward her. "Zipper, give it a rest. Is it really worth starting a fight over? We're all friends here."

She glanced over at Killian and they locked gazes for a moment—those eyes, they were almost mesmerizing—before she looked back at Zipper and stared at him pointedly.

A second later, a toothy grin broke across his scarred face and he chuckled gruffly. "Sure, sure, all friends here," Zipper said, though it hardly sounded sincere. Or true. Killian still breathed an internal sigh of relief, however.

"Fine, let's get this over with then," Winter said. She glanced at Killian again, then down at Lucas. Stamp still rested his hand on Lucas's shoulder and didn't look inclined to move it.

"Yeah," Ridley agreed. He flashed an annoyed look at Zipper before continuing. "The plan is we'll lay low here until nightfall. Then, we'll go out the back where we have some vehicles waiting and escort him out of the city. Once there, we'll hand him off to the convoy that will take him along with a few other special cases to somewhere safe out West. I'm sure Kestrel already told you why we can't tell you exactly where that is."

Killian nodded. He looked over at Lucas. This was it. This was goodbye. Lucas stared around at the group uncertainly. To him, they were just a bunch of strangers taking him somewhere even more unfamiliar. Killian could see his legs were quivering slightly beneath his baggy pants.

"You're sure you can get him out of the city safely?" Stamp asked. He didn't look very comfortable with the situation either.

"We're sure," Winter said softly. "This isn't our first rodeo. We've done this kind of thing before."

Killian took some comfort in that, though it wasn't much. Their eyes met again. They were such a vivid green, so bright and entrancing.

Warning bells suddenly rang out in his head. He reached for his gun before the thought had even finished forming. Everything seemed to slow down all at once. Everyone around him drew their guns as well, Stamp shoved Lucas against the wall and drew his own pistol, and then Killian leveled his on Winter's head, training it between her bright green eyes that were so familiar. Five guns were pointed at his head a moment later.

"I knew I recognized those eyes," he spat. "You were at the club the other night. You're a damn Protector."

"God damn it, I told you we should've made her wear contacts," Zipper said, swearing loudly.

"Shut up, Zipper!" Winter barked. She had her own gun trained on Killian's forehead, as did half the group. The rest had turned theirs on Stamp. Nearby, Lucas cowered against the wall, terror etched across his face.

"Now, we're going to handle this nice and slow," she said, trying to keep her voice calm and steady. "This doesn't have to turn into a bloodbath."

"It wouldn't have gone this way at all if we had just taken their guns like we'd planned," Zipper spat.

"Shut your mouth, Zipper," she barked again. She looked back at Killian. "You know there's only one way this can go down. You need to give us Lucas. Let us take him, and you and Stamp can walk out of here alive."

"You're not taking him," Killian said sternly, gripping his pistol so tight his knuckles turned white. He struggled to keep his hands from shaking.

"You know we have to. If his abilities ever fell into the wrong hands, it would be World War III," she said.

"That's exactly why we were trying to get him out of the city to somewhere safe. He doesn't have to be locked up. He just has to go somewhere that cult can't find him," Killian argued. Beside him, Stamp's eyes darted left and right uncertainly.

They were outnumbered three to one, and all of them looked to be trained marksmen. Their hands were steady, their eyes focused.

"Don't you get it? There's nowhere the Prime Magi wouldn't be able to find him," Winter replied earnestly. "At least we can give him the protection he needs to be kept away from them."

"No, no," Killian said, words beginning to fail him in the face of so many trained guns. There was no way they would be able to make it out of this alive, but he couldn't just hand Lucas over. He had made a promise, first to Skye, then to himself, that he would keep him safe, and that didn't include leaving in a steel box. He had lost too many people already.

"You're not taking him," he repeated.

"Killian, please," Winter said.

"Look, you don't have a choice, asshole," Zipper interrupted. "You're just lucky Winter has such a soft spot for your kind or we'd have just gunned you down at the club and taken the damn kid. It'd serve you right for what you did to Waters and H."

Killian's eyes darted over to look at him angrily, but they instead fell on something just over his left shoulder, out the nearby window. It was some sort of bright light. Fire. He realized what it was just before it hit

The fireball shattered the glass and blasted a section of the frame inward, along with several chunks of brick and plaster. The resounding shockwave sent them all crashing to the floor. Killian landed with a hard thud and felt air leave his lungs. Smoke filled the room as another fireball came spinning through the window. It slammed Skiff square in the chest. He was knocked backward against the wall, and Killian saw a crater in his chest the size of a soccer ball. He knew instantly who it was. The Prime Magi had finally caught back up to them.

The team of Protectors took cover against the wall and fired out the windows. Killian crawled across the floor and found Stamp huddled over Lucas, shielding him from any more fireballs.

"We've got to get out of here," Killian said, his voice hoarse as he choked on some of the smoke. Stamp managed a nod in response.

There was a cry of pain, and Killian glanced over his shoulder to the team of Protectors. Another fireball had hit Lilac. A second later, a loud gunshot rang out, and Silver crumpled to the ground. A sniper bullet had taken off a good chunk of his skull. Winter screamed in anger and aimed several more shots out the window before ducking back down to reload.

Killian knew it was now or never. He sprang up and threw the door open, not looking back as he crashed into the hallway. Several gunshots hit the wall beside him, and he fell to the floor. He didn't even think. He just fired down the hallway and blasted the two approaching Prime Magi. They fell backward, their trench coats riddled with holes, and Killian drew his second pistol from beneath his arm. He walked over to make sure they were dead before waving Stamp and Lucas out. Inside the apartment, the battle continued to rage on.

With Killian in the lead, they rushed down the staircase as quickly as they dared. Even through the brick walls, they could hear the staccato of gunfire and the impacts of several more fireballs. It was utter chaos as people began rushing out of their apartments. There was suddenly a flock of people flooding the stairwell, screaming and running for safety away from the sounds of the battle. Killian shoved through as best he could, Stamp and Lucas right behind him.

Finally, they made it to the bottom of the stairwell and rushed into the lobby. Three more cult members were standing in the entrance, shoving the crowd aside as they struggled to get upstairs. They saw Killian and Stamp at once and neither group hesitated as they opened fire on each other. People dove out of the way, but more than a few caught stray bullets. One unlucky resident took a bullet that would have hit Killian square in the chest. He could pay him only a momentary glance as he returned fire, bringing one of the Prime Magi down. Stamp shoved one panicking woman aside and took a second cult member down. The third ducked behind cover to reload, and Killian rushed forward. He seemed to catch the man off-guard because he raised his gun only a fraction before Killian hit him across the face, then in the stomach. As he slumped forward, the breath gone from his lungs, Killian shot him twice in the head. He crashed into the wall behind him, blood smearing its surface.

People continued rushing from the building, and Killian, Stamp, and Lucas didn't hesitate joining them. Amidst the flow of people, they crashed out onto the sidewalk and sprinted for the alleyway a block away where they had parked the car. Killian caught sight of only a vague shadow perched atop the nearby rooftop, raining lead down on the apartment building. Then they rounded the corner into the alleyway, and all he thought about was escaping.

They dove into the car. Lucas lay down on the floor behind the driver's seat, and Killian revved up the engine. The tires spun for a moment before catching traction and propelling them down the alleyway. He didn't know where it would shoot them out at; they just had to get away.

That was when he saw her. Winter was at the end of the alleyway, pointing a gun at them. She had blood on her jacket, but Killian couldn't be sure if it was her own or someone else's. He didn't really care. He floored the gas pedal.

"What are you doing?" Stamp asked from beside him.

"She's a Protector. She'd do the same to us if it meant getting Lucas," Killian replied, but then he saw the look in her eye. It wasn't threatening; it was pleading. She was begging them to stop.

"Ah, shit," he breathed before slamming on the brakes at the last minute. They slid to a halt mere inches from her feet. She stared at them in disbelief for a moment before Stamp yelled for her to get in. She ran over and climbed into the backseat. Killian didn't even wait for her to close the door before he floored the gas pedal again and skidded out of the alley. Two more Prime Magi were standing nearby and let loose a rain of gunshots at the vehicle. The rear windshield shattered, and Winter ducked. Stamp aimed out the passenger window and returned fire but did not hit either of them. Then they were around the next corner and out of range.

Relief washed over Killian for half a second before a black SUV suddenly slammed into the vehicle's side and sent the vehicle spinning. He barely managed to keep control of the car as they slammed against the curb. Winter hit her head against the door and was knocked unconscious. Killian paid her only a momentary glance before throwing the vehicle into REVERSE and slamming down on the gas pedal. The car launched backward away from the curb, and Killian spun the wheel, putting them into a power slide until the front of the vehicle was back in the right direction. He shifted back into DRIVE and redlined the RPM gauge just as a group of Magi opened fire from the SUV. Killian just barely managed to avoid the rain of lead as he propelled them away from the intersection.

They were only a hundred yards down the road when three more vehicles began pursuing them. Stamp shot out the passenger window but did little more than ping lead off the head vehicle's front bumper. The Prime Magi, however, managed to shatter both side-view mirrors and pelt the car's trunk with a rain of bullets.

Killian swerved and cut through traffic to avoid as much of the gunfire as he could, but the car couldn't take much more. He knew the engine was going to give out at any moment. Still, he floored the gas pedal and took them toward an overpass, trying desperately to come up with an escape plan.

Nothing came to mind, though.

"Stop the car!" Stamp suddenly yelled as they crossed the overpass.

"What?"

"Stop the damn car!" he yelled again.

Killian slammed on the brakes, swerving partially into oncoming traffic. Stamp threw open the passenger door and slammed his palm down onto the asphalt. For a second, nothing happened. Then, a great rumbling filled the ground around them and a crack formed across the roadway. Killian looked up and saw the pursuing vehicles were almost across the overpass. Just as they were about to clear it, a resounding crack pierced the air, and the ground around the overpass seemed to erupt upward several feet, as if there had been some huge underground explosion nearby. The overpass fractured and then, a moment later, crumbled as the ground supporting it gave way. The vehicles pursuing them crashed down to the thoroughfare below, lost from sight.

Stamp slammed the passenger door closed, breathing hard. Killian didn't wait to be told. He hit the gas pedal.

"Stamp, what was *that*?" he asked, unable to contain his shock as they sped down the road.

It took a few moments for Stamp to catch his breath. He looked over at Killian and said simply, "A lot has changed."

Killian barely managed a nod in response. Stamp had always been a talented Geomancer, but that surpassed anything he had ever done before. At least anything Killian had ever seen him do. Clearly, a lot *had* changed, and for Stamp, it appeared to be for the better.

If only we could all be so lucky, Killian thought as he glanced over his shoulder at the still-unconscious Winter and the still-petrified Lucas. If only.

CHAPTER 17

Winter

Killian splashed another handful of hot water across his face. It was a vain effort to get his body to finally stop quivering. The adrenaline still had his heart racing, his vision more than a little shaky.

Stamp and Lucas were suffering similarly. Stamp was pacing about the room, alternating between crossing his arms across his chest and shoving his hands in his pockets. Lucas sat on the couch, his knees tucked up underneath his chin as he rocked back and forth gently. None of them had said a word in almost fifteen minutes, too absorbed in what had just occurred to form any kind of coherent thought. The meet with the Underground was supposed to be the end game. They were supposed to be safe now, but instead they had just been involved in the biggest gunfight the city had ever seen. The news had labeled it as such thirty minutes ago. They had since muted the wall-screen.

Killian turned off the faucet and dried his hands and face with one of the hotel towels. His heart was finally beginning to settle in his chest, though not by much. "What do we do now?" he asked after several moments. He rested his palms on the edge of the counter.

Stamp stopped pacing and looked over at him. He folded his arms across his chest, thought better of it, and stuffed his hands into his pockets instead. A second later, he crossed his arms back across his chest before finally responding. "I don't know what we *can* do," he said. "I've tried calling Skye, but it keeps going straight to voicemail. We have no way of knowing if the Protectors grabbed them. We definitely can't go to the police. We can't do *anything*."

"Well, I know one way we can find out what happened to them," Killian said, nodding to the unconscious form securely tied with duct tape to the armchair. Winter had taken a pretty good blow to the temple and had been unconscious ever since. A purple bruise showed just below her hairline, and a bullet graze had stained her jacket sleeve with blood.

"What exactly are you suggesting?" Stamp asked, not sure if he liked the look in Killian's eyes.

"We ask her," he answered. "Firmly."

"Come on, man, you're not suggesting we—?" Stamp trailed off, disbelief washing over his voice. "I'm *not* torturing her."

"I'm not saying we need to torture her, but, damn it, we need to know what happened to Skye and Kestrel," Killian said. He directed a finger at her. "And she can tell us."

"If what they said was even true," Stamp replied. He glanced over at Lucas before walking over to Killian and lowering his voice. "Look at him. He can't take much more. You go and start getting violent with this chick, and he might lose it altogether."

Killian looked over at Lucas as well. He had been through so much the past few days. So many people had died right in front of him; Killian forgot the impact it might be having on him. He let out a sigh. "You're right. I won't hurt her. But we do need to know what happened to Skye. We can't keep running, and they're bound to track us back here eventually."

Stamp nodded. He looked back at Winter. She was breathing steadily, though her head was slumped and her eyes were closed. "Alright, we can ask her," Stamp finally said after several silent moments. "But do it politely."

"Politely?"

"Just shut up and ask her," Stamp replied, folding his arms back across his chest and stepping aside. He was obviously uncomfortable with the idea, but they really didn't have any other option.

Killian walked over to the armchair and bent over to look at her face. She was still out cold. He tried snapping his fingers to get her to wake up, but her eyes remained closed. Striding over to the kitchenette sink, he filled one of the plastic cups in the cabinet with water and walked back over to her. He turned the cup upside down over her head and she immediately snapped awake. She inhaled sharply and began thrashing about, trying to break free from the tape. Killian stepped backward and watched, his hands clenched tightly into fists.

"Let me go," she finally said, giving up after several minutes of struggling.

"Where's Skye and Kestrel?" Killian asked calmly, ignoring her demand.

She looked up at him, and he saw a fierce fire raging within her bright green eyes. "Let…me…go," she repeated.

Killian shook his head. "Not going to happen. Your little setup nearly got us killed, so now you're going to answer some questions. Where's Skye and Kestrel?"

Winter continued to stare up at him, anger burning in her eyes. Killian didn't flinch away from it. He had a similar rage burning within his own eyes. "Do I need to remind you that we saved your life?" Killian asked. "We could have left you back there."

"I don't know where they're at," she said, cutting him off.

"Bullshit."

"I don't," she argued. "We started tailing them after we intercepted the message about the meet, but then we lost them. We were expecting them to show up at the meet to try to warn you off, but they never showed. I don't know where they're at."

Her eyes suddenly flashed over in Lucas's direction, but Killian stepped in front of her gaze, blocking him from view.

"What do you mean you 'intercepted the message'?" Stamp asked, stepping over.

Winter looked over at him, her jaw suddenly locked. Obviously, she had let something slip she wasn't supposed to.

"Hey!" Killian yelled, drawing her attention back toward him. He tried to look as imposing as possible. "What do you mean?"

"Your cell phones," she said rigidly, her mouth twisting into something between a sneer and a frown. "We've been intercepting all your calls and texts for the past few days. It's how we've been tracking you. Not that it really matters anymore since my whole fucking team is dead!"

She practically spat the last word out like a piece of sour fruit. She began thrashing in her seat again, struggling against her bonds, and let out a loud scream of anger. Killian had to jump forward and cover her mouth to suppress it. Lucas covered his ears, a pained sort of expression crossing his face. After a moment, he ran into the bedroom and slammed the door behind him.

Finally, when she ran out of breath, Winter stopped screaming, and Killian was able to withdraw his hand. His palm was slick with the steam of her breath. Tears started to course down her cheeks, and Killian saw the anger in her eyes had been replaced by something else, grief perhaps.

"They're all dead," she said much more quietly, tears continuing to stream down her cheeks and across her jaw. "All of them. How'd they know where we were? How'd they fucking know?"

"We've been wondering that for days," Killian said. He sighed heavily, recognizing the look now present in her eye. He had been seeing it every day for the past eleven months, every time he looked in the mirror.

"I'm...sorry about your team," he said awkwardly. It was forced and not entirely sincere, but he just couldn't stand here and let her wallow. He knew from experience it wouldn't do her any good, and it certainly wouldn't do *them* any good. He kneeled down in front of her. "We need to find our friends and get Lucas out of here. Can you still track their cell phones?"

Winter shook her head. She inhaled sharply, trying to rid the tears from her eyes. "No. They ditched them after they realized we were tracking them. There's no way to find them now."

Killian stood back up, jamming his hands in his pockets. He looked over at Stamp who just shrugged his shoulders.

"What about the cult, the Prime Magi? You think they've been tracking our cell phones too?" Killian asked.

Again, Winter shook her head. "I doubt it. We've had them under surveillance for a while, since the first time they tried to break Lucas out, but it doesn't look like they're that advanced. They pretty much stick to magic."

"They tried to break him out before?" Killian asked curiously.

"About six years ago. It was right after I started. We'd already realized the threat Lucas could pose if he was ever let loose on the world, but that was pretty much what really put it into perspective. After that, keeping him safe became our top priority. Research on him was abandoned entirely, and we moved him to a new location. It was when we were moving him that we lost his mother." Killian looked at her incredulously, then over toward Stamp. Winter let out a low, sad chuckle. "You know, I really shouldn't be telling you any of this—this is all classified information—but what does it matter now? My whole team's dead. They probably think I'm dead too."

"What do you mean you lost his mother?" Killian asked, ignoring her comment as he tried to wrap his head around everything.

"The convoy that was escorting her got attacked. By the time back-up arrived, she was gone and the entire team watching her was dead. We think the Prime Magi were trying to get Lucas again, but they found his mother instead. I don't know what happened to her after that."

Killian tried to keep his mouth from hanging open. So it had been his mother that Lucas remembered. He looked at the door to the bedroom where Lucas had hidden himself. How was he supposed to handle any of this? Killian ran a hand through his hair and across the bridge of his nose.

"You have to let me take him," Winter said quietly. Killian's eyes snapped back over in her direction. "He's not safe here with you. You know what will happen if the Prime Magi get him. I can see it in your eyes."

"No," Killian said. "He's not going back to living in some box."

"He's too dangerous out here!" Winter yelled.

Killian took a step backward. "He doesn't know his own power. If he loses control—"

"Then we teach him how to control himself," Killian snapped. "We do whatever we have to. But he shouldn't have to live in a box just because your government thinks he's a risk. This is our city. It was made by people like us. This is where he belongs."

He hadn't even realized it meant that much to him, but it was that kind of ideology that had driven so many people from their homes in the first place. It was that kind of oppressive philosophy that had made Blood Haven into what it was, and he wasn't about to let some Protector tell him what was best for one of his kind.

"And what do you think this city will do when they find out he's the one who caused all this?" Winter asked.

Killian stared at her. He suddenly wanted nothing more than to slap her across the face and tell her she didn't know what she was talking about, but a small voice in the back of his head said she did.

"Killian," a small voice suddenly came from the bedroom door. He looked over and saw Lucas standing there, peering through the cracked door. "I'll go with her. If it'll keep everyone safe, I'll go back with her."

Winter looked between them, hope springing across her face.

Killian shook his head, however. "No," he said sternly "You don't have to go back with her. We'll figure something out. We'll—"

"Don't you understand?" Winter said. "There's nothing you can do for him. You can't keep him safe. There's nothing to figure out."

"I'm not letting you take him!" Killian yelled, rage swelling back inside him. Stamp took a step toward him, but Killian held up his hand for him to stop. He looked back at Winter, the fire still burning within his eyes. His voice calmed, however. "He deserves a chance at a life. Just like we all do. I don't know what happened that made him the cause of all this, but he deserves a shot, a chance, at something resembling a life, and I'm not going to let you take that away from him."

The tone in his voice brokered no argument, and Winter just stared at him.

Stamp cleared his throat. For several tense moments, there was utter silence. "So what do we do?" Stamp asked.

"I don't know yet," Killian replied, his gaze still locked with Winter's. "But running has not been working so far, and I doubt that that's likely to change."

"So you plan to fight then?" she asked. "You plan to go up against a cult so powerful even the Protectors have watched only from a distance?"

"I sure as hell don't intend to just lie down and die," Killian responded. "So, yeah, I guess I intend to fight."

Killian looked over at Lucas, then at Stamp. After a moment, he nodded in response.

"You *do* realize that's pretty much suicide, right?" Winter asked. "I looked at your file. I read your history. You have no special training, no military experience. You left the states when you were fourteen years old."

"So what?"

"So you've never gone up against anything like this. You can't handle it."

"And the Protectors can?" Killian asked, drawing a sudden hurt look from Winter's eye. He had struck a nerve, but maybe that was a good thing. Maybe she would finally see his side of it. "It's clear no one can keep Lucas safe for long. Not with the Prime Magi out there trying to get him. Even if the Underground hadn't broken him out, it was only a matter of time before the Prime Magi tried again."

"You don't know that," Winter said, though it sounded weak even to her.

"Seriously? You said it yourself. They're too powerful. They're not going to let anything stand in their way of getting to him. So I say we switch the game up a little. Take the fight to them."

Winter stared up at him for a few moments. Finally, she asked the question that had been eating at her since first meeting them at the safe house. "Why? Why do you care so much about this kid?"

For a second, Killian was taken aback. Then it hit him. Why *did* he care so much about Lucas? He had found him little more than an annoying child, but now he was willing to risk everything for him. A million answers streaked across his mind as he looked over at Lucas, standing in the doorway. It's what his mother would have wanted him to do. It's what Spin would have done. But in the end, only one answer really made sense. Only one answer was believable.

"Because he's my friend," Killian answered firmly.

Winter looked at him incredulously. Even Stamp was a little stunned by his response. Lucas's mouth hung slightly ajar.

"I am?" he asked, his voice tinier than it had ever been before.

Killian managed a slight nod in response, and Lucas ran over, wrapping his arms around him. Winter looked away from the pair. It was obvious by the fleeting look of certainty in her eyes that she was no longer so sure about what to do.

"Fine," she said, looking back over at them after a moment. "So you want to fight. You're going to need my help."

"And we want it because—?" Killian asked, leaving the question open-ended.

"Because I know about the Prime Magi. I know how they work. Today wasn't the first time I've gone up against them." She hesitated before adding, "And because they killed my whole team. I want some serious payback."

Killian looked uncertainly at Stamp. He again shrugged his shoulders. Several seconds ticked past. Finally, Killian led Lucas back into the bedroom and, after a quick word of reassurance, closed the door on him. He stepped back over to Winter, folding his arms across his chest. "How do we know you won't betray us the moment our backs are turned?" he asked, his eyes warning her not to lie. "How do we know this isn't all some ruse so you can grab Lucas? Hell, how do we know you won't kill him just to make sure the Prime Magi don't get their hands on him?"

Winter kept her eyes on his the entire time, contemplating her answer. Finally, she said simply, "You don't."

Killian sighed. "That certainly doesn't inspire a lot of confidence."

Winter suppressed a scoff. "Look, we both know there's nothing I can say that's going to make you trust me. So the way I see it, you have three options. You can kill me and throw me in a ditch somewhere, leave me here and hope I don't find you again, or you can cut me loose, let me help you, *and* be able to keep an eye on me. It's your choice."

Killian had to force himself not to smile. She had guts. He would give her that. Not many people would lay it all on the table like that.

Stamp stepped up beside him and muttered in his ear, "She's got a point. And we could use some help."

Killian nodded. The debate was still raging within him, however. "Fine," he said after several terse moments of silence. "You can help us. But if I even get a hint of an idea that you're planning anything…"

"You'll turn the chip on my shoulder into a battering ram and shove it up my ass? Yeah, I heard," she said smugly.

Stamp snorted and looked up at the ceiling amusedly. "Oh, this is going to be fun," he said.

Killian wasn't sure if he was being sarcastic or not. He rolled his eyes, grabbed his knife, and cut the tape securing Winter's right hand. He then stepped back, crossing his arms.

Winter sent him an angry glare before setting to work freeing her left wrist. Killian stared down at her, a satisfied smile briefly crossing his face.

"I thought you were a redhead," he said suddenly. She shot him a lock of pure death in return.

C H A P T E R   1 8

Branded

Killian continued to stare at the news report. His mouth hung slightly ajar and a ringing filled his ears.

Domestic terrorists.

He said it over in his head again. That was what the news stations had just labeled them in relation to the gunfight at the apartment building. They were also wanted for the destruction of the overpass, though investigators were still looking for the 'explosive device' that had caused the collapse. As the broadcasts continued, there was no mention of the Prime Magi or the Protectors' involvement. Even so, how could the networks think *they* were terrorists?

"Furthermore, if you have any knowledge of the whereabouts of these men, please contact your local constable office immediately. They are considered armed and extremely dangerous," the news anchor continued.

Two facial sketches appeared across the screen. They were rough and some of the details inaccurate, but there was no denying they were likenesses of Killian and Stamp.

"That certainly complicates things," Stamp said. He was finding some difficulty in believing it himself. No doubt he was wondering what Daisy would think. Would she even talk to him again, knowing he had gotten mixed up in all this without telling her? He had not talked to her since just before the shootout at Chaser's club. There was no telling what she might be thinking now, and, since they'd heard the Protectors had been tracing their calls, they weren't about to try to contact her. They had already ditched their phones just in case anyone else tried, and, since they were now being branded as terrorists, it looked like it had been a good idea.

"How could this have happened?" Killian asked, continuing to stare at the screen. His legs suddenly felt weak beneath him, and he reached a hand out to the wall for support.

"It's simple," Winter said from the edge of the bed behind them.

They turned around to look at her curiously. They had moved to a new hotel after cutting her loose. This one wasn't quite as spacious as the Skyway and had an hourly rate instead of a daily. It was reflected in the rough linen bed sheets and the patched armchair in the corner. The wallpaper was peeling, and Killian was pretty sure he could smell mold in the plaster.

"You're both easy targets," she explained.

"What do you mean?" Stamp asked.

"The city council—the Overseers, I guess you guys call them—can't have a bunch of mages duking it out in the streets, especially if this reaches the international networks. They'll look weak. So they're looking to pin this on whoever they can, if nothing else just to be able to tell the world they've got a couple of suspects. And considering you two have now been seen at several of the recent crime scenes, you're the obvious scapegoats. It's all a power play."

"You sure do know a lot about how our city leaders supposedly think," Killian said irritably. He didn't want to believe what she was saying, but as much as he hated to admit it, it made sense.

"We're paid to know how your leaders think," she said. "I'm not saying what they're doing is right. I'm just saying it's how it is."

Stamp buried his face in his hands. "This is a nightmare," he muttered.

Killian placed his hand on his shoulder, trying to be reassuring, but he was just as worried. "We'll get through this," he said, trying to put as much confidence into his voice as he could muster.

"How?" Stamp asked, shrugging his hand from his shoulder. "How can we possibly get through this, Killian?"

"I don't know. We've just got to think of something," Killian said. He knew Stamp was frustrated. This wasn't what either of them had signed on for when they had agreed to help Skye, but they were stuck in this together. They had to keep level heads.

Stamp sank down onto the moth-eaten bed next to Winter.

"You realize even if we do manage to get out of this alive, we're probably going to prison for the rest of our lives," he said. It wasn't a question.

"Not if we hand the Prime Magi to the Overseers instead," Killian replied.

Stamp looked up at him incredulously. "How in the hell are we going to do that? We don't even know where they are."

Killian wasn't sure how to respond. So far, it had been Stamp keeping him in check. Now that the roles were reversed, he really wasn't sure what to do.

"It's okay, Stamp," Lucas said, giving voice for the first time since arriving at the new hotel. He was seated at the head of the bed, his back against the wall. "Killian will think of something."

Stamp sighed, his shoulders slumping. His frustration was far from forgotten. He locked eyes with Killian. "You'd better," he said.

Killian nodded. He only wished he shared Lucas's confidence.

Winter suddenly cleared her throat, drawing their attention back toward her. "Can I make a suggestion?" she asked, though it hardly sounded like she was asking for permission.

"By all means," Killian said, waving his hand across the air. The same slit-eyed expression Stamp often gave him shot across her face. He dropped his hand.

"You have Bloodhounds, right? Mages who can track people?" she asked. "I know I read about them in a report a while back."

"Yeah. They're kind of expensive, though. What's your point?" Stamp asked. Killian, however, had already started to catch on.

"So we find something one of the Magi has touched, get a Bloodhound to put an enchantment on it, and *voila!* We..."

"Follow it straight to them," Killian finished for her. She looked over at him, obviously a little impressed he had put it together by himself.

Stamp, however, did not look convinced. "Okay, that would work perfectly if we had something one of them has touched. Plus, we would need about another twenty grand in chits. I told you: Bloodhounds aren't cheap. And we have to find something specific to the Magi. It can't be something a lot of people have handled. Like a… Like a…" He trailed off, trying to think of a good example.

"Like a bullet?" Winter asked. Stamp's eyes snapped over in her direction and a sort of self-satisfied smile touched her lips.

"I think a bullet would work," Killian said, the same hint of a smile crossing his face as well.

"I know what you guys are thinking and forget it," Stamp said, cutting them both off before they could finish forming the plan in their heads. "We're not going anywhere near there. Plus, we still can't even afford one."

"You let me worry about the chits," Winter said. "That's not a problem."

"Come on, man, they probably haven't pulled any of the slugs from the walls yet," Killian cut in. "We could get in, get out…"

"Uh, I was thinking just I would go actually," Winter interjected. "They don't have any pictures of my face. It'd be a lot easier."

"No. No way," Killian said at once, not even bothering to listen to the rest of her argument. "I'm not letting you out of my sight for a second. I said you could help us. Doesn't mean I have to trust you."

"You're kidding, right?" she asked, her eyebrows high upon her forehead. "You want to walk back into the crime scene that made you a wanted terrorist? Have you completely lost your mind?"

"No, but you have if you think I'm letting you out of my sight. One of us is going with you. End of story."

She continued to stare at him in disbelief, but the firm look in his eye said he wasn't backing down. She looked to Stamp for help, but he merely shrugged his shoulders. Finally, she let out a loud frustrated scoff and stormed over to the small sink in the corner of the room. "Fine," she said more than a little exasperatedly. "You want to get caught, fine, but we're doing it *my* way when we get there. No more blowing shit up just because you feel like it."

"You think that's what I've been doing?" Killian asked.

"Could've fooled me," she said, turning the faucet on to its highest setting, an obvious effort to drown out any further argument.

Killian rolled his eyes, muttering several choice colorful phrases beneath his breath. Most dealt with her gender.

"And you two were getting along so well," Stamp said amusedly. Killian looked over at him angrily. Winter ignored them both.

"Just tell me what we're doing here," Killian said as they pulled into the train station parking lot in the western end of the city. They had commandeered a fresh vehicle from the street outside their hotel; this one ran better than the one they had rented from Carson, even before all the bullet holes, which was surprising due to its rough outward appearance. It was rusted across the roof, and the paint was cracked and chipping along the sides.

"I told you, we're doing this *my* way," Winter repeated. It was obvious she was used to people blindly following her orders.

"I understand that, but I just think it might be beneficial if you told me what the hell we're doing all the way over here," Killian said, more than a little frustrated. It was as if she was purposely making this difficult. Then again, judging by the look in her eye, she probably was. He ran a hand across his freshly shaved face and adjusted the ball cap atop his head in agitation. He hated wearing hats and hated being clean-shaven even more, but it was one of the few ways he had gotten her to agree to him coming along.

Beside him, she let out a long-winded sigh. "We're picking up my team's emergency kit, alright?"

"Alright," Killian said, feeling far more satisfied than he should have. Getting that answer had been like pulling teeth, though.

More than a little exasperated, Winter climbed out of the car without responding. Killian rolled his eyes and followed.

This not being a holiday or the travel season, the train station was fairly empty. They still managed to blend in with the mass of people coming and going through the station. Killian kept his head down and his chin low, not making eye contact with any of the passing travelers.

Winter led them across the atrium, past the ticket booths, over to the rentable lockers. Killian was about to ask where she had hidden the key when they had searched her when he saw they were combination locks. She walked down the aisle on the left and kneeled down at a locker near the center, punching in the code with a hard expression on her face. It beeped after a moment, and the locker door clicked open. Killian stared over her shoulder and saw there was a black vinyl duffle bag stuffed inside, barely able to fit within the narrow locker. With some effort, she pulled it free and slung it across her shoulder. She kicked the locker door closed with her foot. Silently, she headed back outside.

Without incident, and without even so much as a second glance from the station's minimal security force, they made it back to the car and climbed in. She set the duffel across her lap and unzipped it.

As he started up the car, Killian peered over to see what was inside. Several passports were rubber-banded together on top. He counted six—one for each member of her team, he realized. It explained the harsh look in her eye as she pushed them aside. There was also about a week's worth of preserved meals, a few changes of clothes (both male and female), and several silver badges for what looked like Blood Haven's police force. She pocketed one. She also pulled a set of metal binders from the bag and stuffed them into her other jacket pocket. A moment later, he saw a glint of metal as she pulled a small silver pistol from one of the side flaps. He immediately snatched her wrist.

"What the hell do you think you're doing?" he asked.

"Relax," she responded, wrenching her wrist free from his grasp. "If I wanted to kill you, you never would've left that apartment. And I've had plenty of other opportunities since then as well."

She tucked the gun beneath her jacket. Killian felt his own pistol dig into the small of his back. He would let her keep it for now.

"So where to next?" he asked with a bit more acid dripping from his voice than he intended.

"The safe house," she responded, before adding smugly, "unless there's some other place you'd like to get caught."

Killian ignored her comment and backed out of the spot, grinding his teeth. Why couldn't she just maintain her nice, flirty cover from the club? At least then, he wouldn't want to strangle her every time she spoke.

And Zipper said she had a soft spot for mages, he thought with a snort. *Right now, I'd prefer Zipper.*

A cold chill began to work its way up Killian's spine the nearer they got to the safe house. He could see Winter was feeling the same. An uncomfortable look spread across her face, and when they pulled onto the street, she actually kept her eyes from the road. The block was cordoned off by yellow police tape, so they circled the building and parked around the corner. Despite his annoyance with her, Killian gave her a second to ready herself. Her entire team had died here; he knew what that felt like. After several deep breaths, she nodded and climbed from the vehicle.

Killian walked around the front of the car and joined her on the sidewalk. Her eyes were staring past him, however, as he stepped up. Killian turned around, his heart speeding up, when he suddenly felt the cold metal of one of the binders snap around his wrist.

"What the hell are you doing?" he asked. He tried to spin around, but she got a foot under his and pushed him forward against the car, sending him off balance. Before he could struggle any further, the second binder had locked into place and his hands were cuffed behind him.

"I told you, we're doing this my way," she said, her breath hot in his ear as she pulled the pistol from his belt. "And that means not getting either of us caught *or* killed. Just do exactly as I say."

Killian struggled against the binders, but it only served to dig the metal painfully into his wrists. He clenched his jaw.

"Trust me," she said. She snatched the hat off his head and stuffed it into his pocket before grabbing hold of the chain and pulling him along behind her. He nearly tripped over his own feet, and she allowed him to move in front of her. They approached the police cordon and the officers standing there. Killian's heart had yet to slow down.

"You there," one of them called as they drew close. "Identify yourself."

There were three of them, wearing the grey and blue uniforms of the Blood Haven police force. Patches on their arms identified their ranks and their classifications. There was a fire mage, a Lighter, and an Elemental of all things. Killian forced himself to breathe normally as he was marched over to them. The binders continued to dig painfully into his wrists.

"Special Detective Garrote, Third Precinct," Winter said as she drew the badge from inside her jacket and handed it over. It rolled off her tongue so smoothly Killian almost believed it himself for a second. The fire mage took the badge from her and examined it closely.

His back straightened and his tone was noticeably more respectful as he handed it back to her. "What can we do for you today, ma'am?"

Killian wasn't sure how the police force's rank structure worked, but obviously, Special Detective came with some privileges.

The officer glanced at Killian and recognition suddenly dawned upon him. "Holy hell, is this him? Is this the one that blew up the bridge?"

"It was an overpass actually," Winter said, yanking on the binders' chain and forcing a grunt of pain from Killian. He glared at her angrily.

"We hadn't heard he'd been caught. What are you doing back here?' the officer asked, surprise still evident across his face.

"Our friend here says he left something upstairs that might help break this case open. We need access to the apartment where the shootout took place."

"Of course," the officer replied smartly. He pulled the cordon tape upward and allowed Killian and Winter to duck underneath. "Do you need any assistance from me or my men?"

"No, we can manage on our own," Winter said, pulling on the chain again and causing Killian's arms to pop painfully.

"Yes, ma'am." The officer looked at Killian for a moment before returning his attention to Winter. "I hope whatever it is helps get that other scumbag off the street. Men like them that give this city a bad name."

"Oh, you can be sure of that. Thank you, officer," Winter said and she led Killian toward the apartment building's front doors. Killian shot the police officer an angry look as he passed by but wasn't able to hold it for very long as he almost tripped again. The officer snorted and returned to the two other patrolmen, throwing a thumb in Killian and Winter's direction as he undoubtedly filled them in on what he had learned. Killian rolled his eyes and walked into the building beside Winter, his arms at an uncomfortable angle as she continued to hold the chain.

"Did you have to put these on so tight?" Killian muttered.

"Had to make it look convincing. Come on," she said.

They headed up the stairs and, once they were on the second level, Winter unlocked the cuffs. "When we head back downstairs, I'll have to lock you back up," she said. Killian massaged his wrists.

They continued up to the sixth floor and entered into the familiar yellow hallway. There were now several bullet holes along the wall and blood stained the grey carpet. They approached the safe house, and Killian saw there was yellow barrier tape across the door as well. He yanked it down and stared inside the apartment. Beside him, Winter didn't move. She was obviously preparing herself mentally.

"I can go in alone if you want," he offered, not sure why he felt compelled to be nice to her. His wrists ached.

"No, I can handle it," she said. It didn't sound very convincing. Still, she took a hesitant step inside. Killian followed.

The hole in the living room wall had plastic sheeting stapled across it. Narrow beams of light shone into the room through the numerous bullet holes. Killian saw the bloodstains on the floor from where Silver and Lilac had been killed. He also saw the dent in the far wall where Skiff had slammed into it after being hit by the fireball. A sidelong glance at Winter told Killian she wasn't handling it nearly as well as she would have liked. There was an extremely painful look on her face, and she was fighting to keep tears from her eyes. Her hands shook at her sides.

"Zipper died here," she said, staring down at a black scorch mark on the floor. "Took a fireball in the back that would've killed me."

Killian stared at her, unsure what to say. She then looked at a splatter of blood across the far wall.

"Ridley almost made it out. He was right behind me, and then he wasn't." He could tell by the look in her eye she was replaying the events in her head.

Killian tried to get his mouth working, but nothing wanted to come out. What could he say to that?

Finally, after several long silent moments, Winter seemed to snap from her daze and blinked several times, ridding the tears and the memory from her eyes.

"Let's get one of the bullets and get out of here," she said. Killian could do little more than nod in response.

They began searching along the wall for a clean bullet hole that they could recover a cartridge from. As they did, Killian continually found himself glancing in Winter's direction. He knew the resolve it must have taken for her to come back here, and, despite everything, he admired her a little bit. It had taken several months for him to build up the confidence and strength to return to the resort where Spin had been killed, and, by then, it was too late.

After several minutes of searching, Killian finally found a clean bullet hole and began digging out the cartridge. It was embedded deep in the plaster, and it took several minutes of forceful prying before he was finally able to pull it out. He looked at it closely, praying it would be enough for a Bloodhound to get a scent off. Of course, they still had the chit issue to worry about as well.

"Let's get out of here," Winter said from beside him. Killian nodded and pocketed the cartridge.

They walked out of the apartment and rounded the corner of the stairwell when they came face to face with the officer from downstairs. He froze, looked from Winter to Killian, then down to Killian's unshackled hands. He immediately moved to draw his gun. Without thinking, Killian drove his foot outward and connected his boot with the man's gut. An audible exhale of breath left his lungs, and he slammed backward. Winter lunged forward and head-butted him, knocking him unconscious before he could clear his gun from its holster.

"Come on, we got to get out of here before he wakes up," Winter said, already heading down. Killian nodded and followed behind, his heart pounding in his chest. Had their cover been blown or had the officer just come up to help? They reached the bottom of the steps, and Winter removed the cuffs from her jacket.

Killian looked at her incredulously. "You've got to be kidding me," he said.

"The back way's just as likely to be guarded, and if our cover was blown, they'd have sent up a lot more cops," she said.

Killian continued to stare at her. Finally, he turned around and allowed her to re-shackle his hands behind his back. Fortunately, she didn't put them on quite as tight this time.

"I told you, you should have let just me come," she said as she led him back through the lobby and outside.

The two other patrol officers were still milling around outside, chatting casually with one another.

"Find what you needed, ma'am?" one of them called over when they emerged from the building.

"I did, thank you," Winter replied. She gave Killian a hard shove and ducked back beneath the cordon tape.

"You didn't happen to run into Officer Pine up there, did you? He went up to ask something about your precinct."

Winter made sure she kept moving as she answered, "No, we must've just missed him. Tell him to call me over at the station, though, when you see him. I got to get this jerk-off back in lockup."

The officers nodded and gave her a casual wave goodbye. Winter breathed a quiet sigh of relief only Killian could hear and led him back to the car. She unlocked the cuffs, and, this time, she drove as they practically peeled away from the curb. It wasn't until they were several blocks away that Killian breathed his own sigh of relief.

"I cannot believe that worked," he said.

"It almost didn't," Winter replied, her voice taking on a harsh, sharp tone. "You coming along nearly got both of us killed."

"Yeah, well, we're both still breathing so I count that as a win," Killian said more than a little angrily. He massaged the pink lines around his wrists and tried to keep the little voice in the back of his head from admitting she was right.

"Look, I get it. You don't trust me. The feeling's mutual. But you damn well better start listening to me if you want to keep Lucas safe," Winter said just as haughtily. The vein in her neck was tight. "You're playing in hot water, and I don't think you realize just the kind of people you're up against. My team wasn't the first they've wiped out. They are stone-cold killers."

"Yeah, well, I've done alright so far."

They turned onto the highway. By now, Winter's hands were tight around the steering wheel. "We both know most of that was luck," she said. "The only reason you're still alive is because you're good at running and hiding. Fighting these guys, that's what *I'm* good at. You, you're nothing but a glorified deer hunter."

"Shut up," Killian said coldly.

She had struck a nerve. She kept pressing. "You're reckless. You have no idea what you're doing. Worst of all, you think you do."

"I said shut up!" Killian yelled. Winter's mouth snapped closed. She looked over at him and saw rage crackling in his eyes. He suddenly slammed his fist against the dashboard several times before he turned back to her and yelled as loud as he could, "You think I don't know that? You think I don't know I'm out of my league? For Christ's sake, the whole city thinks I'm a damn terrorist! I know this shit is over my head, but what choice do I have? I'm not giving the kid to you, I'm sure as hell not giving him to the Prime Magi, so that means he's *my* responsibility. I made a promise that I would protect him so, damn it, that's what I'm going to do."

Killian was breathing raggedly by now and inhaled slowly through his nostrils. He stared down at his quivering hands.

"Zipper said you had a soft spot for mages," Killian said with a scoff. "Bullshit. I doubt you even consider us human. So until you prove otherwise, just shut up."

By the end, his voice had dropped in volume substantially, and his breathing was coming in ragged gasps. Winter just stared at him, shocked he had completely lost it like that. She fixed her jaw and stared back at the road. She didn't even react when he slammed his fist into the dashboard again. The rest of the drive passed in silence.

CHAPTER 19

Frog

Killian and Winter strode back into the hotel room in almost complete silence. Stamp sat up in the armchair in the corner, obviously having been dozing, and Lucas turned down the volume on the television, an excited look filling his face.

"How'd it go?" he asked.

Killian gave him a look and placed the bullet cartridge on the nightstand. He walked over to the sink and splashed several handfuls of water across his face. Winter dropped the duffel bag to the ground and strode into the bathroom without a backward glance. She locked the door behind her.

"That well, huh?" Stamp asked. Killian flashed him an expression that said he would tell him later.

"So you got one?" Lucas asked. He rolled over on the bed and looked at the bullet. He obviously wanted to touch it but had learned his lesson from Carson's shop and kept his hands away from it.

"Yeah, hopefully, it still has enough of a scent on it," Killian replied. He turned off the faucet and shook the water from his hands. He sank down onto the foot of the bed, the pain in his arm and back flaring up again as he untied his shoes and kicked them off.

"So where to now? I don't know any Bloodhounds," Stamp said.

"I know somebody who does," Killian replied. He lay back on the bed with a groan and stared up at the tiled ceiling. "If we think we can risk dealing with him.”

“Who?”

“Frog.”

“You’re joking, right?” Stamp asked.

“I wish I was.”

“That son-of-a-bitch would turn us over to the cops for a pat on the head, much less the reward they’re now offering.”

“What?” Killian asked, looking over at him.

“Came on the news about an hour ago. Fifty thousand chits to whoever turns us in. Five thousand for any valid information that leads to our arrest. Thankfully, it’s only if we’re alive, or we would have every bounty hunter in the city on us. You know Frog informs; it’s how he stays in business. You seriously want to mess with him?”

Killian rubbed his eyes, exhaustion tugging on him. “That definitely doesn’t make things any easier. I just don’t see any other options. No one else is even likely to talk to us with this terrorist crap hanging over our heads, and Frog’s the only one I know of who might be able to get us into contact with a legit Bloodhound. We’ve got to at least try him.”

“You just… You know we can’t trust him, right?” Stamp asked. “It *was* his tip that led you and Spin to that resort.”

Killian nodded. At the very least, he owed Frog a good hard punch to the ribs. At the most, he would bury him if he tried to turn them over.

“So how *did* it go?” Stamp asked, lowering his voice.

Killian glanced over at him from the bed before sighing heavily. “Let’s just say we don’t exactly see eye-to-eye,” he replied.

“You think?” Stamp asked with a snort.

“She’s obviously not used to people talking back, I’ll tell you that much.”

“Was there any trouble?”

“A little. We ran into a curious cop when we were grabbing the bullet and had to knock him out. Her face will likely be next to ours pretty soon.”

“No wonder she looks so pissed,” Stamp said, his eyes hanging on the bathroom door for a moment.

Lucas joined Killian at the foot of the bed. He rested his hands on his knees, his toes just barely grazing the floor.

"Why can't you guys just be friends?" he asked. "She seems okay to me. She did lose her entire team, after all."

Killian stared over at him and chuckled slightly. "I wish it were that easy, buddy."

"It is that easy, though," Lucas said. "I mean, you didn't like me when you first met me. Now look. You said yourself we're friends. Couldn't you and her end up being friends too?"

"Right now, I'd just settle for being civil," Killian muttered.

At that moment, the bathroom door opened back up and Winter stepped out. Some of the fury had drained from her face, but she still looked quite agitated. Killian had to avert his eyes to keep from scowling at her.

"I still need to get the chits. I assume you two have a plan for getting into contact with a Bloodhound," she said.

"I wouldn't call it a plan so much as a..." Stamp began, but Killian cut him off.

"We've got it. Why don't you go and get the chits, and we'll go meet our contact?" he said as he sat up on the bed.

"Don't want to baby-sit me anymore?" she asked, an eyebrow arching on her forehead.

"Nope, you're a big girl. I'll let you handle it. We'll meet back here in three hours," Killian said.

If Winter was surprised, she didn't show it. She simply nodded and walked back out of the apartment. The door rattled as she all but slammed it behind her.

"If that's what you guys call civil, I'd hate to see one of your arguments," Stamp said amusingly.

Killian shot him a narrow glance and picked his shoes up off the floor. He began tugging them back on. "So, how do we want to do this?" he asked.

"Well, we can't leave Lucas here by himself, and I'm definitely not letting you go alone. You're likely to kill him," Stamp replied.

"You know, I *can* stay here by myself," Lucas said more than a little huffily. "I'm not a baby. I'm thirteen."

"I know, Lucas. It's not your age that worries us. There are men out there trying to find you, and we don't want you to be here alone if they do," Stamp replied calmly.

"But I've been practicing," Lucas said, obviously not satisfied with his response. The two men looked at him quizzically, and he climbed off the bed. He grabbed Stamp's keys off the dresser. "Here, look," he said. He closed his fist around them. When he opened it back up, the keys had turned into a metal knight chess piece. The surface was smooth and shiny and didn't change back when he handed it to Killian to examine.

"That's...incredible," he said, staring at it. It was void of imperfections. He passed it to Stamp. "I've never seen anyone pick it up so fast. Normally, it takes people months, years, before they're able to turn several objects into one thing. I'm... That's just amazing.

Stamp watched as the chess piece turned back into his keys in his hand. Lucas was grinning from ear to ear.

"That's not all," Lucas said. He held out his palm, and a ball of light materialized a few inches above his fingertips. He focused and it grew several inches in diameter, so bright Killian couldn't look at it directly. Lucas threw it against the far wall, and it dissolved as it hit.

"And this," Lucas said. A ball of fire suddenly appeared in the palm of his hand. The flames crackled and popped, and Killian could feel the heat coming off it. He stood flabbergasted.

"How long have you been practicing?" Stamp asked as the fireball dissolved. He stared at Lucas's open palm.

"Just while you were sleeping," Lucas replied. "Well, the light ball I already knew from Loop. The fire and the knight, though, I was practicing for a while earlier."

Killian could hardly believe it. He had to keep his jaw shut forcefully. Unfortunately, he could also feel dread slipping into the pit of his stomach. If Lucas could learn things that fast, people would never stop hunting him for the power he held, the abilities he could one day master. Someone who used his power for the wrong reasons could take over the world or, more than likely, destroy it. It made his legs suddenly feel weak beneath him.

"Lucas," Stamp said, trying to regain his composure as well. He kneeled down so he and Lucas were at eye level. "You have to promise me—both of us—that you'll never use these powers for anything but good. You'll never use them to hurt people. Okay?"

Lucas looked between them uncertainly. He nodded, obviously not understanding why they were both suddenly so serious. Killian nodded as well and placed a hand on his shoulder.

"Let's go see Frog," he said, his voice little more than a grumble. He lost it after seeing the fireball.

"I can't believe she took the car," Killian said, staring around the rust-bucket they had been forced to commandeer. The engine squealed every time they turned, and the seats stank of cat piss. The steering wheel was sticky.

"At least I'll be a whiz at hotwiring by the time this is all over," Stamp said from the passenger seat, his lips tugging upward with the hint of a smile. "That one I did outside Chaser's was the first one I'd done in close to a year. I couldn't believe it when I actually got it to start."

"You were always way better at it than me," Killian said. He let out a light chuckle. "Spin used to get so frustrated when he'd try to teach me, but I could just never get the wiring right. Always clipped them on accident."

Stamp laughed lowly as well. "You were pretty terrible at it. If we left it up to you, we'd be walking everywhere."

Killian nodded before slowly letting out a long, low groan. "I miss my jeep," he said.

Stamp snorted beside him. "I can't believe you still drive that thing. It's old as shit."

"Hey, it's got character," Killian replied. "Not everyone needs to drive around in a shiny new pickup."

Lucas laughed from the backseat, and Killian flashed him a grin. He dropped it almost immediately, however, as he caught sight of where they were. The glass and chrome high-rises had given way to old concrete houses with chain link fences and barred windows. The grass in many of the yards was overgrown, and groups of people loitered on street corners or in the shadows of their porches. They all watched the vehicle pass with the same weary expressions on their faces, and it was then Killian realized they were the only car on this stretch of road.

"We're almost there," he said.

"You think he still lives there?" Stamp asked. He made sure a round was chambered in his pistol before tucking it back into the shoulder holster beneath his jacket. He did similarly with Killian's gun before handing it back to him. Killian left it in his lap. He didn't like the way everyone was staring at them. He pulled the brim of his hat low, shading his eyes.

"He's never moved in the eight years I've known him. I doubt that's changed in the last ten months," Killian responded.

"What does this guy do exactly?" Lucas asked. He was looking out the window, obviously a little nervous. The houses were growing more and more dilapidated the further down the road they traveled, the grass growing higher.

"He's an information broker," Killian said. "People pay him to find out about things. This means he can be either our best friend or our worst enemy right now because he might be able to put us in contact with a Bloodhound, but he also might try to sell us over to the cops or a bounty hunter."

"But you know him, right?"

"No one really *knows* Frog," Stamp replied.

"Frog definitely knows you, though," Killian interjected. "He wouldn't be good at his job if he didn't know everything about you."

"So he knows about what happened to Spin?" Lucas asked.

"He was the first," Killian said, his tone flattening all of a sudden. He sighed. "I'm sure you heard Stamp say it was *his* tip that led us to that nest in the first place. I called him after I made it out."

"What did he say?"

"He asked when I was planning on paying for the tip," Killian replied flatly.

He pulled the car into the empty driveway of the most dilapidated building on the street. Hedges out front were growing across the windows, and the grass was at least a foot tall. The small stone path through the center of the yard was almost completely hidden. As he pulled up and parked, Killian spotted the surveillance camera above the front door and the one at the end of the driveway. He was sure there were at least a dozen others he couldn't see. The siding on the house was rotten and chipping, and the paint color couldn't even be recognized anymore it was so faded. It was a cross between green and grey now.

"Still a shit hole, I see," Stamp said as he climbed out of the car. He waved Lucas out. He popped open the door, but Killian halted him all of a sudden.

"Hold on a second," he said. He yanked off his hat and tossed it to him. "Put that on."

Stamp looked at him questioningly as Lucas pulled on the hat. Killian flashed a glance at the security camera and turned his back. He spoke lowly.

"If he's anywhere near as connected as he used to be, Frog probably knows the Prime Magi are looking for him, and I wouldn't put it past him to tip them off."

"And you think a hat is going to help disguise him well enough to fool Frog?" Stamp asked.

"It's better than nothing," Killian said. "Hell, maybe we should've left him at the hotel, but it's a little late for that now. Let's just go talk to Frog and get the hell out of here. I hate this neighborhood. Gives me the creeps."

Stamp nodded and Killian led the way up to the front door. He rapped on the peeling paint and waited as he heard the camera above his head zoom in. He looked up at it and gave it a casual wave. After a few moments, the door gave a series of clicks, and Killian heard the dozen or so locks disengage from the other side. He nodded to the camera and pushed open the door. It was extremely gloomy inside, but Killian could see the interior of the house was just as spotless as the last time he had been over. The hardwood floor was shiny; there didn't seem to be a speck of dust across its entire surface. The couch and the armchair in the living room had plastic covers over them, and the side table between them practically gleamed from all the polish on it.

As Killian entered, he was hit with the sharp, almost overwhelming scent of cleaner and bleach. It practically burned his nostrils, and his eyes instantly began to water. He suppressed a cough and waved Lucas and Stamp in behind him. They suffered similarly as they stepped through the door, and Lucas actually let out several sputtered coughs.

"Were you raised in a barn? Shut the door!" called a deep croaky voice from the back of the house.

Against his better judgment, Stamp closed the door behind them. Trying to waft the smell away from his nose with little success, Killian led them toward the back of the house. The windows in the living room were covered with plywood panels, the only part of the room not covered in varnish or polish of some kind, and cast an unsettling shadow across the whole house. The air was stagnant, as if nothing had moved in here for quite some time. Killian wondered if Frog even ventured into this part of the house. The only other time he had been here, Frog stayed at his little station the whole time. He doubted this time would be much different.

They walked through the narrow kitchen and saw it was just as clean and polished as the living room. The appliances looked new, unused, and even the magnets on the refrigerator were neat and lined up. The tiny dining alcove had been converted into a workstation for all of Frog's equipment. Six computer monitors displaying a plethora of information rested across a black horseshoe-shaped desk. Sitting in a tall, cushy computer chair was Frog, typing away furiously at his keyboard, obviously researching something for some client or another. Killian searched his multitude of monitors but couldn't be sure which he was working off currently.

Frog's appearance had changed minimally since the last time he saw him. He had a few more grey hairs and had gained a few more pounds, but otherwise Frog looked the same. He had tiny beetle-black eyes set deep into his squishy marshmallow-like face. His double chin was covered in stubble. His skin was just as pasty as ever from lack of sunlight and fresh air, and his gut threatened the burst forth from the tiny t-shirt he was wearing. In short, he was just as ugly as ever. He was also, unfortunately, probably their only hope of finding a Bloodhound.

Frog spun his chair around slowly to face them and said in the croaky voice that had earned him his name, "Ballsy coming here."

"Yeah, well, we didn't have much choice. We need your help," Killian said. He made sure he stood in front of Lucas, blocking him from sight as much as possible.

"As I recall, the last time we spoke, you told me to drop dead and called me a fat piece of shit." Frog looked at him unblinkingly.

Killian hesitated. He had hoped time would erase that from his memory. "Yeah, well, I was upset. You can imagine."

"But now you need my help," Frog said. His snorting sounded very similar to a bullfrog call.

"Yes," Killian said through clenched teeth that he forced off as a smile. He should have known Frog would make this difficult.

"What, run out of friends now that you're terrorists?" The hint of a smile crossed Frog's bulbous lips.

"We're not terrorists," Stamp interjected angrily.

"No, I suppose you're freedom fighters. Revolutionaries fighting for a just cause. What are you fighting for again? They didn't say on the news." Another half-smile. "I doubt Spin would approve of this new direction, Killian."

"Mention Spin's name again and I cut you out of that chair," Killian said.

"Look, Frog, we're not terrorists, alright? We're just trying to get in contact with a Bloodhound and could use your help," Stamp said, trying desperately to diffuse the situation before it got any further out of hand.

Frog regarded him coolly for several seconds, his brow narrow and creased. His eyes flickered between them and then settled on Lucas for just a second. His gaze returned to Killian. Finally, he asked, "What do you need a Bloodhound for?"

"Why does it matter? We're willing to pay. What else do you need to know?" he asked.

"It matters because I have two known terrorists standing in my house, and I *want* to know."

Killian could tell by the look in his eye that he wasn't going to help them unless they told him. He exhaled slowly.

"We're trying to find the men that set us up," he said, holding Frog's hard stare. It wasn't a complete lie.

They held each other's gazes for what seemed like an eternity. Lucas glanced up at Stamp questioningly, but he was too focused on the pair of them to notice. His hand was a twitch away from his gun.

"Okay," Frog finally said, and all three of them—Killian, Stamp, and Lucas—let out internal sighs of relief. "But it's going to cost you."

"How much?" Killian asked, not sure he really wanted to know.

"Two thousand," Frog answered nonchalantly.

Killian almost shot him right then and there. He was pretty sure Stamp actually reached for his gun before thinking better of it.

"Are you kidding me? You've lost your mind if you think I'm paying that much to get a Bloodhound's name."

"First off, it's the best Bloodhound in the city, and he works by reference only. Second, you are wanted terrorists! Be happy I'm not charging you ten to make up for that insane reward they're offering on the news."

"We told you we're not terrorists," Stamp said again, anger biting into his tone again.

"I know, I know, but the media thinks you are and the police think you are, so what's that tell me?" Frog asked.

Killian locked his teeth together so hard he was sure one of them was going to crack. "You owe us—you owe *me*—for what happened to Spin."

"Hey, I only provided the tip. It was you idiots who decided to go in there without a small army," Frog replied.

Killian's hands balled into fists, and he struggled to keep from knocking Frog's head off. He could tell by Stamp's rigid form beside him that he was suffering from the same internal struggle. Finally, with a backward glance at Lucas, he untied the pouch from his belt and tossed it onto Frog's desk. He also pulled out several more chits from inside his jacket, all but slamming them down onto the workstation.

"There's fifteen hundred in the pouch. Here's the other five hundred," he said, withdrawing his hand. "Make the call."

Frog stared at him with a smug, self-satisfied expression and activated the tiny wireless earpiece hidden behind his hair. The person on the other end picked up after a few moments.

"I've got some business for you," Frog said, still staring at Killian with his beady little eyes. "Where do you want them to meet you?"

CHAPTER 20

Wasted

Killian sucked in several mouthfuls of fresh air as they stepped out of Frog's house. It felt like an eternity since he had seen the sun, and it took several minutes for his eyes to adjust. Even though they were in one of the dirtier parts of the city, the air smelled sweet, and it was only after they got back in the car that the reality of their next destination registered.

"The Wastes," Stamp said from beside him, obviously just as uncomfortable with the idea as Killian. He was still rolling it over in his head.

"What are the Wastes?" Lucas asked. He took the hat off and shook his bangs away from his eyes.

"It's the section of the city that never got fully rebuilt after the Terrible Night," Stamp replied. He shot a sidelong glance at Killian, knowing full well what it meant to him having to go back there. It was, after all, the place his mother had died.

Killian didn't say a word as he backed the car out of the driveway and turned onto the road. His jaw was set and rigid, his knuckles white as he gripped the steering wheel.

"Where are you going?" Stamp asked, looking around. "Aren't we going back to the hotel to get Winter?"

"No."

"Killian, she's supposed to have the money," said Stamp. "Frog pretty much cleaned us out. We won't have enough to pay the Bloodhound."

"We'll figure it out," Killian said harshly, his tone barring the way for any further argument. "I'm not going back to get her."

"Look, man, I know she's kind of a pain in the ass, but we need her help."

"Drop it, Stamp."

"Killian, what happened? Did she say something?"

"I said leave it alone, Stamp!" Killian suddenly barked, causing Lucas to flinch in the backseat. "She's not coming."

Stamp stared at him, his mouth hanging slightly open, but he chose not to say anything. After a few moments, he turned in his seat and stared straight ahead.

They followed the highway for several miles into the southern section of the city. They passed the airport and heard the buzz of air traffic overhead as planes took off and landed. When they finally exited, it was into a smoky, detritus-filled haze. The buildings along the narrow streets were all in similar states of disarray, crumbling and broken down; many of their walls were still charred black from the fires that had once consumed them and almost all of them were covered in some kind of graffiti or gang markings. The cars along the sides of the road were just as trashed. The few that still had wheels sat on flat tires. The windows were all shattered, and many of the doors either had been removed or blown off.

If the buildings and vehicles were pathetic-looking, they compared nothing to the area's population. They were ragged and exhausted, wearing scrounged artifacts of clothing, their faces bony and hollow looking. Many had been displaced after the Terrible Night and had never found their way back. Killian knew deep down, looking at them, that if it hadn't been for Spin, he would have ended up just like them—starving, homeless, and hopeless. They had arrived in the Wastes.

Lucas looked out the window with a pained expression on his face and made sure to keep low in his seat. "They're all so sad looking," he said. No one was smiling or laughing; they simply stared straight ahead, motionless.

"They have nothing. Hell, less than nothing," Stamp replied. "Every city has a ghetto, a place where the homeless flock to. The Wastes is Blood Haven's. The cops don't even bother coming here anymore. It's a waste of time. The Overseers refuse to rebuild this part of the city, so what's the point?"

"To help them," Lucas said, suddenly sounding very angry. "How can they not care about their own people?"

"Because as long as the city's wealthy are happy and remain in control, why should they? It's the same anywhere. Even in *perfect* America," Killian replied. He practically spat out the last word.

"I will say this: It's kind of a weird place for a meeting," Stamp said, shifting in his seat. He didn't like the way the buildings all seemed to press in on the street, as if trying to engulf them and trap them here.

"I don't like it either. We'll go to the meet, but if it doesn't seem legit, we bail. Deal?" Killian asked.

Stamp merely nodded.

Killian kept his eyes fixed on the street ahead, refusing to look around. He didn't want to accidentally recognize a location and be forced to relive his mother's death all over again. It was bad enough every time someone mentioned the Terrible Night; being back here made it that much harder.

Stamp checked the address again, scrawled on a piece of paper, and pointed down a street. It had only two lanes, and Killian practically had to weave through the wrecked vehicles on the side just to get down it.

"The address is 51½ Reynolds Street," Stamp said, counting the few remaining address markers on the surrounding buildings. They passed 51 and then 52. He glanced over his shoulder questioningly. There did not appear to be a 51½ Reynolds Street. "Where is it?"

"It's the alleyway," Killian said, turning the wheel hard over and flipping them around. He stopped the car across the street from the mouth of the alley. Cold tingly fingers seemed to crawl up his spine as he stared down it. It reminded him so much of the alley he had hidden in all those years ago as he watched his mother die. It took him a moment to realize his hands were shaking. "This is a bad idea," he said.

"Yeah, well, we seem to be full of those lately. What do you want to do?" Stamp asked. He didn't want to admit just how uncomfortable he was with the situation, but as Killian had said before, they were pretty much out of options if they wanted to find the Prime Magi. This Bloodhound was their only hope.

"Meet the Bloodhound and kill every last one of those trench coat pricks," Killian replied. He popped open his door and motioned for them to follow. There were a few vagrants standing nearby, eyeing the car with keen interest. Killian adjusted his jacket and made sure they saw the pistol tucked into his pants as well as the one holstered beneath his arm. After that, they became much more interested in something on a nearby wall.

The threesome didn't have to watch for traffic as they crossed the street. Theirs was the only working car within a five-block radius. That alone made Killian nervous. The gloomy alley and otherwise foreboding feeling did nothing to calm his nerves. He clenched and unclenched his fists as they strode into the narrow backstreet. Crumpled up newspapers and trash bags lay scattered across the pavement. They walked to the end of the alley where it met the backside of a five-story brick building. It had shattered windows and gang insignias all over it. Two doors led into the building, where Killian guessed workers and loaders had once entered.

He glanced up at several of the windows overlooking the alley and tried to fight the feeling they were being watched. Everything about this seemed wrong. Why would a Bloodhound set up a meet in this part of town? The rates they were known to charge, he could probably afford a place downtown or in the heights. He looked at Stamp and Lucas. They were just as unsure of the situation as he was. Lucas stood close to Stamp and shot him a questioning glance. Stamp, however, was staring all around, his eyes twitchy and alert, his hand poised to grab his gun at the first sign of trouble.

"This has 'trap' written all over it," Killian said.

"You think? I already told you I wouldn't put it past Frog to sell us out," Stamp replied.

"Not a bad theory," said a voice as the door on the right opened. A man in a black vest and tight-fitting cowboy jeans stepped out. He wore brown leather riding boots with silver buckles on the sides. His hair was cropped close to his scalp, and a tribal tattoo crawled up his neck. Yellow-tinted sunglasses covered his eyes, and he wore fingerless leather gloves. Killian saw the stock of a shotgun slung across his back. "Seeing as that's exactly what he's done."

Killian immediately snatched his gun from his waist and trained it on the man's head. "Hold it right there!"

The man stopped in the doorway, a slight smile forming across his lips. Killian didn't like the easiness in which it came.

"Run," he whispered to Stamp.

Stamp hesitated for just a second before grabbing Lucas and sprinting down the alley. Lucas yelled something over his shoulder, but Killian didn't hear what it was. He clicked the hammer back on his pistol, his index finger tight across the trigger.

"I wouldn't do that," the man said.

"Why not?" Killian asked. Sweat beaded across his brow.

The man nodded and four other men stepped out behind him, dressed in similar clothing. The two on the right carried assault rifles, and Killian could see one on the left had a fireball already crackling in his hand. He practically radiated with power, and Killian knew the small baseball-sized flame was far from the pinnacle of his abilities.

"Not unless you feel like being turned over in body bags."

"So you're a bounty hunter," Killian said. It was not a question.

"*The* bounty hunter actually. Drift," he said, and Killian could only guess he meant it was his name. "Frog said you guys are worth quite a bit of money. Fifty-thousand apiece to be exact. Unfortunately, the Overseers want you alive, or this whole thing would have been so much easier. Don't worry, though. Your friends won't make it far. I've got two men waiting for them at your car."

There was suddenly a loud crashing noise, and the ground beneath their feet shook. Killian didn't move. A look of uncertainty flashed across Drift's face before they heard the squealing of tires and a rapid succession of gunshots. None of them sounded like they hit anything, however.

"A Geomancer, huh?" Drift asked, a slight smile cracking his otherwise hard face. Again, Killian didn't move. "Touché. Frog said you guys were good. Oh, well, I'll find them soon enough.

"Speaking of which. That boy, the one your friend was trying so hard to hide; I've heard some pretty interesting rumors."

"Shut up," Killian spat out angrily.

"So they're not just rumors. Interesting." Another smile cracked his visage. "Looks like we'll be retiring early, boys."

The men standing behind him chuckled or nodded their heads in agreement. Drift locked eyes with Killian.

"Do yourself a favor. Put down the gun. The Overseers want you alive, and I'd hate to disappoint them," he said.

Killian's eyes were unwavering as he stared at him. Sweat trailed down his forehead and across his cheeks, burning his freshly shaven face. After a few moments, he lowered the gun several inches so it was no longer trained on Drift's head. His eyes sank toward the ground in defeat.

"Smart move," Drift said and nodded to the mage still wielding the fireball. "Take him."

The man took two steps toward him before Killian snapped the gun back up and shot him twice in the chest, aiming several more shots at the man beside him, before turning to run a second later. The fireball that had been in the mage's hand shot against the nearby wall as he fell and exploded against it, peppering the area with flecks of brick and debris. Drift yelled angrily, and several gunshots zipped past Killian's ear as he bobbed and weaved down the alley, tipping a trash barrel over behind him and blocking a bullet that surely would have taken out his kneecap.

He reached the end of the alley and saw the car was indeed gone. Stamp and Lucas had escaped. He had half a second to breathe a sigh of relief when an arm suddenly shot out from around the corner and caught him in the sternum. His feet went out from under him, and he landed hard on his back, the wind escaping from his lungs with an audible "Oof." His gun skittered away from his grasp. He coughed and sputtered, tasting blood in the back of his throat, as he looked up to see a large man with a cut across his eye standing over him. Drift jogged up behind him.

"Good job, Pike," he said. He stepped over so he stood fully in Killian's view. His eyes darted over to the gun a few inches from Killian's grasp and kicked it away. "That wasn't very smart."

He raised his boot and kicked Killian across the cheek, knocking him out and into a world of darkness.

Killian dreamt of his mother. He saw her windswept hair, the easy smile that often touched her lips, and heard the lullaby she had sung him as a baby. *"Round and round the garden little teddy bear, one step, two steps, tickle you under there!"* she would sing over and over.

Then he saw her running. People surrounded them, and Killian knew they were in trouble. Flames were crackling across the rooftops of all the nearby buildings, and there seemed to be a great panic around them all. A hazy black cloud was behind them. He couldn't see it, but he knew it was death. Wings flapped from within it and static electricity shot out in all directions.

"Round and round the garden," his mother said in a voice too calm for their present situation.

She suddenly shoved him hard to the side, and he fell to his knees in the mouth of a nearby alley. He looked up at her as she turned and tried to get to him, but her feet went out from under her. She fell to the ground with a cry of pain and landed on her hands and knees, her mouth agape in terror. Killian tried to get to her, but she waved for him to stay where he was.

"One step," she said as a person kicked her across the face as he ran past. She fell flat. Killian cried out for her.

"Two steps." Another fleeing person trampled across her body, and he saw blood leaking from the corner of her mouth. He tried to get to her, but again she waved for him to stay back.

"Tickle you under there," she said as a final man stomped across her head, crushing her skull and killing her instantly.

Killian screamed as hard as he could, but no one stopped. They kept running past, trampling his mother over and over. Her hair was ragged and tangled. Her lips were cast downward in a look of frightened panic and pain.

The lullaby she had sung him as a child was now engraved in his mind as a terrible reminder of what had occurred. He screamed and screamed. Then, someone else was screaming with him. It was a much deeper voice, an adult's, and slowly the screams formed into words. *"Aaaaaaahhht's time* to wake up."

Killian snapped awake as ice-cold water was suddenly thrown across his face. His eyes opened, and he immediately tried to lurch to his feet, only to find his hands were cuffed behind him to a wooden chair. They were in some rundown apartment, and it all suddenly came flooding back—the alleyway, Stamp and Lucas fleeing, and his capture. He looked around and saw Drift and the big man, Pike, standing around him. Pike was holding a grimy-looking bucket, the cut across his eye taped and bandaged. The two other men from the alley and a third he did not recognize stood nearby. The one he didn't recognize stood against the window, staring out it as he sharpened a buck knife with a small whetstone. A fire burned in his eyes as he looked over and locked gazes with Killian. He struggled against the cuffs, but they wouldn't give. He was stuck sitting in the chair.

A scratching at the door behind him brought Killian's attention over his shoulder. The door looked like it led into a bedroom. The white paint was peeling and chipped, and a padlock bolted to the frame secured it in place. Tiny fingers worked their way up his spine as his eyes fell to the scratch marks along the floor. They were deep, too deep to be done by human hands.

"You should've just come quietly," Drift said. Killian's eyes snapped back over in his direction. Rage sweltered within his chest. He felt like a caged animal. Unfortunately, like a caged animal, he was powerless to escape. "Then I wouldn't have to hurt you. Well, I'd probably hurt you anyway, but now I'm *really* going to have to put a beating on you. See, you killed two of my best men, and the fire mage, the one you gave two new breathing holes, was Chino's brother."

The man with the buck knife suddenly stabbed it into the windowsill. It wobbled there for a second before steadying. Killian didn't have to ask which one was Chino.

"Now, because of that, you've put me in a rough spot, because Chino here wants revenge, but at the same time you're worth the money only if you're alive. But then I had a revelation. The boy."

Killian's eyes faltered for just a second before he returned them to Drift. A broad smile slowly formed across Drift's face.

"See, I knew the rumors had to be true after the way you acted in the alley, so I called up some contacts of mine and heard the Prime Magi are indeed looking for a little kid matching his description. They're willing to do just about anything to get him too, including, say, blowing up a school." Drift looked quite pleased with himself.

"So you know I'm not a terrorist then," Killian said, returning his eyes to Drift's. "You know the Overseers have it wrong."

"What you are or aren't really doesn't matter to me," Drift replied. "Only what people are willing to pay for you. Or, in this case, for your little friend. And let me tell you, it's quite a lot. Way more than the Overseers are willing to pay. For even a hair of information leading to the boy's capture, the Prime Magi are willing to set me up for life. Life!"

He seemed to relish the last word, and Killian knew there was no way he was going to be able to talk his way out of this. He again struggled against the cuffs, but they wouldn't give. Behind him, the scratching continued, louder.

"So now we get to play a fun little game I like to call the Interrogation Game," Drift continued. "Answer my questions correctly and you get to go to the next round. Answer them incorrectly or refuse to answer and you suffer a penalty."

"Fuck you," Killian spat out. His hands shook behind his back as fear began to work its way into the pit of his stomach.

Drift merely smiled before punching him hard across the cheek. Pain erupted in that side of his face. He had kicked him across the same side.

"You're starting too early, my friend. I haven't even asked a question." Drift massaged his knuckles and shook his hand. "I can already tell this is going to take a while, and I really don't feel like splitting my knuckles, so we're just going to skip ahead."

He walked over to the kitchen counter nearby, and Killian caught a glint of metal as Drift put on a set of brass knuckles. Panic set in completely, and Killian struggled against the chair. He tried to tip the chair over in an attempt to break it apart, but Pike walked over and held it in place.

"Now, you're lucky because we need you to be able to talk, so we'll keep it to body shots for now," Drift said. He flexed his fingers, settling the brass knuckles. "Let's try this again. I'll ask a question. You answer it. Where's the boy hiding?"

Killian stared up at him. He set his jaw and did his best to prepare for the coming blow. He failed miserably. Drift punched him right in the Solar Plexus and knocked the air clean from his lungs. He gasped and doubled over but could only go so far before the cuffs stopped him.

"I wonder how many ribs a person can break before they start choking on their own blood," Drift said.

Killian continued to gasp for air, and Drift waited until he had stopped before straightening him back up. Killian locked eyes with him and tried to keep his gaze steady.

"One more time," Drift said. "Then we start playing *realty* dirty. And you *don't* want to know what that entails. Where is the boy hiding?"

Killian tried to think of something witty to say in return, a joke or an insult, but all that came to mind was the overwhelming pain in his abdomen and that stupid lullaby. *"Round and round the garden little teddy bear, one step, two steps, tickle you under there!"* It was the only thing that came clearly right now. That and the scratching. He was scared to know what was behind that door.

Drift waited a second before punching him in the ribs. He wasn't sure if any cracked, but piercing fiery pain shot across Killian's chest, and he was sure another hit like that would shatter one. Killian felt blood trickle down his palms as his wrists dug against the handcuffs. His fingertips burned as the blood dripped across them.

"Alright, let's try something different. Maybe we're jumping into the main course too quickly," Drift said, wiping sweat across his brow. He straightened Killian back up and stared at him. "Why do the Prime Magi want him so bad?"

"You're a bounty hunter. Why do you care?" Killian asked in a hoarse voice not his own.

The punch to his stomach that followed felt like it knocked his insides around. He gasped for breath and felt hot tears trickle across his cheeks. He tried to fight them back, but they came involuntarily.

"I don't see why you have such a problem with me being a bounty hunter.

We're not that different, you and I," Drift said, straightening up and pacing across the floor in front of him. "From what I hear, you used to be quite the little hunter yourself, killing werewolves, vampires—pretty much any Subby you could get your hands on—all for a penny or two here and there. Hell, from what I hear, you killed entire nests just for a single jar of vamp Dust."

Killian spat a wad of blood-soaked phlegm at the ground. He looked up to meet Drift's eyes but could not raise his head that far. The pain in his stomach was overwhelming.

"Hell, if your partner hadn't been killed, you'd probably be living the high life right about now, like I'm about to, but he had to get himself killed. What was his name? Frog told me, but I can't remember it for the life of me."

"Fuck you," Killian said through another mouthful of blood.

"No, no, that wasn't it."

Drift hit him in the Solar Plexus again, and Killian practically went limp. Questions began to circle within his head: *Why am I fighting so hard to protect Lucas? Why do I care so much what happens to him? What's the worst thing the Prime Magi could do with him?*

Destroy the whole damn world, idiot, a different voice, a much stronger voice, said in his head.

Killian struggled to sit up and slowly lifted his head to look at Drift, bitter resentment burning in his eyes. It was accompanied by the fire of absolute resolve not to tell him a single thing.

Drift seemed to detect this because the smile fell from his face, and he stood a little taller. He hit him again.

The burning in Killian's fingertips began to hurt, and he clenched his fists tightly, trying to quiet it.

"Spin!" Drift suddenly called. "That was his name."

A strange fire slowly settled into his eyes, and Killian knew he wouldn't like what was about to come next.

"Speaking of your hunter days," Drift said, an idea occurring to him as he pulled off the brass knuckles and set them on the counter. "There's something I've been meaning to try, and I think you're the perfect guinea pig. Now, she's a little shy, but I think you'll find she really opens up if you start talking first."

Drift slowly strode around him, and Killian craned his head to follow him. He walked over to the white door, pulling a key from his jeans pocket.

"Boss, you sure about this?" Pike asked, staring at him questioningly.

"Turn him around," Drift answered.

Pike seemed uncertain for a moment, continuing to stare at Drift, before grabbing the back of the chair and turning Killian around. The handcuffs dug deeper into his wrists as he felt every muscle in his body tighten.

Drift unlocked the padlock and pulled it away from the latch. The scratching on the door immediately ceased. A cold sweat ran down Killian's forehead. Behind him, one of Drift's cronies closed the kitchen blinds.

"How you answer my next few questions determines how much of you I let her have."

Grabbing the knob, Drift pushed the door open with his toe and stepped back. It slowly creaked open to reveal a dark room. Blackout curtains must have hung from the windows because no light peeked in. Killian squinted to see through the gloom and managed to spot a figure crouched in the back corner of the room. He could tell even through the gloom that it didn't have any hair. Its skin was ghostly white. Realization settled into the pit of Killian's stomach like a nest of vipers. He struggled against the cuffs even harder, the fire in his fingertips bringing a cry of pain to his lips. Drift must have mistaken it for a cry of fear because he smiled.

"Allow me to introduce Fetch," he said. The shadow stirred at the name. "Now, she's not your usual type, but then, beggars can't be choosers."

"You psychotic son-of-a-bitch! Have you lost your mind?" Killian asked, his breaths coming in gasps as he prepared for the worst.

"Answer my questions," Drift said.

Killian couldn't take his eyes off the shadow. It fidgeted there in the dark. A horrible smell wafted out of the room, like rotted meat and onions. It burned his nostrils.

"Answer them!" Drift yelled. "Where is the boy?"

Killian bit his tongue to keep from telling him. The shadow suddenly lurched forward from the room, faster than he could track. Its eyes were completely black, and its teeth were long and yellow, ending in sharpened points that would surely rip into his flesh with ease. Not a single strand of hair remained on its body. The ghoul was a few feet away when the chain fastened around its neck stopped it short, and it was yanked backward, crashing to the floor. It screeched and immediately scampered back into the room on all fours, the sunlight peeking through the kitchen blinds burning its skin.

Killian continued to breathe heavily, his heart hammering in his chest. His entire body burned, and the sweat coursing across his face and neck practically steamed.

"Damn it, Fetch! What did I tell you about coming out before you're called?" Drift yelled. The ghoul fidgeted again, licking its burned forearms.

"You trained a ghoul?" Killian said. He couldn't even comprehend it, even as the words spilled from his lips.

"Eh, it's a work in progress. You'd be surprised how much she comes in handy. Caught her about a year ago. A lot like training a dog. She gets kicked if she's bad. Treats if she's good."

Killian knew he would end up being one of those treats if he didn't answer Drift's questions. He tried to grab onto that burning resolve he had felt not so long ago, but it felt like it was a million miles away now. He had seen what ghouls did to people when they were hungry. It wasn't pretty.

"See, I knew she would loosen your tongue," Drift said, leaning in close to Killian's ear. "No one wants to die like that. Tell me where the boy is."

Killian's resolve was little more than a flicker now. He couldn't think of a single good reason to keep his mouth shut, yet his jaw locked and he didn't say a word.

"Ay, enough fucking around!" Chino called from the window. He grabbed his knife and pried it from the wood. "Let me do it. We'll get answers and then I can avenge my brother."

Killian's eyes were still locked on the ghoul. He didn't even look in Chino's direction. The fire burning through his body slowly began to circulate back down to his hands. He couldn't even keep his fists clenched it burned so bad. An image suddenly formed in his head of when Spin had taught him how to play Jacks so many years ago. It burned in his mind resolutely.

Chino walked over, holding the knife tightly in one hand, feeling the tip with the index finger of his other. He seemed satisfied with its sharpness.

"Fine, fine. Ruin all the fun. Just remember we need him to be able to talk. No cutting out his tongue," Drift said. He seemed disappointed he wouldn't get to try Fetch out on anyone.

Chino rolled his eyes but nodded nonetheless. Pike grabbed the back of Killian's chair and pulled him back several feet before spinning him around. Chino stopped in front of Killian and sneered down at him. "You're going to pay for what you did to my brother, puto. Where's the boy hiding?"

The image flashed in Killian's brain again, and he suddenly felt the handcuffs fall away from his wrists. He was only vaguely aware of the faint sound of clinking as a dozen metal jacks fell to the ground beneath him.

Chino didn't wait for him to respond. He drove the knife toward his abdomen, and Killian just barely managed to duck out of the way, grabbing hold of Chino's wrist and plunging the knife straight into Pike's stomach instead. There was a gasp of surprise, an anguished groan of pain, and several angry yells before Killian lunged forward and knocked Drift into the kitchen counter. Drift grabbed the revolver from his belt and tried to bring it around on him, but Killian managed to grab his wrist and point it at Chino just as he pulled the trigger. Two slugs hit Chino in the chest, dropping him to the ground. A third ricocheted off the nearby wall and a fourth shot into the bedroom. Killian heard the ping of metal on metal and instantly knew the hell he had just unleashed.

The ghoul immediately lurched forth from the room, leaping onto one of the other bounty hunters and driving its fangs into his collar. He screamed as blood spurted from the wound.

Drift yelled angrily and swung his head forward, hitting Killian in the forehead. Blinding pain exploded in Killian's brow, and he fell backward. Thankfully, Drift had hit him with the soft part of his hairline and temporarily stunned himself, cursing and clutching his head as stars danced across his vision. Killian nearly fell to his knees as he stumbled backward and just barely managed to duck beneath the hard outward strike of the other bounty hunter. Killian knocked him across the jaw, sending him reeling backward, and the ghoul pounced on him next. They both toppled to the floor and teeth met flesh again. There was a glint of metal and the ghoul shrieked as the bounty hunter drove a knife into its side. It bit into him again.

Killian practically crashed into the hallway and stumbled several steps toward the front door when four more gunshots hammered the wall beside him. His feet were suddenly much steadier after that as he raced to the door and crashed through it. The rusted lock gave way, and the door tumbled open, all but falling away from its hinges. He slid across the floor as a staccato of gunfire hit the wall in front of him. He rolled to the side like a log and sprang to his feet, only vaguely aware of the detritus-lined hallway where he now found himself. He raced to the end where he thought he saw an EXIT sign, ran past the stairwell door, turned, and slammed it open.

Screams and more gunshots trailed after him, and he dashed down the metal steps, his boots clanging off them like some kind of horrible symphony. He jumped the last flight of stairs altogether and raced through the open door at the bottom. The tiny lobby was empty, and Killian sped across the linoleum floor and out the two glass doors in front. His heart hammered within his chest as he turned and ran down the sidewalk. Pedestrians jumped out of his way and looked at him in surprise, but no one moved to help.

Killian could practically feel Drift hot on his trail. And he was completely absent of a weapon. It was this thought that distracted him enough to miss the car pulling out of the alley in front of him. It hit him, not terribly hard but enough to send him crashing to the pavement with stars and bright lights floating across his vision. He was sure he had slammed his head into the pavement, and he was sure he had heard someone shout for an ambulance when his world spun away from him once more. Then again, maybe it was just wishful thinking.

He was moving. He couldn't be sure how he knew, he just did. He was also lying flat, and something was across his nose and mouth, keeping his breathing steady. He tried to sit up, but his chest was tight, and his stomach refused to bend. He couldn't even lift his arms.

"Take it easy, buddy. You're alright," a voice said somewhere in the haze that was his mind.

He focused hard and managed to get his eyes to center on the man sitting beside him. He was young and wearing some kind of white and blue uniform. Blue latex gloves covered his hands.

"Help me," Killian said in a raspy voice. His throat felt like cotton.

"We are helping you. You're on your way to the hospital. We're going to take care of you. Can you tell me your name?"

It was then Killian realized where he was. He was in the back of an ambulance. Someone had called for one after all. The crowd that had formed must have scared off Drift and his cronies. But now Killian had a completely new host of problems to handle. They would take him to the hospital. Hospitals asked questions. Hospitals would recognize his face from the news. It was a miracle the two paramedics hadn't recognized him already.

Killian tried to sit up again, but the paramedic beside him rested a hand across his chest. The gentle pressure he applied was more than enough to keep Killian flat. All his strength had left him.

"You have to let me go. People are after me," he said, tugging the breathing mask down away from his face. He knew it was probably a lost cause, trying to convince the EMT to release him, but he had to try. He couldn't go to the hospital. Even if he wasn't arrested right away, the Prime Magi would surely be able to find him there.

"You'll be safe at the hospital. They won't be able to get you. I promise," the paramedic tried to reassure him.

Killian again tried to rise from the stretcher he had been placed on.

"Sir, please lay still," the EMT said, trying to push him back down. Killian's strength was returning, though, and he was slowly managing to sit up. "You probably have a concussion, definitely a few cracked ribs. You need to remain still, sir."

Killian pushed his hand away, supporting his body with his other arm. "I have to get out of here."

"Sir, please," the EMT said. He grabbed a syringe from the workstation beside him and filled it from a small glass bottle. Killian turned just in time to feel the needle pierce his arm. He swept his other arm outward, but the syringe was already empty, and the EMT pulled the needle from his arm. "It's just a mild sedative, sir. You *need* to remain still."

Killian immediately felt himself go all hazy again, and he fell back against the stretcher. It was as if his limbs were made of rubber all of a sudden and refused to obey his commands. A strange sort of fog had enveloped his mind as well, and he couldn't form a clear thought pattern. Beside him, the paramedic seemed to relax and patted him on the shoulder in an effort to comfort him.

"We're almost there. Get you fixed up nicely," he said just before the ambulance swerved to the side hard, sending medical supplies and tools rolling across the workstation. Killian felt the fog clear from his mind a little with the jarring motion. The EMT looked up toward the front of the vehicle. "Bloody hell, Richter, what the hell are you playing at up there?"

"Some bitch just swerved in front of me. Nearly hit her," the driver called from the front. "It's like she didn't even see me. Oh, shit!"

The ambulance swerved again, and they skidded to a sudden halt. More medical tools went rolling across the station and several syringes fell to the floor. Alarm bells rang in Killian's head, but he could barely move.

"What the hell is going on, Richter?" the EMT asked.

"She's got a gun. Oh, shit," Richter said before the driver-side door opened, and a vaguely familiar female voice told him to get out.

Killian managed to look over his shoulder toward the front of the vehicle just as Winter climbed into the driver seat and pointed a pistol at the paramedic beside him. She didn't say anything. She just waved the gun toward the back of the ambulance, and the paramedic caught her meaning. He gave Killian an uncertain glance before dashing out of the rear of the ambulance. He left the doors hanging ajar and Killian saw they had skidded to a halt in the middle of a two-lane street. Several cars were backed up behind them, the drivers craning their heads out their windows as they tried to catch sight of whatever was holding them up. Winter climbed into the back of the ambulance and closed the doors back up, a strange look on her face as she glanced down at him.

Was it concern?

"Bet you're happy I planted that tracker in your jacket," she said. There was a surprising lack of bitterness in her voice. "Next time, don't go running off to an obvious ambush without me."

The comment dripped with conceit, but there was also the hint of a smile to her lips. She climbed back into the cab, and the ambulance began to move again. Killian's head sagged against the stretcher. He knew with Winter watching over him, he was safe.

The same could not be said for Frog.

CHAPTER 21

Betrayed

By the time they switched out the ambulance for something less conspicuous, Killian had regained his bearings enough to start asking questions. His chest ached and his wrists burned from the deep gouge marks across them.

"I put a tracker on you when we went to the safe house, slipped it in your jacket pocket with the hat just in case we got separated or you decided to go wandering off. Good thing I did since that's exactly what you did," Winter explained, the haughtiness in her voice returning. Killian didn't respond. He laid his head back against the seat as she drove them back toward the hotel, taking a roundabout route in case anyone tried to follow them. At his lack of response, she continued. "Anyway, when I got back from getting the money, you guys weren't there. That's when Stamp and Lucas showed up, saying you had gone off to meet the Bloodhound without me and were ambushed by some bounty hunters. I told him to wait there, and I activated the tracker. I almost made it to you before the ambulance, but then they picked you up, and I had to head them off. And here we are."

Killian grumbled a quiet thank you.

"What was that? I didn't quite hear you," she said, cupping her hand around her ear mockingly.

"I said thank you," Killian replied. "Don't push it."

Winter seemed satisfied and didn't. They drove several more blocks before she spoke again. "So, how *did* you manage to escape?" she asked. "I thought

I was going to have to run in and rescue you, but you managed to get out all on your own."

"I'm not exactly sure," Killian said, sitting up in his seat with a low groan of pain. "I somehow managed to morph the cuffs without touching them with my hands. I didn't know that was possible."

"Me neither," Winter replied. "That's impressive."

Killian looked at her, half-expecting a sarcastic smile in return. There wasn't one. Instead, her mouth was a thin line across her face. Her chestnut brown hair was tied back in a loose ponytail, and twin pistols were holstered on her thighs. She also had the sawn-off shotgun peeking out from a shoulder rig beneath her jacket. She had definitely been expecting much heavier resistance rescuing him. He found it touching and definitely surprising. "Thanks," he said again, much more sincerely this time.

She glanced over at him, the faintest of smiles crossing her lips before her brow narrowed and she nodded curtly. It was as though a mask had fallen back in place.

They didn't speak after that. Killian shut his eyes and passed the rest of the ride in a sort of recuperative coma. He woke when they pulled into the hotel parking lot, and she shook him awake. He felt his insides go queasy as she shook him, and he had to force himself not to be sick. He shook his head and motioned for her to wait while he choked it back down.

"Sorry," she said.

Killian shook his head again before climbing from the vehicle slowly. Winter came around the front of the vehicle and, despite his arguing, helped him over to the hotel room door. She leaned him against the wall as she pulled the keycard from her pocket, gave the door four short raps, and unlocked the door. It swung open before she could grab the handle.

Stamp stood there, staring at her. His eyes darted over to Killian. "Jesus Christ," he breathed. He grabbed Killian's arm and helped him into the darkened room.

Lucas was standing at the end of one of the beds. "Killian!" he exclaimed, running over, but Stamp halted him with a raised hand.

Winter kneeled beside Lucas. "Killian needs to rest, okay?" she said.

Lucas nodded solemnly. "Is he going to be okay?"

"He's going to be fine. He just needs some rest." She looked up at Stamp. "Should we call a healer?"

"No," Killian said. "No healers. I'm not trusting anyone from here on out."

"Fuckin' Frog," Stamp said angrily as he helped Killian over to the bed. Killian groaned in pain. "I knew we shouldn't have trusted him. That was so stupid, going to that meet like that. We know better. Spin taught us better than that."

Killian could only grunt in response. His body felt like pure death, much worse than when Chaser had removed the blood tracer from his system, and that was agony.

"He'll get his," Winter said. "We just have to think of some other way to get in contact with a Bloodhound."

"I'm not sure we should even try that again," Stamp said. "Look what happened to Killian."

"No, that's still the plan." He sat up in bed slowly and stared at them. His voice was hard and adamant. "Frog's going to tell us where to meet a Bloodhound, and then I'm going to cut out his heart," he said. His tone didn't leave room for debate.

Winter crossed her arms across her chest and sighed deeply. "I'll run out and get some painkillers. Where do they even sell medicine here?"

"You're better off getting a poultice, maybe a potion or two," Stamp said. "I'll go. You and Lucas stay here with him."

Winter nodded and cast a glance at Killian, but he was barely hanging onto consciousness. Lucas sat down on the edge of the bed beside him. Killian managed a faint smile in his direction before passing out again.

By the time Stamp returned with the potions, Killian was awake again, and Winter was helping him sip water from a plastic cup.

"How you feeling?" Stamp asked, carrying a brown paper sack beneath his arm.

"Like hammered shit," Killian replied. Though his voice was raspy and weak, he seemed much stronger, more alert. His mind was clearer and not so hazy with pain.

Stamp unloaded the contents of the bag onto the nightstand. He had picked up a cream poultice designed to cure all physical pain within an hour of application and three different kinds of potions. One was a muscle relaxant, another to heal bruises and cuts quickly, and the third was supposed to keep him alert and awake.

Winter helped Killian remove his shirt as Stamp unscrewed the top of the poultice jar. Killian didn't feel embarrassed having his shirt off in front of Winter; he was too tired. There was a collective gasp throughout the room, however, as they saw the full extent of his injuries. Almost his entire midsection was engulfed in a deep scarlet and yellow bruise. His left ribcage was also bruised, his disjointed ribs poking against the inside of his flesh

"God, they did a number on you," Stamp said. He handed the poultice jar to Winter, and she looked at Killian questioningly. He merely nodded in return, already clenching his teeth in anticipation. She dipped her fore and middle fingers into the jar and dabbed a clump of the poultice onto Killian's stomach. He immediately cringed—it was icy cold—and suppressed a groan of pain. She slowly began rubbing it in, trying to apply as little pressure as possible while still smearing it into his skin. She then applied some to his rib cage, and he actually barked out in pain, tears glistening in the corners of his eyes. He moaned a garbled curse and bit his lower lip.

When she was done, Winter set the poultice back on the nightstand and held out her hand for the muscle relaxant. Stamp handed it to her, but Killian shook his head, pushing it away.

"No, not the relaxant. Just the other two," he said.

"Killian, you need to let your body heal," Stamp said, but Killian shook his head again and waved for the other two. "I'm not taking a relaxant and getting all loopy. Frog's likely to move once he hears we made it out. I'm not letting him hop out of this."

Winter looked up at Stamp, and, after a drawn-out sigh, he nodded. She grabbed the healing potion instead and unscrewed the top, tipping it against his lips. He drank almost the entire bottle before he swallowed wrong and began to cough. Winter pulled the bottle back and waited for him to stop.

"Those sons-of-bitches," he sputtered out. He finally finished coughing, and Winter saw tears had formed in the corners of his eyes again. This time, they didn't appear to be from pain, however. "God damned assholes."

Several tears streaked across his cheeks. Winter had been wondering when it would finally come, when the reality of what had occurred would set in. He inhaled sharply in an effort to halt the tears, but several more trickled from the corners of his eyes.

Stamp and Lucas didn't say anything, and Stamp actually turned around pretending to look at something on the blank wall-screen. Winter set the potion bottle back down on the nightstand and leaned forward so her face was only a few inches from Killian's. She kept her voice low, barely a whisper.

"It's okay," she said in a surprisingly soothing voice. "It's over. You did great. You did so great."

Killian would have expected something like this from Skye or maybe Loop, not the woman he had hated so passionately just a few hours ago.

Another spiral of tears coursed down his cheeks, and she wiped them away with her thumb, continuing to speak soothing words. Finally, he managed to get himself back under control. He wiped his nose and eyes with the back of his hand, and Winter gave him the rest of the potion. Stamp remained silent the entire time.

"We're going to get them, Killian," Lucas said from the foot of the bed. "We're going to get them."

Killian nodded wearily and drank the energy potion without any further incident. Winter screwed the caps back onto the bottles and moved to stand when he caught her wrist. "Thank you," he finally said. He held her wrist firmly, and she knew it wasn't just for the compassionate words. It was for everything she had done. He had finally forgiven her for the safe house. Or at least as much as he was capable of right now.

Winter nodded, and he released her wrist. She walked over to the sink in the corner. She turned on the faucet and ran her hands beneath the water as if she was washing them, but they both knew she was trying to hide the tears threatening to overwhelm her as well. She had been suppressing the reality of her own situation and the loss of her team so much that she had almost forgotten. Helping Killian had almost been like saving one of her own. She splashed a handful of water across her face and stared into the mirror.

"So," she said, turning off the faucet and drying her face, "how are we going to handle this Frog character?"

The plan ended up being rather simple, and a few hours later, after Killian felt more like his old self, they loaded up and headed out. The poultice and potion combination turned out to be really effective. He still felt sore, like he had just been through a rugby match, but the bruises across his midsection and ribcage had faded substantially, and he had regained full range of motion, though his stomach still gave a twinge of pain whenever he twisted.

Stamp elected to drive, despite the fact he hated doing so, and Killian sat in the passenger seat, his shotgun resting between his knees. They were quiet as they drove through the city. The sun had disappeared beneath the horizon several hours before, and a twinkling night sky was overhead. Hardly any clouds obstructed the view, and the glimmering half-moon was bright and shiny.

They entered the neighborhood with a much different attitude than earlier that day, and the residents seemed to pick up on it. They all but averted their eyes as they drove past. Stamp stopped the car several houses away from Frog's and let Winter out. She pulled her pistols from her thighs and disappeared into the darkness of a nearby side yard. They drove up to Frog's and stopped the car at the foot of his driveway. A grey SUV was parked there.

"Looks like Frog has some company," Killian said. He climbed from the vehicle, the shotgun held aloft before him. He blasted the security camera above the door, tearing it to shreds, and then fired three more blasts at each of the door hinges and locks. Stamp walked up beside him, and, between the two of them, they were able to kick it clean away from the frame. It tipped forward into the gloomy confines of the house, and Stamp waved Lucas over to join them. He kept low and all but hugged Stamp's side, just as he had been instructed on the way over.

Killian moved through the house swiftly. He saw a shadow in the corner of the living room and blasted him as he drew his gun. Killian recognized him as one of Drift's cronies, his neck and forearm bandaged, which meant only one thing.

His theory was proven when he busted into the kitchen. Drift stood next to Frog, their hands already raised. Winter stood behind them, her guns trained on the back of their heads. The other remaining bounty hunter lay at her feet.

Damn she moves fast, Killian thought before Stamp walked in and called the house clear.

"You sons-of-bitches, have you lost your minds?" Frog said in his normal croaky voice.

Killian had never heard a more annoying sound. "No, but you did when you set us up to get ambushed," he said. He wasn't sure who he wanted to kill more right then.

Drift stared at him with a stony expression. He was obviously not used to being on the receiving end of this sort of thing and wasn't sure how react. Frog sputtered angrily, his beady eyes bouncing between them. "I'll make sure every news station in the world gets a picture of your faces," he continued to say. "There won't be a place you can hide. I'll shut down the airport. I'll kill every boat in the harbor. You won't be able to move without…"

Killian pulled the trigger and blasted Drift in the shin. He hit the floor immediately and screamed in pain.

"What… What…" Frog obviously wasn't sure what to say. The Killian he had known wouldn't shoot an unarmed man he held dead-to-rights.

"He was blocking my line of sight," Killian explained. Frog looked between Killian and Drift, his mouth hanging open and his twin chins jiggling in fear. Drift writhed on the floor and continued to scream and curse.

"Now hold on just a second," Frog said. "You can't do this. I control every network in the city. If I die, every informant in the city dies with me. You need me."

"I don't need shit except a Bloodhound's name and where to meet him. How quick you give me that determines how quick I let you die."

Frog could see by the look in Killian's eye that he wasn't bluffing. His hands were stock-still, and the barrel of the shotgun didn't give the slightest tremor. "I'm not giving you shit unless you promise to let me live," Frog said.

"Stamp, take Lucas into the next room," Killian said, his voice surprisingly calm. Stamp looked uncertain; he had never seen this side of Killian but nodded and led him outside regardless. Killian turned to look at Winter. "You got him?"

She nodded and Killian stepped over. Frog was practically vibrating in his seat. Killian raised the shotgun and slammed the stock across Frog's knee. He screamed in pain and clutched his knee. Saliva flew from his mouth, and Killian stepped back.

"You don't bargain!" he yelled. "You sold me out! You sold Stamp out! You owed us more than that!"

"I'm sorry. The money was too good," Frog cried. Tears were flooding his cheeks and dripping across his t-shirt. "They offered me half the reward if I sent you their way. I'm so sorry!"

Killian stepped forward and shoved his shotgun across Frog's throat, forcing his head back, so he looked up into Killian's face.

"Are you sorry about what happened to Spin? Huh? Are you?" Killian was screaming at the top of his lungs.

"Yes, yes," Frog continued to cry. "I'm sorry for what happened to Spin. I didn't think he would actually take it."

Killian pulled the rifle back suddenly, all but lurching backward. "What? What did you say?"

"Nothing, I'm sorry," Frog sputtered, keying in on what he had said. "I'm hurting. I don't know what I'm saying."

"No, what did you say? What do you mean you didn't think he would take it? Why the fuck would you give him a tip if you didn't think he would take it?"

Killian pointed the shotgun at his head, the gears in his mind turning quickly.

Frog was openly sobbing now. Killian had shattered his kneecap. He would be lucky if he ever walked right again.

"I'm going to break your other kneecap if you don't tell me what the fuck you meant!" Killian barked. Winter still had her guns trained on both Frog and Drift, though the latter had passed out from pain and blood loss. Killian wasn't concerned.

"They paid me," Frog finally sputtered out.

"For what?" Killian brought the shotgun barrel a few inches closer to his face, his finger tightening across the trigger in anticipation.

"To give him the tip. They said he was too good and was killing the competition. So they paid me to tell him about the resort and make it sound like a cakewalk."

"Who?" Killian asked, his voice sharp and rigid.

"I don't know. It was all anonymous." Killian brought the shotgun even closer to Frog's face, his finger a twitch away from pulling the trigger. Frog flinched back. He could feel the heat radiating off the end of the barrel. "I swear! They never told me. Everything was done remotely, backdoor email accounts and such. I never knew!"

Killian stepped back, hardly able to believe what he was hearing. All this time, he had thought it had just been an accident, a mistake on their parts. He had never thought someone might have orchestrated the whole thing. His stomach almost bottomed out.

"Why didn't they just kill him? Why didn't they just kill both of us?" he asked. His tone had flattened completely.

"They said it had to look like an accident. If they killed him outright, too many people would start asking questions. I guess they thought you would just leave the business if you made it out alive." Frog finally managed to get the tears to stop and sat up in his seat. "I'm sorry, Killian. I really am. The money was just too good. It was never personal."

Killian's eyes shot up toward his at that and before he knew what he was doing, he raised the shotgun back up and blasted him in the face. The chair pitched backward from the force of the gunshot and blood splattered the wall behind him. Winter watched flabbergasted, her mouth hanging open as she stared at him. Killian stood there with the gun still raised, his mind barely able to catch up. His heart hammered within his chest.

"Killian, the Bloodhound," Winter exclaimed, finding her voice. Killian blinked, then looked down at Frog's dead body.

"Shit," he said. "Shit, shit, shit!"

He dropped his shotgun onto the kitchen counter and pulled the keyboard from the small drawer in the desk. He ran a search on one of the monitors for Frog's list of contacts. It took several minutes of searching before he finally managed to dig it up amidst the plethora of other files and data logs. Frog had information on nearly everyone and everything, but he didn't have time to look through it all. He found the list of contacts. It had over three hundred names and phone numbers listed on it but no job titles. Killian printed it off, grabbed it up off the printer, and tucked it into his jacket before thinking of something else. He typed furiously at the keyboard, some of the keys sticky with blood, and ran a search for Spin's name. It came up with only one thing, an email sent to an address that was no longer active. It had only one line of text on it: *"The deal is done. He took the bait."*

Killian instantly felt a fresh wave of anger erupt within his chest, and he wished he could kill Frog all over again. He pounded his fist against the desk.

"Killian, someone probably heard the shots and called the cops. We need to get out of here," Winter said.

"Yeah, right," Killian said, the fire in his chest burning out almost as fast as it had erupted. He suddenly felt ten years older. He grabbed a rag from the kitchen, as immaculate as ever, and wiped his fingerprints from the keyboard and the shotgun. He dropped it on the ground beside Drift after making sure it was empty. He would let the police come up with their own theories, hopefully leading them off his trail for a few days.

"What do you want to do about him?" Winter asked, indicating Drift. Blood had pooled around his leg and darkened the hardwood floor. "Sure you want to leave him alive?"

"No, but I've done enough killing today," Killian said. "We got what we came for. Let's just get out of here."

He turned and walked out of the kitchen, through the living room, and outside to Lucas and Stamp. He heard a single muffled gunshot come from inside before Winter joined them as well, not saying a word about it. Killian knew she had killed Drift, maybe to keep him from talking to the police or maybe just to ease his passing since Killian was pretty sure he was going to bleed out before the police arrived anyway. Regardless, he didn't mention it and neither did she. Lucas looked at them uncertainly but seemed to sense it was best to keep quiet.

They all loaded back up into the car and drove away, passing a group of speeding police cars along the way. They didn't stop as they drove past, and a few minutes later, they couldn't hear the sirens anymore. Killian stared down at his hands and the blood he would never be able to wash off them. Sure, he had killed before, but this time had been different. It hadn't been self-defense or an act of necessity. It had been murder, plain and simple, and regardless of reasons or justification, he was now a killer. He wondered what Spin would think of him.

"Somebody set Spin up to die," Killian said, finally looking up from his hands. "The resort, the hunt, it was all a setup."

"What? Who set it up?" Stamp asked, looking over at him in pure shock. He barely managed to keep his eyes on the road.

"I don't know," Killian said, looking out the window at the vast expanse of lights around them. "But when this is all over, I'm going to find out."

CHAPTER 22

Bird's Eye View

It took hours of cold calling numbers on the list before they finally got in contact with a Bloodhound. His name was Hawk, and it took some convincing (plus an extra 20 percent on top of his usual rate) for him to agree to meet them the next day. Killian could have kissed Winter when she said she had finally found the right number.

"I don't always cold call numbers, but when I do, I make sure I call every single one before finding the right one," she said. She chuckled, but Stamp and Killian didn't join her.

"That must be an American thing," Killian said, glancing at Stamp.

"Oh, come on. I know you were born in the 90s. You *have* to know what I'm talking about," Winter said.

"Not a clue," Stamp said. Killian shook his head as well. Winter rolled her eyes and laid back on the bed.

Killian sank down onto the bed beside her, trying to force a smile onto his face. He couldn't stop thinking about what Frog had said and what he did to him in return. Even while running down the names on the list, his mind had been preoccupied by it. His hands felt like they were slick with blood, and he constantly found himself wringing them out with water in an effort to clean it off. He wondered if he would ever feel clean again.

"You alright?" Winter asked lowly. Killian nodded, but the forlorn look in his eye prevented her from believing him. She sat up. "I would have done the same thing if I had been in your shoes. Almost anyone would have."

Killian nodded, though he hardly felt reassured. Sure, he had gone there with every intention of killing Frog, but now that he had actually done it, especially so easily and without hesitation, he felt sick to his stomach. He had known Frog for years. Hell, Spin had often referred to him as a friend, and Killian killed him. Gunned him down in front of the same workstation where he had provided them so many job and tips. Of course, it was also the same workstation where he had set them up.

"So what time's the meet?" Stamp asked, leaning against the dresser on the far side of the room.

"Three o'clock," Winter replied, "which means we can get some sleep tonight and move out fresh tomorrow."

Stamp nodded. "Does anyone mind if I catch the shower first?"

Killian and Winter both shook their heads. Lucas shrugged his shoulders. Stamp dug some clothes out the bag they were all sharing (Winter had bought them each a few outfits earlier that day) and walked into the bathroom. They heard the shower come on a few seconds later.

Killian sat on the bed, not really looking at either of them. Lucas looked like he wanted to say something but for once was at a loss for words. Winter let the silence hang until it grew uncomfortable before moving and turning on the tiny wall-screen.

"I'm going outside," Killian said, and stood up from the bed as she turned it on. He didn't pay the news broadcast a second glance as he snatched his jacket off the dresser and headed outside. He closed the door behind him before Winter could respond.

The inky night sky was still bright with twinkling stars, and Killian stared at the shining moon overhead. Not too long ago, it would have meant hunting a vampire or a pack of ghouls. Now it was just a reminder of how drastically his life had changed.

He walked to the corner of the building and stared down the street. It was nearly empty of traffic. Only the occasional car buzzed past. It all seemed like a lifetime ago, hunting werewolves and killing vampires with Stamp and Spin, teaching the occasional lesson at Skye's academy, and dating Daisy with the thought of marrying her one day.

Spin taught him many things. He taught him how to kill vampires and ghouls, werewolves, and skin-walkers. He taught him how to survive in a world wrought with new mysteries every day. He taught him about loyalty and always watching out for those who watched out for him. Spin's teachings kept Killian from running for the hills now. But Spin never taught him how to deal with this kind of loss, both physical and emotional. Killian suspected it was because he himself had never learned to deal with it. It probably had been a contributing factor to why he dropped his guard around the little girl in the resort. Some part of him had wanted it to be his own daughter, so much so it blinded him from the truth.

Killian sighed and stretched his arms above his head. Everything had changed. Daisy was with Stamp, Skye's academy was gone and she was God-only-knew where now, and Spin was dead. On top of that, his actions had led to alienating every contact in his book and to Loop getting shot. Killian suddenly wished he could punch something. His mind was a whirlwind, and he couldn't get the rollercoaster of emotions to stop.

The door to the manager's office opened nearby, and a young girl walked out carrying a stack of white bath towels. She had dark skin and long black hair. A pale frilly dress flowed down to her knees, and she wore white leggings underneath. She smiled at him as she rounded the corner and walked past him. Killian managed a slight nod in response, his mind a million miles away.

"I know who you are," she said in a small, dreamy voice. Killian spun around and saw her standing there, staring at him.

"What did you say?" he asked.

"I said I know who you are." A look of surprise flashed across Killian's face. "Don't worry, I'm not going to turn you in," she quickly reassured him. "I know you're not a bad man. My mom hasn't made the connection—she doesn't really watch the news—but I recognized you right away. I'm good like that, with faces I mean. I can tell when a person is lying or if they've done bad things. I know you didn't do the things they say you did."

Killian looked at her questioningly, more than a little confused. "Who are you?"

"Acela. My mom owns the hotel," she replied.

"Oh," was all Killian managed to get out.

"Don't worry. I just wanted you to know your secret's safe with me and that if anyone comes looking for you, I'll make sure my mom leads them away."

"Why would you do that?" Killian asked. "You don't even know me. Maybe I am what they say."

Acela merely shook her head in response, smiling brightly. "No, I can tell. You're not one of the bad ones."

She turned to head up the nearby steps but stopped and looked back at him again. "That boy you're with, you're helping him, huh?" Killian nodded slowly and she smiled again. "Good. He needs friends. I can tell."

Again Killian could only nod in response. A second later, a woman's voice called Acela's name. Her mother.

"Coming!" she called back. She smiled again and waved goodbye. "Well, see you."

"Thanks," Killian said, halting her at the base of the steps. She nodded and flashed another smile before jogging up.

She was halfway to the top when she suddenly halted and called back, "If he ever needs another friend, I'm around."

With that, she was gone.

Killian rubbed the bridge of his nose. It seemed Lucas wasn't the only one who needed a friend. He debated leaving but decided he would rather a lonely teenage girl make the connection than a sleazebag at the next place. They would stay here for now.

A few minutes later, Winter stepped out of the room and walked over, her hands jammed in her jacket pockets.

"Who were you talking to?" she asked.

"The owner's daughter. She's nice," he said.

A worried look crossed her face, but she didn't say anything about it. "You okay?" she asked instead after a moment.

"No, but I will be," Killian answered. He knew it was stupid to take a young girl's word for it, but maybe he wasn't one of the bad ones. He was just forced to do some very bad things. He snorted lowly, suddenly wondering how many convicted murderers had said that same thing before they went to prison.

"There's something I've been meaning to say to you. I should've said it a while ago," Winter said. Killian looked at her expectantly and could tell she was a little uneasy about it.

"Thank you," she finally managed to get out after a long breath, "for stopping after the ambush at the safe house. You had every reason not to, but you did anyway, and I've pretty much made you regret it every minute since."

Killian blinked at her. He wasn't sure what he had been expecting, but that definitely wasn't it. He rubbed the back of his neck.

"Um, yeah, no problem."

"You going to be out here much longer?" she asked.

"For a little while, yeah," he replied, looking back up at the night sky.

"Mind if I join you?"

"Be my guest," he said.

Winter stepped up beside him, her hands still jammed into her jacket pockets, and stared up at the night sky as well.

"So," she began, more than a little awkwardly. They had never really had a normal conversation before and neither was sure where to even start. "Terrorists, huh?"

Killian looked at her with the hint of a smile tugging at the corners of his mouth. It was the first real one since leaving for Frog's.

"Don't think that just because you saved my life you're off the hook. I still hate you," he said.

"I still hate you too," she replied. "But, like it or not, we're stuck in this together so we better make the best of it."

Killian looked at her, really looked at her since that first time at the club, and saw just how beautiful she was. The way the moonlight gleamed off her pale skin, giving it an almost surreal glow. Her eyes were like jade orbs that twinkled almost as brightly as the stars overhead.

"That's the smartest thing I've heard you say all day," he said, and once again, the mask was lifted for just a second as she smiled lightly.

Hawk had agreed to meet them in a bar a few blocks from Neutral Bay. As they drove toward it, they smelled the saltwater coming off the tide and heard the horns of the sea traffic. Stamp agreed to stay with Lucas at the hotel, so Killian and Winter made the trip to the bar alone. They didn't talk much the majority of the way. Killian had had a very restless night of sleep and was still feeling more than a little battered. The bruises had come back in force, and his whole body felt like putty. He let Winter drive and she was more than willing. Killian got the impression she was used to taking the lead, and, right now, he wasn't about to argue. He was done being in charge.

They parked in the narrow parking lot next to the bar, and, at a glance from Winter, Killian pulled on the baseball cap, making sure the brim was low enough to shade his eyes. He checked the pistol tucked into his pants before climbing out of the car and joining Winter. They walked around to the front of the bar and stepped in.

It smelled of peanuts and stale beer. It wasn't a dive, but it wasn't exactly upscale either. Killian also detected the acrid scent of turpentine, which meant they were more than likely brewing their own alcohol. A pool table was in the back, flanked by a wall of red leather booths. A long wooden bar rested on the opposite wall. Hundreds of bottles were racked behind it. There were only a few patrons, and the bartender was busying himself cleaning up behind the bar. A man with bright red hair sat in the corner booth closest to the door and eyed them wearily as they walked in. Hawk. Killian could tell by his long pointed nose and his hardened gaze at everything.

He nodded to Winter, and they walked over. Hawk raised his hand to halt them when they were a few feet away.

"That's far enough. I know who you are. I'm not helping a known terrorist," he said. Killian and Winter exchanged glances.

"Terrorist?" Winter asked, putting on her best confused expression. "Who exactly are you talking about?"

"Him," Hawk said, regarding Killian coldly. "He's the one that blew up that bridge and shot up that club. I don't know how you convinced Frog to give you my number, but I'd recommend you lose it. Jackal, see them out."

A large man rose from the booth behind him, hidden by the bench's high back, and ushered them toward the door.

"Come on, we're willing to pay you. We already agreed to 20 percent above your normal rate," Killian tried to argue. Jackal, however, stood in front of him and blocked his path. Since he was at least a foot wider and a head taller, it didn't leave much room for persuasion. He grabbed him by the arm and wrenched him back forcefully.

"I'm not a terrorist," Killian said angrily, struggling against his grip. "I'm just trying to find someone."

"Your next target?" Hawk asked from over Jackal's shoulder.

"I'm not a damn terrorist!" Killian barked, and actually managed to slip from Jackal's grasp. Before he could think better of it, he punched him hard across the jaw. Jackal fell a step backward before he moved to seize Killian around the throat.

"Hold on," Hawk said suddenly. Jackal practically froze, his arms still extended toward Killian's neck. "Not many people have the balls to hit Jackal once they see how big he is. You must really lose it when people call you a terrorist."

"Only when people call me something I'm not," Killian said, taking a step away from Jackal's reaching hands.

"Fine, you're not a terrorist. You're not looking for your next target," Hawk said, his voice dripping with sarcasm. "Who are you looking for then? Jackal, go ahead and step aside. I can't see them."

Jackal did as commanded and stood beside the booth, folding his arms across his chest.

"The assholes who are trying to kill me," Killian answered.

"Isn't that everyone in the city right now?" Hawk asked. There was obviously meant to be some humor in his question, but his face remained expressionless.

"Very funny. I'm talking about the people who started this whole thing. I want to find them so I clear my damn name," Killian replied. Beside him, Winter kept silent. It was obvious everything banked on whether or not

Hawk believed him.

Several seconds ticked past. Time seemed to move in slow motion before Hawk finally spoke again. "Who am I to get in the way of such a noble cause?" he asked. He motioned to the bench across from him. "Take a seat."

Killian and Winter both breathed sighs of relief, and Killian sank into the booth. Winter remained standing. Her eyes drew toward Jackal. He stood rigidly, waiting for instructions.

"Thank you," Killian said.

"The money and the item, please," Hawk said curtly. Killian dug the bullet cartridge out of his pocket. It was zipped in a plastic bag. Winter pulled a pouch from her jacket and dropped it onto the table. Hawk weighed it with his hand, seemed to be satisfied, and picked up the plastic bag. He stared at it for several seconds. "Here's how this is going to work. I take the item and the money, and I call when I've found the location of whoever handled it last."

"Well, that'd be me," Killian interjected.

"What?"

"I handled it last, when I dug it out of the wall," he explained.

"Great, makes my job that much easier," Hawk replied, his voice dripping with sarcasm once again.

"You can still do it, right?" Winter asked.

"I don't charge as much as I do for my good looks," Hawk replied. "Of course I can still do it. It's just going to take a little more time. I'm also going to need something with your scent so I don't pick up the wrong trail. The hat will work."

Killian pulled it off without argument and tossed it onto the table. He would be glad to be rid of it.

"Anyway, as I was saying, I'll call you when I've got an address. After that, I'm not responsible for what happens. We won't speak again unless you want to hire me again. Don't even try until you've got your name cleared. Got it?"

"So you just take the money, and we wait for your call?" Killian asked, with more than a little uncertainly.

"That's the deal. Take it or leave it. I don't work on faith."

"But we're supposed to pay on faith?" Killian asked skeptically.

"Be happy I'm willing to do it at all. I could lose my head just for talking to you, much less helping you out. Take it or leave it."

"We'll take it," Winter said before Killian could argue any further. She scrawled a phone number down on one of the cocktail napkins and handed it to him. "Call us there. Any time."

She practically pulled Killian from the booth and dragged him toward the door by one arm.

"Cute pet by the way," Killian said with a pointed look at Jackal before Winter forcefully pulled him out the door.

"You must really enjoy getting your ass kicked," she said as they strode back to the car. "That guy would have put you through the floor."

"I can handle myself," Killian said. "I don't need you babysitting me."

"Are we really doing this again?" Winter asked. "I know you can handle yourself. I've seen you handle yourself, remember? I would just really rather you didn't have to."

That took Killian by surprise. He had been expecting an argument, not a pseudo-compliment. He was still wondering about it when they pulled out of the parking lot and headed back to the hotel. Did she actually care about him?

CHAPTER 23

Waiting

Killian's eyes continually drifted over in Winter's direction the entire ride back to the hotel. For whatever reason, her words had really struck a chord in him. There was just something about the way she had said it, as if she had admitted she actually cared about him. Given the way they had treated each other over the past two days, it came as a bit of a surprise. Killian forced his eyes forward as they pulled into the hotel parking lot and tried to push it from his mind.

"So you want to tell me why you were staring at me the entire ride back?" Winter asked as they climbed out of the car. Killian froze.

"Oh, um, no reason," he tried to answer. It sounded hollow even to him. She didn't look convinced.

"Uh-huh," she responded.

They went to their hotel room, and Killian unlocked the door, keeping his eyes away from hers. They entered and Killian immediately got a bad feeling in the pit of his stomach. Lucas and Stamp were not inside. Their beds had been made up, and all their gear was still splayed out around the room, but they were gone.

Killian drew his gun instinctively and checked the bathroom. Winter searched around the room.

"They're at the pool," she suddenly called.

"What?"

Killian walked back out of the bathroom, and she handed him a scrap of paper. *Went to the pool* was scrawled out in Stamp's neat handwriting.

"I didn't even know this place had a pool. Did you?" Killian asked. Winter shook her head.

They walked back out of the room and turned the corner toward the manager's office. When they walked in, the bell above the door gave a jingle.

"Be out in a minute," a female voice called from the back room. Killian and Winter stood there waiting at the counter. A few seconds later, a tall, pretty, black woman strode out of the back room. She smelled of laundry detergent and bleach. Killian saw the resemblance immediately. Acela was a spitting image of her mother.

"Can I help you?" she asked.

"Yeah, where is the pool?" Killian asked.

"It's on the backside of Building C," she answered. A smile suddenly split her face. "Oh, you're that couple looking after your nephew. My daughter told me all about you. She said you would be stopping by when you got back."

"Uh, yeah," Killian said, managing a smile in return.

"They're all over at the pool right now. That boy is really sweet." Killian and Winter both nodded. "Well, I wish I could stay and chat, but I've got to finish this laundry. No one told me when I opened this place it would be so much work. Is there anything else I can do for you two?"

"No. Thank you," Killian said and, with another smile, she disappeared back into the adjoining room.

Killian and Winter walked back out. "Has Stamp lost his mind?" she asked. "He knows better than to have Lucas out in the open like this."

"Let's just go make sure they're alright, honey," Killian replied. She shot him a narrow glance in return. He of course recognized the dangers of it, but he also knew Lucas was a kid. He needed to get out sometimes and just have some fun.

They walked the short distance to Building C and saw there was indeed a sparkling blue pool on the other side. Stamp was sitting on a lawn chair on the side while Lucas and Acela swam around. It was obvious she was teaching him as she demonstrated how to float on her back. Despite his amazing magical abilities, Lucas seemed to be having a rough time with it.

Killian and Winter opened the white metal gate and walked into the pool area. Stamp stood as they walked over. He was still fully dressed, but he had kicked off his shoes and socks, standing barefoot in front of them.

"There you guys are," he said. "How did it go?"

"About as expected," Killian replied.

"Care to explain this?" Winter asked.

"That girl, Acela, came by the room a little while ago, said she'd met you last night and asked if Lucas and I wanted to go swimming. I was going to say no, but Lucas had pretty much already accepted. I knew if I didn't let him, he was just going to try to sneak out anyway. Figured at least this way I can still keep an eye on him.

"He needs this," Stamp added.

Winter looked like she wanted to argue—she obviously didn't approve —but Killian spoke up before she could. "You're right," he said, looking over at Lucas and seeing how happy he was. He was laughing and looked like any other kid right then. "He does need it."

Killian cast a sidelong glance at Winter and, after a moment, she nodded begrudgingly. She sat down on one of the canvas chairs, staring around like a sentry. "What's the matter? Don't feel like going for a swim?" Killian asked, looking at her amusedly.

"You can't hide a gun in a swimsuit," she responded curtly.

"I don't know about that. I do alright," he said slyly.

She looked at him sharply, and he tried to keep the smile from forming across his lips. "You're an idiot," she said. There was no hostility in her voice, however, and Killian could tell her attitude was forced.

"Killian, you're back!" Lucas suddenly called from the water.

"Yeah, I'm back," he responded, casting another sidelong glance at Winter before walking to the edge of the pool. "Having fun?"

"Yeah. Acela has been teaching me how to swim. I'm not very good yet, but she said no one learns to swim in a day."

"She's a smart girl. Just be careful, all right? There are still people out looking for you," Killian replied.

"I know, I know. Thanks," he said, wading back to Acela. She smiled at Killian, and he nodded appreciatively. Stamp was right. Lucas needed to be a kid sometimes, and he could tell Acela was just looking for a friend.

"So how *did* it go?" Stamp asked when he walked back over to the row of lawn chairs and sat down.

"He's going to call with an address," Killian replied. "Should probably be a day or two."

"I meant how did it go with you two?" Stamp said, looking between him and Winter. He kept his voice low, so she couldn't hear. "I notice neither of you is trying to shoot laser beams out of your eyes anymore. That's a good sign."

"You got me," Killian replied honestly. "One second, we hate each other. The next, we're almost friends."

"Almost?"

Killian shrugged his shoulders. He glanced over at Winter and saw her eyes continually draw back to the pool longingly.

"She's more human than she likes to let on," he said. "I think she just doesn't like people knowing it."

"Can you really blame her?" Stamp asked, glancing at her as well.

Killian shook his head. A moment later, he stood up and pulled off his jacket. After unbuckling his shoulder holster and setting it down on the chair, he yanked off his shirt as well.

"What are you doing?" Stamp asked.

"Going for a swim. Lucas isn't the only one who's been through a lot the past few days," Killian responded. He kicked off his boots and socks, and set the gun tucked into his belt on the chair as well.

Without saying anything further, he ran over to the side of the pool and dove in. As soon as the cool water hit him, everything from the past week seemed to fade away. All his worries, all his pains and aches, evaporated from his body, and all that remained was the water around him.

He broke the surface with a sharp exhale. He was still wearing his jeans, and, although they constricted his legs somewhat, he was able to swim around pretty easily. He looked up and saw Winter staring at him with a surprised expression on her face. Her mouth was hanging slightly open.

"What's the matter? Never seen a man with his shirt off before?" Killian asked.

"Never seen a man so stupid," she responded sourly. She looked back toward the buildings, and Killian just snorted.

He paddled over to Lucas and Acela. They were both smiling widely. Lucas bounced up and down, the tips of his toes barely grazing the bottom of the pool.

"Killian, you can swim?" he asked.

"Of course I can," Killian replied. "And Acela and I are going to teach you."

Lucas exclaimed excitedly. They spent the next few hours swimming around and teaching him how to float, the basic breaststroke, and the doggy paddle. He struggled and failed miserably several times throughout the day, but he refused to give up, and Killian was genuinely proud of him when he managed to make it to the other side of the pool without assistance. He looked up toward the edge of the pool and saw Stamp smiling proudly as well, and even Winter looked pleased. She dodged his gaze, however, when she noticed he was looking at her.

As the sun began to set, they climbed out of the pool and wrapped themselves in heavy towels. Killian shivered and Lucas looked waterlogged, but he was smiling all around.

"Thanks so much for teaching me," he said to Acela.

"Of course. It was fun. Hardly anyone uses to pool anymore," she replied. "My mom's going to be wondering where I am, though, so I better get going. I can't believe she let me go this long."

Lucas nodded, and she waved goodbye. He stared after her retreating form until she disappeared around the side of the building.

Killian looked down at Lucas amusedly. He knew right away Lucas had a crush. He spared him the embarrassment, however, and decided not to say anything. Gathering up their gear, they headed back to the hotel room.

They smelled of chlorine; Killian and Lucas desperately needed showers.

He let Lucas go first as he continued to dry himself off. When he had disappeared into the bathroom and they heard the shower running, Killian turned to Winter and prepared for the impending verbal thrashing.

Surprisingly, there wasn't one.

"I hope you two know what you're doing," she said simply as she sat down on one of the beds and pulled her shoes off.

Killian and Stamp shared momentarily looks of confusion before Stamp replied, "I hope so too."

The call came early the next morning. The sun was just barely peeking over the horizon, and tiny snippets of light were coming through the edges of the thick curtains. Stamp and Lucas were still asleep, murmuring softly, but Killian and Winter were both wide awake. They had been tossing and turning all night. Winter snatched up the phone almost immediately, trying not to wake Lucas, and pressed it to her ear. A moment later, she grabbed a piece of paper from the nightstand and copied down the address. After a quick word of thanks, she hung up.

"They're in the Rocks," she said quietly.

"That complicates things," he said, suppressing a groan of dismay. It was a very upscale district of the city. She nodded.

Neither said anything else as they rolled back over and tried to go to sleep. Just like the rest of the night, however, it eluded them.

When the alarm went off at 9:00 a.m., Lucas and Stamp awoke feeling rested and refreshed. Killian and Winter both felt like the walking dead.

Every time either of them had tried to relax into a slumber, they relived their respective nightmares. Killian was either jumping into the canyon, the words replaying in his head, or running down a street and seeing his mother get trampled to death. Winter was too scared of reliving what had happened to her team. She couldn't close her eyes for more than a few seconds without it flashing across her mind. If only she had thought to get a potion that allowed them dreamless sleep; then maybe they could get a full night of rest.

"You look like shit," Stamp said as he dressed.

Killian shot him a look and told him about the address.

"It would be in the Rocks," Stamp replied, understanding the implications of it as well. Higher class meant higher security, more cops. He looked up at the ceiling and let out a long exhale.

"It's smart," Killian said. "They're hiding in plain sight, and there's no way we're dumb enough to come after them there."

"They obviously don't know us very well," Stamp replied, the corners of his mouth tweaking upward.

"Still, it might be good to leave Lucas here," Killian said. "I don't want to have to keep an eye on him while we're doing this. It's going to be risky enough taking them head-on."

"Good point. Who's going to watch him, though? There's no way I'm sitting this one out."

They looked over at Winter, and she immediately began shaking her head. "No way. Those assholes killed my whole team. There's no way I'm staying behind."

"I can stay here by myself," Lucas piped up. "I already told you I can handle it."

Killian wanted to say no, but they were kind of stuck between a rock and a hard place. They really didn't have much choice.

"We could ask Acela to keep an eye on him. She seems smart enough," Stamp suggested.

Killian looked over at Lucas and saw he was already nodding his head in agreement. He glanced at Winter unsurely. "What do you think?"

"I think this has bad news written all over it," she replied, "but if none of us is willing to stay behind, we really don't have much choice. If this works, we won't have to worry about anyone watching him ever again."

Killian nodded, though uncertainty was still splashed across his face.

"I'll go ask her," Stamp said and headed out. Lucas joined him, obviously excited to see his crush again. Killian and Winter both exchanged concerned glances after the door was shut behind them.

"You really think this is a good idea?" Killian asked.

"No, but like I said, what choice do we have? We need to take out the

Prime Magi if Lucas is ever going to be safe. It's going to take all three of us, if we're lucky, and we can't be worrying about him while we're inside. I don't like it, but it's our only real option, and I doubt this girl would turn him over."

"I'm more worried about them being here alone if any of the Magi come looking for him," said Killian.

"Look, it's been two days since we've moved over here. If they haven't come looking for him by now, I doubt they're going to." A bit of sharpness leaked into her voice, and Killian could tell she was trying to contain it.

"I know you really care about him," she added. "We're going to get them. We're going to finish this."

Killian nodded. He picked his gun up off the nightstand and tucked it into the back of his pants. Summing up his courage, he turned back to look at her, noticing again how truly beautiful she was.

"I know we've had our differences the past few days, but I really do appreciate your help in all this. Maybe when this is all over, we could..." He trailed off at the look in her eye.

"I don't think that's a good idea, Killian," she said. "What you're feeling, it's natural. I saved your life and now you feel like we have something. Trust me when I say that isn't the case. We just need to get this done and then things can go back to normal. We can go back to our lives and forget any of this ever happened. Okay?"

Killian couldn't even nod in response. He just stared at her. Her response had come so quickly; it was almost as if she had been rehearsing it. Was he that obvious, that detestable, she had felt the need to rehearse it so there wouldn't be any argument?

Before he could say anything, the door opened, and Stamp and Lucas walked back in. "She says she needs to take care of a few things and then she said she can look after him," Stamp said. Lucas looked positively gleeful.

"Good," Winter said, and Killian finally managed to get his head working. He nodded.

Stamp noticed the strange look in his eye but didn't say anything. He waited until Winter had gone into the bathroom to take a shower before walking over to him, making sure to keep his voice down. "You alright?" he asked.

"Fine. Why?"

"Because you look like someone just throat-punched you. You sure you're okay with leaving Lucas behind?"

Killian made sure to keep his eyes from Stamp's. "It's not that. I'm fine. Let's just get this done. Then everything can go back to normal."

Stamp stared at him quizzically for several long seconds before nodding. He set to checking his gear and Killian did the same.

Winter was right. It was a bad idea. Hell, less than a day ago, he had hated her guts. What the hell was the matter with him, thinking it would be a good idea to get involved with someone now? He pushed it from his mind as best he could and, when she walked out of the shower drying her hair, regarded her with the same neutral expression he reserved for drying paint. She noticed, but chose not to say anything, and began gearing up.

And forget any of this ever happened, Killian repeated internally. She would definitely be the first thing he tried to forget.

CHAPTER 24

Tumbling Rocks

The address Hawk had given them turned out to be a very fancy, luxurious hotel. A tall steel and glass tower, it looked out over the harbor and the opera house across the water. Private balconies stretched across the length of the building. Bellhops stood ready outside the front doors, and valets drove the guests' cars around to the private parking garage beneath the building. The guests themselves were definitely upper class, sporting expensive suits and fine jewelry. The lobby sported plush rugs and decadent furniture, all situated beneath a grand, sparkly chandelier that cast a dazzling glow across the whole room. The receptionists behind the check-in desks were well dressed and wore broad smiles, answering every question with cheerful voices. Security cameras watched everything, and a small detachment of guards rotated around, covering the angles the cameras couldn't.

"If you wanted a place to hide, this is definitely it," Killian said, staring at the building from across the street.

"How in the hell are we going to get inside? Better yet, how are we going to find them? There's got to be a hundred rooms in this place, and that Bloodhound didn't tell us which one," Stamp said.

Winter didn't say anything. She simply sat there staring out the car window, a quizzical look on her face. Suddenly, she popped open her door and got out.

"Where are you going?" Killian asked.

"I'm going to go find out what room they're staying in," she answered. She unbuttoned the top several buttons of her shirt to reveal a fair bit of cleavage and shook her hair from its ponytail. It fell across her shoulders. Killian forced himself not to stare at her.

"You know the receptionist won't tell you where they're staying; it's against policy. Plus, we don't even have a name," Stamp said.

"Don't need a name," Winter answered, adjusting her bra, so she looked at least a cup size larger. "And I'm not asking the receptionist."

She turned and walked across the street. She added a sensuous sway to her hips and thrust her chest out. They watched as she strode up to the bellhop standing by the door and began speaking to him. He looked young, even from this far away, and he smiled broadly when she walked up to him. They couldn't hear what she was saying, but she was laughing and smiling a lot, and the bellhop tried everything he could to keep his eyes away from her chest.

"What do you think she's saying?" Stamp asked.

"I'll blow you for some info," Killian answered flatly. Stamp looked over at him, and Killian shrugged his shoulders. "No idea."

"So you guys are back to hating each other?"

"Nope. We're being civil," Killian replied, and Stamp could hear the acidity in his voice. Before he could ask about it, however, Winter touched the bellhop's arm, thanked him, and began walking back to the car.

"Room 517," she said as she climbed back into the car. She pulled her hair back into a ponytail.

"How did you find that out?" Stamp asked.

"Told him I was looking for my boyfriend and was trying to find out what room he and his fraternity buddies are staying in so I could break up with him. Said he'd be able to recognize him by the dumbass trench coats he and his frat brothers always wore."

"That worked?" Stamp asked incredulously as she fixed her bra and buttoned her shirt back up.

"It helped that I told him he could buy me a drink at the hotel lounge when he gets off if he helped me," Winter replied. The corners of her mouth tweaked upward, and Stamp chuckled.

"That still doesn't help us with getting inside," Killian cut in. "How are we going to get past the security? They'll recognize us from the news the moment we walk in."

"Not if you look the part," Winter said. "Security isn't going to look twice at a couple of guests turning in after a long day of sightseeing."

"And how exactly are we supposed to look the part?" Killian asked, shooting her a suspicious stare.

Winter dug into her jacket pocket and pulled out a leather pouch. It rattled heavily with chits. "Feel like doing a little shopping?"

She smiled slyly.

Killian rolled his eyes and shifted the car into gear, pulling them away from the curb.

When they returned to the hotel over two hours later, they were dressed to match the hotel guests. Killian wore a slim-cut black suit with a matching necktie, loosened around his collar, and shiny dress shoes, Stamp wore a grey three-piece with an open collar, and Winter dazzled all in a form-fitting knee-length charcoal dress and pointed black boots. She had let her hair down again, and a sparkling jewel necklace hung around her neck.

"I sure hope this works," Killian said as the bellhop opened the door for them, and they strode into the lobby. The bellhop smiled at Winter, and she winked back.

"It will," she said. They were all carrying large vinyl travel bags, no doubt loaded with clothes and outfits for a few days' vacation. At least that's what Killian hoped they thought.

True to Winter's word, though, no one looked at them twice as they walked across the lobby. The security guards paid them a cursory glance at best, and the guests they passed along the way nodded curtly or else ignored them entirely. To them, they were just another group of traveling corporate execs or tourists on vacation. They had no idea the bags were actually loaded with weapons and gear, and that, even now, Killian was carrying two guns on him.

They walked over to the reception desks and set their bags on the floor in front of the counter.

"Checking in?" the young woman behind the counter asked. She flashed a brilliant smile.

"Yes. Two rooms, please," Winter said, smiling just as brightly. Killian wondered how many hotels like this she had checked into over the years, how many missions she had done just like this back in the states. After a moment, he decided he probably didn't want to know.

"How long will you be staying with us?"

"Three days," Winter responded. Again, it rolled off her tongue so smoothly that Killian almost believed it himself. The receptionist obviously did and began typing into her computer.

"We have two suites available on the fourth floor, overlooking the harbor," she said. Winter nodded in agreement. "I'll need your passport as collateral while you stay with us please."

Winter dug into the bag at her feet and removed the passport from a side pocket. She handed it over, and Killian recognized it as one of the ones from her team's emergency kit. It contained an alias, no doubt.

The receptionist opened the passport and stared at it for a moment, before nodding and flashing another radiant smile.

"It will be $300 a night. If you require currency, we have an exchange just off the main concourse where you may withdraw either chits or bills. Here are your keycards, rooms 409 and 411. I hope you enjoy your stay."

Winter smiled appreciatively and handed one of the key cards to Killian. He tucked it into his pocket with a sideways glance at the receptionist before picking up his bag.

They walked over to the row of elevators and pushed the call button. Killian stared at his reflection in the chrome doors as they waited for it to arrive. A young man with tired eyes and a few days' worth of stubble stared back at him, a man he barely recognized anymore, thanks to all that had happened over the past few days.

As the doors beeped open and an elderly man stepped off in front of them, Killian steeled himself, ready to end this, ready to go back to his life, and forget any of this ever happened. As Winter and Stamp stepped into the elevator in front of him, however, he wondered if he could even return to his old life. Did he even *want* to?

Flashing Winter a look, Killian stepped into the elevator beside her, feeling a slight rush when her arm brushed against his.

Regardless, it was ending today. No matter what. The doors closed and they traveled upward.

Stamp checked his watch. "Well, if Carson keeps to his word, the cops will be on the other side of the city, investigating that bomb threat right about now."

"If he wants to get paid, he'll do it," Killian said, putting as much confidence into his voice as he could muster. On the inside, his heart hammered with nerves.

They arrived at the fourth floor and stepped off. Finding their rooms, they headed in and locked the door behind them. Killian had half a moment to stare around at the decadent room before they began to gear up. They set the bags on the kitchenette counter and immediately began pulling out the gear. Winter removed her boots and yanked on a pair of jeans. Stamp unzipped her dress, and she let it fall to her ankles where she kicked it off. She was wearing a tight black tank top underneath. She pulled on a shoulder rig loaded with ammo clips and buckled a tactical holster onto each thigh before pulling her boots back on.

Killian noticed for half a second how tight her shirt was before he tugged his necktie off and shrugged out of his jacket. A gun was holstered beneath his arm and another was strapped to his ankle. He rolled up his sleeves and holstered another pistol on his hip, trying all the while to quiet his thundering heart. He dug into one of the travel bags, pulled out the sawn-off shotgun, made sure it was fully loaded, and snapped the breach closed. He dumped several shells into his pocket and looked at Stamp. He was still fully dressed, a nervous look on his face.

"You alright?" he asked.

"Oh, yeah, I'm great," Stamp replied, sarcasm dripping from his voice.

"You're going to be fine. They're more than likely going to have someone guarding the door, and we can't let him tip off his buddies," Killian said. Stamp nodded and Killian patted him on the shoulder reassuringly.

Once they were fully geared up, each of them nodded.

"Shame we couldn't make better use of this room," Stamp said, staring out the windows and the beautiful view below. "Daisy's always wanted to stay at a place like this."

"And she can once we get this done," Killian said. He threw a sidelong glance at Winter, and she nodded. "We kill these son-of-bitches, and I'll personally pay for your stay," she added.

Stamp nodded, gave one last sigh, and followed them out the door.

Thankfully, they didn't pass any other guests along the way and made it to the stairwell door without incident. It was unlocked, and they headed up to the next floor. They stacked up on the door as Stamp tried to shake off his nerves.

"You've got this," Killian said and handed him a thin knife.

Stamp nodded again, a little more confidently this time, and looked up at the ceiling. He exhaled deeply before grabbing the doorknob and walking into the hallway, the knife concealed against his wrist. Killian waited several seconds before peeking around the corner.

True to his prediction, a man in a brown duster was standing outside one of the doors about halfway down the hallway. Stamp walked toward him casually, the Magi regarding him with a weary stare. Stamp took two steps past him before lunging forward suddenly and driving his elbow hard into the trench coat's nose. He stumbled backward. Stamp grabbed him by the back of the head and drove the knife hard into his abdomen. He let out a garbled moan, and Stamp covered his mouth. A moment later, he sagged against his shoulder, and Stamp lowered him to the ground slowly.

Killian and Winter left the stairwell and walked over to Stamp. He looked a little green in the face.

"You okay?" Killian asked lowly.

"I've never killed anyone that close before. Vampires sure, but people…" He trailed off.

"I won't say it gets easier because it doesn't," Winter said, her voice barely a whisper, "but if we do this, you'll likely never have to again."

Stamp nodded and readied himself, pulling off his jacket. He had a pistol holstered beneath his arm as well, and Killian handed him the sawn-off shotgun. "Let's get this done," he said.

They nodded and stacked up on the door. Stamp stood on one side. Killian and Winter stood on the other. Her breath was hot on the back of his neck. She held up her hand, three fingers extended.

Three...

Killian thought of all that had happened over the past few days, all the things he had been forced to do, and he suddenly felt very angry.

Two....

They were going to pay for this. They were going to pay for all the lives they had taken trying to get Lucas. They were going to pay for Loop getting hurt, even if it hadn't been them who had pulled the trigger directly.

One....

And last but not least, they were going to pay for turning him into this.

Winter clenched her fist, and Killian banged on the door. He waited, a breath caught in his throat as he heard footsteps approaching the door from the other side. He heard them lean against the door to look through the peephole and then unlock the two deadbolts that prevented them from just kicking the door in. A moment later, it opened, and Killian grabbed the man standing there. He yanked him out of the doorway and threw him against the opposite wall. Winter blasted him with twin gunshots to the chest, and Stamp shot both barrels of his sawn-off into the hotel room. There was a cry from inside, and Killian lunged into the room, firing shots at the two Magi sitting on the couches in the living room. One of them had been reading a magazine. The other was cleaning his gun on the decadent glass coffee table. The one reading the magazine fell back against the cushions as a gunshot knocked him in the chest. A second hit him in the shoulder, and he was dead before he fell flat. Killian missed the other one who dove for cover behind the couch. Winter missed as well.

As Killian moved forward, he saw there were three more standing in the dining area. The room was a luxury suite and, as such, was as large as some apartments. It also hosted a huge balcony where two more Magi were smoking cigarettes. Killian had just enough time to dive behind the kitchen counter on his left before they all opened fire on him. A fireball hit the overhead cabinet behind him and blew the wooden doors clean off. Winter took one of them out with two precise gunshots before diving behind the counter as well, sliding to a halt beside him.

"There's a few more than I was expecting," she said. She fired a shot over the counter blindly.

"No shit. I don't see the big one, though. The somatic. Whatever the fuck his name is," Killian said, firing several shots over the counter as well. He ejected the spent magazine from his pistol and slammed a fresh one in.

Stamp fired another spray from both barrels and caught the fire mage in the shoulder. He immediately rushed to the bathroom doorway opposite the kitchen and took cover inside. With slightly shaky hands, he popped the breach on the shotgun, ejected the spent shells, and loaded two fresh ones.

The Magi began spreading out across the living room and dining area, flipping the dining table on its side for cover. The fire mage hid behind it, his shoulder a bloody, tattered mess. A hail of gunshots hit the overhead kitchen cabinets and wooden splinters flew in all directions. Killian cursed as one bullet zipped right over his head and pinged off the oven behind him.

Winter crawled to the corner of the kitchen counter and peeked around, surveying the area. Several bullets whipped past, and she ducked back behind cover. She popped back out a moment later and returned fire and was rewarded with a sharp cry of pain. One of the Magi taking cover behind the couch had caught a bullet to the ear and fell back flat.

Winter crawled back over to Killian. "There're six of them still able to fight. The ones behind the couch won't be a problem. We just need to punch through the frame. The cushions aren't going to stop lead. It's the ones hiding behind the table I'm worried about. I just hope they don't have much ammo," she said.

Killian nodded. He jumped up from cover for a second, fired three shots, and ducked back down as a fresh wave of bullets hit the cabinets behind them.

"That's a good way to get shot," Winter said.

"It's also a good way to get them to waste their ammo," Killian replied smartly, and she had to acknowledge the logic in his words.

"We can't afford to wait them out. Security's bound to have called the cops by now."

"Doesn't give us much time," Killian said.

"I wish we had some grenades."

"I might be able to help with that," Stamp said from the bathroom door. They looked over at him questioningly, and he responded by grabbing the potted plant from the bathroom counter. He scooped out a handful of dirt from the pot.

"I've always wanted to try this," he said, and threw the handful of dirt into the dining area as hard as he could. It plumed out as it hit the floor and became little more than a thin coat of powder.

Killian was just about to ask if that was his grand plan when Stamp pressed his palm to the floor and closed his eyes. At first, it seemed nothing happened. The Prime Magi continued to fire at them, and Killian kept his head low. Then, the layer of dirt began to vibrate. It gathered together back into a handful and rocketed forward like a wave, hammering into the table in the shape of a fist and sending it crashing backward. The Prime Magi hiding behind it lunged from cover. The fire mage, however, wasn't quick enough, and the table knocked him backward. He hit the ground hard. Killian and Winter immediately popped out of cover and shot two of the Magi as they dove for fresh cover. Winter shot the fire mage as well before ducking back behind the counter.

"That's three left," she said.

Killian nodded and looked over to see Stamp breathing heavily. The trick had obviously taken a lot out of him. "You alright?" Killian called. Stamp nodded, managing to fire another blast from his shotgun before bending over to catch his breath.

"Let's finish this," Winter said, reloading her pistols. Killian nodded and pulled the pistol from beneath his arm. He was sweating profusely and his heart was like a rabid animal, but his hands had never been steadier.

"I'll pop out of cover and fire at them. When they return fire, you slide out from the side and blast them," he said.

Winter nodded, and Killian let out a heavy breath. A moment later, he jumped up from behind the counter and emptied both magazines into the couch, pulling the triggers as fast as his fingers would allow. The Prime Magi kept their heads down, trying to avoid the onslaught of lead as best they could. When his guns clicked empty, Killian ducked back behind cover. The Prime Magi jumped up almost immediately to return fire. Winter was ready, though. She lay on her side at the corner of the counter, her guns already trained on the top of the couch. She blasted them as they popped out. Two went down with clean shots to the chest. The third just barely managed to duck back down in time. Killian recognized him from Jo Jack's shop. He was the one traveling with Saxos.

"Leave the last one alive," Killian said.

"What?" Winter asked disbelievingly.

"He'll know where their leader is."

After a moment, Winter nodded. She obviously didn't like it, but she understood why they needed him alive.

"Throw out your gun, and we'll let you live," Killian called out.

"Fuck you!" the Magi called back and fired several shots over the couch.

"You can't make it out of here alive. Even if you manage to kill us, the cops are on their way."

"Go to hell."

Several more shots hit the cabinet behind their heads before they heard his gun click empty. Killian heard a mumbled curse.

"You're empty. Throw the gun out and you can live," Killian tried again. There were several moments of terse silence. Killian waited with bated breath, his heart still pounding somewhere near his ears.

"You'll let me live?" the man called.

"We'll let you live."

A moment later, Killian heard the clatter of the man's gun hitting the ground nearby. Stamp glanced around the crook of the bathroom door, saw the gun laying nearby, and nodded at them.

Killian rose from cover slowly, his gun held aloft before him and trained steadily on the top of the couch. Winter crouched at the corner of the counter, her gun trained evenly as well.

"Come out slowly," Killian said.

The man peeked his head out, saw their guns trained on him, and rose with his hands up. Sweat dripped across his brow. Killian could see he was nervous.

Killian stepped out from behind the counter and moved toward him slowly, his gun still trained on the man's head. He was a dozen steps away when a long ice sickle suddenly appeared in the man's hand.

"Killian, look out," Winter yelled just as the Magi lunged it at his chest. Killian dove out of the way and felt it split the air next to his head, grazing his neck before shattering against the wall behind him. Winter and Stamp both opened fire, shooting him in the chest multiple times. The glass window behind him shattered as he collapsed to the ground.

Winter rushed over and kneeled beside Killian.

"You okay?" she asked as he rolled over onto his back. The ice sickle had drawn a long line of blood across the side of his neck.

"Yeah, I'm okay," he answered and allowed her to help him to his feet. The cut burned fiercely. "Damn ice mages."

"We don't have much time. The cops will be here soon," she said.

"This isn't all of them," Killian said, looking at the corpses spread out around them. "Saxos isn't here."

"Check the bodies," Winter called over to Stamp. He looked exhausted but nodded and set to searching the bodies for some clue of their leader's location. Winter joined him.

Killian grabbed a paper towel from the roll on the counter and pressed it against his neck in an effort to halt the bleeding. He spotted the door next to the dining area and walked over to it. He kicked the fire mage onto his back to make sure he was dead before grabbing the doorknob tentatively. Just to be safe, he drew his gun, letting the paper towel fall away from his neck. Killian opened the door sharply and aimed his gun inside. It was dim —all the lights were off and the curtains were drawn—and there was a strange aroma in the room. It was a bedroom. A huge king-sized bed occupied the center of the room, and an ornate porcelain basin rested on the dresser against the far wall

It didn't look like a decoration.

Killian took a hesitant step inside, his heart rate revving back up, and recognized the scent as someone who hadn't bathed in several days. He covered his nose and moved to hit the light switch. It was only then that he saw the form laying across the bed. It looked far too thin to be human; its arms were stretched out and tied to the headboard, giving it the shape of a large Y.

Killian flipped the light switch on and couldn't help the gasp that came to his lips. It was a woman, her eyes closed. He walked over slowly, not sure if she was alive, when he saw her chest rising and falling steadily. She was wearing a plain black t-shirt and shorts. As Killian drew nearer, the smell grew stronger, and he was certain it came from her. He also saw the faded white-lined scars across the insides of her thighs and biceps. Bandages wrapped her wrists, and Killian could see that blood had leaked through and stained them pink. There were also several scarlet stains on the sheets and across the floor next to the bed. Killian drew his hand up to his mouth in disgust. Not because of her appearance or condition, but the fact the Prime Magi could do something like this to someone.

It was only when he stood right next to her that he saw how thin her hair was and how hollow and sunken her eyes were. As a floorboard creaked beneath Killian's foot, her eyes slowly opened. They were hazel, and he recognized them almost immediately. He had seen them before, and, as he stared at her, he recognized so many of her other features. Her long nose, her angled jaw line, her thin lips. Winter appeared in the doorway and gave a startled gasp.

"Oh, my God," she said, her hand drawing to her mouth as well.

The woman's eyes stared into Killian's, and with a feeble, quiet voice, she said, "Help me."

Killian nodded and immediately set to untying her wrists from the headboard, all the while unable to take his eyes away from hers.

They were Lucas's eyes. She was Lucas's mother.

CHAPTER 25

The God Mage

"Get her some water," Killian yelled.

Winter nodded and disappeared back out the door.

Killian managed to untie the woman's left wrist and set to untying her right, barely able to believe this. He figured the Prime Magi had killed her when they grabbed her instead of Lucas. He had never thought they would keep her captive all this time instead.

As his eyes drew back toward her bandaged wrists, though, he got a sickening feeling in the pit of his stomach that she hadn't been kept solely as a hostage.

Killian finally untied her right wrist, and her arm fell to her side limply. She had almost no muscle in them at all.

"You're going to be alright," he said. "You're safe now."

"You have to get me out of here," she replied weakly.

"Don't worry. You're going to be okay."

Winter rushed back in with a glass of water, and Killian took it from her hands. He tried to bring it to the woman's lips, but she shook her head away from it.

"You don't understand," she said.

Killian tried to hush her and bring the glass to her lips again, but she suddenly lunged forward and grabbed him by the sides of head.

"You don't understand," she said again. "They know where he is."

The bottom of Killian's stomach suddenly fell out. He dropped the glass to the floor, and the water splashed outward.

"They know. He has gone to get him." Her tone was shaky like an old woman's, but the strength had returned to her voice. She released Killian's head and fell back against the mattress weakly.

"Who?" Killian asked. He could tell by the look in her eye that he didn't want the answer.

"Saxos, the God Mage," she said.

Killian stared at her for several long heart-pounding moments, his heart hammering in his ears. Then, without another word, he swept her up in his arms and carried her toward the door. She weighed almost nothing at all, and it wasn't even a strain to carry her. Winter looked at him questioningly.

"We have to get back to the hotel now," he said. After a moment, Winter nodded, not needing an explanation.

"Stamp, we're leaving," she said. Stamp looked up from the body he was searching, saw the woman cradled in Killian's arms, and tried to speak.

"I'll explain later," Killian cut him off. "We need to get out of here now."

Stamp nodded, and they exited the suite. They entered the elevator already on their floor and hit the button for the second floor. The ride down seemed to last an eternity. Killian could practically feel the adrenaline coursing through his veins. His breaths were short and sharp, and his heart still hadn't settled back into his chest.

What have we done? Killian thought over and over. *What in God's name have we done?*

The elevator beeped, and they stepped off, heading for the stairwell door. They passed a family of tourists on the way, and, although the family looked at them curiously, no one said a word.

They entered the stairwell and walked down the steps swiftly. Lucas's mother breathed steadily against Killian's chest, her eyes on him the entire time.

When they reached the bottom, Stamp was the first one through the door, followed closely by Winter and Killian. He glanced into the lobby and saw three police officers talking to the receptionist. She pointed toward the elevators, and the three of them immediately ducked back into the stairwell.

"Shit. What do we do?" Stamp asked.

Killian looked around for another way out, but there weren't any other doors out of the stairwell. They were trapped.

Winter suddenly dashed back up the flight of stairs and disappeared around the corner. Killian was just about to call after her when a loud ringing suddenly filled the entire hotel. She had pulled the fire alarm. She joined them a moment later, and they waited for a few moments as people suddenly came rushing through the lobby. The police officers were unsure how to handle the mass of people—they were obviously the first responders—and simply waved everyone toward the exits, more concerned with the possible fire than the shootout upstairs. When people started spilling from the stairwell as well, Killian, Winter, and Stamp joined the crowd and rushed through the lobby. The police officers didn't even look at them as they strode past. A moment later, they were back outside. Unlike the rest of the guests who gathered in the valet area, however, Killian, Winter, and Stamp headed down the street. By the time they reached their car a block away, Killian's arms were starting to grow tired, and he was happy to set Lucas's mom down in the back seat. He climbed in beside her, and Winter and Stamp loaded into the front. Winter floored the gas pedal and propelled them out the narrow backstreet.

"As fast as you can, Winter," he said. She nodded and barely slowed when she turned onto the highway access ramp.

"You're Lucas's mom," Killian said as they weaved through traffic, shooting across lanes like a bullet.

"Yes... Lucas..." She said his name as though she had not heard it in some time, savoring its sound.

"How did they find him?" Killian asked. "How do they *keep* finding him?"

She didn't reply. She merely held out her bandaged, blood-soaked wrists, and Killian suddenly understood. He had always heard there was blood magic out there and people who were desperate enough to use it, but he had never come face to face with it before. It was the darkest of practices, reserved only for the truly evil.

"So that's how they've been doing it," he said quietly, his voice suddenly lost.

"Yes. They've kept me this whole time on the off chance he one day would escape or someone broke him out."

Killian's eyes shot up in her direction. He understood what she was implying. It was their fault this had happened. By breaking Lucas out, her suffering and his capture was on them.

"I don't understand," he said. "Why did they take so long to find him this time? We've been in the same place for two days."

"I was too weak. It takes a very strong magical aura to perform the ritual. I'm the only one who can do it since I'm his only true blood relative. Saxos can't. Their connection is too impure," she said.

Killian suddenly felt sick to his stomach. Saxos was Lucas's father? Even worse, he had been cutting her open every day to try to get to Lucas. Every time they had shown up, she was somewhere bleeding. Lucas's own mother had been used against him.

"Winter, how far are we?" Killian called to the front seat.

"Five minutes," she said, swerving to avoid an eighteen-wheeler merging onto the highway.

Killian looked back at Lucas's mother. "It's going to be alright. We're going to get him. Lucas is going to be fine."

"Shayla," she filled in.

"Lucas is going to be fine, Shayla. We're going to get him," he repeated. Unfortunately, even he could hear the doubt in his voice.

They exited the highway at a jarring speed and slid through the intersection. Winter pushed the car to its limits. They narrowly dodged a van turning through the intersection, and a thunder of horns suddenly blasted them from all direction. Winter kept her foot pressed down on the gas pedal. They raced down the narrow streets and slid through the corners like they were in some off-road derby. The engine squealed and made all sorts of grinding noises. Killian knew she was pushing the RPM gauge to the absolute max it would go.

Finally, they skidded into the hotel parking lot, and Killian jumped out before she had even brought it to a complete halt.

"Killian, wait," Stamp called, jumping out after him.

Killian was already at the door to their room, however, his gun drawn. He slammed through it with his shoulder, busting the meager lock off. He rushed in and immediately saw the room was empty. The bathroom as well. He sprinted back outside, passing Stamp at the door. He chased after him as he ran around the corner to the manager's office, hoping, praying Lucas would be there. He knew even before he opened the door he wouldn't be.

His feet touched something wet and sticky as he walked inside. He looked down and saw a pool of blood coming from behind the counter. A sick feeling erupted in the pit of his stomach again. He walked over to it slowly, his heart in his throat, pounding fiercely.

Please no, please no, he thought over and over as he rounded the corner of the desk.

A set of cold dead eyes stared up at him from the floor behind the counter. It was Acela. She had been shot in the head, blood leaking from the back of her skull. Killian stumbled backward, immediately throwing up his hand to stop Stamp from coming any closer. He halted in the doorway.

Slowly, Killian managed to steady his feet beneath him and look through the open door in the back. There was still a load of laundry going, and, there, in front of the rumbling dryer, was a charred corpse. Killian knew it was Acela's mother right away.

He stepped back from the counter slowly, a ringing suddenly in his ears. Stamp still stood in the doorway. "What is it, Killian? Is it Lucas?"

Killian shook his head. Everything seemed to overwhelm him at once, and his head was suddenly swimming. He rushed out of the manager's office into the parking lot and vomited all over his polished dress shoes.

It took him several minutes to stop, his head rolling and his stomach doing somersaults. Winter walked up, supporting Shayla underneath one arm.

"They've taken him," she said. It wasn't a question. Killian stood up straight and wiped his mouth. He nodded slowly.

"What do we do now?" Winter asked.

Killian couldn't bring himself to respond. He merely stared at Shayla. She was right. This was their fault.

His fault.

"There is something," Shayla said weakly. "But I will need time, rest."

"Do we have time?" Killian asked.

"Yes. Not much but enough. They can't perform the sacrifice until the next crescent moon, and they still have to find a focusing point rich in magical energy."

Killian looked up at the sky instinctively, despite the fact that the sun was still up. "How long until then?"

"A day. Maybe two," she responded.

"What sacrifice are you talking about?" Winter asked. "Who are they sacrificing?"

"I will explain everything soon, when I'm stronger. We need to get away from here, though," Shayla said.

Killian nodded, a small flare of hope lighting within his chest. They weren't lost yet. Not completely.

"Tell us everything," Killian said, handing Shayla a glass of water. They had checked into a shabby motel, and she stretched out on one of the lumpy beds, two pillows propping her up against the headboard. She drank deeply, draining the glass.

Killian leaned against the wall, crossing his arms across his chest. Stamp sat in the armchair in the corner, his hands folded beneath his chin. Winter stood near the window, half-expecting to see the Prime Magi again every time she looked out. Killian knew they wouldn't come back. They had already gotten what they wanted.

"Before I begin," Shayla said, setting the glass down on the nightstand, "please understand that even then, Saxos was more powerful than you can ever imagine. He was every girl's fantasy—and worst nightmare. Try not to judge me. You don't know what he was like."

Killian, Stamp, and Winter exchanged uncertain glances before nodding.

Killian's heart was already beating swiftly.

"It all started about fifteen years ago," Shayla began. "Saxos was a pretty well-known archeologist back then, an expert on ancient mythology and lore. I was just a TA in one of his classes with a schoolgirl crush on him.

"He had just returned from a dig in Belize, I think. I can't remember. He came back…different. Harder. He said he had learned of an ancient ritual that could bring the old powers back to the world. Magic, he always called it. It didn't take him long to decipher the texts—Saxos was a genius when it came to that sort of thing—and an obsession quickly grew within him. Completing this ritual became all he could think about, and he began collecting what he would need for it: the bone of a god, the tooth of a saint, the feather of a phoenix. No one thought he could do it. Not the professors he taught with, nor his fellow archeologists he had once called friends. After all, how could you get the bone of a god, the feather of a phoenix? Phoenixes are creatures of myth, and gods aren't even physical beings. But Saxos understood it was all in the way you looked at it. A phoenix symbolizes renewal, consecration, virginity. He took the blood of a virgin—the feather of a phoenix."

There was a long pause, and Killian guessed who the virgin had been. Shayla was lost in the memory for a moment before she blinked several times. He could see the hint of tears glistening in her eyes. She didn't cry, though. Killian doubted she could anymore after all she had been through.

She continued. "The bone of a god he took from an Egyptian pharaoh, a *divine* king. The tooth of a saint was the easiest I suppose," she said. Killian felt the sickening feeling in the pit of his stomach again. The more he heard, the more he wanted her to stop, but he *had* to know. He needed to know what he was going up against, what kind of monster he was going to face.

"By the time he had gathered all this, he had built a huge following around him. Other students, a few teachers, runaways mostly. He called it a family, but it was really a cult. I was one of his followers, his *first* follower really. I was blinded by his charm. I didn't see what it really was. He could hypnotize you with his words, quoting Plato, Aristotle, Shakespeare. He promised to make the world a better place where people would no longer be judged by their wealth or their looks but by their true power. We were hooked. We wanted to change the world. We wanted to make it a better place."

Shayla's voice caught in her throat as she fought back a flood of emotions. Killian knew the story was going to get only worse from here. He glanced over at Winter and saw she was no longer looking out the window. She was staring at Shayla as she fought to continue her story.

"I had been in the cult about five months when he came to me one night and asked if I was willing to be the focusing point for the final ritual. Once I learned I wasn't going to be sacrificed or anything, I of course accepted. The chance to make the world a better place, to bring power to the world like it hadn't seen in a thousand years? I wanted it and was willing to do almost anything for it.

"The ritual wasn't complicated. It required five men to lie with me in one night while Saxos chanted some words in another language, burning the items he had gathered in a fire beside the bed. When the fifth man had finished with me, Saxos took his turn, and I knew this was it. The focusing point of the ritual he had talked about. We were bringing power to the world like it had never seen. Afterward, I was fed the milk of six nursing mothers, and we waited. We waited for nine long months for the baby to come."

Killian could barely believe what he was hearing. How had something like this happened and no one heard about it?

"But as time went on, I began to question things," Shayla said. Killian could tell the story was reaching its climax. "We seemed to hurt more people than we helped, taking when we should have been giving, and then I heard Saxos one night, talking to a few of his key followers about what he intended to do with the power, and what he had to do to the baby to get it. He wanted to reshape the world how he saw fit but not in a good way, not in a way that brought peace to the world like he had promised. No. He wanted to *rule* it.

"Then I heard about the sacrifice. The end of the ritual was killing the baby, *my* baby, during a crescent moon. Only then would the powers be released into the world, and magic would return."

Shayla sniffed loudly, trying with everything she had to keep the wall up, to stop the flood of pain from washing over her.

"But magic did return," Stamp suddenly interjected. "How did it come back if Lucas wasn't killed?"

"What you see is only a small teardrop of what could have been released. When I found out what Saxos planned to do with my baby, I ran. I knew I wouldn't make it far on my own, so I turned myself in to the authorities. I told them what Saxos was planning and what would happen if he ever got his hands on my baby. They agreed to protect me and Lucas, and I gave birth in one of their facilities behind a three-inch steel door and plate glass windows. It didn't matter, though. Nothing could stop the burst of magical energy that came out of me when I gave birth to Lucas. It penetrated the walls and spread out to every corner of the globe. Magic returned to the world but not as Saxos had predicted, not as he wanted. He and he alone was to get power, but instead the whole world did. Every person, even if they've never displayed a single ounce of magical energy, has it coursing through their veins. All thanks to Lucas. He gave the power to the whole world."

"But what will happen if Saxos sacrifices him now?" Killian asked. "Will he get the power?"

"I don't know, and, to be honest, I'm not sure if Saxos does either. But I think he's willing to try just about anything to get it back, including murdering his own son," Shayla said.

Killian felt tiny fingers dance across his spine. He rubbed the bridge of his nose, barely able to process all he had just heard.

"You said you had some way of getting him back," he managed to say. "I assume you mean blood magic."

"Yes," Shayla said. "I need time to get some of my energy back, but once I do, we can perform one of the rituals and locate him, hopefully in time to stop Saxos from performing the sacrifice."

"How long do you need?" Winter asked.

"A few more hours," Shayla replied. "By then, I should be strong enough to perform the ritual."

Killian nodded. He looked to Stamp and Winter, and they both nodded in return. After a moment, he excused himself and walked outside. He needed to process all this. It was so much to take in. The moon was shining overhead, and he saw that it was still a bright half-circle. In a day or two, it would turn into a crescent. They had to find Lucas before then and stop Saxos. They had to kill him. Then this would all be over.

Killian sighed heavily and leaned against the railing, gripping the crossbar tightly. No matter what, this was still on him. Lucas never would have been taken if he had just put his foot down, voiced his concerns about leaving Lucas alone. Then he never would have been taken and Acela and her mom wouldn't be dead. Their deaths were on his head, hanging within his mind amidst all the other mistakes he had made in the past few days. He suddenly realized how tightly he was gripping the railing and released it. His knuckles slowly regained their color.

"You okay?" Winter asked as she stepped out of the hotel room behind him.

"What do you think?" Killian asked.

Winter stared at him, not sure if his anger was directed at her specifically or the world in general.

"We're going to get him back," she said. "He's going to be alright."

"He never would have been taken in the first place if we had just been a little smarter," Killian said. "I knew it was stupid to leave him there, but I did it anyway. What the fuck was I thinking, listening to you guys?"

"Killian, it's no one's fault," Winter said.

"Yes, it is. It's our fault. He was our responsibility, and we blew it. It's my fault for not saying no," he replied.

"Killian…" Winter tried to take a step forward, but he raised his hand to stop her.

"Please, just don't, okay? I don't need any more of your sympathy," he said. "You made it clear how you feel, so don't give me any more of that shit."

Winter halted in her tracks, staring at him. He could tell he had hurt her. He could see it in her eyes, behind the mask she wore so often.

"I said what I did because I thought it was best for the both of us. I didn't say it because I wanted to hurt you," she said.

"Well, it really doesn't matter now since we lost Lucas," Killian replied, "so just back off."

Winter stared at him for several long moments before crossing her arms across her chest and planting her feet.

"No," she said sternly.

"What?"

"No. You don't get to make me the bad guy just because I hurt your feelings. I said what I did because we needed to focus on what we were about to do. Just because you want to cry about it doesn't mean I'm the bad guy, and just because we lost Lucas doesn't mean you are either. So stop beating yourself up about it. We're going to get him back, we're going to stop Saxos, and we're going to get through this."

She turned on her heel to go back into the room but stopped all of a sudden. "And for the record, just because I said no doesn't mean I don't want it too."

"What?" Killian asked, not sure if he had heard her right.

Winter spun around, walked up to him, and, before even he knew what was happening, kissed him hard on the mouth. It was tight and over quick but pleasant nonetheless.

Before Killian could respond, she turned on her heel and returned to the hotel room. Killian stood there for several minutes, staring at the door. Strangely, the small flicker of hope burning in his chest brightened just a little.

Blood for Blood

The moon was over halfway across the night sky when Shayla finally proclaimed she was strong enough to perform the ritual.

"I'll need a map of the city, a very specific one that shows all the streets and buildings, sawdust, and foxglove petals. We'll sprinkle the sawdust across the map and place petals at each of the four corners. I'll then cut my wrists and allow my blood to spread across the map. It takes a lot of focus so you *must* remain silent while I perform the ritual. Blood will cover the entire map except for wherever Lucas is being held," she explained.

Killian, Stamp, and Winter exchanged concerned glances, but they nodded nonetheless.

Stamp headed out to get what they needed, though Killian wasn't sure where he was going to find sawdust and foxglove petals at this time of night. He didn't exactly know of a twenty-four-hour apothecary.

While he was gone, Killian and Winter paced back and forth across the room, too anxious to really speak, and Shayla continued to rest. Killian wondered if she would ever fully recover from all she had been through.

As the hour mark ticked past on the nearby clock, Killian stopped in front of Winter and said what had been on his mind since she had left him on the porch.

"Thank you."

"For what?" she asked.

"For saying what you said back there and for doing what you did,' he replied. "I needed it."

"Which part?" she asked.

"You know which," he said. He added, "although the other part was pretty nice too."

Winter nodded and managed a faint smile in return. The mask had finally slid down all the way, and he could see she was hurting just as much as he was. Fear, worry, anxiety—all of it was present in her bright green eyes. She was right, though. They were going to get through this. One way or another, this would all be over soon.

Stamp arrived back in the hotel room almost two hours later, carrying a small paper sack and looking rather frazzled.

"Sawdust and foxglove petals—not easy to get at three in the morning," he said.

"Where'd you go?" Killian asked.

"Sutherland."

"Damn," he said, knowing it to be a pretty good drive away.

"Yeah. Even then, I had to break into an apothecary just to get the foxglove petals," Stamp said.

"Well, we're already terrorists. Might as well add breaking and entering to the list." There wasn't any humor in his voice.

They woke Shayla and laid the map across the floor beside the bed. Killian sprinkled the sawdust across it while Winter arranged the petals at each corner of the map. Shayla steeled herself.

"Now remember," she said. "I must remain focused during the ritual. You must stay absolutely silent."

The three of them nodded and, after a moment's hesitation, Killian handed her a small knife. She stared at it for several long, terse seconds, muttering beneath her breath. None of them could hear what she was saying, but Killian doubted it was English. Then, drawing in a sharp exhale of breath that made each of them cringe in anticipation, she slit her wrists. It wasn't deep, but deep enough to cause blood to slide down her wrists and across her palms in long, steady trails. She placed her hands over the map and allowed the blood to run down her fingers and drip onto the map. Shayla continued muttering beneath her breath, the words coming more and more swiftly.

Killian watched with bated breath. At first, the blood seemed to pool in the crease marks, but then the map seemed to flatten itself and the fold marks disappeared. The blood spread out evenly after that. When it was finally completely covered in her blood, Shayla stopped chanting and waved her hands over the map in a sort of figure-eight pattern. Blood continued to drip across its surface. Killian waited, looking desperately for a blank spot on the map, but he didn't see any.

A grunt of pain suddenly escaped Shayla's lips, and Killian's eyes snapped over in her direction. She was sitting there on the edge of the bed, her arms suspended over the map. She began moving them again very slowly, but again a grunt of pain escaped her lips and she stopped.

"Something's wrong," she said. She tried to stand, but an invisible explosion seemed to go off right next to her, and she was suddenly thrown backward onto the bed. Killian and Stamp rushed to her side while Winter grabbed tissues to stop the bleeding. She pressed them to her wrists.

"They're blocking him," Shayla said.

"What?"

"Lucas. They're blocking him, making sure I can't use the ritual to find him," she answered.

"How are they doing that?" Killian asked.

"I don't know. Saxos has always had his ways, but I don't know. I can't break through it."

Killian stood from the bed, anger already beginning to take hold. Could they not beat this guy? Was he always going to be a step ahead of them? He ran his hand across his scalp angrily. "There's got to be something we can do," he said, his tone rigid, determined. "We cannot let this asshole win. Anybody got any suggestions?"

Winter stared up at him. It was obvious she was out of comforting things to say. Right now, she couldn't find her voice at all. Stamp stood there beside the bed silently, his face reflecting what they were all thinking. They were out of options. Saxos was going to win, and Lucas was going to die.

Killian fought every urge he had to yell, to scream. He wanted to tear the room apart piece by piece, yell at his friends for giving up, but he couldn't. On the bed, Shayla sat rigidly, her eyes unblinking.

"Winter, call Hawk," he said suddenly. "We've got one of Lucas's sweat jackets. He can use it to track him."

"We don't have enough money," she said, her voice flat and defeated.

"Then I'll make him do it. I'm not giving up."

"There's not enough time," Shayla said quietly, her voice returning to its weakened state. "But I know something else that might work."

"What?" Killian asked, falling to her side immediately.

"Something much stronger than blood magic," she answered and turned to stare piercingly into his eyes. "Black magic. Death magic."

He didn't have to ask what that entailed. He could tell by the look in her eye.

"You're... No. There's got to be some other way," Killian said, shaking his head.

"There isn't."

"You can't kill yourself. We'll think of something else. Lucas *needs* his mother."

"No, he doesn't. He needs you to save him. And you can if I do this." She raised her hand, and Killian saw she was still clutching the knife. He caught her wrist before she could bring it to her throat. Her hand was shaking, and tears glistened in the corners of her eyes once more. Slowly, Killian realized his hands were shaking as well, and the taste of blood had slithered into his throat. Fear wrapped itself tightly around his stomach.

"Let me do this," she said, staring up into his eyes. "I have done nothing for him his entire life except ensuring a life of running and hiding. Let me do one good thing for him, so I can honestly call myself his mother."

Killian looked at Stamp and Winter, but they seemed just as unsure as he was. He locked eyes with Shayla, a fierce battle raging within. Thoughts of his own mother and the sacrifice she had made for him permeated within his skull. Finally, after several heart-pounding moments, he nodded slowly and released her wrist.

With his assistance, she rose from the bed slowly and stood over the map. Her knees were shaking now as well, and Killian steadied her as best he could with a hand on her shoulder. Tears glistened on her cheeks as she prepared to make the ultimate sacrifice for her son, the same thing his mother had done for him. Slowly, she raised the knife to her throat, and muttered several words beneath her breath.

"For Lucas," she added just loud enough for Killian to hear, before she raked the blade across her throat.

She dropped the knife, and, at first, Killian wasn't even sure if she had cut her throat. Then blood began to pour from her esophagus, dripping down across the map. She fell to her knees, clutching her throat. Tears continued to course across her cheeks as she choked on her own blood, staring up at Killian. He realized then that tears were running down his cheeks as well.

More and more blood fell across the map until it was so thickly covered that the map couldn't even be seen anymore. And still more kept flowing until finally, as the life drained from her eyes, Shayla collapsed to one side. Blood continued to pool around her neck, and a final tear streaked across her face.

Killian stood there, staring at the map, his hands shaking at his sides. In all his life, he would never forget the sacrifice she had made for her son, the sort of courage she had possessed. He would never know anyone that brave ever again.

Killian continued to stare at the map, waiting and waiting. His hands shook more violently. *Come on. Come on,* he thought anxiously.

"Come on!" he shouted down at the map, but still no bare spots formed across the map. Nothing was happening.

"Shit," Stamp breathed from a far off place.

Killian's whole head seemed to be spinning, and he suddenly let out a loud, harsh scream. "Come on!" he yelled again.

"Killian…" a vaguely recognizable female voice said. He suddenly punched the wall as hard as he could, drowning out whatever else she was going to say. A loud ringing filled his ears. As unbearable defeat began to wash over him, Killian pushed past his two companions and slammed out of the room. He let out another harsh cry of anguish and practically fell to his knees beside the car.

He punched the rusted passenger door, and pain immediately shot into his fist.

How had it come to this? How had they tried so hard and still lost? It was like a punch to the stomach that wouldn't stop hurting. Again and again, Killian wished Spin were still alive. He would know what to do, but he let him die too. Killian choked back another piercing scream, his voice all but lost now. He had failed. He had given his word and broken it.

"Killian," Winter said, jogging out of the hotel room behind him. "Killian, it's going to be okay. It's going to be alright."

Her voice was hollow, and Killian could tell even she didn't believe her own words.

"No, it's not," he said, his voice dripping with acid. "It's not going to be okay. We lost. The bad guys won. End of story."

He refused to face her. He sat there on his knees beside the vehicle his hands clenched into fists in his lap.

"They haven't won yet. We'll think of something else," she tried again.

"What don't you get, Winter? We're fucked. We have no idea where they took Lucas. They're going to kill him, and it's our fault. *My* fault."

His voice broke apart, and tears began to course down his cheeks at the last words. He punched the car door again and felt his knuckles split, warm blood dripping across the back of his hand.

Winter walked over so she stood in front of him. He could tell by her posture she wasn't going to move until he decided to face her. He slowly rose, and she immediately pulled him into a tight embrace. At first, he struggled, but then he relaxed into her and put his arms around her. He could tell by her wet cheeks she was crying too.

"We're going to get him back, okay? We're not out of this yet," she said.

Tears continued to steam down his cheeks. She kissed one of them away with a soft peck. Before he knew what he was doing, Killian kissed her neck, then her cheek, and then pressed his lips to hers. There was a moment of comfort in which everything seemed to fade away, her lips pressing against his in a wonderful sort of bliss, before she suddenly pulled back, staring at him.

"I'm sorry," he said awkwardly, his voice still short and broken. "It just happened."

Several terse, silent seconds ticked past. Then, she leaned forward slowly and pressed her lips back against his. Her mouth was warm and inviting, and, in just a few short moments, he felt everything begin to fade away again. He could tell she was feeling the same thing because she wrapped her arms around his neck tightly, and their kiss grew even more heated. Her body pressed against him firmly, forcing away even the slightest gap between them.

Not thinking of anything but her soft lips and warm body, Killian opened the car door, and the two of them all but fell onto the passenger seat. Killian was on top of her at first, but as they pulled their legs inside and closed the door behind them, Winter got up and straddled him. Their lips were pressed tightly together, and Killian could feel her grind against him. She was still crying—he might have been too—but they couldn't bring themselves to stop. All their worries were gone. Inside the car, there was nothing but the two of them and desire. A desire for comfort, a desire to forget, and they could give one another that. They could help each other forget.

Killian ran his hands across her back and over her breasts, enjoying the rich, natural curves of her body. He could tell she was enjoying it too. She moaned into his mouth sensuously.

"It's been a long time," she said as she finally released his mouth from her own. She was breathing heavily.

"Same here," he said in a gruff voice.

"You remember where everything goes?" She was sweating, and Killian could tell it wasn't just from the heat.

"I think I'll manage."

Winter raised herself off him slightly and unbuckled her belt, pulling her pants down to her ankles. She slid her underwear down as well, and Killian had a momentary view of her womanhood before setting to work on his own pants. She waited patiently as he fumbled with his belt and fly before finally managing to get his pants down. He was erect and ready. Winter slowly lowered herself down around him, cringing as he entered her, and moaning as he slid all the way in. Killian gripped her buttocks tightly as she began to move up and down.

It didn't take long before they began to fall into a rhythm. Killian slid her shirt up, revealing her tight-fitting bra, and yanked it downward. Her large, shapely breasts fell out. They were just as pale as the rest of her body, and he explored them with his mouth as she continued to thrust against him. She moaned loudly as Killian ran his tongue against her again and again. Everything felt so good; he could feel the climax building up inside him.

Finally, after what seemed like an eternity, she slammed down against him, and he released inside her, a single, silent breath escaping his lungs as ecstasy overtook him.

For the longest time, they just sat like that, wrapped in each other's arms, hoping the world would just go away for a few more minutes. As he looked at his watch, however, and saw it had been nearly an hour, he nodded to her. She planted one final kiss across his lips before climbing off him. She pulled her pants back on and fixed her shirt and bra. Killian yanked his own pants up. The windows were fogged over, and Killian felt a rush of fresh air hit him as he climbed from the car. Winter joined him, and they stood staring at the sky for several long moments.

"We're going to get him back," he said rigidly. "I don't know how, but we're going to get him back."

It was as though a fresh wave of determination had hit him. He wasn't willing to give up. Not now. Not ever.

Beside him, Winter nodded.

When they walked back into the hotel room, they found Stamp sitting on the edge of the bed, staring at the map. He hadn't moved Shayla from her spot on the floor, and, for that, Killian was grateful. He shouldn't have to do that on his own. No one should.

"You alright?" Killian asked as he strode over. Stamp was staring at the map, not moving.

"It worked," he said, his voice barely above a whisper.

"What?"

"It worked. The blood ritual worked. Look," he said, pointing at the map.

Killian immediately rushed over and stared at the map. It took him a moment to see it, but when he did, it was clear as day. He didn't even have to look up the address. He had been there many times before. It was Skye's academy. They had taken Lucas back.

CHAPTER 27

War

Killian still remembered the day the academy opened. There was a great ceremony held in Skye's honor. She cried. Killian cheered. Spin stood there with the same stony expression on his face he always wore. They celebrated that night with a party at the opera house ballroom. It was the first time Killian had ever worn a suit, and he remembered it feeling just as uncomfortable as he had expected. Still, it was for Skye so he had tolerated it. She had looked beautiful in her long flowing gown as toast after toast was made in her honor. She was giving the children of Blood Haven a future, a safe way to learn how to control their abilities before the streets could swallow them up. Her academy was the first of its kind, and she had put her soul into making it great. A fire burned in Killian's stomach at what it was being used for now.

He stared up at the main building through a set of binoculars. The sun was just beginning to rise, its orange and pink tendrils just barely grazing the horizon. They still had about an hour of darkness left.

"Why here?" Stamp asked from beside him. "Why would they take him back here?"

They lay at the foot of the hill looking up at the academy, hidden amongst the tall yellow grass. It was a shell of its former self, a far cry from how it had looked the day of the ceremony. Though the firefighters had saved the frame of the building, it was little more than a skeleton now. It had been stripped, gutted by the flames. The walls were black and charred; the windows were shattered and broken. Even the grass on the soccer field had been burnt to ashes.

"Shayla said they needed a place rich in magical energy to be the focusing point for the sacrifice," Winter said. "Think about how many kids got trained here, how much energy went through this place."

How much love, Killian added silently.

Skye had built this place on the principle of helping the city's youth. Now it was being used to destroy it.

Killian passed Winter the binoculars and let her survey the area. There was a single Magi walking around the outside of the building. They couldn't be sure how many more were inside. One thing was for certain, though: this was definitely the place. Killian could practically feel the energy. There was a static electricity in the air he had never felt before. Gusts of wind ridden with ash swirled past, and Killian knew, deep down, there was evil here.

"So what's the plan?" Stamp asked.

"We're going to kill them." Killian answered, making sure his pistol was fully loaded and chambering a round. His voice was quiet and gruff, and determination burned in his eyes.

"Finally feel like going hunting?" Stamp asked.

Killian nodded.

An hour later, as the sun beamed a bright, narrow strip across the horizon, Killian and Stamp set off through the grass. They stayed low, crawling on their hands and knees. The sun shone across their backs, and the blistering heat seemed to trap itself within the stalks of tall grass. Killian's back hurt and his shoulders burned, but he kept his head low and his eyes forward. Sweat trailed across his face and down his back, and the dirt crunched beneath his hands.

As they neared the edge of the grass, they dropped down onto their stomachs and crawled the rest of the way on their elbows, moving forward an inch at a time. Killian could just barely see the patrolling Magi through the grass. He slowed. The slightest sound could give them away before they were ready.

They halted a few feet from the edge of the field, staring though the narrow slits in the grass. Stamp was about an arm's length away, clutching the double-barrel shotgun tightly. His face glistened with sweat and dirt smeared his cheeks. Killian glanced over at him and gave a nod.

As the trench coat walked past the academy's front doors, Stamp picked up a small rock from the ground and threw it over his shoulder. It landed with a thud, and the Magi immediately froze, his head snapping around to look out across the field. His eyes searched the grass. Drawing his gun, he walked over slowly, scanning. There was a quiet *pop*, and he suddenly fell limp. Killian rushed forward and grabbed him before he hit the ground and dragged him backward into the grass. He lowered him out of sight as blood pooled across his chest. The *pop* came from the hunting rifle they had bought back at Carson's. It felt like a lifetime ago.

Winter lay at the base of the hill, a towel wrapped tightly around the barrel to suppress the shot. It seemed to have worked. As they lay there watching the front doors, no one came running out. Several seconds ticked past before Killian gave another nod, and he and Stamp burst forward from the grass. They covered the short distance to the front doors quickly and stacked up on either side. The doors had been broken apart by the flames, and Killian peeked into the foyer. The reception desk was little more than a pile of ash and rubble. Black scorch marks climbed the wall, reaching toward the ceiling like thin gnarled fingers.

Another Magi stood in the corner of the room, smoking a cigarette. He blew puffs of smoke toward the ceiling. He yawned several times in the short time Killian watched him, and his eyes were rimmed in red. It seemed he had drawn the short straw for watch duty.

Killian glanced at Stamp, his eyes darting toward the ground. Stamp nodded. He bent down and scooped up a handful of dirt. As the trench coat finished his last drag of the cigarette and ground it beneath his foot, Stamp threw the dirt through the doorway. It formed a sort of wave in the air and hit the Magi across the face, knocking him back a step and blinding him. Killian rushed through the door, pulling the knife from his belt and stabbing it into the man's gut. He gasped and Killian quickly covered his mouth with his hand. A moment later, he sagged against his shoulder, and Killian lowered him to the ground. He finally let out a breath.

They made sure the rest of the foyer was clear before Stamp walked to the door and waved. Winter rose from the cluster of bushes she had been hiding in and sprinted up to the house, covering the distance quickly. She was breathing only slightly heavier than normal when she joined them.

"Good work," she said, glancing at the dead Magi. Killian nodded and tucked the knife back into its sheath.

"Head to the roof and give us some cover. We might have to get out of here fast," he breathed. He pointed to the stairwell door next to the entrance to the west wing.

Winter nodded and disappeared through the door, hardly making a sound as she went.

She's scary good at this, Killian thought and flashed Stamp a look. He seemed to be thinking the same thing.

While Stamp checked to make sure no one was creeping along the west wing corridor, Killian walked over to the double doors behind the reception desk. He creaked the left one open and looked out into the courtyard. The sun had still not reached up over the main building, and the resulting shadows cast a gloom across the entire quad. Killian saw the fountain was still intact, though the foliage around it and the benches had all been reduced to ash. A few trench coats milled around, yawning or stretching as they woke. Many were sleeping on foldout cots or sleeping bags on the ground. The remnants of a few small campfires could be seen.

And then Killian saw him. Near the dragon statue at the back of the courtyard, in a small cage that looked like it was meant for an animal, Lucas lay sleeping. Even from this distance, Killian could see the enchantment they had lined around him in chalk. It glowed, thanks to the revelation charm around his neck, and he recognized it almost immediately as a negating barrier, killing all magical energy trapped within and blocking a mage's abilities. Killian could tell it had zapped Lucas of all his strength as well. He looked far thinner than when he had seen him last.

Killian's hand clenched into a tight fist, his fingernails digging into his flesh. He whistled to Stamp softly. He crept over, and Killian nodded out into the courtyard.

After a moment, Stamp saw Lucas. "There's too many of them for us to take head on," he said, counting at least eight. "How do you want to do this?"

"I say we split up, attack them from both sides. I'll take the east wing, you take the west," Killian offered.

Stamp thought about it for a moment. He stared at Lucas, his grip tightening around the shotgun. He nodded.

"Wait for my go," Killian said. "Then unleash hell."

Stamp nodded and they separated, heading in opposite directions. They halted at the doors to their respective wings, and Killian gave him a thumbs-up. After a second, Stamp returned it before pushing the door open and disappearing. His heart already pounding in his ears, Killian did the same.

It seemed a lifetime ago when he had walked this hall last. He moved slowly, his pistol held aloft before him. A few rays of sunlight gleamed through the windows on the right. Killian glanced into each of the classrooms on his left, making sure they were empty before moving on.

When he reached the very last door at the end of the hall, he froze, staring through the small shattered window. It was Skye's classroom.

"The sacrifice will be both of yours to make," the words suddenly echoed in his head. He had a flash of the dream and the black shroud before he pushed the broken door open.

Her classroom had been hit the hardest. The flames had spread across the plants like a plague and engulfed the ceiling. The skylights had shattered. Shards of glass hung from the window frames like jagged teeth.

Killian felt a fresh wave of anger hit him. He could hear the Prime Magi talking out the distant windows. Their voices were only murmurs from this far away, but he could imagine their conversations, talking about the coming sacrifice or what they intended to do when it was over.

Killian gripped his gun a little tighter and turned to head back down the hall. He needed to find a classroom with suitable cover. Skye's classroom, with its high, arching windows and multiple skylights, would not do the trick.

He had taken two steps when one of the nearby double doors opened, and a Magi stepped in. Both of them froze as the door clicked shut behind him. Then, just as the Magi opened his mouth to call for help, Killian dashed forward and slammed against him. He drove his shoulder hard into the man's chest just as he drew his pistol from its holster. Killian grabbed his wrist and tried to wrench the gun free from his grasp. The Magi pulled the trigger, however, and a repertoire of gunshots echoed down the hall, sending a ringing through Killian's ears. He finally managed to knock the gun from the Magi's hand, but his own pistol slid from his grasp as well. They both clattered against the floor. Killian ducked beneath the man's outward swing and elbowed him in the cheek. The next second, a fireball erupted from the man's palm and slammed against Killian's shoulder, sending him spinning to the floor. He landed with a cry of pain, his shoulder smoking. The flame had burned right through his jacket and singed the flesh beneath. His gun lay a few feet away. Ignoring the fierce pain, he rolled to the side just as the Magi summoned another fireball. His fingers closed around the pistol, and the Magi threw the fireball. Killian came up on one knee and had enough time to fire a single shot before he was forced to dive out of the way. He felt the heat of the flame as it spun past him. He aimed back at the Magi, but saw he had already fallen to his knees. Blood was spreading across his shirt and, a moment later, he pitched forward.

Killian sucked in a mouthful of air as he stared at the dead Magi. He had just enough time to realize it was Q, the Magi he had fought back at his apartment building, before a sudden barrage of gunshots rocketed the area, forcing him to dive out of the way. The entire academy was alerted to his presence. They fired from the windows in Skye's classroom, raining hell down around him. Killian had no choice but to run. He sprinted down the hall back toward the central wing, firing over his shoulder blindly as several Magi chased after him. As he neared the double doors leading back into the lobby, he dove to the floor and fired at the three men racing after him. He emptied his clip, and all three of them crashed to the floor, multiple gunshots hammering into each of them.

Killian ejected the spent magazine and slapped in a fresh one. He rose to his feet and pushed through the double doors behind him. His breath came in short gasps, and his heart was pounding as he raced around the reception desk and slid to a halt next to the doors leading into the quad.

A moment later, they slammed open and two Magi raced in. Killian shot them both in the back. They toppled to the ground in a crumbled heap. Holstering his pistol, he grabbed the assault rifle one of them had been carrying and checked the magazine before shouldering it. He peeked out into the quad. Gunfire was hammering the area from all around. Winter rained lead down from the nearby rooftop. She had killed three already, though she was forced to take cover as the Magi on the ground finally realized where she was. They were also contending with Stamp. He had taken cover in one of the classrooms in the west wing and was firing from a narrow window. Killian could just barely see the muzzle flashes.

Killian narrowed his gaze and spotted Lucas again. He was still curled up in the cage, trying to keep his head down. The Prime Magi were split up trying to deal with attacks from both sides. There was an empty lane of fire through the middle. Killian summoned up his courage and prepared to make a run for it.

Just then, the doors to the east wing slammed back open, and three more Magi sprinted in. They opened fire on him, and Killian bolted out the door, firing several shots over his shoulder. He ran as hard as he could as bullets split the air around him. Dirt flew in all directions, and a fireball flew past, so close it all but singed the tip of his hair. It was a war zone.

Killian slid to a halt next to the fountain and took cover against the cracked stone. He fired back toward the main building, driving the three trench coats back into cover. They ducked out of sight, and Killian hopped over the small retaining ring that had once kept the water from spilling out.

It was bone dry now.

A well placed bullet to the top of the fountain sent concrete scattering in all directions, and Killian hopped over the other side. His shoulder was on fire. He gritted his teeth as he neared the cage holding Lucas, his feet pounding the dirt and loose gravel.

Lucas looked up suddenly, as if able to sense his presence, and Killian saw the fear on his face. He locked eyes with him.

Something huge suddenly slammed into him, and Killian was knocked off his feet. He slid across the ground, his head spinning and every bone in his body aching. He had just enough time to realize he had dropped the assault rifle before someone grabbed him by the back of his collar and picked him up off the ground.

It was Saxos. He stood taller than Killian remembered. He no longer wore sunglasses, and Killian saw his eyes burned bright orange. It was unnatural and sent a shiver through his spine.

Saxos held him up with one arm and reeled his fist back, punching Killian hard across the jaw and sending stars dancing across his vision. His brain felt like it had been knocked around, and blood flew from his mouth. Saxos brought him close, so their faces were only a few inches apart.

"The boy is ours," he said in a voice very similar to the one Killian had heard in his dream.

Bang!

A gunshot suddenly slammed into the back of Saxos's shoulder, causing him to stumble. Killian looked over and saw Winter crouched atop the roof, aiming through the scope. A small smile flashed across Saxos's face, and he threw Killian as hard as he could. Killian flew through the air like a brick and crashed through one of the windows of the west wing. He slammed to the ground, the breath gone from his lungs, and slid across the room before finally coming to a halt against the wall. His brain felt like mush, and he spit out a mouthful of blood. Everything was spinning, and, as much as he tried, he couldn't get his eyes to focus.

The ground suddenly trembled, and dust fell from the ceiling. Stamp had just caused a miniature quake. Apparently, he wasn't doing well either.

Killian managed to roll onto his back, allowing some oxygen to seep into his lungs, and struggled to pull the pistol from his ankle. His hands shook as he barely managed to close his fingers around the gun's grip. He drew it just as a Magi stepped into the room. Killian aimed and pulled the trigger. The first shot hit the wall several feet to the man's left. The second and third hit above his head. The fourth finally connected with the Magi's shoulder, and the fifth hammered him in the abdomen. He slumped to the ground.

The sound of crunching glass brought Killian's attention back around to the window. Saxos suddenly slammed his foot down on his hand, breaking several of his fingers and causing the gun to fall from his grasp. He screamed out in pain, trying to wrench his hand free from beneath Saxos's foot, but it was no use. Saxos weighed too much. He bent over and grabbed Killian by the collar again, lifting him off the ground. This time, Killian couldn't even struggle. His legs dangled limp beneath him, and the pain in his hand prevented him from trying to punch Saxos in the face. Blood dripped from his mouth, and his entire body was on fire.

"He is ours to do with as we please," Saxos said, and punched Killian across the jaw again.

"He is ours to sacrifice." Again, Saxos fist slammed across Killian's jaw.

"And he is ours to use to reshape the world."

Saxos drove his fist hard into the underside of Killian's chin, causing his head to snap backward. He saw glowing stars and wondered if they were real little ornaments hung to decorate the room, or just figments of his imagination.

Saxos reeled him back again and threw him across the room. Killian slammed into the chalkboard and dropped to the ground. He lay next to a pile of debris. Chunks of plaster and stone lay across the floor, and Killian reached out toward them, feeling them with his hand. He scooped up one piece of rock and transformed it into an arrowhead. It was rough and pitted, the edges uneven and jagged. He threw it over his shoulder weakly, and it landed near Saxos's feet. Saxos looked down at it and chuckled. Killian picked up a small piece of plaster next, and it morphed into a tiny knight chess piece. This time when he threw it, it thudded against Saxos's chest. He laughed again and began walking over. Killian grabbed a large rock and had just managed to close his fist around it when Saxos picked him up again.

"Play time's over, Elemental," he said, his lips peeling back in a wicked smile.

"You know why I hate weather mages so much?" Killian asked through a mouthful of blood. His mind was foggy as he remembered the look in the vampire master's eye when he had asked him the same question. It had been amused. Then he focused on the look in its eye when he drove the stake through its heart.

It had been fear.

Pure, unadulterated fear, and Killian had caused it.

He gripped the rock a little tighter, felt its edges turn smooth, and slammed it into Saxos's chest. He screamed as the stake pierced his chest and dropped Killian to the ground. It had just barely missed his heart. Blood spread across his shirt as he grabbed the stake and tried to wrench it free. Killian picked up another rock, and it suddenly transformed into a stone knife. He sliced Saxos's ankle open, and the Prime Magi toppled to the ground, screaming even harder. He was still holding the stake planted in his chest, even as it turned back into the rock and spread the wound open even further. Trails of blood poured from his mouth, and he could barely keep his eyes open as Killian stood up in front of him slowly.

"He's not yours," Killian said before raising the knife above his head and driving it down into Saxos's collar bone. Blood spurted from the wound almost instantly, and Saxos's eyes opened wide, spread in the same look of fear that had crossed the vampire's face just before he died. A moment later, his strength left him, and Saxos toppled to the side. He choked as blood filled his throat and lungs and gasped for breath, his mouth opening and closing as he tried to get air into his body. He looked like a fish caught on dry land. A few seconds later, the life vanished from his eyes, and he lay completely still. Killian stood over him, his broken hand hanging limp at his side. The knife in Saxos's neck transformed back into the rock and fell to the ground amidst a pool of blood.

"He's not anyone's," Killian said. He stepped over Saxos's body and walked toward the window, determination burning inside him.

"On the contrary, he *is* mine," a slithery voice said over his shoulder.

Killian turned just in time to see the ice sickle pierce his stomach, wrenching him backward. He fell against the wall as the old man stepped into the room. Killian vaguely recognized him. He had seen him somewhere.

"I've been watching you, Nicholas Riley," he said. "You possess a will to live that I have not seen in a long time. Not even my dear friend, Zakary, possessed that will."

He indicated the man lying at Killian's feet, the man he had believed to be Saxos. His eyes darted up to the old man's in shock.

"That's right," he said, smiling wickedly. "*I* am Saxos. And I am no somatic mage as so many would believe. *I* am the God Mage."

Killian could hardly believe his ears. All that effort and it hadn't even been Saxos. This old man with wispy white hair and thick eyebrows, with bony arms and spotted skin, was the God Mage. He tried to speak, but the blood pooling in his throat prevented him.

"You're probably wondering how such an old man rose to such great power in the first place. I assure you, I wasn't always this way. The ritual never said anything about the side-effects it would have if it wasn't completed properly. It never said I would lose my youth if I didn't sacrifice my son as it entailed. But have no fear. Once the ritual is completed, my youth will return, and the power that is rightfully mine will finally be bestowed upon me."

He took another step forward, and Killian suddenly realized where he had seen him. He had been stalking him since the beginning, first outside Skye's academy after it had been blown up. He had been posing as a lone reporter, keeping his distance just in case any of the others asked questions. Then he had nearly ran him over outside Jo Jack's shop. His face had shown no signs of fear or shock when Killian had sped past. Finally, he had walked right past him in the hotel where they had fought the Magi and discovered Shayla. He had been right there. And Killian had let him go.

Killian felt weak, sagging even further against the wall. His head rocked to one side, and he stared out the window. The Prime Magi were still firing up toward Winter, but there were only a few left and she had driven them into cover. Lucas was still huddled in his cage. He looked over and saw Killian standing in the window. A huge smile broke across his face and hope washed over him. Then he saw the blood dripping from the corner of his mouth and the ice sickle protruding from his stomach. His mouth slowly fell open and tears filled his eyes.

Summoning up what little strength he had left, Killian swung a leg over the windowsill, determination still burning within.

"Now, now, Nicholas. You can't run off just yet," Saxos said. "We were just starting to get to know each other, and I have been so looking forward to this."

Fear gripped Killian as he moved to get his other leg over. He stopped, however, as his breath suddenly grew very cold. He looked down to see another long, thin ice sickle was sticking out his shoulder. It had pierced him in the shoulder blade and gone all the way through. Dripping blood sheathed the tip of the sickle in red.

Killian looked over his shoulder and saw Saxos standing there, another ice sickle formed in his palm.

"Now please, good sir, don't make me use another one," he said.

Again, Killian looked out the window. Lucas stood with his hands wrapped around the cage's bars, sobbing uncontrollably. Killian felt his legs go numb, and he fell back through the window, landing at Saxos's feet.

There was suddenly a loud scream, and Killian swiveled his head around. It was Lucas's voice. Saxos regarded him with a slight, amused smile.

"He'll cry himself hoarse if he keeps that up," Saxos said, clucking his tongue. "He really has taken a shining to you."

Killian could only stare up at him, more blood leaking from between his lips, his breath frigid.

"You must understand why I have to do this," Saxos continued, meeting his gaze. "It's my right. I performed the steps, I did the ritual, I've made the necessary sacrifices. Lucas was *made* for this. It's the only reason he exists."

"He wasn't *made*," Killian sputtered through mouthfuls of blood. "He was *born*."

"Oh, don't be coy with me, Nicholas. We were all made. All of us with these powers were made the moment I unlocked the door and let magic back in. In a way, you are all my children. And soon, when I wipe out your little friends and perform the ritual as it was meant to be performed, you will all be my subjects, and I will be your God."

"There's only one God I know of," said a voice from the doorway. Killian slowly swiveled his head around and saw Stamp standing there. "And you're not him," he said.

Saxos turned and immediately threw a barrage of ice sickles at him. A dozen split the air, and Stamp dove to the side. His hand swept across the floor, scooping up a handful of dirt and rock. He rolled to a stop and threw it into the air just as more ice sickles formed in Saxos's hand. A fireball crackled to life in his other. Stamp would not be able to dodge them both.

Just as the dirt began to cascade back down, however, Stamp threw his fist into the air and brought it down like a hammer. All at once, the dirt and rock and debris around Saxos rose into the air. He had half a moment to stare around at it in wonder before it slammed down in the shape of a fist, smashing his head down into his shoulder and breaking his neck. He immediately crumbled to the side.

Stamp breathed heavily as he rose from the ground and ran over. He was pretty torn up, cuts across his face and arms. He had taken a fireball to the thigh, his pant leg charred, and the skin beneath was wrinkly like old hamburger meat.

A sort of euphoria washed over Killian as Stamp helped him up. The edges of his vision got all bright and shiny. He looked up and saw Winter atop the distant roof. She was still firing at the Magi but stopped when she saw him through the window. She yelled something, but he couldn't be sure what it was. Stamp helped him over. He was saying something as well, but again Killian couldn't hear what it was. Everything was getting so bright.

He looked over at Lucas, still standing in the cage, wringing the bars. Tears glistened across his face. Killian managed a faint smile and mouthed the words "It's over."

His vision went completely white, and he felt the life channel from his body like water down a drain. He knew he was floating just outside his body. Everything was so bright, and something was pulling him away. Before he could float away, however, a loud scream suddenly pierced through the veil, and a crack formed across the void. A moment later, it shattered altogether, and Killian was back in the building. Stamp had set him against the windowsill and was trying to stop the bleeding around his wounds. He halted, however, as a bright orange light suddenly exploded from within Lucas's cage and consumed him. He screamed from somewhere within, but it wasn't from pain. It was from rage. The Prime Magi stopped firing their guns as they watched what was happening. Several showed signs of fear. Winter took several steps backward atop the roof and even Stamp looked uncertain.

Suddenly, the orange light retracted into a small floating ball and then shot up toward the sky in a narrow spiral. They could just barely make out a dark silhouette within the cylinder of light. It was thin and small, and Killian knew it was Lucas. He stood completely still, and Killian could tell his clothes had disintegrated.

The cylinder of light suddenly exploded outward again and consumed the entire quad. Killian squinted to see through the bright light and just barely saw the dragon statue suddenly explode into rubble. Screams came from the group of Magi. Screams of pain.

A loud roar suddenly echoed from nearby, and, as quickly as it had appeared, the orange light vanished. Killian blinked to get his eyes to adjust, and he gasped at what he saw.

The remaining Magi had transformed. They were no longer men, but creatures. One had long, curved tusks sticking out from its bottom lip, and his skin had turned pewter grey. The other two had shrunken several feet and had long pointed ears. Their teeth were yellow and sharp, and their skin was murky green. They stared at each other in shock and fear.

Another loud roar pierced the air, and Killian looked back toward Lucas's cage. Except there wasn't a cage anymore, and Lucas had vanished. He had been replaced by a huge black dragon. Killian could barely wrap his mind around it. Its eyes were dark red, and its massive scaly wings looked to be at least forty feet across. It took up the entire back half of the courtyard. Its teeth were each the length of Killian's arm and looked razor sharp.

"My God, what is that thing?" Stamp asked. Killian could only shake his head in response.

The three former Magi screamed in fear and ran toward the main building. They stumbled as they tried to adapt to their new bodies. The two smaller ones with the pointed ears struggled the most.

The dragon roared again, and a spiral of fire suddenly erupted from its mouth, engulfing them in flames. They screamed and crumbled to the ground. The third Magi, the one with grey skin and tusks, had nearly made it to the door when the dragon bounded forward and grabbed him with one of its massive front claws. The ground shook beneath its feet as its wings opened and launched into the air, taking the screaming grey Magi with it. When it had flown about fifty meters into the air, the dragon opened its claws and dropped the Magi to the ground. He screamed until he hit the ground with a sickening crunch, and Killian was forced to look away.

High in the air, the dragon flew several circles around the academy, its huge wings flapping in the wind. A few moments later, it lowered its head and flew back toward the academy. Atop the roof, Winter took cover behind an air conditioning vent, fear vivid across her face. Stamp crouched low next to Killian, one arm across his chest.

The dragon landed back in the quad, and the ground shook again. It looked up at Winter with its scarlet eyes, and she practically shrunk beneath its gaze. How could they fight something like that?

Slowly, it turned its head to look at Stamp and Killian. It took several steps toward them, covering a dozen meters in the span of a few steps. Stamp slowly scooped up a handful of dirt from the ground behind him.

The dragon saw it and roared. Stamp threw the dirt through the window, using his abilities to turn it into another small wave. It hit the dragon across its scaly face, and it fell back a step. It roared again, and Killian was sure it was about to burn them alive, but then it looked directly at him and somewhere deep in its scarlet eyes, he saw Lucas. He saw the innocent way he looked at everything, the joy that washed over his face when he laughed, and the pain he had come to know so well. Killian knew, buried somewhere within this monstrous creature, Lucas still existed.

Before he could try to stop it, however, the dragon launched into the sky, soaring high overhead and disappearing over the wall of the academy. Killian stared after it, unable to comprehend how it was possible, how any of this was possible. His head slumped against the window, and he looked over at the creatures the Prime Magi had become.

What had happened to Lucas? What had they unleashed upon the world?

Stamp said something, but his words were lost as the ringing filled Killian's ears once more. The white void slowly returned, and he felt himself lifted from his body.

"The sacrifice will be both of yours to make," the words echoed in his head once more. Killian finally understood.

CHAPTER 28

Sacrifice

There was white all around. He felt warm, safe. He saw his mother. She was humming the nursery rhyme she had sung to him as a child.

"Round and round the garden little teddy bear, one step, two steps, tickle you under there!" she sang over and over.

Killian tried to get to her, but she was always just out of reach. Then she vanished, and Spin stood there. He was saying something, but his words seemed to be lost in a sort of haze.

The white began to fade. It grew dark, and Spin's words slowly grew audible, but it wasn't his voice. It was Stamp's.

"Not sure if you can hear me, buddy, but we need you back," he was saying. "We need you back really bad."

He suddenly felt himself dragged backward and everything went dark.

Killian gasped in a mouthful of air, his eyes snapping open. Stamp was standing over him and he gasped as well.

"Nurse, nurse! He's awake," he called out the door, and Killian was vaguely aware he was in a healing ward.

A moment later, however, everything grew fuzzy, and he slipped back into the darkness.

When Killian awoke the next time, it was dark outside. The moon shone brightly out the nearby window. He was still in the healing ward, though he had been moved into a different room. There was an old flat-panel television in the corner, and flowers decorated every flat surface in the room. Several had the messages: GET WELL and BEST WISHES attached to them. Someone slept in an armchair in the corner. She was small and had short black hair.

Killian sucked in mouthfuls of air and tried to sit up, but wires and leads connected to his chest and arms prevented him from doing so. He tried to rip one of them off, but a nurse suddenly came rushing in and forced him to lie back flat.

"Sir, it's going to be okay. You need to rest," she said. She injected something into his IV, and he instantly calmed. Exhaustion overtook him, and his eyes seemed to drag themselves downward. The woman in the chair strode over and held his hand as he drifted back off.

Killian's eyes fluttered open again sometime later. Gum was crusted across his eyelids, and his throat was dry. His tongue felt like cotton.

"I was wondering when you were going to wake back up," a familiar voice said.

Killian looked over toward the window and saw Stamp standing there. He had never been so happy to see anyone in his life.

Stamp walked over and placed a hand on Killian's shoulder. "Welcome back," he said, a small smile crossing his face.

"What happened?" Killian asked in a hoarse, croaky voice that wasn't his own.

"Later," Stamp said, pouring some water into a cup and handing it to him. "For now, you need to rest."

Killian drank the cup dry and set it down on the small table beside his bed. He looked up into Stamp's eyes.

"Stamp, what happened?" he asked again, his voice sounding a bit more like his own.

Stamp sighed. He looked around as if to make sure no one was listening and dragged a chair over. He leaned forward so his elbows rested on his knees and interlaced his fingers in front of his mouth.

"What all do you remember?" he finally asked. Killian had to think about it for a moment before answering. Had it all been a dream?

"I remember attacking the Prime Magi at Skye's academy. I killed Saxos, their leader. No, it wasn't Saxos. He shot me?"

"It was an icicle. Went through your back," Stamp said, and Killian suddenly remembered the pain, the cold. He felt his stomach instinctively, remembering how the icicle had protruded from his abdomen, dripping with blood. "The healers were able to patch you up pretty good, but you lost a lot of blood. We weren't sure if you were going to make it. Then you dropped into a coma. The healers said if you came out of it on your own, you'd be fine."

Several seconds ticked past. Stamp leaned forward so only Killian could hear. "Do you remember what happened to Lucas?"

It all suddenly came rushing back, and Killian knew it hadn't been a dream. He nodded slowly, and Stamp let out a long exhale.

"What happened to him?" Killian asked.

"We don't know. He just changed. People are already coming up with their own theories. Some are saying he's the antichrist. Others think he's the next form of evolution for mages. He's gone, though. Hasn't been seen since he flew away from Skye's academy. I don't know."

"How long have I been out?" Killian asked.

"About five days. I was beginning to think you wouldn't come out of it at all when you suddenly woke up."

"I..." Killian thought about telling him he had heard his voice, but he decided against it. Some things were just better left a secret. "The Magi?"

"Gone too. It looks like we wiped them out. If any are left, they're probably in hiding. The Overseers launched a pretty huge manhunt for them, but they didn't turn anything up."

"They changed," Killian said, remembering the strange creatures they had become.

"Yeah," Stamp said. Again, he looked toward the door, and Killian knew he wasn't supposed to be telling him any of this. "They're not the only ones. Hundreds of people all over the city did as well. Some people are even hearing reports of it in other parts of the world too, but they're keeping it very hush-hush. Something's happened. Lucas did something."

"A second Change," Killian said lowly.

"What?"

"He caused the first Change by sending a pulse of magical energy out across the world. I can only assume that's what this is as well."

Stamp rubbed his eyes. He looked like he hadn't slept in days. "I don't know. The city's in a panic. A lot of those who changed have fled. It was getting violent. People were chasing them through the streets calling them monsters and hell spawn. We thought it might turn into another Terrible Night, but the Overseers managed to get everything under control. Those who stayed in the city have been moved to special cordons in the city so they can be protected, but the whole thing sounds like bullshit to me. I think the Overseers are just trying to keep them off the street. They're saying it's a whole new strain."

"What are they really?" Killian asked.

"Really?" Stamp asked. He struggled to find the right words. "They're goblins…trolls, orcs, gargoyles. Pretty much every mythical creature ever written about, they've become. I've even heard some people talk about seeing nymphs hiding in the parks, but I don't know how true that is. It's crazy out there. I can barely believe it myself."

"How are neither of us in jail?" Killian suddenly asked, noting the fact he wasn't handcuffed to the bed.

"Well, when the cops showed up, they tried to arrest us. They didn't even want to call a healer for you, but then the Overseers showed up. They seemed to have figured everything out for themselves by then and made the cops take you to a healing ward. There was a press conference yesterday, and the cops issued a public statement saying it was the Prime Magi who had caused all the chaos, and we were just innocent bystanders caught in the crossfire. A bunch of the first responding police officers were awarded medals for bravery and all that nonsense. Our involvement has pretty much been swept under the rug altogether."

"Figures," Killian said, scoffing. "Still, I'll take it over handcuffs."

Stamp nodded. He stood from the chair, interlacing his finger atop his head and looking up toward the ceiling. He sighed heavily.

"Is Winter alright?" Killian asked, trying not to sound too concerned.

Stamp saw the look in his eye, and the hint of another smile crossed his lips.

"Winter's fine. A little banged up like the rest of us, but she's okay. Skye's alright too. She's been here every day in between meetings with the Overseers. I'm sure she'll be by in a little bit. Loop, too. She stayed last night."

Killian nodded. So that's who it had been.

There was a light knock on the door, and he looked over to see Winter standing there. He wasn't sure who he had been expecting, but he was pleased nonetheless.

"I see someone's awake," she said, walking over. "How are you feeling?"

"Alive surprisingly."

"Yeah, you gave everyone a bit of a scare. It's good to see you up and around, though," she said. She stopped several feet short of the edge of the bed. She looked like she wanted to come closer, but a quick glance at Stamp made her stop. Killian wondered what was going on.

Stamp suddenly cleared his throat awkwardly. "I'm going to go grab a coffee and leave you two alone," he said.

He walked out of the room, and Winter mouthed "thanks" at him. He nodded before disappearing out the door.

"What was that all about?" Killian asked when she walked over to the edge of the bed and sat down on it.

"Skye hasn't exactly been happy that I've been coming around. She seems to think I'm still going to try to arrest you or something and hasn't allowed me to be alone with you. But I've already talked to my superiors, and they recognize we can't do anything about Lucas now. Mission over."

"I see," Killian said, already reading the look in her eye.

"They've, uh, recalled me back to the states. They allowed me to stick around until you woke up, but now that you have, I've got to go back," she said.

Killian could tell by the strained expression on her face that she was trying to sound nonchalant about it, but he knew she was upset. He reached out and placed his hand atop hers. After a moment, she turned her palm over and clutched his hand.

"I take it Stamp told you about everything that happened?" Winter asked.

Killian nodded. "Then you understand a lot of people would be very angry with you if they ever found out what really happened up there, how involved we all really were. You need to be careful; you need to watch your back."

Her voice began to shake, and Killian saw the mask disappear from across her face. She wiped a lone tear from her eye and squeezed his hand even tighter.

"I'll be okay," Killian said. "I promise."

"You'd better," she replied. She smiled slightly. "I can't keep saving your ass all the time."

Killian snorted. "I'm pretty sure I saved you just as many times as you saved me."

Winter chuckled and, a moment later, leaned forward and kissed him softly on the lips. It didn't last long, and there wasn't nearly as much passion in it as the last time they had kissed. Killian knew what it was. It was goodbye.

Winter slowly pulled back and wiped several more tears from her face. "Take care of yourself, Killian."

She stood from his bed slowly and released his hand. It fell to his side as she turned and headed toward the door.

"Hey, there is one thing I've been wanting to ask you," Killian suddenly called after her. She stopped and turned to look at him.

"What is it?"

"What's your real name?" he asked.

Winter stared at him. After several long moments, a small smile broke across her face. "What's yours?"

"You already know mine," he said.

"Touché." She locked eyes with him and finally said, "It's Sarah."

"Nice to meet you, Sarah. I'm Nick."

With one final smile, Winter disappeared out the door, and Killian knew he would never see her again.

Stamp was pushing Killian across the healing ward grounds in a wheelchair when Skye showed up. It was a bright, sunny day outside, and it felt amazing to have fresh air blowing across his face. Tall trees rose around the cobblestone path, and the grass was neat and trimmed.

Loop had already turned up earlier in the day. She had apologized for not being at the academy to help them, but Killian had hushed her and told her it wasn't her fault. They had hugged, and she spent the next half-hour telling him about how much she hated Barker. He had chuckled and forgot for a short time all that had happened. For that, he would be forever indebted to her.

The shock of losing Lucas had made Killian's head spin, but as it sank in more and more, he felt depressed more than anything. They had failed. After everything they had gone through, they still failed. Sure, they had saved Lucas from being sacrificed, but look at what he became instead. Killian wondered if the Lucas he had known even existed anymore or if he was just a shadow trapped in the dragon's scarlet-colored eyes. It made him sick just thinking about it.

Skye came around a bend in the path and approached them tentatively. Killian wasn't sure how to feel, finally seeing her. He had felt a range of emotions toward her ever since waking back up—anger, betrayal, regret, sadness. She had pretty much tricked them into looking after Lucas, knowing full well he had caused the first magical outbreak, yet she didn't say a word about it. He understood why, but it still angered him that even after all these years, she still felt she couldn't trust him. A small part of him was also still angry that she had broken her vow to never use her abilities on him.

She walked up slowly, holding a small white teddy bear she had obviously purchased from the healing ward gift shop. He knew, with the exception of a cactus from Loop, that all the flowers in his room were from her.

"Hi," she said, coming to a halt a few feet in front of them. She was wearing the same tan leather jacket she had worn the last time he saw her, and her honey blonde hair fell across her shoulders.

"Hey," Killian said, not sure what to say. Stamp looked between them.

"I'll, uh, leave you two alone," he said, setting the brakes on Killian's wheelchair and walking back up toward the healing ward. Killian shot him an annoyed expression, but he kept walking.

Killian and Skye sat there awkwardly for several long moments. She clutched the teddy bear very tightly and bit her lower lip nervously.

"I'm so sorry, Killian," she finally said. Killian stared up at her. "I never meant for you to get hurt or for any of this to happen. I was just trying to do the right thing. If I had known breaking Lucas out would have caused all this…"

"You would have done it anyway," Killian said, cutting her off. She looked at him, and he sighed heavily. "It's okay. It's how you're wired, I suppose. I know you didn't mean for me to get hurt."

Skye's grip on the teddy bear slowly loosened.

"I just want us to be friends more than anything. I just got you back. I don't want to lose you again," she said.

Killian looked down at the ground, trying to find the right words. They weren't coming easily.

"I don't know if we can be," he finally said. He had thought long and hard about what he would say to her when he finally saw her again, but even now he found the words difficult to get out. She was his oldest friend—he had known her even before Spin—and yet she betrayed his trust in a way worse than even Stamp had.

"Not now anyway," he added, "not when everything is still so fresh. You didn't trust me. You kept me completely in the dark. And you broke your promise to never use your powers on me."

"I know, and I'm so, so sorry, but I had to do it. You and Kestrel were going to end up shooting each other," she said. Tears were in her eyes now. They threatened to spill over onto her cheeks at any moment, and she gripped the teddy bear harder than ever.

"I just can't look at you the same way anymore," Killian said.

"So you can't forgive me, but you can forgive Stamp?" Skye asked. "After what *he* did to you?"

It was petty and a weak attempt at guilt, but it was all she had. Killian couldn't meet her eye. There was some truth in her words, but he just couldn't do it. He just couldn't let it go so easily.

"It's different," he said in a quiet voice. "After everything I went through, you weren't there, Skye. You didn't see."

"If I could have been there, I would have, but I had other responsibilities. I had to look after the children from the academy. They had nowhere to go, and the Prime Magi started targeting them as well in case we tried switching Lucas out with one. We had to stay underground," Skye said.

Killian felt a sudden flash of anger. So while he had been out risking his life trying to keep Lucas safe, she had been hiding in a hole with Kestrel? She saw the anger in his eyes and knew she had lost the fight. Her voice was very quiet as she said, "I'm truly sorry for what happened, Killian. If I could put myself in that wheelchair instead, I would in a heartbeat."

"Please, just leave," Killian said, refusing to meet her eye. He was afraid if he did, he would blow up on her or forgive her. He wasn't ready to do either.

Skye tried to fight the tears back, and, for a minute, Killian didn't think she was going to leave. Then she walked over and set the teddy bear in his lap and pecked him on the cheek softly.

"Goodbye, Killian," she said and, with that, she was gone.

For the longest time, Killian just sat there, replaying all that had happened in his head, wondering if there was some other way he could have done things, some different path he could have taken that would have prevented Lucas from changing into that terrible monster. As he remembered the words in his dream, however, he knew it had been decided long before he even met Lucas. Some higher power had been at work, and it had willed Lucas into becoming the dragon that killed those Prime Magi so easily. There was nothing he could have done.

Stamp walked back down about an hour later. He looked around for Skye, but when he saw the look in Killian's eye, he decided not to ask.

"There's someone else who would like to see you," he said instead. He rubbed the back of his neck awkwardly. Killian craned his head around and saw Daisy standing there. She looked as beautiful as ever. A yellow flower held her rich black hair away from one ear, and her dark eyes sparkled. She walked around in front of him.

"Hey, Daisy," Killian managed to get out. She was the last person he expected to show up.

"I, um, wanted to come see how you were doing," she said. Killian stared up at her, not sure how to respond. "So how are you?"

"I'm okay," Killian replied. "I guess."

It seemed neither of them was very sure what to say. Stamp stood there, looking between the two of them.

"Babe, can you give us a minute?" Daisy asked. After a moment, Stamp nodded and headed a little further down the path. She turned to look back at Killian, her hands folded in front of her. "I just wanted to say how sorry I am for what happened between us. It wasn't your fault. I never should have pushed you to talk to me like that…"

"Daisy, stop," Killian said, holding up his hand. She stopped speaking and stood there nervously. Killian sighed. "You did exactly what you should have done. You tried to get me to open up, something I desperately needed to do, and I rejected you. It's my fault what happened. It's taken me a long time to realize it, but with all that's happened, it seems stupid to hold something like this over your head. I'm not saying I'm okay with it, but I do understand it, and maybe one day I'll be able to accept it."

Daisy stood there shocked for several long moments. She couldn't believe what he had just said.

"Thank you," she finally said, a broad smile splitting her face. Killian nodded, and she hugged him. It was warm and gentle, and Killian knew there wasn't anything sexual about it. It was a hug between friends, and, for the first time he could remember, he was okay with that.

Daisy waved Stamp over. When he saw the look on Daisy's face, he smiled too. "Thanks, man," he said, and he and Killian clasped hands. Killian nodded. Stamp's eyes suddenly flashed over at Daisy's, and a dark look passed between them. She nodded.

"Killian, there's something we need to tell you," she said, looking back at him. Killian glanced between them and wondered for a moment if they were about to say Daisy was pregnant.

"Your jeep was blown up," Stamp said.

Killian stared at him for several long moments. He hadn't been expecting that. "What do you mean?"

"A couple days after you got to the healing ward, we called for a tow truck to go pick up your jeep, and when the guy tried moving it; well, it blew up," Stamp said, staring down at him.

"Somebody had put a bomb on it," Daisy added.

Killian could hardly believe what they were saying. Someone had planted a bomb on his jeep? It was like they were playing a practical joke on him. Then he remembered what he had learned about Spin's death, and it all became clear. Whoever they were, they knew Killian had learned the truth, and they wanted him dead because of it.

Killian's hands slowly clenched into fists in his lap. He was going to find out who they were, and he was going to kill them.